I0657408

BURNT TREE JUNCTION

THE ACCLAIMED HISTORICAL FICTION SERIES

- VOLUME 3 ANTHOLOGY -

# LACE COLLAR

## CHESTNUT COTTAGE

## JOANN KLUSMEYER

innovo
PUBLISHING

Published by Innovo Publishing, LLC
www.innovopublishing.com
1-888-546-2111

Providing Full-Service Publishing Services for Christian Authors, Artists & Ministries: Hardbacks, Paperbacks, eBooks, Audiobooks, Music, Screenplays & Curricula

**BURNT TREE JUNCTION: HISTORICAL FICTION**

VOLUME 3 (ANTHOLOGY)

## LACE COLLAR
—
## CHESTNUT COTTAGE

Copyright © 2022 by Joann Klusmeyer
All rights reserved.

No part of this publication may be reproduced, stored in a retrieval system, or transmitted in any form or by any means electronic, mechanical, photocopying, recording, or otherwise, without the prior written permission of the author.

ISBN: 978-1-61314-679-8

Cover Design & Interior Layout: Innovo Publishing, LLC

Printed in the United States of America
U.S. Printing History
First Edition: 2022

—

Has God called you to create a Christian book, ebook, audiobook, music album, screenplay, film, or curricula? If so, visit the ChristianPublishingPortal.com to learn how to accomplish your calling with excellence. Learn to do everything yourself, or hire trusted Christian Experts from our Marketplace to help.

# CONTENTS

What happened should never have happened to any girl, but the product of this calamity was taken over by a doctor who saw great potential. And there was that lace collar that had been lovingly made for a child not yet born.

Something needed to be done for the youngest of humans who had the misfortune to be born without protectors. Hence, the creation of Chestnut Cottage. Also, it is well known that angels were created as messengers for their heavenly Boss, as well as put in charge of the Boss' special creations, humans. So it would seem natural for the angels to be near where a number of brand new humans were created who seemed to have no other protector.

PART I

# LACE COLLAR

## THE PASSING OF CECELIA HADLEY

Her daughter, Isabel, and 10-year-old granddaughter, Olivia, leaned over the frail body of old Grandma Cecelia Hadley. Her end was near, and last words would surely be forthcoming, momentarily.

A weak wave of the hand, skin seemingly translucent from departing life, old Miss Cecelia got her daughter's attention, "My lace collar… the black one…."

"Yes, mother. What about it…?"

"Put it on me with my pink silk dress for the viewin'. Uh…"

"I certainly will mother. You will be beautiful."

The old face turned aside. That was not the response she wanted. "Listen to me, Isabel. Take off the collar, and do not bury it. Save it for Olivia's little girl. It's all I can give her."

"Yes, mother. We'll save it for Olivia."

The pale hand waved again… with a sign of exasperation. "Let me say it, Isabel. Not Olivia. For Olivia's little girl."

With a painted-on smile, the frustrated daughter, Isabel, agreed. "For the little girl. Yes." She nodded her head with assurance. Yes. Olivia was just a little girl.

With an insistent whisper, the dying woman repeated. "Olivia's little girl, to remember me by." It was all she could manage.

Her life had become much too complicated. The silk thread of the collar was black, as anyone with two eyes could see. So why would the package say something unheard of like 'ebony'? No matter. If her daughters, Isabel and Ophelia, just got it right....

"Olivia's girl," the old woman repeated with poignant insistence. And with that, she closed her weary eyes and passed, as she had lived her life, gracefully, and with dignity she entered into the land of her reward.

Young Olivia wiped her knuckles into her damp eyes, and Isabel tried to smile through clamped lips. "Ramblin', that's what she was, darlin'. She was meanin' you to have that collar, Livie, bein' the last thing she crocheted on her fingers."

Olivie sniffed and nodded. Grammie Izzy was wrong, of course, but now was not the time to tell her. Old Grammie Cece said what she wanted to say, and the collar was to be kept for a little girl who was not here. Not yet. Olivia was certain of that.

Olivia did not need a black crocheted collar to remember Grammie Cece with. She had sat with Grammie as her feeble fingers created the lacy thing of beauty, with its rose petals, shiny black webbing, and twining leaves. She had been there as the old hands slowed, and then finally struggled to finish the collar.

"For your little girl," Grammie Cece had said. "It's all I can leave her."

"It's enough, Grammie. She'll love it." And to the nine year old, it had all seemed possible. It didn't matter what Grandma Isabel said. It would all work out.

Momma Ophelia and Olivia had sat in the kitchen as the neighbors prepared Grammie Cece for her last 'visit' with the neighbors who she had loved for so many years. The tiny community of Enterprise was very close knit as were most of the small clusters of houses at the turn of the century in Northern Arkansas.

Cecelia was buried in the field with the daisies, where other marking stones stood, and life went on. Isabel rinsed the collar and shaped it on a towel, marveling at the skill that had created the three-dimensional roses on the network of black.

Most unusual it was, and patterned after Cecelia's artistic mind… and then it was packed with petals of marigold and lavender, which were known to be repugnant to moths and other nibbling insects. Packed away… with the very few precious items of the household.

Olivia knew exactly where it was, and it would stay there and be fresh and new for her own little girl. Some day. The whole idea seemed a fantasy, like the promise of Santa Clause, Snow White and the Dwarfs, and The Old Woman who actually lived in a shoe.

Tiny, tiny people living in a shoe! Imagine that!

## DOCTOR DAVID HARPER

Doc Harper had a lot of time to think. Much more than he wished. Seemed like he had spent at least ninety percent of his life on the roads and by-ways that extended out from Ridge Road like so many legs of a centipede.

Ridge Road crawled along, endlessly, striving to stay on top of the ridges as long as possible. Having to cross a hollow created a nightmare of sticky clay roads that were attack by rushing ditch water… a nightmare for struggling horses attached to any kind of load, and by a million weary steps of anyone on foot.

The doctor, however, was drawn along in comfort behind a pair of mules. Today it was Puller and Pancake. Pokey was having the day off. On something as important as the doctor's buggy, a spare animal was needed, so there were always two strong mules ready to go. So, today, the mules knew to go straight ahead until being told to turn. There was nothing for the doc to do but think.

Where every leafy road or by-way led off Ridge Road, the doctor would see the scenery in his mind and know every living person who lived there. Also, some of those who were no longer living. Old Miss Cecelia Hadley was one of those. So memorable, she was. She knew where she was going, and she was ready. She took advantage of the doctor's visits just to chat and reminisce. Lovely lady, she was.

And the granddaughter. Sweet child. He had pulled her through chickenpox and mumps, but the measles had just about done her in. Thin as a reed now, she was, and with not a lot of reserve strength.

It was from her he'd heard about the fancy, ebony-colored collar. "For me," the girl had explained, with a pleased smile, "to keep for when I have a little girl. I'll name her Ebony Lace and tell her about Grammie Cece makin' it for her, special."

Doc had raised eyebrows at the name. "Does your momma know about the name?"

"Sure does. She says I got time to change, but why'd I change when I got it right, already?"

Made sense… you'd have to admit. The girl had more to add.

"Momma's always get to choose the name for the babies, and that's what I get to choose. She'll get to have the collar, and it's only been wore once."

Doc had nodded, agreeably. Didn't pay to argue with females of any age, unless it was about a life or death matter. He hadn't lived for well over thirty years and not learned that.

The general health of his community was never far from his attention. His 'doctor's eye' assessed everyone, it seemed, even before a greeting was spoken. Just one of his curses because so many people didn't want to know about their trouble. Didn't want to do what might alleviate their distress.

But that girl, Olivia, must be getting on to thirteen, now. She had completed Miss Temple's school but continued to attend to help the teacher with the little ones. Gave her something to do. She was not needed at home, as so many girls were, so she was available.

Loved plants. Studied leaves and flowers, and noted which attracted their own special insect. Word was that she practically cared for the family Herb Garden by herself. All the mints and a few of the flowering preventatives like the cone flower for colds, and rosemary for allergies. Not only that, she drew pictures of the plants and made a scrapbook.

The Hadley farm adjoined Doc's parent's horse farm, where Doc still lived in his own house. Alone. Here he was easing up on three dozen years and still hadn't found time to search for a lady who would put up with doctor's hours. All hours of the day or night he must answer the bell. What lady would want a life of that?

Some decades ago he had built a four roomed cabin on the driveway to his parent's house. A loud chiming gong was attached to the gate post, along with a note box for a message. For night calls, the messenger could bang the gong to wake up the doctor, thereby saving a few seconds of time. The Doc would have clothes and shoes on by the time the 'someone' reached the door… because a night call always meant an emergency.

So today he was coming home at about four o'clock, the sun having sunk low and reflected silver off the surface of Blue Lake. He had cleared the 'hanging saddle' of the mountain where Forum Ridge became Ridge Road. He could see the Hadley's drive just ahead and his own about a quarter of a mile farther on.

He saw a flash of color on the ditch ahead. Clothing? Someone resting by the side of the road…? Well, he could give them a short… WHAT was that? A flag? Something… what was it?

He drew closer. The 'flag' had stopped waving and was crumbled into a pile of flowered fabric.

"WHOAAA mules!" The eight hooves on the road stopped immediately. Doc Harper leaped out and hurried to the heap of fabric just in the edge of the trees. A person…?

"Oh, Dear Lord, have mercy! It's little Olivia!" Too weak to speak, she just groaned softly as he moved aside her torn dress to reveal a pair of blood-soaked shoes peeking from a red-stained pettislip.

"Oh, Dear Lord!" his agonized lips repeated.

A quick search of face and arms did not reveal the source of the blood, so there was one other place for the injury. Carefully gathering the tiny thirteen-year-old frame into his arms, he carried her to the buggy. The second seat of the vehicle was a permanent bed, just for this purpose, though it was seldom used. He placed the small body there.

Back at the reins, he turned the mules around and hurried them back to the Hadley Lane. For the almost quarter of a mile of it, he sorted through his mind for the reasons this could not be what he instinctively knew it was. There'd be no early supper and bedtime today.

When he approached the house, Ophelia stepped out to greet him and invite him for a cup of tea. But when he lifted the tangled armload from the rear seat, she screamed an ear-shaking volume of horror.

"NOOOO! She got run over! I told 'er about that road!"

But no, it was not a broken leg or a skinned thigh. Doc Harper spent a night of desperation to save her remaining blood, and maybe repair the damage. Not possible. Though he pushed the knowledge from his mind, he knew that the trauma this girl had experienced would mean that she would never have a natural born child. If, indeed, she lived.

It was touch and go whether she would have a life. Any life.

Isabel and Isaac had no time to grieve, attempting to hold their daughter together. Ophelia lived and breathed for that girl and was inconsolable.

Morning came, and the girl was still breathing… barely. The blood loss was immense. Doc had Isabel spooning warm willow tea into the bloodless lips, hopefully to replace some of the liquid loss. Dehydration was a real threat in cases like this.

Pulse was weak and thready, but continued. The girl, for all her miniature build, was a fighter. Maybe it would be enough. He had a memory picture of the impish smile when she confided her name for the child she would have. Well, there'd be no problem about that. No child… for a certainty.

Leaving a sedative for Ophelia, Doctor David Harper repacked the contents of his doctor bag while Isaac harnessed the mules to the buggy. He climbed aboard, and hardly had the strength or heart to wave a hand at the distraught grandfather.

He'd get a little sleep and be back to see them. Everyone was important to a doctor, but near neighbors like the Hadley's seemed a bit more important. Old Isaac and his own father had swapped out duties for years, helping whichever of them needed the help at that moment.

Doc's father raised Clydesdale carriage horses. Or rather, he provided the pasture and barn and let them raise themselves. Made a pretty good living selling to Fayetteville, Eureka Springs and Berryville.

Pulling into his yard, he loosed Puller and Pancake into their pasture, separate from that of the Clydesdales, and stripped the buggy's back seat bed of its blood stained sheets.

Warm milk and the bed. A doctor couldn't afford to dwell on the problems of the day that might keep him from the sleep he would need the next day.

## THE DAY AFTER THAT

When the Frisco engine puffed its way out of the station and struggled up the next hill, an undocumented rider was spread-eagled on the roof of number five car, holding to the handholds against the swaying as the locolotive plunged down the track.

It had been a sudden decision. Very sudden. A quick trip to the house, a change of clothing and to grab the small amount of money he had handy. Without being seen, he disappeared, running through the woods. He dashed out of the brush of the ditch and ran down Ridge road as far as his breath would let him.

Before he reached the small valley town of Wishbone, he had found a leafy bed among the oaks and spent the night.

Morning came. Raking the broken leaves and twigs and a couple of caterpillars from his dark, curly hair, he brushed his clothing with a bushy weed.Considering that he'd done the best he could about his appearance, he headed into the town.

Buying a fresh-baked roll from the bakery, he pocketed the rest of the money to buy a ticket, once he reached Eureka Springs, about 8 miles down the track.

He hated it that he had to leave behind his fancy bow and arrows in his haste to get away, but it had seemed best. It wasn't his fault, actually. He hadn't wanted to spend another minute in that God-forsaken place where there was absolutely nothing to do… but work. He'd been rather forced to come here, and he didn't like work. He shouldn't have to do what he didn't like.

For the first few days of the stay, it was fun to take his bow to the woods. He'd killed a number of birds and one small fur-bearer he couldn't quite identify, and then he had broken one of the arrows.

No matter… he had another arrow.

Then he aimed at and hit a half-rotten log with a satisfying 'thunk' and tried to pull out the arrow. It had stuck on something, so he placed a well-shod foot against the log and pulled all his weight against it.

A sudden separation of the arrowhead from the shaft propelled him backward against a nearby tree, doing minor, but painful damage to his back. Even worse, his expensive arrow was totally hidden in the pithy center of the log, impossible to remove.

In a bout of rage, he broke the shaft of the arrow across his knee and pitched the splintered parts away. Lips firm and eyes narrowed, he looked for something else to break.

And there on the road was a flash of color.

If he hadn't been so mad or if the arrow had not broken, he'd have thought twice and not done what he did. But now that he had done, it was time to move on. Quickly. He didn't like this dopey, dreary place anyway. Too far from everywhere. Time to split.

And now he was swaying on the top of number five box car. The wind tossed his dark curly hair this way and that, but no matter. He was leaving boredom behind him, along with any other trouble that might have attached itself to him if he had stayed.

Stinking old Clydesdale horses, anyway? Who'd ever want to inherit a business like that? Surely his grandparents could leave him something more appropriate. Like money.

It was early afternoon when Doctor David Harper blinked himself awake with the niggling thought that something dreadful was awaiting him. It was. The memory of yesterday settled in with a vengeance. Oh, Dear Lord, please don't let it....

He looked in his mirror, and a growth of whiskers greeted him, along with hair standing every which way. Not as much hair as he used to have, but he still had quite enough for a thirty-five year old. No matter that it was silvering over his ears.

True. When the light was just right, silver sparkles showed among the darker waves of his hair. No matter. He'd earned every one of them.

He splashed himself awake with cold water, and proceeded to repair the growth of the night. Face not bad looking. Good DNA, he thought with a smile. They'd finally given a three-lettered name for the human interior matter that identified one person as being different from another. That had just come out in one of the papers he subscribed to.

So, blessing those Harpers back in Ireland, who had insisted they learned to play the harp just like old King David in the Bible, his DNA helped him learn. Fact is, they, the Irish Harpers, insisted that it was because of them the Irish flag had the tiny golden harp on it. The old folks seemed to set a store by that link with the past… and the Bible. And it might even be true. Some of it, anyway.

Leastwise, that little harp on the Irish flag had to come from somewhere, didn't it? And that had been the time of his pa's grandpap.

But then the potato famine had hit Ireland, and the whole family had moved. Boarded a sailing ship to the new country, landing in a place called Jamestown over on the coast. Some family members restlessly headed west, and the hills of Northern Arkansas had finally stopped them.

So now… cheeks smooth-shaven and black wavy hair tamed… Doc crawled into a clean shirt and tossed yesterday's shirt into a pail of water. Maybe the stains would come out. Ma was good at that sort of thing.

Today, it would be Puller and Pokey, giving Pancake the day off. He pulled out onto Ridge Road and turned left. The Hadley farm just ahead.

A cloying sense of dread enclosed him… tightened around him, suffocatingly dense. The neat farmhouse just ahead. Old Isaac… sitting on the porch, feet on the ground, knife whittling curls of wood to toss to the ground. Waiting.

"Knowd you'd be along. She's still a'breathin' Doc. You thinkin' what might'a … well, something in the woods, maybe? They was sticks and twigs in 'er hair."

"I tried not to think, Zack. Just couldn't put two and two together and make sense of it. Fact is, though, there was another someone involved. Certain to have been."

The stern-faced old man kept whittling, and Doc sat beside him for a minute to offer maybe a bit of comfort. The other man was suffering immensely… silently… internally. His stiletto-sharp knife was plunging into the evil flesh of that 'someone' instead of the hickory stick.

"How could something happen to our little girl? Her Ma's been right. She shouldn't'a been on the road alone, but who'd'a thought of somethin' happenin'…?"

Doc clapped a sympathetic hand on Isaac's shoulder and entered the house. In the dimness of the room, the girl on the bed appeared totally bloodless. The wrist, thin as a sapling, beat with a feather-sized pulse. Better than nothing.

"You tried to feed her anything?"

"No, Doc. Waitin' for you to say what."

'First thing'd be beef broth. Like you been doin' with the tea. We'll see what tomorrow looks like, and then maybe add egg yolk. You got the beef where you can get it right now?"

"Quick as I open up a jar. Got it handy, thinkin' that'd be what you wanted done."

While Isabel was out of the room, Doc pulled aside the blanket to check his handiwork. Pads were packed efficiently. Only minor blood spots. Best that could be expected, but time would tell if his best had been good enough. There was so much of the human body that was inaccessible. One did what one could, and sighed, wishing they could do more. Just one of the woes of being a doctor.

Skin dry. Needed liquid in the absolute worst way.

Isabel returned with luke-warm broth. A careful spoonful touched the girl's lips, and she managed to deal with it, somehow. A few drops. Then a few more drops. Have to do better than this, right quick.

With careful fingers, he softly massaged her throat. Maybe tomorrow she would come around… and be able to swallow, but then would also come the pain, and he might have to put her out again. A delicate balance that doctors had to make.

His mind turned over one of the discoveries pushed forward when he was in training over two decades ago. Pain causes stress, and stress hampers healing. The papers he now received bore that out, and various kinds of preparations were being tested.

He did all he could do. Then, Doc gave Isabel a friendly 'shoulder' hug, and walked away. The girl was in the best hands possible. Stable pair of grandparents.

Ophelia, the girl's mother, was lucky to have had her parents so well able to help her when her husband, a policeman, was killed in a robbery.

Doc turned his attention to his own day. He had a troublesome pregnancy just down the road toward Wishbone that he'd promised to check in on. That was not his favorite type of stop, but Enterprise had no midwife with that specialty, so he did what he could. It was just that he couldn't spend the waiting time that some patients hoped for.

Thoughts came back to Olivia.

Poor, unfortunate girl. Lost her Pa. Now she had certainly lost the little girl that would be named Ebony Lace... even before she could get born. Just didn't seem fair to her or Isaac and Isabel. Doc had long since quite trying to out-guess God's judgment or selections of who should get well. That was one thing not required of him.

On the way back home, he stopped where he had picked up small Olivia. Halting the team, he stepped into the woods. Scuffed leaves. She had obviously crawled to the road, the pain of standing up and walking being just too much to bear. He stopped at about a hundred yards in. She had crawled a long way. Such a determination in that small body. Going any farther could not stop what had already happened but she did her best.

Doc stopped and went back to the buggy. Somehow he didn't want to see any more of what he could not undo. He could only deal with the result, no matter how it happened.

Back to the Hadley farm. Isaac was out in the stables, but Isabel sat watch over the patient. Eyes bloodshot and worried. Ophelia was there, red faced and sniffing.

Time to get something straight. "Isabel, I'm leavin' you somethin' I want you to take. Now. You get some sleep and let Ophelia sit watch. You're gonna be needed later and for a long time, and I don't want you gettin' down from lack of sleep."

He had said it firmly and in front of Ophelia. They were going to have to work together during this crisis, and Isabel would never be cross with her daughter. So now Ophelia would realize she had to be brave.

"Isabel, show Ophelia how you fed her. I'd like you to stir a raw egg yolk in the next cup of broth. Also, wipe her face and neck gently with a soft cloth in warm water. Maybe help her retain some moisture."

He moved toward the door, assuring them, "I'll stop in tomorrow. Just keep up what you're doin'."

The ladies nodded… and he was gone.

## THE HARPER MEN OF ENTERPRISE

Horses were a valuable commodity in every part of the country. One wishing to breed the animals could choose from the small donkeys, mainly used for transporting, to the full sized mules bred especially for their strength in pulling and their perseverance in heavy farm work.

Or there were the lighter boned saddle horses, and these were popular both on the farms and in town. Having a good, fast saddle horse meant you could get somewhere quickly… and then there were the Clydesdales.

Thought to have originated in New Zealand, they were co-opted by the Scotts with their rugged mountainous terrain. The handsome strength and even temperament of these animals made them popular for transmitting fancy carriages through city streets. One might say that the Clydesdales, and the Clydesdale-blends, were a sign of prosperity… maybe even wealth. They were an expensive horse to own unless their tremendous strength was economically used.

To have a pair or two of these handsome animals in a city paddock used only for transporting fancy carriages went a long way toward telling the world (and your neighbors) that you had 'money to burn' and had no need to economize. In this case, they became a 'luxury item' and therefore very desirable among certain classes.

Doc Harper's father seized early onto the value of breeding these animals and chose black for his signature color. The broad backs, glossy coats, as well as the hoof fringe that many considered attractive, gave them a sale price well worth the time it took to produce the curved neck, lowered chin and prancing gait expected of a carriage horse

So David Harper, Senior, picked a grassy lowland near the west end of Blue Lake for his place of business. When one had breeding stock and the ability to train, one then had the sale of a half a dozen animals per year made a tidy income.

As a boy, Doc Harper became proficient with the animals, but decided to leave it for medical training.

For his own use, Doc preferred the no-nonsense appearance and ability of the mountain mule. Many of the places his buggy must go had roads hardly more than trails, and they often crossed muddy streams. As a doctor, he would be prepared to go anywhere, and the reliable mule filled the bill.

The fenced-off a pasture apart from the Clydesdales was perfect for Pokey, Puller and Pancake. This trio of animals may have been among the top tier of pampered mountain mules and Doc wanted it no other way.

He had been twenty five when he returned from the nearest medical training facility. His mountainous location was very hard on buggies, but that was just one problem of the occupation. There was no hospital to work from, so he had to go where the sick or injured were.

That left David Harper, Senior, to work alone, as his daughters opted for the nearby towns. Working long hours and entertaining grandchildren for the summers when they wanted to come. Not a bad life for the elder Harpers.

So for half his life, the blue-eyed, dark-haired younger Irishman followed his heart… which took him up and down Ridge Road, and made him a part of every family. The dark wavy hair now showing threads of silver around his ears, and a few in his beard.

Now at thirty seven, he was the rather surprised owner of the hair and beard when he looked in the mirror and shaved. Where did the time disappear to…? And why hadn't he done so many of the things he intended to do…?

There was a time that he would have chosen and courted a young lady, but there was always something else demanding attention. And when he would have taken her for a ride in a 'courtin' buggy', he was forcing his way through the brush and vines to a woodcutter who had met with a flying axhead. Blood, flowing, was immediate, and courting could happen tomorrow. But it didn't.

By lamp light, he scanned a pamphlet he had picked up from his mailbox, words containing the latest word on pain killers, the newest of equipment for a country doctor's pack, and the continuous debate as to whether there was there any value in the herbal medicine that was often the only health product available.

And the birthdays had flown by.

The horrible attack on young Olivia brought him up short on his reminiscing. He had actually attended at her birth when Ophelia had come to her parent's farm for her 'lying in'. Olivia's mother had married just after Doc had returned with his diploma, printed on 'sheep skin parchment' as were other valuable documents of the time period.

Beautiful Ophelia… married, and having a baby…? Surely not, and, my, my how time flies. She was only three years younger than Doc.

But then he hardly turned around until he regularly saw Ophelia's little girl walking the roads, inspecting the vegetation with dedicated interest, and watching the insect life, slipping quietly up to a butterfly, or picking blackberries into her mouth.

Quite, charming child. Polite. Loved everything. Was the darling of Miss Tillie at the school. Doc would wave to her, and occasionally offer her a ride. Usually, she preferred to walk and see what she could see.

And now she hovered between life and death… closer to death, actually. The attack had done irreparable internal damage, and it was certain that she would never see her own little girl who would be named 'Ebony Lace', because of the keepsake collar crocheted by her grandmother. Shame… actually.

Doc had wondered, fleetingly, whether Olivia had by now become a 'woman'. Thirteen was usually the bridge age. And he sincerely hoped she hadn't as she was certain to have trouble. Now or later.

Terrible attack.She must have put up quite a fight, for such a mild child, and then to crawl so far to reach the road. The girl was a fighter, though. She might even pull through this tragedy.

The last few yards of her crawl would have been accomplished by the sheer force of determination... hard-headedness. For a fact, there was obviously more tenacity in that little thing than he would have expected.

She had hung on for three days, now, but if she didn't come around immediately, she would succumb to lack of nourishment and liquid. Isabel did her best, but teaspoons full at a time...? Frustratingly slow.

It was a light day today, and he turned Puller and Pokey in at the Hadley lane. Isaac met him with hollow eyes and wrinkled a pulled-down face. Bad news. She hadn't come around.

Doc nodded. Time to do something. Even if it hastened the worse. Isabel sat by the bedside with her bowl and spoon. A washpan of water stood by, showing that she had just been 'bathed'. The sorrowful woman stood and let Doc have her place.

He looked in under the pale eyelids. A flutter of nerve movement. Hmmmm. Well, let's try the feet. Lifting the cover revealed bare feet still as death. Holding her ankle, he pulled the back of his fingernails along the sole of her foot. Once.

Twice... then the girl arose out of her coma with a scream of unearthly, rasping pain, dredged up from the depth of her soul. A scream, and then another, weak arms flailing and head turning from side to side.

Doc watched, not sure what to do next. No matter. The girl immediately fell back into the unconscious state. Doc decided to take the arousal as a good omen. Let her rest for an hour or so, and then try the sole of her foot again.

He didn't need to. A half an hour later, she opened her eyes, tears flowing and whispered 'Ma...? Ma...!'. Isabel busseled out of the room to get Ophelia while Doc held both her hands in his.

"Shhh Shhhh! Momma's coming."

Eyes closed again. The slightest move, however, brought screams of pain. Her throat was so raspy and dry she had trouble swallowing. She begged for the pain to go away, as Ophelia stroked her arms, legs and feet.

Doc worked up the courage to ask Isabel the question that plagued him. "Is she...uh, has she reached her... periods?"

Brightly, the girl's grandmother answered, "She has! Two months back, now."

Doc nodded, but groaned, inwardly. Time would tell, as it had in so many other instances of this type. There was so much the doctor wanted to know and dreaded knowing.

He needed to leave the Hadley home. Swallowing his agony, he left Isaac with a smile and a pat on the shoulder. He stepped into the buggy and tapped the horses with the reins.

As he neared his own cabin, Puller sounded off with a 'He-haw He-haw' and was answered by Pancake out in the pasture. One of the Clydesdales lifted a head and pronounced a whinny.

Sounds of home. Maybe he could take a nap. He checked the Note Box by the gong. There was a note. Zillah Fry was in the throes of one of her headaches.

*"Would Doc bring something when he came that way?"*

Turning the animals around, he headed up the hill. Zillah's worse headache problem was that she was married to it, but what could Doc do? Bring her a few hours of comfort? That's what. A few hours of comfort from the bottle of liquid that would put her to sleep.

And the pair of mules plodded up the hill to the Fry's house.

## MISS OLIVIA DALTON

She had opened her eyes, screaming. "HELP ME! STOP HURTING ME! GO AWAY AND LEAVE ME ALONE!" Her eyes, now uncovered, searched for a sight of the animal that had attack her.

She knew all the small animals of the woods and the timid deer, and she even knew the wolf pack. A scream and a tossed stone always sent them away. They were well-fed and, anyway, humans were not their meal of choice.

But this animal was different. It crammed her sweater into her mouth and over her eyes, and held her wrists in an iron grip. What animal could do that? And it threw her on the ground on rough sticks and small rocks and tried to... what was it doing? She strained to remember, and then the faint pictures melted away.

She had a moment of puzzlement before she lapsed again into the blessed land of nothingness.

Young Olivia had been carefully reared. Protected as a princess, and she adapted well to that treatment. She loved everyone, and they loved her… or at least admired (and possibly) envied her. No one ever tried to hurt her.

The animal that had attacked her seemed to have a voice and ordered her to do things she didn't understand. She had fought it by kicking when she had a chance, but that only made the animal madder. Finally she lay back and turned her mind off. She was obviously going to be eaten alive, and nothing could change that.

But later, when she would have looked up into the trees, she was lying in a bed of pain with her face in dead leaves with sticks in her mouth, and the best thing to do would be to get out of it if she could. She stood and promptly fell forward onto her face. Then she remembered nothing.

She did not remember the sharp sticks and rocks that had ripped her stockings into rags, and she did not feel the scrapes and cuts on her skin. Instinct rather than reason had told her to crawl… and go uphill. She would have no memory of this trip which must have taken more than an hour.

She would not know that after Doc had done what he could, he allowed Isabel to remove the sticks, clean the wounds and apply salve to her knees, elbows and palms. She had a slice from a sharp object down her cheek and neck, doubtless from a brier.

When she had reached the bar-ditch by the side of the road, a brief consciousness cleared her mind and told her she must wave her hand, the universal signal that one would like a ride. Possibly she saw and recognized her good friend Doc, but then her body allowed her to lapse again into the nothingness.

She knew no more until she woke up in the bed of pain with the impulse to get out of it, somehow. Strong arms held her shoulders, and a soft voice told her, "There, there, sweetie. You're safe now."

That reassurance let her retreat again but only for a half an hour. Eyes open again, she recognize Doc and Grammie Izzy. She was safe. Someone would do something to whatever was hurting her.

Her throat hurt so bad she could only whisper, but she was thirsty. Really thirsty.

Something about that made Doc and Grammie very happy. "Only a little water at first," Doc had said. What was wrong? Why couldn't she have very much water? And she had undoubtedly hurt herself, somehow, though she never took chances and seldom fell. She didn't climb into the trees or anything, but the slightest move was painful in a place where she had never had pain before.

No one could really explain to her what happened, or listen when she said an animal in the woods attacked her and wouldn't let her get away. Why were they not concerned about that animal… and find it… so it didn't attack the littler kids on their way home from school?

And then she got so tired she couldn't think anymore.

The half cup of water was reason for rejoicing as Doc and Olivia's relatives discussed and re-discussed it. If she could just eat and drink, she had a chance, though all agreed it would take time. And maybe it was just as well that she thought she was attack by an animal. At least for a while.

Doc rejoiced in her life, but knew from deep within his soul that the worse was yet to come. There'd be a time when she must know the truth, pleasant or not, and she would be fortunate if the worse result would be no little girl named 'Ebony Lace'.

But first things first, and leaving Isabel in charge, he left to make his rounds. Being by her side would not help her now, and anything to be done could be done by Isabel.

As Pancake and Pokey negotiated the hardly passable trails and ducked the hanging vines, Doc filtered facts through his mind. All of her careful rearing was of no value now. It was as though a delicate and well-tended flower had been crushed under a boot. Or a brisk shower of rain had dashed a monarch butterfly against a stone.

In one afternoon, she experienced one of the worst evils of the world, and who would do such a thing… and so near her own home? A stranger… but what stranger would somehow be waiting in the woods just when Olivia happened along?

No matter. Life must go on.

He stopped in on her most days, for a while, and was relieved that at least she showed improvement. Slow. The three days of coma had left its mark on a child who had very little natural reserve. He encouraged her to stand up for a while each day, even though it 'hurt awfully, Doc.'

Then he encouraged (insisted) that she go to the table for her meals. The short walk and time sitting along with her family, and the sight of food before her might encourage her to eat more. Maybe it did.

Miss Tillie missed her at school. Missed her terribly. She was such good help with the little ones that required so much time. The teacher brought whatever story books she could manage and asked her mother to provide her with drawing paper and encourage her to draw plants. It was something she did well, and it might draw her mind aside from herself.

Doc encouraged the drawing. He also wanted her to write a note to accompany the artwork. A few sentences about what that plant was good for. He even dropped off a paper that had been sent to him that had sketches of medicinal plants and their uses. It occupied her for a while, but she was inclined to sleep for long periods.

It was three months later when he sent her family from the room and examined her as best he could without frightening her. What he thought he learned lay in the pit of his stomach like a volcanic rock tossed up when northern Arkansas was formed. Gray and hard. Rough and cold. The thing he had feared had indeed happened… somehow… and now it must be dealt with.

He decided, however, to wait another month. So far, her family had not worried because a crisis could easily have put her off schedule. He'd wait and be absolutely sure before he upset them. There'd been no morning sickness, seemingly, but it didn't always happen.

It was in the fourth month that he gathered her three relatives together in the parlor. To their wide-eyed gaping eyes, he offered one ray of hope. There was something that could be done, but she would need to be taken to the hospital in a larger city than Eureka Springs. What needed to be done required skill and equipment not available to him.

Doc watched as sober faces moved side to side. Such an indignity was just not acceptable. Not after what she had been through already. He could see that the dear people did not understand, though he spoke as clearly as possible.

Perish the thought, they insisted. Babies were lost... yes... but were not ripped out before they had a chance to be born. And at her age, it would take parental insistence, not just permission.

So, now the next thing would be to tell the girl what was happening to her. She was a smart young lady, and deserved to know. But she was not smart about how it happened. Her education had been sketchy along that subject, as it seemed there would be a lot of time for it later.

In addition, she could not even think of her attack being from other than an animal? Why would a human even... ? Well, that was a good question, and the answer was unacceptable.

The gossip grapevine passed the information from one end to the other of Ridge Road as quickly as a winter freeze-up could cover every twig and stone with a casing of ice. Did you hear... ? Right here in our woods... ? Strangers oughta be shot... !

'Now, you girls listen. Don't you never be alone on the road for no reason. See what can happen...?'

'There ain't no way that little splinter of a girl can... Well, just look at 'er!'

From that time on, Olivia was never free of her puzzled look. Yes, she knew there would be a baby. A girl, of course. Her name would be Ebony Lace. She insisted on a pencil and Doc's note book. "My little girl will be Ebony Lace, and she will be beautiful like the picture of Grammie Cecelia."

She had taken the faded and dim tintype photo of her Great Grandmother Cecelia and insisted Doc look at it. It was possibly one of the two or three pictures taken of her in her lifetime. About twelve, Cecelia would have been at that time and was dressed in ruffles and bows. And very beautiful, it was plain to see.

The girl struggled through the fifth month and moved painfully into the sixth. Sometimes she whispered to Doc that she 'couldn't hardly breathe' when she sat on the soft sofa. Doc had no trouble believing it. Doubled over in the softness of the pillows… of course she couldn't breathe. It was amazing that the baby could.

At the beginning of the seventh month, she could not stand without help. Doc fought with what he knew should be done and what he was not permitted to arrange. So he did his best. She must eat six meals a day and have at least three eggs every day. Without fail.

By the eighth month, her legs went numb unless she was stretched out in bed. She insisted on listening to Doc's stethoscope to the 'oomph, oomph' that registered in her ears. A faint smile. Ebony Lace was talking to her. She tried to read, but her hands cramped when they held the book.

With a lump in his throat, Doc told her family. "Any sudden pain she has, come and get me. In the night or wherever I am. I'll try to keep you in touch of where I'll be. Don't wait until morning."

Isaac, seeming to have aged ten years in the last months, followed Doc to the buggy. "Wanted to ask you somethin'…away from the women folks. There ain't no good news, is there?"

Again Doc swallowed the lump. "No good news, Zeke. There just ain't room inside her for what's growin'. If you get a chance, prepare the women folks that it ain't good. I'm thinkin' it'll about do Isabel in, the way she'd taken care of Olivia. Do your best." And he turned away and climbed in the buggy. It wasn't good for the family to see the doctor in tears.

Doc lost a lot of sleep, being sure there would be a midnight call. There was something about it, the doctors and nurses all agreed, that made babies start to move in the night hours. Mostly, they could wait until morning, but he didn't want to risk it for Olivia.

And two weeks into the eighth month, it happened. The gong rang out in the night air, with strike after strike. Old Isaac on the saddle horse beat on the disk of metal six times, and then went galloping to the house, maybe to help get the buggy ready.

In ten minutes flat, Doc was on the way, Puller and Pokey moving as fast as their legs and the dark road permitted.

He burst into the house with his stethoscope in his hand. The girl on the bed was screaming… and gagging, gasping for breath.

Hands on the heaving abdomen told him the final picture had already been painted. There was nothing he could do to stop what was heading at them, bright and roaring as a train coming into a tunnel.He couldn't stop it any more than he could a have stopped the Frisco engine out on the tracks.

The three good-hearted, loving adults stared at him, hands outstretched grasping for some word of hope. Doc moved the stethoscope here and there, and the stead 'oomph, oomph' sounded. And then it sped up to a stead 'oomph.oomph.oomph'.

Doc again dealt with the growing lump in his throat and turned to the three. "I want all three of you to go to the parlor and sit down. I mean 'sit down'. I'm coming in to talk."

They turned and left, and Doc drew his sleeve across his eyes. No matter what the news, it was not good to see tears on the Doc's cheeks.

He faced the three pairs of eyes. "My good friends, the worst has happened, and there is absolutely no hope. I can take away her pain, but it will not stop what's going to happen. She is too small, and not strong enough to do what must be done."

A startled gasp from Ophelia. A stead gaze from the other two. They knew and trusted Doc, and there was more to say. Shaking their heads would not make it go away.

"You must think quickly and decide. You have two choices and neither are good. Olivia's heart is already struggling, and the damage already done is going to take her life. Here's what you must decide, and decide right now.

"I can remove her pain, and you can bury both Olivia and Ebony Lace, or I can attempt to save the baby. It is very risky, and there is not much chance of success, but I can try. So far, the baby has a good heartbeat, but she is going into stress. What has to be done, must be done immediately."

He looked at all three, individually. The faces of the mother and grandmother were as though carved from stone. He turned to Isaac who managed to whisper, "Save the baby."

Doc looked back at the other two and saw a painful nod of their heads. He turned to go back to Olivia, screaming in pain. Isaac followed him to the door and laid a hand on his arm.

"Doc, what're the chances?"

Doc answered, "Honestly, maybe one in ten."

And he told them, "I want you all to stay outside the room. Ophelia, get a large dishpan and line it with soft blankets. Put it in the oven to keep warm. Isabel, wash your hands the very best you can and wait outside the door."

Isaac looked up. "And me…"

"You have to pray, as best you ever did."

Doc closed the door behind him, and from his bag he took the small vial and the needle. Three more screams, a couple of groans and the room was quiet.

Doc caught his lower lip between his teeth to steady himself, took his seldom-used scalpel in a firm hand. He swiped his sleeve across his eyes and dealt again with that lump in his throat.

With the sharp edge of the knife, he lay the point against the now-quiet abdomen and made the first incision. He was totally on strange ground and was not even sure how deeply to cut. He hoped Isaac was praying.

Olivia was gone. At rest. A quick check with the stethoscope. A reassuring 'oomph oomph', faint but definitely there. Another movement with the scalpel, pushing deeper. Now! He reached down with both hands… into the still-warm flesh… and lifted away the perfect little girl, still attached to her mother. He called, "Isabel! Come in slowly."

The door cracked open, and the old woman paused. Doc told her, "I want you to back up and come toward me, slowly. I want to hand you the baby. Do not turn around."

And louder he said, "Ophelia, bring the pan… quickly."

Stepping backward, he put the tiny girl into the hands of her great grandmother. "Hold her until Ophelia brings the pan, and both of you go to the kitchen. Quickly! Cover her and wait for me."

When the women were gone, silently, from the room, he drew together the damage from his scalpel and took a few stitches. He spread the sheet over the placid, peaceful face. The image of her under the sheet must not be allowed in the minds of those who loved her. Only her face.

Then he joined the family in the warm kitchen. All three of them stood around the dishpan staring down at the tiny scrap of humanity that whimpered softly… and actually lifted a small hand, arm seeming to be no bigger than Isaac's thumb.

Doc sniffed, and felt a thrill of relief. Looking up to the Power above, he mouthed, 'Thank you'. To Isaac he said, "Go to the buggy and bring the box from between the seats."

Isaac was instantly gone. Doc took the dishpan and set it on the table. Folding back the blanket, he looked at the perfect little body. His first thought was, 'Olivia would have been proud.' Then, there was that lump again.

Doc had been in business a lot of years, and no one, it seemed, was ever prepared for the mother to be lost. He had packed the box in order to be prepared. Among the other items in it were a few softly worn diapers (very small) two bottles with nipples, a small bottle of clear oil.

"She must be cleaned. Ophelia…?"

The distraught lady shrank within herself. "NO! I CAN'T"

He turned to Isabel, the rock. "Take one of those flannel squares and the oil, and clean the creases very softly. Her skin is about as strong wet tissue paper. "

He handed Ophelia a diaper. "Tear it in fourths. We need tiny diapers."

Then he took his book to record the date and time of the birth. It was the duty of the doctor or the midwife, and the registry was insistent that it be done quickly.

Isabel took her assignment seriously. "Poor little tyke. No momma. And she ain't even got no name."

Doc expected this and he was ready. "Here's an idea. I've never given my name to a living soul, and I'd love to share it with this little girl. Her name will be Ebony Lace Harper. Any objections?"

Silence for a minute. Then Isabel… "Ebony…? For a little mite like this? What'll we call 'er? Eb…?"

Doc was ready again. "How about Bonnie? That means beautiful in the old country, and this little girl is very beautiful to me." He touched the damp haze of dark hair on the pink skull, smoothing it. When he lifted his finger, the hair bounced back into its naturally curved shape.

A very long sigh. Curley. Just what he had feared and dreaded. He boarded the buggy and clicked to the horses.

"Well, they'll just deal with it someway", he told the trees around him. Puller and Pokey expressed no opinion. One step after the other.

He waited a day to let the family absorb the situation, as much as possible, and came back to see if the little mite was still breathing. She was, but mostly from the dogged determination of her great grandma. Milk, a drop at a time. Rocking and humming. Changing the miniature diapers.

She looked at Doc. "Can't hardly find a place in my mind to put it all. This here little thing is a month and a half too little. The thing is, she don't seem to know it. I ain't hardly put 'er down, thinkin' I might not get to pick 'er up again, and her still breatin'. How does someone this little even live?"

Ophelia had totally folded. She took to her bed and refused to get up.

Doc told Isaac, "Now when arrangements get made, you'll all be goin' to the buryin'. I'll stay here with Bonnie." He made a point of using the baby's name.

"But, Doc, I was of a'mind…."

"No, Zeke. The women folks'll need you with 'em. I'm stayin' with the little girl that came at such a high price… paid by all of us."

"Yeah, Doc, but it ain't her fault. Thanks."

## BONNIE HARPER

Little Olivia Dalton was laid to rest in one of the most heavily attended funerals in the memory of the communities around Enterprise. It was almost as if by attending the funeral, the residents of the surrounding communities hoped to somehow negate the brutal attack. Hoping their attendance would make the horror disappear.

But the gossip grapevine blossomed and bore fruit in the form of a million speculations.

"Couldn't'a been a local, that girl bein' barely thirteen."

"I don't know. Evil seeds sprout and grow everywhere."

"Wonder who it was?"

"Don't we all… 'cause then we'd do somethin' about it."

"No way to know… fer sure."

"Less'n he confessed… which he wouldn't."

"Reckon it don't really matter, no more. It ain't like anyone'd be comin' to claim the little one that just got born. That'd be the important thing."

"I been over to pay my respects and saw that baby. Why, she'd fit in a shoe box and still have room to rattle around."

"'Spose someone that little could ever have a whole mind when it grows up?"

"Don't know, but don't call that baby and 'it' around Isabel. She'd go plain rabid."

"Heard Ophelia couldn't handle it. Came completely undone. Makes sense, though, with her loosin' her man the way she did and left with the little girl, and her gone, too."

"Hmmm, well, I'd think that'd make 'er more possessive of that baby."

"Didn't though. You'd think it was Isabel's baby. 'Course, old Zeke is plum foolish over it, I mean her."

"And that name. Doc Harper sorta took over. Seems like that girl told 'im ahead'a time what she wanted, and she wrote it in his book."

"And that last name. Doc Harper's. Said it might'a been that as well as any other, with no one knowin' anything."

"You don't think he'd…?"

"Never. Why he's almost forty, if he's a day."

"No, he's nearer thirty seven… bein' the same as when we was in school."

"Don't know's that'd matter. 'Course I'd never believe he'd'a…"

"But someone did."

"Fer a fact, fer sure."

"Word was, the girl didn't see who it was. Thought it was a wild animal and wouldn't be talked out of it."

"Likely best that it be left that'away."

Ophelia had her Pa take her and her buggy over to the nearby town of Wishbone where she found a room and got herself a job.

First it was floor cleaning at the hotel, and then her ability got her a promotion to room clerk. A personal room in the hotel came with that job, if the person was to want it.

Worked out well for some, and Ophelia was quick to take it. It wasn't long until the attractive lady of 35 attracted the gardener who kept the gardenias and roses in beautiful condition, and kept the ground under the magnolia tree swept clean of blossom debris.

He also was paid with an apartment back up the hill behind the hotel where he moved with his bride. When word filtered back to Ridge Road, there was a lot to say over the gossip grapevine.

"Seems Ophelia Hadley, I mean Dalton, found 'erself a fellow."

"Wouldn't'a thought otherwise, her bein' as pretty as she still is."

"Wasn't she alone for about ten years after her man was shot?"

"Not alone. She was with 'er folks."

"Well, I fer one, am glad for her. What she's been put through… that's a lot for any one person."

"Yeah, but Isabel and Zeke went through it, too, and them at their age stuck with a kid the age'a Bonnie."

"I don't reckon they think of it as bein' stuck."

Marsie, with a smile, "Should'a heard her braggin' when that kid sat up by 'erself. Come time she takes a step, likely Isabel'll put it in the papers."

"The way I hear it, Doc Harper stops in to check on that girl every week or so. Cute little tot, she is. Dark curly hair all over her head. Isabel keeps it combed all the time. Sometimes ties on a ribbon… and her barely a year old."

"Has it been that long?"

"Bet your boots, it has."

"Law Sakes, how time does fly!"

Small Bonnie was a bit behind her mother in standing, but caught up at sixteen months. At seventeen months, she took a step, enjoyed it, so she took another. At a year and a half she ran. And ran.

The problem with that was that when she ran, someone must run after her. Isabel chuckled and shook her head. "That youngen! Blink once and she's gone. Like a butterfly on a tulip… breeze comes and she's off and gone."

Zeke was nodding. He'd had his share of running. "And here it is tomato season, and Isabel was aimin' to get some put up. So I have to let the hay go and hang onto the girl." He smiled, fondly, but that did not get the hay in.

Isabel added, "And we cut down a lot of the garden, just the two'a us and her. Didn't need so much, don't you know."

Doc looked from one to the other. "Could be I could help. I'm out to see Nelda and Sam Wainwright. Their daughter, Dorothy, up in Joplin… she get's to worryin', her folks livin' out there alone. Wants me to check on 'em every week or ten days and see it gets done whatever they need.

"So if I was to take Bonnie with me, Nelda'd love to see 'er. Doesn't get too much of'a chance to see somethin' lively as that girl."

"But you in the buggy… do ya think she's be safe. She's so…."

"Certainly would… if I tied her to the seat."

So that was the beginning of Bonnie's travels with Doc Harper. A belt for her waist and a hook on the seat held her firmly, and still gave her a good view.

The grapevine was quick to pick up on it.

"I saw Doc over to the store. Had Zeke and Isabel's kid with 'im."

"Yeah, heard that got started so Isabel could get her tomatoes canned."

"Believe me, I could'a used help like that. Reckon I could get Doc to pick up my youngens?"

"Don't get yer hopes up."

"Doc seems to set a special store by that youngen."

"Could be on account'a the way she got here… him bein' there and all."

"Wonder who could'a done that to the girl."

"Reckon we'll never know."

At two and a half Bonnie began to talk. Doc played games like when he held up his hand and counted his fingers. She held up her hand, and he helped her a few times. ONE TWO THREE FOUR FIVE.

Then he would point to his middle finger and ask her its name.

"One, two, three. It's THREE!"

He bought a box of dominos. She could ride for a mile or two counting the dots. During the busy summer, she went with him on a number of selected rides. There was corn to shuck, peas to shell and green beans to snap. Isabel insisted on passing a few jars of whatever she canned to Doc... in gratitude.

Couldn't no one ever say the Hadley's took freebees.

Winter came and Bonnie missed the rides. Doc stopped by when he could, with new games. Like a puzzle that made a picture if she got the blocks in the right place.

He brought wooden ABC blocks and a copy of the alphabet on a large cardboard. At three and a half, she could line up the blocks without looking at the cardboard. Next she learned B O N N I E.

BINGO! Her mind snapped into place. If the blocks made one word, they could make more words, and she demanded to see them. Doc found himself stopping in three or four times a week before making his rounds. Isabel added him to the breakfast table, and her biscuits were a lot better than his! Sorta worked out good... both ways.

At five years old, Doc brought her some little books he'd ordered. The books had stories of three or four sentences, and pictures on every page. That was also the first year she could attend Miss Tillie's school as her momma had.

One thing different. If Doc could not take her to the school, Zeke swung her up into the saddle in front of him and got her there. Safely. He always picked her up after school, too.

Too much could happen if he didn't.

## MISS BONNIE HARPER TURNS FIVE

Bonnie, thanks to Doc Harper, could very well know when she turned five. Fingers on one hand. Easy.

She also knew that at five years old she could attend Miss Temple's school, if... the grownups who ruled over her permitted... and if Miss Temple had room for her and agreed to take her. Otherwise, she would have to wait a year and then Miss Temple would have to take her, so why not now, and get it over with?

Miss Tillie Temple well remembered the pleasant, studious but easy-going personality of Olivia (no one just said, right out, that

Olivia was Bonnie's mother. Unthinkable!) They left it more like Bonnie appeared by some mysterious means, best left undiscussed.

Miss Temple had been devastated by the loss of Olivia, both on a personal and helpful level. So the idea of whether to accept Bonnie never lingered a moment in her mind. That taken care of, it was only left for Zeke and Doc Harper to determine how she got there. Not a problem.

So Isabel ordered fabric from the catalog store up at Burnt Tree Junction. She picked the mother of several well-dressed daughters, (four, to be exact) and offered a swap of skills. A common practice in the mountains.

She settled on Mrs. Carpenter, as the seamstress, selecting the styles she thought suited Bonnie the best. Puffed sleeves, full skirts and wide sashes, and Isabel sorted out four dozen of her best canned pickles… the Carpenter girls adored Isabel's pickles at community gatherings where food was served.

Three dozen of the jars would be beet pickles, and one would be of the mild 'bread and butter' variety so tasty on sandwiches. All 48 jars would be returned to Isabel, of course. The gift of food never included the jar or the casserole dish unless specified clearly. Glass canning jars were not only expensive and highly breakable, there was the bulky transportation costs in getting them home from a nearby town.

In due time, seven new dresses appeared, and a light-weight unlined coat for the in-between weather.

It had been a matter of community interest whether Isabel would permit Bonnie to have the earlier, five-year-old year, but wise minds thought she would. Both Isabel and Bonnie were getting older, and were affected in totally different ways. Bonnie was no clone of Olivia… she was quicksilver to Olivia's sweet gum resin (relaxed, solid and mild), and she was afraid of nothing.

Miss Temple was also getting older. Though she was looking forward to having Bonnie, she was unprepared for her demand for attention and for answers to her questions, of which were endless. Miss Temple did not have many children like her, which was not to say she might have enjoyed them.

There were those who came close, but her best memory went back to when she was in the classroom, herself, and a classmate by the name of David Harper was much the same way. And here was Bonnie Harper. The teacher knew the reason for the name, but still… there was something that dwelt in her mind, causing a bit of itching, occasionally.

The gossip grapevine picked up on conversation of their own students in that one-room class, and passed on bits of interest.

"You recall, don't you, of Doc's ma sayin' that sittin' next to him was a mite tiring, him being like a 'worm in hot ashes'?"

"I do for a fact! My Ma and grannie got a charge outta that description picturin' a bucket'a ashes bein' taken out. Never said how that worm would'a got in that bucket, but it'd do some squirmin' for sure."

"Isabel started 'er out with seven new dresses. Imagine that!"

"Could be on account'a her getting so' dirty. Wouldn't hardly be wearin' the same dress two days, runnin'. Rides right up there in the saddle with Zeke, comin' to school. Likely got dirty underthings, too."

"I'd reckon."

And as she got older, Bonnie's appearance began to change. Olivia was such a slim, splinter of a girl, there was talk she'd have to 'stand twice to make a shadow'.

Not so, Bonnie. Well filled out and fast moving was an often used description of girls like her. Also said, was that "no grass'd ever grow under her feet!"

When she was eight years old, Isabel showed her the pictures Olivia had sketched and colored. Bonnie studied them intently and demanded paper. There was a lot of drawing paper left from that furnished by Doc, so Bonnie began.

Flowers from the garden appeared on the paper. Mint plants for making tea were documented. Doc found a descriptive circular on tea plants that had been sent to him, and passed it on to her.

With the circular, she now had a list of ailments that were best helped by what tea. Most of the community knew, or thought they knew, but to have a picture and also a list would have been a help.

When Bonnie was ten, she had perfected her drawings of garden tea plants and put them on separate sheets to bind into a book, but when Doc saw them, he immediately knew of a use. There were not enough, actually, to create even a small book, but if she would make two pictures more, to total a dozen, he'd take them to the newspaper in Wishbone Hollow, the Wishbone Cryer, and he'd see what they suggested.

Easily done, he took the twelve sheets to the printer. The typesetter peered critically at the pictures and counted the sheets. "You thinkin they'll ever be more than these?"

Whereupon Doc shrugged his shoulders and nodded. He guessed there might be… why the question?

"'Cause, for a few dollars I could put these on one sheet to be folded, and print off a hunnerd or so. It'd take another 20 pictures like these to make any kind of'a book that that'd be thick enough to bind. Better to have about 30 more."

Wheels spun in Doc's head. If he had all of these drawings and descriptions on one folded sheet, it would make a perfect handout to young girls and new customers. He could plainly see that ten did not fit economically on the page and two more would be only an afternoon's activity for the girl. Especially if they were mushrooms.

Most of the way home, he considered which 30 items would fit best for the book, which he knew he ultimately must have. About six of the new items could be the additional non-poisonous mushrooms… so abundant in the woodland. There were those who bypassed harvesting that nutritious fungi because they couldn't tell if it was a safe one.

Raising the total to forty items, it could include the spring greens like poke, goosefoot, wild onion and lettuce, along with other well-knowns. Also, it could contain the edible flowers like the hibiscus, violet and buttercup. Bonnie loved to sketch flowers.

He titled the sheet of twelve items 'GARDEN TEAS OF NORTHERN ARKANSAS', complied by Ebony Lace, assisted by Bonnie Harper. The girl loved the two names… making it look like she helped herself. Could have. The ten-year-old bounced excitedly on her toes and demanded a sheet for everyone in her school to take home.

Mrs. Erlicht, whose farm adjoined that of Mrs. Putman, commented, "Sight how that youngen'a Isabel's can put a picture on paper to look like it could be picked off and used. Could'a had a lotta help from Doc Harper, wouldn't ya think?"

"Could be, 'cept for the drawin'. I recall David Harper bein' quick with answers and regular with homework, but not to draw like this. As I recall, David couldn't draw flies without honey on his hands."

Mrs. Erlicht agreed. "Fact is, though, I thought I'd tack a sheet'a these on the kitchen wall to refresh what I already know."

And the talk continued from Burnt Tree Junction both ways east and west on Ridge Road.

"Ebony Lace...? You know of any family by the name'a 'Lace'? Don't think I have. Now Bonnie Harper... I know about her. She 's the...."

"Yeah. From Olivia Dalton. It'd'a been hard to miss that a'happenin'."

"'Tween you and me, I wouldn't'a thought that could'a happened. Either to her, or with no one knowin' who was... only...."

"I hear she held onto the idea of it bein' a animal, clear up to the time'a her passin'."

"Best that'away, I reckon."

And it was late in the year that a hot spell that came on in October. Everyone knows that the last planting of hay has to be brought in by then, and sixty-two-year old Zeke was in the field with his mule and cart, wielding his machete and scythe.

He ran out of drinking water that he had brought to the field, but he wanted to get enough on the cart for a load before going back to the barn. It took longer than he thought, and the mule, cart, and hayfield began to circle and blurr before his eyes.

Hayfields are not supposed to tip sideways, so he sat down in the cart on the hay and lay the pitchfork beside him. He'd rest a minute, and then he'd go to the house for water, full load or not. Zeke closed his eyes, thinking he was getting too old to be in the field alone, and it happened. Quietly, peacefully, and without fuss... the way Zeke had lived his life... he passed on to the next.

He would never again bring in the hay, because at the ripe age of sixty two, he departed gently on to his reward.

The mule waited for two hours, and then he leaned into the trace and brought hay and owner to the barn. He reached the water trough and drank his fill. Then, just for the thing of it, decided to lift his voice in a resounding bray. The rusty-hinge sound of his "he.. haw… ehaw… ehaw.. ehaw" brought Isabel's attention to the time of day.

"There's Zeke, bringin' in the hay. He'll be hotter'n a two dollar pistol. That mule bellerin' likely means there's no water. I'll go draw some."

That was the moment Isabel's life of devastating losses took on another hit. Leaning against the loaded hay, she bent forward onto the faded overalls she had washed so many times. Arms around him and tear wet face on the bib of his overalls, she poured out her anguish to the hens, scratching in the barnyard, and the mule, still hitched to the wagon.

She had not one thread of desire to draw another breath, and begged with her tears to be taken on with her life's mate, but it was not to happen. But if she refused to make a move, perhaps the Powers that were, might relent and take her because there was nothing left in life for her to do.

Prayers are always heard and answered, though not always the way they were prayed. Seemed there must have been something left for her to do, because school had let out, and Doc was riding toward her on the short driveway, bringing Bonnie home.

Doc mostly lifted Bonnie to the ground and insisted she go to the house, out of the boiling October sun. He removed the clips and freed the mule, and then looked in the house for Isabel. A sodden heap of tears was what he found.

"Bonnie, listen to what I say. You are gonna have to be a big girl for me right now. Grammie Izzy needs you to be in the room with her. She mustn't go outside or even into the kitchen. I want you to pour a pitcher of water and take in into her room, and then shut the door.

"If she comes around, offer her a drink. I'm going for help, and I'll be back. Don't be afraid. Remember, it's time to be the big girl that I know you are."

She looked at Doc, her face wet and red. Tears hung on the tips of her eyelashes, sparkling in the light from the window. Dew drops of agony. But behind the wet, the red and the sparkling, a determination shown through.

"Yes. I can take care of Grammie." With that, she uncurled from the heap on the bed she was, planted her feet firmly on the braided bedside rug, and walked determinedly to the kitchen for the water pitcher. Doc watched, satisfied. She'd be all right.

As he headed to the house of his parents, he mused. The life of a Doctor was, by choice, one of witnessing tragedy and bearing pain and agony, and he wondered why some people seemed to get more than their share.

Two days later, Zeke was lovingly placed beside Olivia.

Ophelia and her new husband looked on. Bonnie eyed Ophelia warily, but the older woman made no attempt at friendliness, past a simple greeting. Isabel was still drowning in the sea of her total sorrow, and Doc's parents were trying to hold everything together.

Doc was required to make a call on a first-baby case, where he thought there might be difficulty. Leaving his parents in charge of Isabel, he put Bonnie in the buggy behind Pancake and Pokey, and they left.

Bonnie was ten and a half.

He had never brought her on a birthing call, before, but what was a year or two… or ever four or five…? He was not absolutely certain that he might not need help on this one. Someone for errands.

Bonnie, herself, had sterilized everything in his birthing bag and placed implements it in their linen napkins to stay clean. For the last year or so, it had been a chore she enjoyed, and, truthfully, one he had often found tedious.

The girl rode silently beside him, staring mostly out the windshield at gathering darkness of the road ahead. Doc glanced from the corner of his eye and watched her features, solid as though cast in marble. Only the blink of her eyes, and an occasional swallow in her throat indicated life.

She and Grandad Zeke had a special feeling for each other, and Doc knew Bonnie would have to break... but that she was determined that it not be now, when Doc depended on her. Doc nodded with satisfaction.

She was made of good stuff. Hands folded in her lap over her favorite blue dress with white dots and white lace on the collar. Dark, dark hair pulled back into a clasp at her neck, pulled so firmly that the curls were stretched out into waves until escaping below the ribbon. Lashes dark on her pale cheeks when she blinked.

Carmelita Wilson's young husband was pacing back and forth in the front yard, like a wild beast in a cage. Another buggy was in the yard, the horse still in the harness. The friend had obviously just arrived.

That would be Bessie May Coleman. She lived across Ridge Road and east a quarter of a mile, almost over into Garland. The girls had been friends since Miss Temple's school, and were close neighbors.

As they approached the house, Bonnie reached for and lifted the birthing bag... actually a small suitcase... and possessively set it in her lap, wrapping both arms around it. Doc watched. She was leaving no question that she was going to be there when he needed her... a part of the mental tie between herself and Doc.

Cliff Wilson rushed to meet the buggy, both hands reaching to shake Doc's. "Oh, Doc, I was about to... I mean, I knew about the funeral and all, but she's painin' somethin' awful, and I ain't for certain Bessie's gonna make it, neither, for tearin' up till she can't rightly see what she's doin'."

"It's all right, Cliff... we're here." Vaguely, he realized he had said 'we' instead of 'I'.

In the house, he found Bessie sitting on Carmelita's bed, leaning over her and sobbing. Carmelita was shaking in agony, obviously frightened and as tense as a fiddle string. The two young people with her were no help.

Doc lined up his thoughts. First, get rid of Bessie. Next, use an anesthetic. He didn't like to do it. Natural childbirth was best, when possible, but the shape Carmelita was in... well... one must set priorities.

He sent Bessie to the kitchen for a pan of hot water and to make a pot of tea. Cliff was set to removing the mules from the harness. Doc needed a white smock and turned to take it from his bag, and the bag was lying open on a chair. The smock was held in Bonnie's sturdy ten-year-old hands, opened, so he had only to slip it on.

He made no comment, as Bonnie took out the starched apron and put it on herself. She watched as Doc lifted out the small bottles and set them on the stand beside the bed.

Morphine. It had been quickly brought into use in the war, to ease the death of the dying and to give the badly wounded a chance at being repaired. Wonderful stuff, but terribly addicting. Reason enough not to use it unless absolutely necessary. Bonnie watched… hardly blinking.

Scolopine. A extract of belladonna… the death angel plant. First used to quietly dispose of an enemy, it was found to have a numbing quality if used in smaller quantities. Often dangerous. Somewhat of a guessing game to determine the dosage, taking into account the size of the intended patient.

In childbirth, it was especially dangerous for the baby. While quieting the pain of the mother, the much smaller body of the baby was the victim as the drug acted on the tiny nervous system… creating 'sleepy baby' situation.

The preparation rightly earned the name, 'twilight sleep'.

Doc felt that it's best use was a 'promise' that a painkiller was coming, and then holding off as long as he thought the mother could stand the pain before administering it. A baby 'crowning' was considered a safe times and sooner to be used only in a dire emergency.

Carmelita might be an emergency.

The pan of warm water appeared, and Bonnie watched as Doc carefully washed his hands and dried them on a towel from the bag. He turned to the medicine bottles, and Bonnie dipped her hands into the soapy water and then dried them on the same towel.

She watched as the liquid from the bottles was poured, tiny drops at a time, into the tube of the hypo needle. Then she watched as he set the needle aside and dipped a cloth in the water, wringing it out. He wiped the warmth across Carmelita's tear-wet face murmuring that she was doing fine.

Carmelita responded with a scream. "IT HURTS! DOC, DO SOMETHIN'!"

Doc's soothing voice answered. "I will, Carmelita. Help is on the way. Just a little longer." In the midst of her screams, he examined the bulge. Active. Birth before midnight… maybe a lot sooner.

"Bonnie, wring out the cloth in warm water and message her arms. Bessie, bring hotter water. Cliff, look for the blankets she made, and make sure they're ready. Then, I want you and Bessie to go to the kitchen and each have a cup of tea, and don't come back in until I need you. I'll call when I need you."

With a look, a mixture of surprise and relief, the two adults left. Bessie returned with hotter water, and added it to the pan. Bonnie wrung the cloth and carefully massaged Carmelita's arms. The room was so warm from the October heat, that the moisture quickly dried and cooled her skin.

Then she moved the damp cloth to Carmelita's neck and forehead. It seemed to calm her slightly. Doc completed his examination. "Carmelita…?"

"Huh", between sniffs and whines.

"You're doing a really good job. I have some things that will help you, but they are not the best for the baby. So I want you to keep doing what you're doing, and I want you to count to five, very slowly, over and over. You're very brave, and this is a hard job. But I know you can do it."

Bonnie, with her sketchy and erroneous views of childbirth, listened carefully. Carmelita didn't seem to be working, but Doc said she was. So she must be.

Internal activity slowed, as it often does, and the exhausted girl finally dozed, quietly. Doc motioned Bonnie to stop with the washcloth. She sat on a nearby chair and studied her hands… folded together in her lap.

Doc studied her. What would she do when the actual birth happened? She was only ten… but a solid ten, brave, serious ten… and obviously considered herself a part of the answer. Would this be the time? Nodding to himself, he agreed. Yes, sooner or later, she would be helping him, so why not now?

It was eleven o'clock when Doc went to the kitchen. Cliff and Bessie were both leaning forward on the table, asleep. Exhausted from worry. Wonderful! The folded blankets were stacked nearby, and cups of cold tea were on the table.

It was going to be soon. Carmelita was restless, groaning, and straining. "Bonnie, when I tell you to, I want you to go get Bessie and the blankets. Try not to wake Cliff. Tell Bessie I need her to come in but not to make a sound. Can you do that?"

A firm nod. "Yes."

No hesitation. No questions. No sign of fear. Yes, it was time.

Carmelita began to weep, pathetically… dismally. A few more minutes, and her pain would stop. Doc watched and monitored the contractions. Now!

He caught Bonnie'a eyes… she was watching his every move and expression. He picked up the syringe and dabbed at Carmilita's skin with the sterile cotton. A quick flinch, a tense jerk, and then blessed relaxation. She turned her head on the pillow and sighed.

Doc examined again. He had a fear of administering too quickly, but not this time. He felt the tension of her abdomen smooth out and the internal contraction push. In the lamplight, he saw a spot of hair.

With hands on her abdomen, he stimulated the contractive action. To Bonnie, he whispered, "Go call Bessie, and come right back."

Bonnie was gone, and back immediately, and at his side. "Now watch," he told her. And she stared transfixed, refusing to blink.

Then quickly, a small head appeared and slid into Doc's hands. An arm… and magic! There was the baby!

Bessie appeared with the spread blanket. "Here, Bessie. Hold the blanket here." Bessie blinked her sleepy eyes, but held the blanket as Doc transferred the damp little bundle to her.

"Bessie, lay the little fellow on his mama's stomach. We have more work to do. Bonnie, take the water pan to the kitchen, and bring clean water."

A half an hour full of busy minutes, Bonnie hovering.

Then it was over, and the mess was removed. Used cloths and towels laid aside, and a clean little boy was snuggled in the blankets.

"Bonnie, go call the baby's Pa."

The exhausted young man reacted to a shake of the shoulders. With an excited grin Bonnie whispered, "You got yourself a little boy!"

Cliff startled awake, realized what she said, and dashed to the bed. The pink creature in the basket was whimpering softly and turning his head from side to side. A tiny fist escaped the blanket and flapped about.

The impressed papa wiped a sleeve across his eyes and sniffed, touching the silky hair with a calloused finger. Bessie watched, fidgeting to again be holding the basket. It was her turn. Babies, she knew about. It was just a friend in labor that had her torn apart.

Doc watched papa and friend, nodding with satisfaction. Carmelita slept peacefully. He could leave the little fellow in good hands, and tomorrow he would bring the paperwork and check mama, who would then be awake.

"Bessie," he asked, "Could you make a cup of tea for Bonnie and me, and we'll be on our way. Peppermint, if you have it."

Eager for something to do, she bustled into the kitchen. Five minutes later she had the tea. Bonnie stolidly and importantly sipped the tea, looking from one to the other of the adults, sober and thoughtful. It had been a horrible day and an exciting evening. Her ten-year-old brain was going into overload.

Cliff reattached the mules to the buggy and lit the lanterns. Bonnie repacked the birthing bag and carried it to the buggy. By the time they reached Ridge Road, she had wilted across the bag and was sleeping soundly.

Doc watched her in the light of the lanterns. Dark wisps of curls across her forehead, ribbon messed up and spirals of hair trying to escape. Eyes closed. Efficiently, small hand with fingers spread protectively across the birthing bag. It would be interesting to see what she said tomorrow and the days that would follow.

It could go two ways. She could have been frightened of the whole scene but more likely, hooked forever on the magic of birth of new life…as he was. Only time would tell.

## ISABEL DALTON

After two days of being sheltered by the elder Harpers, they went home. Isabel sat up in bed after another sleepless night and took stock. When one gets blindsided and battered into the earth, then one must plan how to rise again.

But the fact was, at going on sixty three years old, a body doesn't expect what she just went through. After a sick spell, maybe… nearing a hundred years of age, quite likely. But Zeke was a robust sixty five. It really couldn't have happened… but it did.

So… she must somehow manage her farm. Little Bonnie was there, all alone. No, of course not. Doc had her with him, and he wouldn't leave her. And he wouldn't let her go back to school… not yet.

Thinking to do.

Fact One: She really couldn't manage the farm alone.

Fact Two: There was no way on earth that Ophelia and her new husband would take over.

Fact Three: She had Bonnie to take care of for the next eight or ten years.

Fact Four: She had absolutely no idea of what she could do and was reluctant ask for help.

But Fact Five loomed the largest: Decisions must be made: post haste.

At this moment, Doc was returning from a call up Ridge Road at Burnt Tree Junction. The small cluster of houses surrounding this point had just about everything but a grocery store. It even had a catalog store where anything could be ordered from baby chickens to dress material, to fence wire, and it was even possible to order a whole house.

Of course that would be impractical, here in tree-studded northern Arkansas. But one could order a house, if one wanted it.

Carl Potter's son had stopped in and left a note that Pa wanted to see him. Not for himself, actually, but Pa wanted to talk to him about the pains Mellie, Carl's wife, was having. It had been an easy call.

Doc had prescribed a B-one Vitamin pill that he kept in stock, but that was not the best of it. Mellie Potter was one who just didn't know how to stop. She tried to take on the cares and duties of the world, and Doc just had to put her to bed. Make here stay.

A week would do it, he thought. During that time, she wasn't to be on her feet more than 20 minutes at a time or more than five times a day. Carl and the boy would do the house work and the cooking.

(That, of course, would be the biggest incentive he could give her to do what he said and get well.) Carl never bothered to learn to cook, of course, and the boy would live on eggs and biscuits, which he made. Passable quality.

Miss Mellie immediately decided to do just what Doc said… so she could get back to taking on the cares of the world.

As he climbed back in the buggy and Bonnie slid in from the other side, he looked at her and winked. Bonnie winked back. Sharp younguen, putting things together in her mind, the way she did. Like they said in the mountains, "didn't no grass grow under that girl's feet, and no cobwebs grew in her mind, neither."

They clopped along toward Enterprise in silence, until they were going down the last hill before home. Bonnie waited until the buggy passed Doc's driveway and moved on toward hers.

"What's gonna happen with me, Doc?"

Doc drew in a dreaded breath and rode silently for a couple of minutes. What did one say to a ten-year-old, with the kind of honest relationship he had with this one?

"Well, little Miss, I'm thinkin' that'd be for Grammie Isabel to say."

Only a moment's hesitation. "She ain't gonna be able to say nothin', Doc."

True assessment. Silence for a quarter of a mile, and the team turned without direction into the Hadley Lane. Doc knew Bonnie was absolutely right. Zeke had been the decision-maker, and he was a private person about his business. It would have been the last thing in the world to have told Isabel what to do if he was no longer with her. Think on it…where else would he be if not with her?

But Bonnie had a right to know. "Right off hand I think she might talk with Ophelia. She might have an idea, don't you think?"

No hesitation this time, either. "No. She'd say for Grammie to find a place in town and bring me with her."

Doc nodded. The girl had been doing some thinking, and she might have it figured out. "So, how would you like that?"

"I ain't goin'."

That got Doc's attention. "You… what…?"

"I ain't gonna leave Miss Tillie's school. She wants me there."

"But, Bonnie, sweetie… you…."

"I'll talk to my friends, and someone will let me stay with them until the end of this year."

All right. It wasn't that he was surprised… it was just the Doc hadn't thought it through from Bonnie's point of view. Best he nip this in the bud immediately while he thought about it.

If just until the end of the year… seven months… would pacify her, there should be something. Some way, "My dear, let's think about this some more. We'll talk with Grammie Isabel, and then…."

"No. I'm not going to Wishbone, and I don't want to be dumped on Ophelia. She doesn't want me. If you don't want me to ask my friends, then can I stay with you?"

"Uh, well, yes… but we haven't talked with your Grammie."

"Doc, we know she can't stay here on the farm. Not without Grandad."

Her ten-year-old voice carried the definite finality of a forty-year-old. Well, that'll be something to decide now that Isabel is up and around.

And Isabel was now up and around. The elder Harpers would like to have asked her about her plans, out of caring for her, but it was just not the kind of relationship they had. Isabel didn't offer and they didn't ask.

Maybe their son could do better. With hesitation and reluctance, they bade goodbye and rode away. They met their son just turning into the lane.

"Whoa! Whoa, there!" And both teams were stopped.

"Bonnie, stay in the buggy. We're goin' on home. I just want to say something to my Pa."

Bonnie rested her hands in her lap. They could say what they would, but she was not going to live with Ophelia. She'd run away first. She felt a lot better now that she had told Doc what she wanted.

Doc swung back up in the buggy and clicked to the mules. Bonnie studied his expression.

"Grammie ain't talkin', is she? She's gonna have to be told what's best. I wish someone could stay with us, to help but everyone wants their own farm, don't they?"

What could Doc do but nod. In the last two days, he and the girl had learned to read each other quite well. He had brought her home from the birthing, asleep on the buggy seat. He had managed to get her into the house and into her room.

He had wandered through the spotlessly clean house and located Ophelia's old room. Cool room. Fresh bed sheets. He stretched his exhausted body across the spread and was instantly asleep… but not for long.

He awoke with a start. Barnyard sounds coming from a different direction. What was…? And gradually reality dawned in his foggy mind. After about 10 minutes with a pair of wide open eyes, he decided he was hungry.

A quick check of the kitchen turned up nothing that didn't need to be cooked. A small sound drew him to the door of Bonnie's room. Sounds of sniffs and snubs… muffled and soft.

Bonnie was crying. Doc felt his heart being twisted and wrung out by the sound of it. So brave all evening, and now she had broken. Should he go in to her?

His hand against the doorknob, and he hesitated. Would she want him to intrude on her obvious grief, when she had been so brave all evening? Likely not. There were some things one hid more deeply from those who loved them most. Strange, but human. If she had wanted him to see her tears, she would have let him.

He forced his feet to walk away. He remembered seeing a pile of fresh-picked cantaloupes on the back porch. That would be just about right for a snack. Tiptoeing through the door, he failed to skip the squeaky board. Cringing at the piercing screech, he went on, selecting by the feel, two ripe melons.

Back in the kitchen, he put them on the table. Isabel would have said, "No, put them over here and wipe them off." No matter.

Slicing them open, he scooped the seed cluster into a bowl and settled down to the table. Small sound, and he looked up.

Bonnie stood in the doorway, face flushed but dry and hair pushed somewhat into place. "Is one of those for me?"

Doc nodded at the rightness of his decision. She would have hated for him to see her cry, "Sure thing! Slide on up here and we'll have a picnic."

The face acquired a somewhat forced smile. Seating herself, she picked up a spoon with her solid, little girl hands. So entirely different from the dainty, small-boned ones of her… of Olivia. Strong hands. No nonsense hands.

Where Olivia's drawings were delicate sketches showing veins and serrations on the leaves, Bonnie's were strong, with bold lines. It was like her drawings were lifting themselves up to the viewer… wanting to be seen. Their bold lines had transferred beautifully onto the sheet made by the printer.

With only a delicate sniff, Bonnie applied herself to the melon. Then she returned to bed, and he went back to Ophelia's room. The sun was high before they woke up. Much needed rest for both of them.

Together, they took care of the animals. Not much conversation. But the evening meal, ham, sliced off the hanging meat in the smoke house, and fried potatoes, somehow got together without Isabel's help. Doc was no great shakes as a cook, and Bonnie would not have been encouraged (permitted) in Isabel's well run kitchen. No matter.

Bonnie had a wonderful appetite. She heaped the ham cubes and potatoes on her plate, surrounding them with sliced onions, fresh from the fall gathering. She chewed thoughtfully, studying Doc's expressions.

"Grammie'll have to sell this farm 'cause she can't take care of it and I'm not big enough."

Doc let the sound die out on the air. A rooster flapped on a fence porch and sounded forth with a possessive crow. The hens scratched and clucked, paying him no mind.

A bumble bee zoomed toward the screen door and crashed against the frame. He lay on the porch buzzing his balance back, and then he took off… going somewhere. Doc gathered his courage.

"That's possible. We'll just have to wait and see what she says."

"No! I want to stay here. If I don't say somethin', I'll be carted off to Wishbone. I can't go there."

Doc bravely asked, "Why not?

"'Cause you'll be here, and I won't, and you need me to help you. Do you have any more patients expecting to get a baby…?"

So that was it! At least part of it. She had witnessed a birth, and she had been bitten… as he had been, buy the magic. It could only be magic. Of course, all of the earth was created by the greatest Magician of them all… so why shouldn't it be magic?

So now what? The fact was, in a couple of years she WOULD be a great help. But what were they going to do tomorrow… and the next day?

So they came home from the trip to the Potters. Bonnie had reiterated her firm decision to stay in Enterprise, in this house, with whoever would make it possible for her to do so.

And Isabel had come home and now… well, she must make plans. She sat at the kitchen table with her teapot. Elbows on the table, chin in her hands, eyes trying to focus on the window. She turned when Doc and Bonnie entered.

Gaunt and hollow eyed, she appeared to have shrunk several sizes. Maybe she weighed a hundred pounds… if she had a few rocks in her apron pockets. She did, however, realize that there would have to be great changes.

"Doc, you got a minute to sit?"

He did. Bonnie sat beside him.

"Would you be havin' a way to know what this here place is worth?"

"Lock, stock and barrel…?" A common phrase meaning that the owner would essentially just walk out with the clothes on their backs and the money in their pockets. "You sure?"

"Pretty much. Maybe take my bedding. Pillow and such."

Doc nodded. It was a good place, but he shouldn't quote a price, right off, like he'd been thinking on it. "Miss Isabel, I'll check around. Should have somethin' in a day or two."

And he wanted to say something else. Should he? A doctor was treated special by most communities, like the preacher and the school teacher. And she had brought him into the subject on her own. Surely he had the right to speak up.

"I've been thinkin'. You needin' to get Bonnie back and forth to school, I need to stay over here and take care of that while you make plans. I spent the night in Ophelia's room… is that's all right?"

Isabel lifted the cup wearily to her lips and nodded.

"So I'll just run over and check my mailbox. Then we can talk more if you want."

Bonnie's eyes followed him out. They registered approval from the dark depth of them. Doc was coming around. She'd just wait and see if more words were necessary. He needed her, and he just needed to realize that.

## WISHBONE HOLLOW, HERE SHE COMES

It took some delicate positioning of words, but Isabel Hadley was a realist. She couldn't stay on the farm; she needed a SMALL place in a town, with not much demand on her, and she needed something to fill her mind or she would go crazy, faced only with her thoughts.

Doc had told her that her place would bring $600.00 easy. Maybe a bit more if she left most of the furniture.

The one thing she did well, and loved to do, was care for a house and cook. That was also one thing that was always needed in the cities, large or small: someone who could keep house and cook.

Not only that, older ladies were valued much higher than younger ones often looking for something to do until they married. Ophelia joined into the plans only to nod. Whatever was decided would be good, as long as they realized it couldn't be with her. What space she had would be needed for the baby she would be having in the spring. Certainly no room for an old woman and a girl who reminded her of the worst agony in her life.

Wishbone Hollow was nestled between two mountains whose sides were peppered with houses. There was a liberal sprinkling of 'two-rooms and a porch' cabins, put up to sell to vacationers. Would two rooms be enough for her and Bonnie?

Doc realized it was his turn, "It wouldn't be very good for Bonnie to move her to a new school in the middle of the year. Think about this... I can get her to school, and here's something else.

"I always thought I'd buy a place of my own, some day. Just never got around to it. And this one, right here by my folks, that'd be about the best I could find. Suppose I buy this place and move over here, so Bonnie will have her own room and what she's used to."

Bonnie's eyes flitted excitedly from Doc to Grammie. Isabel's eyes were dull and sunken, and her weariness and despondency was plainly written on her face. She nodded. "If you could arrange it, I'd be grateful. For this year. Maybe."

Ophelia be-stirred herself and located a cabin. Town property was priced high, but no matter. The two-roomer was perched on a ledge in back of the grocery store. It had spring water and a good outhouse. Fence all around for safety. It could be had for about two thirds of the income from the farm, leaving a tidy sum for security.

Finding a job was just a matter of deciding which one she wanted. Someone else's house? Well, she'd make it her own. If they didn't like it, she'd find a better place. The very thought of such bravery on her part gave her a bit of energy. Sort of a head-lifting and spine-straightening. Ophelia assured her it was true... that she could pick and choose. Wealthy folks had better things to do than keep house.

Not only that, there was a room for her at the big house of the Kilpatricks. She could stay over anytime she wanted. She could move in permanently... but no, thanks, she'd keep her two-roomer. One needed to have a place that was strictly theirs. So nice of Mrs. Kilpatrick.

White dress uniforms trimmed in blue just like the dining room curtains and the table cloth. Blue candles.

Mrs. Kilpatrick was used to having servants. She explained to Isabel what she wanted and when she wanted it. After that, it was up to Isabel. How could the desolate widow have asked for more? She had a choice and took the best one.

Isabel was an original salt-of-the-earth person. She sincerely did not like what happened to her, but it had happened. If she had been pitched into a lake with floating sheets of ice, she sincerely would not like it, and she would have a choice. She could give up and die or set herself to swimming out.

So she moved into the Kilpatrick's kitchen and made it her own. Mrs. Kilpatrick, a busy woman with social causes, was thrilled with her good fortune. Neat as a pin about herself and the house, was this new employee and a very good cook in addition. Small suggestion (ham and green beans) would set her to planning the meal and what would go with it, and it might end up with peach cobbler or a spiced apple tort.

Isabel made each duty last as long as possible so that there would be no free moments, except to thank her Dear Lord for Doc, one of the few persons she would trust with Bonnie. Truth be told, Isabel was having trouble dealing with the generational difference. Bonnie was so different from Ophelia or Olivia.

And now, Bonnie could come for a visit and amuse herself during the day until Isabel came home… usually after dark. It would work… it had to.

So the day the wagon, pulled by a pair of his Pa's Clydesdales (they need the exercise, son) unloaded the last of Isabel's belongings into her two-roomer, was a turning point. Bonnie, who had insisted on coming, even if it meant another day missed at Miss Temple's school, was very quiet.

It was still October, and the ice cream store in Wishbone was still open. Doc guided the huge animals down the narrow mountain road to main street and the ice cream store. The flavor for today was chocolate.

The pair, Doc and Bonnie, sat at the picnic table in the shade of shop, concentrating on the dark, cold sweetness in their bowl. Silently. Ten and a half was too young for such an uprooting as Bonnie had experienced. Looking at the tiny house where her beloved Isabel would be living made Bonnie sick to her stomach.

Her mind just couldn't grasp it all. She spooned the coolness into her mouth with dogged seriousness, as if it was a duty to be completed before her life could again become normal. How could the farm be complete without Isabel, and how ever could she and Doc manage alone? Too much… entirely too much.

Doc watched her from the corner of his eye. He was getting used to that viewing position. It was clearly time to pull her attention away from the happenings of the day.

And there was Isabel.

Poor, unfortunate Isabel had been slashed apart from all she knew by the ax of inevitable circumstances. Isabel's life had formed Isabel into who she was, and now all the known anchors of her life had been cut away… and she was adrift. It was clear that she would survive, but she would be changed. That was unfortunate for her… and also for Bonnie.

He had done all he could for Isabel and would continue to do… but his highest concern was for the little girl riding beside him. He, himself, was responsible for her life and breath. All he would have had to do was NOTHING, and there would have been no Ebony Lace, and he, Doc, would carry no blame. The matter would have been past and gone, but he had not let it… therefore he was responsible.

"Miss Bonnie, I've made a decision."

The girl brightened and turned, expectantly, as though he could make the horror go away. Catching her lower lip in her teeth, and squinching her dark eyes, she bored her gaze into him.

"You must learn to ride Sparky." The young filly with the reddish cast to her chestnut coat was the pride of the pasture.

"Ride…? Sparky…?"

"Yes. I can't be there all the time, so you will need a way to get to school… safely."

"But I… ?" But she couldn't even form the question.

"We will make a way. I know your concern. Girls do not ride a horse safely if it has to gallop. We will make a way. Grandad Zeke has trained her to the saddle, and you will learn to ride with the saddle. You will be seated IN the saddle with one foot on each side. I have thought a lot, and for us to live at your house without any one to help us, this and several other things have to happen. We'll do what we can… what we have to."

The girl's sad dejection had been pushed aside to make room for this new problem. She would ride Sparky with a saddle and not a dogcart, as most girls would do. Doc had said it… and it would come true.

They returned the bowls to the shop and climbed aboard the wagon. The two Clydesdales climbed the steep road out of Wishbone Hollow with no more effort than grazing in the pasture. They turned east on Ridge Road, and the flint gravel crunched under their wide hooves.

Heads up, they walked almost in step, necks curved. They were an excellent pair of carriage horses, and would be advertised for sale in the spring. The October sun was lowering behind Blue Lake and it would be totally dark by the time they reached home. Three hours, at least. A lot of time for thinking.

Doc had no recriminations over Bonnie's ability. A few evening's training, and Sparky could spend the day in the school's corral with the two or three other transportation animals. At ten and a half, and Bonnie being who she was, she could easily manage the saddle for this year.

So what if her knees were visible below her skirt? So… on to the next problem. He gave her a half an hour of leaning back on the comfortable padding of the buggy seat and staring out on the starry sky and the darker outline of the treetops.

Then, "Another thing. You and I are going to have a new relationship with each other. From now on, I will be referring to you as my 'niece'. I will be Doc, or Uncle Dave, whichever is most convenient at the time."

The dark eyes turned to him with just enough starlight and reflection from the lanterns to create a shining spark. A glow of intense interest, mixed with puzzlement. Of course she would wonder why, and she deserved to know.

"It's necessary. Either we are related somehow, or you were a rescued orphan… or it will be necessary to adopt you. You know, of course, that I gave you your last name, and if you wish, I can adopt you. Actually, I like the 'niece and uncle' plan. Give it some thought and we'll talk about it later."

About ninety seconds later she tapped his arm. "I've thought about it, Uncle Dave. And that makes you have to look out for me the whole rest of my life." The words were spoken plainly and soberly, but then she ducked her head into a giggle, totally representative of her age.

He turned to watch her with her face hidden in her hands but fingers so that she could peek through them. Then, "I mean it, you know."

A tickling thrill of relief spread down his arms. She was still a little girl but she understood it. She would understand more… as years went on.

Another twenty minutes of silence, except for the soft steps of the Clydesdales and the grinding crunch on the limestone flint of the road.

He turned to her and saw her lashes rise and fall. Deep thought? "Bonnie, are you awake."

"Yep."

"Hold up your hand, palm toward me."

Without a question as to why, she stretched her right hand across her chest and presented her palm. Of course he hadn't needed that. He knew exactly the size of her hand, but it was a good conversation starter.

"Very good. You can put it down now. Your hand is barely big enough, but we'll make it work."

"For what…?"

"At my cabin, I have a small gun, usually referred to as a baby Winchester. It was given to me when I was a bit younger than you, and now it will be yours to learn on. Up until recently, you were safe enough, but this concern would have happened even if Grandad Zeke had lived. We even talked about it.

"You, like every other girl in the world, needs to know how to protect herself when she has to, and sometimes that will mean using a gun. We will be workin' on it of an evenin' or when we can, but you will need to practice a lot. We must have you ready to hit whatever you shoot at."

Enough for now. But it seemed best to introduce all the things that would change, and get it over with. It would help her get over the loss of Isabel.

He watched as Bonnie held up her right hand in front of her face, studying the size of it in the lantern light. Big enough? If Doc said so, then it must be. And somehow she was not surprised, though she thought she should have been. Doc was different. Like a part of his mind was inside hers, or some other such silly idea.

"…baby Winchester," she repeated. "I haven't seen it, have I?"

"No, because you shouldn't have seen it. There was no need, but now there is."

That was enough.

And she was not even surprised when the fourth change was brought up.

"Bonnie, you know, of course, that we will have to have help. You're too little to be alone as much as I will have to be gone. I am sorry to have to move someone into our house, but I don't see another way right now.

"I plan to advertise for a young couple to come and live in the house and help take care of you, with cooking, transportation, and I hope a few other things that Grammie Izzy might have done for you. The man will take care of the animals and garden, and may even help you get used to Sparky. But one thing for certain, when the weather is bad… or for any other reason you cannot ride Sparky, he will take you to school in the buggy, and pick you up."

A good two miles of silence followed. "Will I keep my own bedroom?"

"If that's what you want, we'll try to work it out."

"How about if I have the whole upstairs for my own, with nobody else comin' in, less'n I ask 'em?"

Hmmm, well, an even better answer. "I don't see why that wouldn't work. One thing, though. The summertime, it's rather hot up there for sleeping?"

"Oh, I'd not sleep in the bedroom. I'd go out on the upstairs porch."

The porch. About 6 feet by 9 feet and stretched across the south end of the house. Boarded up 3 feet from the floor. Sloping roof. Be no trouble to add a mosquito screen.

Bonnie again, "But, Doc, could I still be downstairs when I wanted to?"

No hesitation. "Absolutely. It's your house and you can be where you want to be, except in the couple's bedroom. That sound all right?"

"Sure does, Uncle Dave!" And another fit of giggling behind her spread fingers. Then a small confession. "I been wantin' to sleep out there for a long time, but Grammie wouldn't hear to it."

Jolly good show! She hadn't had much to giggle about lately. "Well, you're older now, and likely she'd let you if she was here. And remember, we don't have to tell her... do we?"

Bonnie watched Doc's expression... then answered with a slow, decided shake of the head.

Such changes. Isabel, in all her sadness and slight build, was made of steel. She would make changes in the lives to the Kilpatrick's that they could not have imagined.

Bonnie was adapting to a whole new set of rules and making a massive step up in maturity. Jolly good!

And himself? Maybe his changes would the greatest of all, them being unexpected as of only a year ago. The responsibility for a young lady entering the most difficult and exciting period of her life. Please, Lord, let us have a couple answer my add that contains a lady in her twenties... who knows more than I do.

Please, please, Lord.

## COUPLE TO WORK FARM, LIVE FREE

It meant another trip to Wishbone to put an advertisement in the Cryer. It was faster, this time, because he saddled Sparky, hoping to give her a bit of schooling on the way.

> WANTED: Couple to work on farm. Hard work. Varied duties. House furnished. Live free. Salary $20.00 mo. and every bit of it will be earned with muscles and sweat.
> Ridge Road East, Hadley Lane

He had thought long and hard on the wording of the ad. Twenty dollars a month was top pay for a job with house and garden. He wanted to make sure it was known that this was no easy job. The 'muscles and sweat' should rule out those expecting something for nothing.

He'd decide when he talked with the applicants whether he trusted them with his new possession.

*Now, Lord, here's where I'm expectin' a lotta help from you. Is that all right for me to do? I know that fellow we both know named Gideon, he had a chance to test you... but could you send me the right ones first off, so we don't have to waste time? I'd thank you and be grateful to you forever. Amen.*

The Wishbone Cryer came out on Friday just in time to catch the weekly mail distribution on Ridge Road. Doc read his contribution and nodded sternly. Sure enough, it sounded properly demanding. A good warning.

Saturday dawned with no time to test the baby Winchester. Someone over to Chinquapin Cove had a kid with a broken leg. In two places. Doc hated calls like this. Compound breaks were so hard to set, and so precarious with active boys... keeping them off the leg long enough to let it heal.

He loaded Bonnie aboard (be sure to take paper and pencil, or a book. I've got no book, Uncle Dave. Then the paper'll have to be enough.) The call was bound to be a long one, just getting there and back.

Pokey and Pancake ducked their heads under the hanging vines and plunged through the grassy shortcut. It was either that or go another two miles. No matter to the mules. They did what they did and were well fed. What more could a mule want?

Bonnie leaned back against the seat and ducked limbs that whipped in the sides and studied Doc's face. She was good at what she did. She could tell Doc would have liked to turn this down, but he didn't. She found herself wishing this was going to be a birthing, but she'd never seen him 'set' a broke leg. That would be fun, too.

In due time they reached the house. The cry of a young child met them at the yard gate. Bonnie waited in the buggy, as she was told to do, and picked up a pencil and looked around for something to draw.

But here came a girl about her age. "Hi! I didn't know there was a girl comin' with the Doc? He said you could come in if you was a mind to. I'm Carolyn, and I'm in the sixth grade."

"Hi! That's the same grade I'm in! Can you climb in and talk with me?"

"Sure can, and then we can go have cookies Ma just made. She thought they'd be good for Lucy and make 'er stop cryin' but it didn't. So we got lots'a cookies."

"What's wrong with Lucy to make 'er cry?"

Carolyn's eyes widened in surprise. "Oh, she's who had the broke leg. Broke in two places and her leg ain't hardly long enough to even HAVE two places." And the ridiculousness of what she said set her to giggling.

Bonnie giggled, peeking at Carolyn through her fingers. "You know what? Doc was thinkin' it'd be some big old teenage boy with the broke leg. Ain't that a joke on Doc!"

"Yeah, and he grinned and said it was just a 'green stick' fracture, and he'd have it fixed in no time. Do you know that a 'green stick' is?"

"Sure I do, when it's for fur certain a stick. Don't know about a leg. It almost impossible to break a green stick. They splinter and bend, don't they?"

"Then let's go watch. I don't get to see much, livin' way back here like I do."

So they slid off the buggy seat, paper and pencil forgotten.

Lucy, aged two, had stopped crying and was watching Doc with great interest as he wrapped her leg in the funny cloth and painted 'mashed potatoes' on it.

Doc grinned at her every so often, and Lucy grinned back. She'd never had this much attention since her brother hit her in the head with her doll bed because she told him to 'go away!' Broke the doll bed, but Pa fixed it.

Excitement over, Bonnie and Carolyn sat at the table eating the oatmeal raisin cookies. Giggling at everything that was being said. In the parlor Doc could hear the giggling, and prolonged the procedure as much as possible. Maybe it wasn't going to be so bad, taking her with him so much.

Trouble mainly happened with families, and families had youngens, and a fair number of them might be girls. He sighed… thank you, Lord. Everything helped.

And then a tray arrived with cookies and tea while he instructed the parents to keep her off the leg for a couple of days, at least. The parents groaned, not certain that it would even be possible. Lucy ran her own life.

And finally he must drag Bonnie away from Carolyn. Not much chance they'd ever see each other again. In 1913 northern Arkansas, folks could live five miles apart and never meet, because there might be three ridges and two hollows between. Too bad.

Entering Hadley Lane, they could see the strange buggy near the house. Good thing they'd left Chinquapin Cove when they did… someone else obviously needed them.

But no. A wide smile and a head of curly red hair that could stand a haircut greeted them. Hands outstretched, he reached for Doc's hand to shake. "Hope we ain't too late, Sir. Came quick as we could. I'm Dan Scott."

"Too late…? Doc was clearly puzzled.

"The Cryer, Sir. We saw the ad and came quick as we could. Likely should'a waited till tomorrow, but it being Sunday, we allowed it best to come on. The job ain't been took, has it?"

Oh! The ad! "Not yet, why not come right in. Is that your wife in the buggy?"

"Yes, Sir. I'll get her. You'll want'a meet her, too."

You bet! He sure did. She was a major part, as far as Doc was concerned. Bonnie ran ahead, opened the door, and headed for the kitchen. One thing she had learned was the first thing to do was to poke up the coals in the stove and put on the water for tea. No cookies. Sorry.

Doc talked, listened, and tried to size up the pair. Maybe twenty two and twenty five and due to be parents in a short while. Looked strong. Certainly talkative.

"When we saw that ad, Iris and me, we thought it sounded like just what we was lookin' for. My Pa, he's got a spread back past

Blue Lake. Good and big, with lots'a work, but our family… well, Pa's luck seemed to run to havin' boys. They's three older'n me, and two more down past me. So what chance'd I have at somethin' of my own?"

Hardly pausing for breath, he continued, "I know about muscles and sweat and animals and crops and any kind'a machinery you got. To tell the truth, it was the $20.00 that we thought might be a misprint. Was it?"

Doc had time only to shake his head, "Cause we were determined that you'd be so happy with us that maybe we'd have a whole year, and then we'd have somethin' toward havin' our own. Or maybe even two or three years. When we saw no one home, I wasn't wantin' to prowl around, but I looked over the fence and back'a the house."

"You got a real good place here. I know you knew that, but I just loved lookin' around and seein' what was here. And the house looks big, is that where we… we…?"

The entrance of the tea tray interrupted the discourse. Doc got a chance. "Yes, the house would essentially be yours. My niece, Bonnie, will have the whole upstairs, and I'll need a room at the back. The thing is, I'm a Doctor and on the road a lot. The other thing is, my niece cannot be left here alone, and she is a very important part of this job."

Bonnie set down the tea and went back for the sugar and cream.

Dan Scott butted in with a whisper. "Forgive my bein' so bold, but we was thinkin' you might be where the girl was… where there was a girl…? I don't mean nothin', but we was hopin' it was so, 'cause we'd love to take care'a that little girl."

Doc drew in a breath and was about to speak, not knowing what to say, when Bonnie returned. Iris, sipped her tea.

"Bonnie, is it? The tea is lovely. I was just sufferin' for somethin' warm and wet. And it's gettin' a might chilly. Did you help grow the tea plants?"

Bonnie stood and stared transfixed at the yellow hair under the white bonnet, the crocheted wool cape and the roominess of the skirt. Her eyes strayed toward the lady's lap and jerked back to her face. She must not be rude. The lady smiled.

"My name's Iris, and yes, I'm gonna to have a little one. Do you like babies?"

Bonnie was speechless. Doc pushed a chair close behind her, and she backed into it. Bonnie, the honest, confided, "I don't really know, ma'am… I mean Iris. I ain't never really got to be close to one, but I'd sure like to find out."

The men looked from the girl to the young women, not more than ten years older. The red haired young man took the pause as an opening.

"Mr., I mean Doctor Harper, is it? Saw the name on the box back there and remembered it from… well, we heard about you. I think I might say that livin' in that house with you two'd be a pleasure for us. I see seven or eight rooms, easy, and we been livin' with my family, and it was always a crowd. My Iris, she'd love to have a big house like this to work with. Cleanin' and cookin' if you was to need that done. Couldn't find no one better'n her. Your little niece bein' here, and that'd make it even better. Someone to be with and do for, like doin' up her pretty school dresses."

Iris smiled and watched her husband, nodding agreement to every word from his mouth.

More from Dan Scott. "Saw that good lookin' mule out back but didn't go in to him. I sure like havin' mules, and I see you got two more. Always thought mules were smarter'n either horses or donkeys. Like they took over the brains'a both. But here, I'm about to talk a leg off you, as my Ma would say.

"Would it be rude to ask when you'd be makin' up your mind? We're just really wantin' a place like this, but we'd need to keep lookin' if you wasn't sure we could do it." He trained a pair of sky blue eyes on Doc.

Doc glanced over at Iris, who smiled and wrapped a protective arm around her abdomen. Then back to Dan who had moved to the edge of his seat, in his nervous anxiety. Lord… are these the ones?

It seemed the Lord wanted him to make his own decision. "I might tell you that you're the first one here. You sound all right and if you're ready to start, you can bring your things Monday, and we'll try it. At least a few months, and if it works out, we'll talk further."

Bonnie touched Doc's sleeve. "Uncle Dave, can I show Iris the house?"

Doc nodded. Watching Iris stand up, he judged, maybe six months. That'd let her get started before the baby came. Could it possibly be this easy to handle this most important venture? Everything connected with this house, and Bonnie had been so hard… how could this possibly be so easy?

The ladies walked away, and Dan asked, "Doctor Harper, could I put your mules up? You're likely tired, and I'd love to do it 'afore we leave. Seems your little niece likes my Iris. She'll be so happy about that. She's from across the hollow and had to leave her two sisters. Fact is, Doctor, we'd fairly love to take care'a that little girl."

Yes, Doc was tired, but he worked with Dan to get the animals put up. Another half hour and they were gone… the buggy making its way down the lane, and Bonnie practically dancing on her toes. "Doc, did you notice! She'd gonna have a baby!"

Doc could only smile and nod. Please, Lord, don't let her be disappointed! Please…. please… please!

The buggy pulled out onto Ridge Road and began to climb toward Burnt Tree Junction. Danny reached toward Iris, gently tugging her closer to him.

"Well, what do you think of the girl?"

Iris drew in a ragged breath and pulled her sleeve across her eyes. "That girl's got herself a lotta tears that ain't been shed. What made us think this here add would be those people? There was so much said back when it happened… and then nothin'. Things like that don't just go away."

Another mile. "Don't know, baby. Maybe it was that we was due a good thing. That there farm back there is a poor man's dream come true. Figgered to have to work five years to earn enough for what I want for us. That could be the place. He'd be needin' someone to be there till that girl gets to be eighteen or married, don't you think?"

Two miles of silence as Iris tucked the quilts closer around their feet. "Seems to be kickin' up a little breeze from the north."

"Could be more'n a little breese. Startin' December, it's time. Just so it don't get so bad we can't get over there Monday. I'm thinkin' that if it looks bad in the mornin' we'll just head on over there. Then we'd be there, and I could start work Monday."

Iris nodded. "Maybe we should go tomorrow if it isn't blowin' in bad. We could wait in the yard till they get back from church."

"Good thinkin'."

## THE COMING OF IRIS SCOTT

Iris was a light-hearted ray of sunshine. Daniel Scott knew, from the time he saw her, she was the one who would make his dreams possible.

Uncomplicated and agreeable to his aggressive personality and fierce dreams. She would not 'talk him down' as the saying was, when he made concrete and definite plans. He would climb the ladder of success by determination and hard work, and she would hold the ladder for him… not an easy job, actually.

Essentially buried among seven brothers of a very close family, he knew he would break out of the pack, and the discovery of Iris, her family, newly arrived in the Arkansas mountains, made it possible. He had thought he would be working alone, but there she was.

Oval face, dimples and wispy, yellow hair… she met most days with a wide-eyed pleasure for what it might bring. It brought Dan Scott from a mile down the trail.

Married a year, now, they had spent the time with his family, a mob of individuals, coming and going, here and not here, and working together to be successful. Dan wanted individual success, and, surprisingly, Iris had dealt with the tedium of waiting. Of continued talk. Of putting figures on paper and scratching them out. Of impatience when it seemed no success would be found. Of the weekly perusing of the Wishbone Cryer whose want-ad section made it the most important voice between Eureka Springs and Berryville, northern Arkansas.

Then he read Doc's communication. Hadley Lane. Why did that ring a bell in his mind? The way he consumed the double page flyer, Dan had, what might be said, his finger of the pulse of Ridge Road and all its tributaries.

Hadley Lane. Wasn't that where small quips indicated a terrible problem and the association with a popular doctor. Then, checking in the gossip grapevine by his sisters and mother, many details were filled in.

A lot of 'Tsk Tsk' sympathy was discussed, and then cast aside. It was nothing they could personally assist, so they had turned to their own lives. Now here it was. Hadley Lane. A Doctor. A 'baby' who must be ten years old... or so. Could it be...?

It was! It not only was, it was the clear and profound indication that this was the right move for the younger Scotts. The Hadley family was well known. And solid. Common sense told Dan that was the kind of friends to make because he knew himself to be a kindred soul.

To find Iris, who was happy to dream his dreams with him, was content to be a firm rung of his ladder to success. Well trained in the duties of house-keeping and contented to perform them. That was an important facet, and her discouragement at being thrown into such a large family that she became lost, was another.

And then Iris saw Bonnie. Somehow she saw the girl as her opposite and oh! what good times they would have together! She could take care of this wonderfully large house (alone) and have the sister (she had left behind) and the pleasant feeling that she had added to someone's life (surely there was something to teach her). So the house on Hadley Lane had a whole colorful bouquet of inducements. And the crowning centerpiece was her husband's excited happiness after all his careful planning, and his disappointments.

Sure enough, a 'blue norther' was blowing in from Missouri and they usually lasted at least three days. Best they pack up necessities that a buggy could hold and get back on the road. Anything missed could be gotten later.

So there they were in the yard, bundled in piles of blankets. Side panels of the buggy had been pulled down, and that buffered some of the wind, but not the cold. Mitten'd fingers circled the mugs of hot liquid from their canteen... now growing cold.

The heated stones at their feet were reduced to tepid, and the poor animal in the traces was hunched over, facing the blast of wind as much as he could. A thin trail of smoke arose from the farmhouse chimney, but the door was locked tight. As they had expected. On Sunday morning, the Hadley's (Harper's ?) would have been gone to church. No matter.

They'd soon be home. If not, Dan, the provider, has decided to pull on into the shed behind the corral fence. To protect the horse, and maybe be a bit for themselves, but the act of crawling from under the warm quilts to get there would be a dreaded venture.

So they'd wait just a little longer, pink noses, tingly fingers notwithstanding.

And up the lane came Sparky pulling the small buggy and hurrying toward the warmth of the shed.

"Look, Doc! Someone else looking for the job."

Doc sincerely hoped not.

Today was one of the many times he would be relieved and thankful when he saw the mop of red curls on top of the sun-browned face, barely past his teenage freckles.

Bonnie ran excitedly to the buggy and helped Iris untangle from the blankets and rushed her into the house. Together they poked up the coals and had the kettle on. Ham and eggs were the quickest, and Iris was free with her praise of the wonderful stove. Not like the monster she had helped to deal with, over at the elder Scotts.

"Bonnie, honey, you and me, we're gonna do some fun cookin' on this here stove. You know how to make caramel popcorn? This here's the kind of a day for that." She didn't seem to need an answer.

Bonnie knew about the caramel corn, but Isabel never made it. The few times she spent with friends, it was either that… or taffy. She set on the plates, and Iris slammed a skillet full of drop biscuits into the oven.

With a wink at Bonnie, she whispered, "Them's the quickest, and it don't do no good to keep a hungry man a'waitin'." And that was the first of many pieces of advice she slipped to Bonnie.

The caramel corn came about, immediately after dinner, as there was no dessert prepared. "Bonnie, honey, you get the pan ready and spread out the popcorn. Then you have the soda measured out, 'cause this here syrup's gonna start to foam, and it's gotta be poured right then."

The fellows finally had a chance to get acquainted over coffee and crunchy clusters of home-grown popcorn. Iris confided, "This coffee's so good. I sure like a cup'a coffee with somethin' sweet. Didn't have it over at the Scott's 'cept for holidays and birthdays. Cost too much for that mob'a folks. It was always tea."

In the flurry of warming the house, Bonnie had tossed her winter coat on the wicker settee. When she picked it up to hang, Iris told her, "Wait, honey. Let's see that coat. Appears you just about out-growed it."

Truer words were never spoken. It was short, and a lot of dress-tail showed under it, but it was the sleeves that were the concern. "Look at that! You're gonna freeze your wrists, goin' to school."

With expert fingers, she examined the wool, lifting the lining and holding it to the light. "Honey, this here's good wool. Ain't even faded a bit. Now, if we was to cut about six inches off the bottom, bein' shorter wouldn't matter none, and then make cuffs for the sleeves, that'd fit you right good. What'da'ya think?"

Bonnie, in a whirl of ideas, thought it was wonderful. And before school on Monday, she had a smart, finger-tip jacket.

The community church in Enterprise drew from a rather wide area, and Sundays were so often visiting days. Several families met at one place, had lunch and caught up on what was happening. Today they met at the farm on Joe Cotton, conveniently close to the church.

"Sure was glad to see Doc and the girl. They been so tore up lately, hadn't seen hide nor hair of 'em."

"Yeah, and the more time that girl spends with Doc, the more she seems to look like 'im."

"Sure, and there was talk for a while. Nobody that knowd Doc believed it, though. Doc'd never...."

"If Doc was to have eyes on that girl, he'd'a waited till she got some size on 'er."

"And if that little one was his'n, he'd'a taken it from the start. Knowin' Dave Harper like I do, he was fair, but no one pulled the wool over him."

"But somebody was to blame." A silence while the ladies thought of some way to get out of the current subject.

Marcella took a sliver of pumpkin pie, and ate it, holding it in her fingers. "I need this like I need…"

"Another youngen?"

"You're right there!"

And Annabeth just couldn't let it pass. "The girl's puttin' on a shape. Isabel and Ophelia with that tiny build, and then her… uh, Olivia bein' such a little bit'a nothin'…."

"Un huh, and Ophelia havin' to make over everything she had, just to make it fit."

"Hear Ophelia's in a family way with the new fellow. What is she now… thirty five…."

"If she's a day."

Apparently the subject had not been talked out sufficiently. "It was good'a Doc to buy the Hadley place. That'away the girl gets to stay put. They's been enough changes in her life."

"That's the truth. The thing is, though, how's he gonna get her to school and back and keep up with his doctorin'?"

Finally, Ida had her chance. "I know how. My Eldon saw in the Cryer that Doc advertised for help. A couple, he said. And he'd pay $20.00 for the right one. He's gonna be deluged with fellows wantin' the job."

"Do tell! At that price, he'll get the pick'a the lot."

"He wouldn't never do no less, when it comes to that girl."

"I hear he's callin' her his niece. Seems strange."

"Well, I 'speck he had'a do somethin'. Couldn't hardly be haulin' her around and her not kin. Even if she ain't."

The oddity of Eleanor's comment went by un-noticed. That was just Eleanor. Everyone knew what she meant.

While at that moment, Doc was showing Dan the baby Winchester. "I aim to have her be a perfect shot. It'll take you and me, both, and a few boxes of ammo."

Dan examined the 'toy' with interest. It lay in the palm of his hand like a trinket. He fitted his bulky fingers against the trigger. "Be good enough to learn on… fer a fact. I'll set up a target till you get a chance to put up what you want, and we can spend a while about every day. Iris'll like to watch."

And Iris was enticed into the upstairs (where no one but Bonnie was permitted to be!) and pronounced it a wonderful apartment. And the lovely porch in the summertime… ! Lucky girl you are!

Bonnie followed Iris down the stair steps smiling at the walls, and mentally caressing all the thoughts inside her head.

## THE COFFEE CHAT

On during the winter and into spring the coffee clichés and afternoon teas the ladies conversation turn to the situation on Hadley Lane. Doc had moved his gong and note box about halfway to the road. Close enough to hear it from the house, and far enough to give him a chance to get dressed and bring the mules around.

Eleanor wondered, "I hear the fellow helpin' Doc is busy showin' Bonnie how a gun works. Seems strange to be havin' sometin' so dangerous and her only what… she must be twelve by now."

"Is she learnin' good?"

"I hear she is. Doc's made a believer outta her that she has to."

"If Isabel was there, she wouldn't be."

"But Isabel ain't there, but she was when Bonnie's… when Olivia wasn't no older's Bonnie. Such a little splinter of a thing. Just a'walkin' on the road."

"Seems to me a girl oughta be took care'a better'n that."

"You remember Olivia. She was took care'a like she was a hot house flower. Who'd'a thought that on Ridge Road. Not two miles from 'er house, that… Well, all I can say is, I'm glad he's there."

"Yeah, and that fellow and his wife, they seemed to look at Bonnie like she was their little sister… leastwise it seemed that way in church."

"So she's gonna take a gun with her when she rides that horse to school?"

"Reckon so. She'll do what Doc says."

"Isabel seems to be getting' along. Had no chance to do anything else."

"It's gotta be hard on her, but she's got that job. And for a fact, she couldn't stay on the farm without help, and she'd not even be able to tell the 'help' what she wanted done. She was one'a them girls that was 'took care of'."

A moment of silence and some head's nodding. Some girls were 'took care of' and others were tossed into life, 'sink or swim." And look at Isabel when she lost Zeke? She managed to 'swim' but at what cost?

And the beautiful Ophelia? She crumbled at what happened to Olivia, and hadn't even the strength to be glad she had Bonnie. Both of the ladies in Bonnie's life faded out under tragedy.

"Lucky to have Doc, for sure," Annabeth summed up.

"My Susan says that Bonnie'a got a hand for drawin'. You 'member her.. uh, Olivia was the same way. Made pictures of plants and things. And now Bonnie does the same thing."

And Cora added, "I heard the same thing. Fer a fact, though, she didn't get that from Doc, and there ain't no amount's teachin' that could change that. Over a year ago he had her make that sheet of tea plants, remember? I still got that and it's been handy about them mushrooms. I keep forgettin' which is safe and which ain't."

"I hear Dudley Jones is cuttin' wood for Doc on the shares. One rick for Doc and two for him. He's got a passel'a oak, walnut and hickory. Good wood."

"Yeah, and Dudley was heard to say that it was a pleasure to work for Doc... him bein' so patient when Dud didn't have the money right off for the cold medicine and things. And the bill for when Dora had that last kid. Gonna be the last, I hear."

"Well, I'd say seven's enough, but it don't always work that'away."

Mable grinned, dimpling at the piece of news she was about to pass on. "My Katie said when the boys at school heard that Bonnie was let to bring a gun to school, they said 'could they get a look at it'. Katie said Bonnie put her hands on her sides and looked them boys in the eye, and said, "The only way you're gonna get a look at my gun is when it's pointed at you. And I'm a really good shot."

And Francine, "Was she a'braggin'?"

"Could'a been, but them boys didn't know that and wasn't takin' no chances. Fact was, Bonnie was told it went in the teacher's desk until she started home. She's wearin' dresses with good full skirts that the new lady helped her make. She puts her leg over that saddle just as good as any boy, sayin' Doc told her it was the only way to be safe and keep control on the horse if he had to gallop."

The ladies get-togethers were such a wonderful way for the isolated farm wives to 'hash things out' and get the 'latest scoop of news". It was a couple of decades later that the subject of so many of these chats, penned this descriptive rhyme.

THE COFFEE CHAT

By Bonnie Harper.
They sat around in friendly chat,
Discussing mostly this and that... and a hat.
When then a neighbor's wayward lad
Was seen to act in ways quite bad. Oh, t'was sad!
With eyes aside they thought a while
And put this in their mental file. Some with a smile.
Each took a piece of chocolate cake
A firm decision each must make... with no mistake.
The first one knew what should be done
With every child beneath the sun. She had none.
She looked around as though to try
To look each lady in the eye. And heaved a sigh.
Another said, "When all is done,
"A mother must control her son." She had one.
The next one thought the matter through
And 'thus and so' she thought she'd do. She had two.
Another said, "Now let me see...
These things work out differently. She had three.
The coffee pot, near empty now,
An answer must be found, somehow. Without a row!
The minute hand made one more round
The ladies made not one small sound...
but thoughts abound.
One smoothed her apron on her hips
And raised her coffee to her lips. With quiet sips.
"I've seen boys act this way before
"I'd have to think the matter o're. She had four.

Another said, "I don't contrive
"Fixed rules for boys. They're too alive." She had five.
And then one had a thing to say
Before she stood to walk away. Much work today.
"Boys do these things just for the kicks
"It leaves their mothers in a fix." She had six.
One lady's thoughts were far away,
The windows framed a sunny day…
with squirrels at play.
She watched a tiny nesting bird.
She hadn't even said one word. She barely heard.
"I guess," she said, "there's no rule give.
"We do our best and trust to heaven." She had seven.
Then there was nothing more to say,
So all the ladies went away, to start their day.

The rhyme of the Coffee Chat was the first of many that were to be written about the pioneers of northern Arkansas. But that would be in the future. Just now, Bonnie was busy collecting thought and impressions, without actually knowing it.

It was life seen through the eyes of a twelve-year-old. Nothing special, except that it was HER life.

## GORDON COOPER SCOTT

Christmas had come, and school was out for two weeks. It was decided that Ophelia would bring her mother out to the farm for a few days, and Iris was excitedly preparing for the visit.

Isabel had thoughts of the old times when she was in charge of the kitchen, the food, and the caring for the people. Now it would be different, but when she saw the attractive, pregnant lady skillfully managing the stove and serving tasty food, it wrenched her heart.

Yes, she was glad Bonnie was taken care of. No, it was painful that it was not by her. The poor, 'carefully brought up by the rules' lady had no ability to accept the change. She was dismal at the sight of Bonnie and Iris, so close and companionable, and she powerless to do anything about it, while being unable to remember it was caused by no fault of hers.

So, after two days of being treated like a guest, and trying to talk with Bonnie, not understanding any part of her current life, that Isabel humbly requested to be taken back to town. Not feeling well, she guessed.

So the mules pulled the wagon to Wishbone and left the dispirited lady in her two-roomer, and stopped at the hotel where Bonnie and Doc enjoyed a cup of steaming chocolate with marshmallows. Bonnie bought some new ribbons to tie back her hair and two packages of buttons requested by Iris.

Doc picked up a number of bulky items, loaded them in the wagon, and turned Pancake and Pokey up the street that led to Ridge Road. It was a silent trip of disappointment. No happy moments together with Grammie, because Grammie was no longer the same person. That seemed to be the trouble with being molded by things outside the body, out of one's own control, rather than from what was within. But it was all Isabel knew.

Bonnie looked at Doc in mournful sadness, and he could do nothing about it. It was with great relief when the mules turned in at Hadley Lane. From the note box, Doc took a scrap of paper. Bonnie did not even ask who it was, and he changed the mules to the buggy and was gone.

Iris was anxiously waiting for Bonnie, because she wanted to make the ginger flavored cookies that looked like little people… head, arms and legs that stuck out. She had colored frosting in red from beets, green from the juice off spinach but she had not blue. No matter. They'd just dress the cookies with the colors they had.

But she did pull a couple of late carrots and shaved one into strips. One of the cookie persons was going to have red, curly hair. They positioned the candy hair with tweezers, giggling excitedly. Bonnie had cut a pattern of a tree, and they baked 'tree' cookies. They were decorated with the scraps of the frosting.

Doc returned as the last giggling batch of cookies came from the oven, steaming and frosting smeared, looking delicious. Bonnie seated him with hot tea and the least messy of the new cookies. Together the ladies cleaned up the mess while Doc sipped the tea and ate cookies. He closed his eyes and turned his head toward the ceiling. He mouthed, Thank you, Lord, for Iris. When I can say it better, I'll thank you again.

It was in March that Iris' activity was somewhat hampered by the lump in her abdomen settling into a more comfortable position. She didn't get much sleep, and often attended to her duties with bleary eyes and a certain waddle to her usual brisk walk.

When she could, Bonnie watched and studied, and became breathless with impatience. If pains started in the daytime, she told Miss Temple, she would miss a day of school. And Miss Temple had responded, "Do you think she can't have that baby without you?"

Soberly and seriously, Bonnie told her. "Yes."

And Iris was wonderful about answering questions. Loved to, it seemed. And she was free to let Bonnie put her hand where the baby was kicking, and Iris would put her hand over Bonnie's hand and press, making the little elbow (knee? heel? head?) move under the pressure.

The dark eyes under the brush of curls, and the blue eyes beneath the wispy yellow hair locked in a heart-pounding gaze of excitement. Magic! Had to be!

And then the storm came. There was the myth that a storm brought babies, and doctors were inclined to think it was true. Doc, however, was close at hand when the pains started for Iris.

In a serious moment, Bonnie had queried Doc about the medicine in his needle. It obviously stopped the terrible pain, so why did Carmelita have to go through so much before he gave her the shot. Doc had explained to the eleven-year-old as though she was twenty.

Having a baby was natural, and most of the time it went well. Yes, it hurt, but it was a hurt that was bearable for most mothers. If Doc did not use the needle, the new mother could be one of the first to see the baby. Not so with Carmelita who slept through the first hours while Cliff and Bessie admired the little fellow.

And the cruel, hard facts were that what seemed to help the mother certainly did not help the baby, and must NOT be given until the very end. And Bonnie nodded understanding. She, herself, had seen (just a peek) of the top of the baby's head before Doc had put Carmelita to sleep.

All of this Bonnie had carefully and fully explained to Iris, who listened, gladly. Iris' mother had said she would come when the time was close, but when she learned that a true and educated doctor was within 'spittin' distance, if the wind was right' she'd just wait until it was over and come to see the finished product.

It was good news for Bonnie. She was convinced that she would be enough encouragement for Iris. There were three others along Ridge Road who would come around before summer, and Bonnie wanted to be experienced and ready.

So, Iris had waddled through the preparation for supper, and wasn't hungry, she insisted. Good, thought Doc. A sure sign.

From then on, Bonnie stuck to Iris like a coat of paint. Keeping her moving if she could manage it. Then it was time to count. Doc's watch had a clear black and white face with minutes clearly marked. Silently, with gazes locked, they waited. Ten minutes.

Had to get better than that. So they'd go out and see how the baby chickens were progressing.

When Doc saw that Iris enjoyed sewing, he sent the pair of them up to Burnt Tree Junction to the catalog lady. They were buy cloth and also to order 200 baby chickens to be delivered to the depot in Eureka Springs. Doc would have been notified of the day they would be there, and they were. Cheeping and pecking hungrily at each other's eyes.

He bought some baby chick food and encouraged Sparky to make haste and get them home. So now the number of live chicks had been reduced to 170, at best count. Better than expected live rate. And now they raced around inside the pen like so many chicken dinners and nests of eggs.

Bonnie watched Iris from the corner of her eye. She saw her throat move as she swallowed a contraction. No pain yet... just pressure. They walked to the garden to decide where the tea plants would be this year. Iris was walking slower. It was time to... what... ? Go to the house? Maybe.

By 8 o'clock, pains were regular at five minutes. At four minutes Doc said she must come to the bedroom. The space between five and four had been very close.

She was gowned, and the bed protected, and Dan sat at the table before a cup of cold coffee and suffered. It wasn't fair that Iris should have to do this alone, was it? Well, go tell that to God.

Two minutes. Bonnie was a jittery as a possum out on the limb of a persimmon tree. Doc said nothing. He sat by the lamp and read some papers he'd gotten in the mail.

Bonnie watched Iris. She caught her breath and clamped her hand over her mouth. "No" whispered Bonnie. "You have to breathe." Iris took a long breath and groaned, drawing herself into a painful knot.

Now Doc was interested. A groan. One minute. This was going to be a quick delivery. His favorite kind. The long hours of waiting were boring, dreary and painful for everyone.

Tears filled the blue eyes, and Bonnie wiped them away. "Oh, please, it hurts!"

Bonnie pushed back her hair, "But not for long... remember?"

She followed it with, "You don't want the baby to get medicine. That's why you hurt, so the baby won't have to."

A loud cry escaped her lips and another one. Doc told her, "That's all right. Be as loud as you want. Noise won't hurt that baby."

Doc motioned for Bonnie, and they saw wet, red hair. Bonnie could not hold back a giggle. It was fast from then on, and Bonnie held the blanket for the damp and wriggly creature. "Hold tight' Doc had said, and she did.

A loud wail and a flailing of arms, and Gordon Cooper Scott demanded his place in the world. He was separated from his mother and snugged into a dry blanket. "Take him to the kitchen. Dan's suffering more than Iris."

Dan took the bundle while tears of relief soaked his day-old red, curly beard. Hugging the little creature, he made his way into the bedroom to Iris, and Bonnie took the mess to the outhouse.

Doc met her as she returned and pointed to a chair at the table. "Let's leave them alone for a while. And that, Miss Bonnie, is about the easiest delivery you will ever see."

Years later, Bonnie was to hear that statement in her mind, but now she was just giggly happy. Doc watched, nodding. She's hooked on the magic.

The decision had been made that if the baby was a boy, he would be named Cooper from Iris' family, and Gordon from an ancestor who fought for Scotland's independence with the McDonalds.

Tough Cappy (from Captain) Scott had commanded his company with discipline and strength. If weak and wobbly soldiers went to war, they were more likely to come home behind the drums.

The battle over, the soldiers returned to base and family, signaling their fate before them. The flute and bagpipes sent their music out over the Scottish hills, and the family danced for joy at the sound.

But the somber beat of the drums told a different story. Someone, who had eagerly waited for a loved one, would have waited in vain.

Old Cappy Scott, it was said, had a record of the flute and pipes return because of his wise decisions. Because of his training. Because his men refused to let him down. Because he constantly told them they were the greatest company in the history of the world, and somehow made them believe it.

So the new squirming red-faced, arm-waving bundle of humanity had a lot to live up to. He would 'test' himself in his own set of mountains, and likely fight another war for his country.

Freedom was not free, some wise person said.

## BONNIE BECAME THIRTEEN

The Baby Winchester, though a reliable weapon, was not a tool adapted well to Bonnie's sturdy hand, but it was a weapon of necessity, and she willingly aimed, shot, listened to suggestion, and was cheered on by Iris, leaning against the fence outside the practice field. When she was able to hit the backdrop of the target board, Iris clapped and hurrahed while Bonnie, herself and Dan, her part-time teacher laughed.

Baby Gordy made an interesting plaything. She had not the fascination with baby tending that occurred with many of her age and older, but he was fun. He had his own kind of magic that continued. He learned to stand on wobbly legs, to demand a bite of whatever Bonnie was eating, and a few other accomplishments.

When he was six weeks old, Bonnie had a birthday. For reasons known to the whole community, not much was actually made of her birthday, because it always brought up thoughts of 'that time'.

At a Sunday dinner gathering, Lizzie mentioned, "I recall this was the time… I mean, last week Bonnie turned twelve."

Short silence, then Eleanor, "Wouldn't'a been if she'd been full term."

Lizzie the peacemaker offered, "She couldn't never have been full term. The way I heard it, it was either start to breathe on her own or die."

Eleanor was insistent. "Still and all, from the time she was started, she'd'a been needin' six more weeks ta have her right birthday."

And from Nancy, "Well, whenever it was, she'd done herself proud'a makin' up for it. With Isabel and Ophelia bein' so small built, and worse was… uh, well, the thing is, I note she's fillin' out good as any other twelve-year-old."

"Well, anyway, Miss Iris gave her a party. They didn't want to bring in her Gran and Great- gran on account'a the memories, I reckon. But Doc drove all the way over into the boonies and brought a girl named Carolyn that Bonnie met on a doctor call."

"Imagine that! I know who that girl is. All the way over there, and takin' 'er home. Doc sure sets a store by that girl."

"Good thing somebody does."

"Right. The time I tried to put myself in her place, I couldn't"

"She's finishin' up school this year, ain't she?"

But Iris who considered herself in charge of parties and celebrations had none of the recriminations about the date that happened twelve years ago. All she cared was that she now had Bonnie, and they had so much fun.

Bonnie wasn't especially excited, but it was easy to have fun when Iris was in charge. She knew Bonnie's favorite food… squirrel dumplings. Iris made dumplings so light that they could 'float on air if the breeze was right'.

And she had asked Doc, privately, about a girl named Carolyn that Bonnie really liked… and would it be possible to have her here for the day? It was the best present Iris could think of.

That meant three trips for Doc over across a hollow and two hills, but no matter. Again he raised his head, after making the trip to gain permission, and spoke to his Maker. Thank you. Thank you, for Iris.

Then Iris sent Bonnie and Dan to the woods for at least six squirrels… they were such little scrappy things after they were skinned. Maybe get seven if they could.

Dan with his rifle and Bonnie with the baby Winchester headed out. Bonnie hit a few tree trunks and brought down a fair amount of bark chips, but no squirrels. Dan knocked eight of them from their meal of new spring shoots, and they carried them home.

Anyone… absolutely anyone… knows you never serve stewed squirrel the day you put it in the pot. It's got to simmer on the back of the stove for a day along with an onion or two (depending on the size). Much of the flavor of squirrels was in the bones… just like the marrow of beef bones. In fact, some cooks cracked the leg bones to speed up the process. Not Iris. She was an artist at the cookstove, and nothing was to be hurried.

Bonnie wanted bread pudding made out ofcinnamon rolls and raisins. And she'd pick the greens, popping up along the fence rows, and they'd be cooked in bacon grease and layered with boiled egg halves. If Iris was going to do this… might as well do it right.

When Bonnie woke up Iris called her down stairs and handed her a brand new skirt of red and blue checks, trimmed in red lace. She must put it on now because she was not allowed to do any work.

"But what if Doc…?"

"Too late. He was up and gone an hour ago."

"But…"

"Oops, I've got to get a pail of water."

"I'll get it."

"No. Go work on your drawings. Breakfast'll be ready in a minute."

It was a little more than a minute when the very unexcited birthday girl heard a squeal of happiness and someone clomping up the stairs.

"CAROLYN!"

That's how the day started, and it ended with Bonnie and Carolyn chattering in the buggy seat behind Doc. The only thing that marred the day was that Carolyn's family was moving. Bought a place over on Echo Mountain, a good twenty miles in the wrong direction.

But now Bonnie was thirteen.

Her skirts were lowered enough inches to reach mid-calf, the prescribed length for her age. No more riding a'straddle Sparky.

Local modesty demanded that a lady on horseback, if she MUST be on horseback, was to crook one knee around the saddle horn and attempt to have both legs on the same side.

Doc didn't think it was safe, and Sparky was puzzled over the unbalanced weight and the odd way the left rein rubbed the cheek hair. Everything had been good, up to now. He got to trot up the road and spend the day with other horses in the school corral. Then sometimes he got to gallop back down the hill and usually got a treat of some kind.

No more.

Bonnie had spent most of the year working on the drawings of herbs, edible flowers and medicinal trees. Forty two pages were a lot. Sometimes she and Iris walked through the woods to get another look at a certain plant. You could see it… and see it… but when you wanted the lines to be exact so someone else could recognize it, another look might be in order.

And she liked to bring the paper down to the kitchen table. Iris would hover and watch, exclaiming over the magic of it all. She just had to make a mark, and it was always the right mark. Magic hands, for a fact.

At one point she put Bonnie's hand outstretched on the table and her own beside it. Iris' slightly plump, smooth hand had tapered fingers and small, dainty nails. Bonnie's was sturdy, knuckles more prominent, and finger ends squared off… no other way to describe it.

Bonnie had never given consideration to the shape of her hand. It was there to use so she used it. It seemed a normal thing that some folks could do certain things better than others.

But Iris decided to tackle the puzzle. "Bonnie…? You may find it hard to believe, but I went to school with a girl with hands like yours, and you know what? She could draw, too. Maybe not as good as you… but a whole lot better'n me."

Bonnie studied her hand for a minute. "But you know what? It'll make sense to you if you remember what my embroidery looks like beside yours. And remember teaching me to knit. Never got past the first stitches, and it looked… well, you took it out when you thought I wouldn't notice."

Iris had to grin at that.

And there was no more school for Bonnie. She made her garden of tea flavored plants and finished all forty two pages of the book. With index and title page and the other pages the editor said had to be there, the book turned out to have forty eight pages and a cover.

Doc took it to the printer. Printer said it had to have a name, well, how about USEFUL AND MEDICINAL PLANTS OF NORTHERN ARKANSAS. Too long, the printer said. So how about MEDICINAL PLANTS OF ARKANSAS.

That was better, the printer said.

It'd be ready in six months. What she'd do with a book, Bonnie had no idea. To make up the right number of pages, she'd had to go to trees like the willow for pain killing, and sassafras for a soothing tea. The acorns from the oak were edible and sometimes processed to add to coffee grounds.

Oh, well….

But there were Doc's trips. All of them. She went on every call whether there was to be a baby or not. Somehow she managed to fill the days.

If Doc had been a seaman, he might have thought of her as a ship without a rudder, being pushed before the wind… or maybe by the tug boats in a harbor. But Doc was not a seaman.

Rather, he occasionally thought of her as a butterfly in the rain, hanging under a leaf until the shower passed. Not knowing when that would be.

Or more clearly the animal with a broken leg. Like the fox, dragging a leg to the den and packing dirt… hopefully wet dirt… around the break and staying perfectly still for the bone to re-knit. Silently bearing the hunger and thirst. Not knowing if or when the healing would be.

But what could he do? A lollipop or a new pair of shoes wouldn't do it. Thank you, Lord, for Iris. A bit too old for a sister, and much too young to be a mother, she filled in for both. In the summer that Bonnie was thirteen, Iris produced a chubby, blue-eyed girl with blond ringlets tinged with pink… a true 'strawberry blond'.

Another easy delivery. Iris had no time or inclination to bother with pains. Sure it hurt… get it over with, and there was the baby! If everyone was like her, who would need Doc!!!

And Bonnie went on to her fourteenth birthday amid comments around the tables at Sunday teas.

"I can't keep from noticin'' the changes in Doc's niece."

"What way… ?"

"It's hard to say, but she don't seem to catch a body's eye like she used to. Times she's in a group, she didn't used to be so silent. What happened to all her words?"

Leticia Smith nodded. "Could be she's just bein' above her age, and tryin' to be what he really is?"

"What is she, really?"

"Who knows, less'n she starts to talk."

"Well, now, she ain't silent all the time. When my Eddie broke his arm, that girl sat down by him and looked in his face while Doc fixed it.She told him a story that she made up on the spot. Eddie didn't whimper, and his eyes were glued to hers for a whole half an hour. Fer an eight-year-old boy, that's a long time."

There was a silence while this was digested and stirred into the mix of common knowledge. So there were certain folks she responded to. Reason for thought, for a fact.

"Well, maybe it's just LITTLE boys she cares about. Don't see 'er around the bigger ones."

"That's right! And her fourteen. You'd think…"

"It don't do to think when it comes to Bonnie. You think you got her pegged, and she proves you wrong. Most'a the folks around here didn't expect 'er to even live."

And it was during the last months of her fourteenth year that Doc sent her up to Burnt Tree Junction in the little buggy. She was to get some white cloth that washed well and was stiff enough without starch. She was told to make a white dress like nurses wear… no, make two while she was at it.

And another thing. She needed a few aprons. Ones that looked nice, he told her, not like his that she had been wearing. Likely there was a way to 'pretty them up' a bit? Maybe a spot of lace or something?

There was, and Iris knew instantly and exactly what to do.

That amazing Wards Catalog was as thick as a Bible and referred to with reverence almost equal to that of the Good Book. Iris excitedly turned the pages to the fabric. Right there it was… and look over here at all kinds of aprons. Which did she like the best?

Bonnie chose one, and the order was on the way. In a mere three weeks… maybe a day or two sooner, the package would be hanging on the Harper mail box.

The land bordering Ridge Road was settling fast and Doc was kept busy. That included Bonnie, and Doc had begun to wonder how he did without her.

New babies seemingly rained down in the spring showers. There was Myrtie Mason with her first on practically the same time as Louisa Barker with her second. Louisa had a bad time with her first, a breech delivery, and it looked like there would be a repeat.

Doc hitched up the small buggy and sent Bonnie up toward Burnt Tree Junction to sit with Myrtie. Bonnie's first year at school had been Myrtie's last, and Myrtie had helped her learn to add and substract.

Myrtie's mom would be with her, and first babies were almost always slow. Also, it was not always that the mother's calendar was exact.

So… Myrtie's mom was on the way, Myrtie's man had said, but she wanted Doc to be there. Doc weighed priorities, and decided on Louise who was certain to have trouble. It would be an all-night watch, for certain.

So he left, and noted with dismay that a cloud bank was building up in the direction of Oklahoma. The Barker place was low set, with a low-water bridge across the small creek. Low-water bridges were perfect for a shallow creek, but mountain creeks could rise in a matter of minutes. When that happened, water would be a foot to a foot and a half deep over the bridge, and if it was muddy, it was hard to tell where the bridge actually was.

The weather held until he crossed the Plum Creek and drove up to the house. Louisa was crying and red-faced with fear that Doc couldn't make it.

Relief dried her tears, and a cup of raspberry tea seemed to help, likely more mental than physical. Later, he would prescribe chocolate for its small cocaine content. Chocolate made with water and a fair amount of honey. Seemed to help some distraught mothers.

And he settled in for the night, glad he did not have Bonnie along and that he would be headed up to Myrtie's first thing in the morning. He had been quick to note that Bonnie had a 'bedside' manner that seemed to put at ease the childbirth fear, and that was good in this case, as Myrtie had been a favorite 'older girl' to her.

A light sprinkle peppered down on the buggy top as Pancake pulled the small buggy onto Ridge Road. Puller and Pokey had been selected for the Plum Creek run. Bonnie became a bit anxious as the shower built up into a downpour as they passed Garland Community. One more mile. Come on, Pancake.

Pancake came! He really didn't like to trot, but he was galloping when the reins steered him onto a side road. Myrtie's husband was pacing the yard for the Doc's arrival and had the wagon shed open for the buggy.

He lent an arm to help her down, and demanded, "Where's Doc?"

"He'll be on quick as he can. Someone was in trouble."

Rob Mason was not satisfied but what could he do? To make it worse, Myrtie's mom wasn't there yet, and it appeared that the clouds had unzipped and were dumping their entire contents on the inhabitants of the Junction.

Myrtie's mom was on the way, but due to rising water, she had to go a good five miles out of her way. No way to get word to Myrtie. She'd just plunge on through the deluge and depend on a higher Power to take care of her little girl. Of course, that 'little girl' belonged to the higher Power as well as to mom, but mothers have trouble remembering that.

Myrtie was sitting at the table looking highly uncomfortable. Glad to see 'little' Bonnie, dressed in white with the entire bottom foot of her skirt dripping water. She, like Rob, was dismayed that Doc was not along.

With fearful eyes, she begged Bonnie, "What'll we do if he don't get here? I'm gettin' what I think is a pain every ten minutes. I ain't never had a baby, and my mom was supposed to be here. I'm sure glad to see you, but what'll we do?"

Bonnie stepped out of her wet shoes and walked in her stockings to the table and sat down. "First we need to think about this. One way or another, we're gonna have this baby."

"You ever done this without Doc…?"

"Dozens of times." (She did not mind that she'd stretched the truth a bit.) "I know exactly what to do. I have the chocolate drink that Doc wanted you to have, but we have to wait until you're down to three minutes." (She had to guess at that. She didn't remember Doc ever timing it, but she could only have it once, so any comforting effect must be a held until badly needed.)

"Really, Bonnie…? You know what to do? Seems strange, and me teaching you how to add."

The memory brought a fleeting smile to each of them. Bonnie sent Rob back to the wagon shed to get her bag… outfitted identical to Doc's and that had been done just a week ago.

While down at Plum Creek, Louise had struggled through the night, and in the early hours Doc had manipulated the back-side of the little girl to let her legs appear. Now, just slow things down to get the chin in line away from the umbilical cord. Touchy, anyway to look at, and rather hard on the mother.

Ted Barker leaned over her, holding her hand and counting with her. ONE TWO THREE FOUR FIVE and then again ONE….

At six o'clock the little girl yelled her indignation at such
indecent treatment while her parents laughed with delight. Two little
girls. And both of them breathing. Thank you, Doc.

"Well, there's the sayin', storms bring babies and little animals.
If you got a cow or goat ready to deliver, you likely got another baby.
Now, Ted, you been through this before, so I'm gonna leave you in
charge. I've got seven miles between me and another little one comin'
down with the storm."

Ted, cradling a snugged bundle in his arm, waved to Doc with
the other one. "See ya. Doc. Be careful of Plum Creek."

It was friendly advice, but totally un-needed. Doc dreaded that
low-water bridge almost as much as Louisa's breach pregnancy. First
off, Puller and Pokey reared their heads at the dark brown water,
not wanting to step where they could not see. Doc insisted, so they
stepped into the water.

By a careful watch of the vegetation beside the road, he guided
them to where the bridge should be. Water almost three feet deep,
and the bridge was down there somewhere. He'd been over this
hazard before, so he rather knew where to go, but the mules did not.
Each step was a hesitation until they felt the rocks of the bridge…
the water rushing between and over them.

And that was when the loosened half-rotten log broke loose
and barreled downstream, rolling and bucking toward Puller. He
reared to avoid it, hind hoof coming down outside of the bridge in
three foot water.

Pokey strained backward to hold him up until he could get his
footing, and the sure-footed beast managed, but the buggy swayed
and one wheel went over. The jarring as the buggy sunk down to
the axel… the wheel spinning loose as the water ran through the
spokes. All of the buggy contents slid to the down side. Birthing bag,
medicine bottles and all.

With a groan, Doc slid down the seat and into the water. He
could have a broken wheel, and most certainly a bent axel… maybe
broke instead of bent. Too far to go back to get Ted, and both mules
were now on solid rocks, standing in a foot and a half of roiling
water.

Standing in water up to his hips, Doc spun the wheel and heaved a sigh of relief. Still in tact. Leaning up to his chest in the water, he examined the axel. Not broke but somewhat bent. Not much, but enough to make travel difficult. No way to straighten it and no way to keep from traveling on a wheel at a fifteen degree angle.

Only one thing to do. The mules had their heads reared back and ears laid low, registering concern and extreme nervousness. For a pair of placid mules, this was not good. He'd just have to see if he could lift the wheel back to the bridge and move ahead just enough for the buggy to move to the center of the platform of loosely spaced rocks.

Turning his back and lowering himself into the water, he grasped the wheel behind him, with both hands. He had to lift… move forward a little… and keep the wheel from turning in his hands. It was somewhat like trying to keep popcorn in the pan without a lid.

"STEADY, NOW!" he warned the mules. 'WHOAA ! HOLD IT. STEADY. POKEY !! Pull on out!" Lifting with every ounce of strength, he hoped the mules… Pokey, at least… understood a little of what he was saying. Moving toward the mules, he searched for a firm footing. Dear Lord! I can't be let to slip!

Flitting through his mind was how often he called on help when he was in trouble and wondered if he had been thankful enough when trouble had passed him by. Certain not to have been. I'll do better, Lord.

And the strange way the mind can work, while searching for footing, moving the whole weight of the buggy and quieting the horses, he thought of Bonnie, seven miles away with a first timer.

Pokey lifted his head in a resounding and meaningful whinny, and lunged forward, pulling the wagon in a line and barely catching the spinning wheel. It settled onto one of the bridge rocks… just barely.

Holding to a pair of spokes in each side of the wheel hub, "Go Pokey," and the mule shifted weight and moved over making room for Puller to stand.

"WHOA !" and the pair stopped… glad for a command they understood. "HOLD IT !" and they did until Doc could get back on the bridge and into the buggy seat. Level at last. Soaked to the collar he squelched when he moved, and his shoes squenched, but he was back in business… the bridge straight before him, and the other side of Plum Creek in sight.

And now the drenching rain let up. Thank you, Lord. He had a two mile muddy road and five miles of flint gravel between him and where he needed to be and wasn't sure that the axel would last that long. The whole buggy wobbled like a person with a sore foot.

Thank you, Lord.

While up near Burnt Tree Junction, Myrtie's mom was within two miles of Myrtie's house, but her horses were exhausted from the climb through the mud. They were still moving but not very fast.

Myrtie counted down to three minutes, and Bonnie stilled the tremors of fear that started in the back of her head and rippled down her back. She squeezed her eyes shut and remembered Myrtie leaning over her, whispering encouragement and pointing to the right chubby fingers to add to the other chubby finger… and Myrtie's genuine excitement when Bonnie got it right.

Now it was her turn to encourage Myrtie. She could do it, and she would. She protected the bed and put Myrtie between the sheets. The chocolate drink was history, and the fight was ahead. Rob Mason was searching from window to window as if that would bring either Doc or mom… if he just looked hard enough.

Bonnie watched the clenched jaws and saw the tiny beads of perspiration. She leaned over to Myrtie, "Listen, you have a hard job to do, but we can do this. Nature is on our side. If you want to scream or cry, you do it. One thing I can promise you, everything is goin' the way it should. Nobody ever said it was easy, but it's possible."

And Myrtie screamed, tugged on the towel that was tied to the headboard. Her mom had told her to do that. She also told her that some folks put an ax under the bed to 'cut the pain', but when she had tried it, it hadn't helped a great lot. So Myrtie labored without the help of the ax.

As Doc pulled his wobbly buggy onto Ridge Road, Bonnie assisted a tiny girl into the world. With the last push, Myrtie heard the first yell from her daughter. Bonnie laid the little body on the skirt tail of Myrtie's flannel gown. Myrtie reached down and closed her hand on the tiny arm and held to it.

Rob caught both of the miniature feet in each of his calloused hands and grinned at Myrtie. "You did it, Baby! You did it!"

Bonnie finished and sent Rob to the kitchen with the flannel wrapped bundle while she settled Myrtie in a more comfortable position. There had been four hours of labor, and it had seemed forever, but now it seemed a mere minute. On a sheet of paper she wrote the time. She didn't have scales, but who would argue with 6 pounds 7 ounces?

Name? Myrtie drew in a breath and looked into Bonnie's eyes. "I have a request. I know what I want to name her, but I didn't expect it to be you who helped. If you don't want me to, I won't."

Apprehensive, Bonnie stuttered. "W-w-what, is it?"

A moment of embarrassed hesitation, then, "We, all of us, know what your birth name is, and when I heard, I thought, 'if I have a little girl, I would like her to be named Lacey.' Would that... I mean, do you mind?"

Relief poured over her body. "Oh, Myrtie, I think it would be a wonderful name for her. And if I had anything to do with it, I'll be proud and never forget it."

Lacey Lou Mason,
6 lb 7oz, 8:03 am,
19 April 1914.

Doc could enter it in the book.

While Doc, the axel wailing miserably at every turn of the wheel, turned at Hadley Lane and moved his equipment to Dan's small buggy. Hooking Sparky between the shafts, he hurried up Ridge Road, water coursing down in a dozen rivulets. Sparky knew what 'hurry' meant and the buggy was light.

It was 9:47 when he turned in at the Mason's drive. Sodden, but having dripped off the worst. Muddy shoes left at the door. Rob met him at the kitchen door with a proud grin, a pink flannelled bundle at his shoulder.

"Sorry, Doc. Lacey just couldn't wait for you!"

Bonnie sat by the bed as Myrtie leaned against the pillow, both ladies sipping chocolate… made with milk, this time.

Somehow, Doc wasn't as surprised as he had expected to be. He examined the little girl and her mom and pronounced them in good shape. As he pulled out onto Ridge Road right behind Bonnie, he sensed that a fork in the road had been reached, and Bonnie would turn squarely into the way her life would go. Not today… or maybe not even this year… but there is something about being touched by the magic. It does not leave one unchanged.

While Bonnie, traveling ahead of Doc down to Enterprise shivered with fear as she realized what had happened. She had never heard the expression 'the bravest soldiers are the most frightened after the battle'. But if she had, she would have understood it thoroughly.

Pancake happily pulled the buggy out onto Ridge Road. He fully knew that down the road was home and likely a scoop of corn.

Doc pulled in behind her with Sparky in the harness. Thoughts whirled. He had checked baby and mother. Couldn't have been better.

The magic happened. There was nothing, and then there was something. As God had said, 'Let there be light', light had appeared. Magic. No other word for it.

Bonnie rode along behind Pancake letting him choose his pace. Thinking of the day and its emotions, she shivered from head to foot. Wet shoes on the floorboard at her feet, she pulled her sock feet under her dress and watched the sky, now clear of rain.

Two miles down the road the tears began to flow. Rivers down her face. Bent forward into a puddle of sobs that lasted for the better part of three miles. Then a determined swallow and a swab across her face with a sleeve. Stop it! Enough!

By the time she had reached Hadley Lane, the redness of her eyes was fading and she straightened her clothing and painted a smile on her face. Iris would want to know how she got on. She would know that Doc had not made it to help, so she would be concerned. She deserved a good story.

Iris was a wonderful listener.

Looking to the southwest at the late afternoon sky, Bonnie marveled at the brilliant reds and golds streaked across the horizon. It was as if the sky was apologetic about the storm. "Sorry about this morning. It just seemed like the thing to do. Perfect weather to bring babies."

And Bonnie knew there was something to be done, and now was the time. Not today, but the first thing in the morning she would get with it.

Iris met her with eager eyes. "By yourself! Oh, you lucky, lucky girl!"

Bonnie nodded agreement. Call it luck, or call it magic. No matter.

## THE STORM AND ALEXANDER HARPER

The storm that had beset the mountains of northern Arkansas moved on to the north, as storms do. It passed through the town of Blue Eye, the town claiming to be in Missouri, but actually almost straddled the Arkansas line.

The fury built up strength as it climbed north, spilling water by the bucket, not caring a whit what it fell on. It was just a matter of chance that an eight car passenger train was rounding a curve heading toward the Missouri town of Joplin.

Around the mountains of Arkansas and southern Missouri were the sudden roughness of terrain in the path of progress, but the trains would not be stopped. The roadbed for the tracks was hacked out of the rocks and clay as it rounded, rather than topping, the hills. The outside of the track was held level by wooden trestles created from logs of trees a foot and a half thick. Made to last for decades.

The mountain of the upward side of the hill was composed of boulders and ledges of thick, gray volcanic residue in whose fertile depth trees grew quickly. Generally this strengthened the hillside as roots of giant trees cradled and bound together the rocks and clay. One large tree had grown where the soil was shallow, but had weathered storm after storm, and finally grown so tall its tip caught the brunt of the wind that came around the mountain.

As the Arkansas storm advanced onto the Missouri landscape, the wind loosened the tree and toppled it over, exposing the loose sheet of stone clutched in its roots.

The weight of the stone broke from the hold of the root and began to slide, aided by a layer of rain-softened soil and shrubbery. As it slid downward it gained speed. Ordinarily, it would have passed over the railroad bed with only minor damage to the rails, but not this time.

The eight passenger train came around the curve full speed just as the sheet of stone passed over number four car carrying 38 passengers. It struck just above the side windows of the train, cutting cleanly through the metal and peeling back the top of the car like the shiny tin of a can of sardines.

The force of the jolt shook cars three and five, laying them over on the siding, tossing passengers about like so many beans in a baby's rattle. Number four car tipped on its side, dumping its passengers over the low side of the track like potatoes dumped from a basket. The damaged car slid a short way and stopped wedged against a wall of massive stone.

The lighter (younger) passengers were pitched out into space, landing mostly in the fast moving creek below, now swollen into a raging river from the storm. Sixteen-year-old Alexander Harper, along with nine others like him, landed in the water, took stock and headed for the bank in a strong Australian crawl.

The smaller, lighter passengers were caught in the current and flung downstream, depositing them torn and bleeding on banks and submerged vegetation. Nine-year-old Rita Harper was no match for the strength of the water, and was eventually picked off a bush that had caught her clothing but not before she had tumbled over and over under the foamy water.

Mr. Thomas Harper along with nineteen others were dashed to the ground before the car had begun to slide, and he was identified only by his clothing. His remains and that of his daughter, Rita, were consigned to a later crew as attention must be given to the living.

Estella Saande Harper was discovered lying head down by the river, her heart still beating. She was carefully scooped onto a trauma board, head blocked with padding. Her limp arms and legs were attached to the board, and she was gently carried over the quarter of a mile of rough terrain to the rescue train. The only good thing that Estella had going for her was that she was not conscious, and it would be a few hours, at least, before she found out that she was totally paralyzed.

On the rescue train, Alexander sat beside trauma board of his silent mother and stared ahead as the train puffed its way to Joplin, Missouri. He was dry eyed and in shock as he sat on the edge of the seat and stiffened his body against the rocking of the car. His mind had passed into blessed un-knowingness.

He looked out at the clearing sky with unfocused eyes. By the time the train reached Joplin, the sky had turned to a brilliance of a meteor, purple and red streaks playfully rippling across the horizon. It was like it said, "Sorry about that."

Night fell, and the one hundred thirty two passengers who survived were farmed about into every hospital or trauma ward where medical personnel performed their magic, or passed them onward to their eternal reward. Alexander was put to bed on a floor pallet under the influence of a strong sedative. Tomorrow would be another day.

Back in Arkansas, Bonnie Harper awoke with a vague sense of something needing to be done. Something that had reached its time. Blinking the sleep from her eyes, she rolled from the bed and sat up. Yes. There it was.

Dressing quickly, she moved a chair to the closet and reached high on the tip top shelf for the tin box that had come with crackers in it. Opening it, she picked up the faded tintype of a girl about twelve years old. So old and dim it was, it was hard to make out the features, but the sight of it tugged at her heart.

Putting the photo back, she lifted out the cloth-wrapped bag that wafted the aroma of lavender. Putting the tin box back, she stepped from the chair and went down her stairs with the bag. Maybe she'd wait and let Iris enjoy it with her when she opened it, over a decade after it had been closed.

The table had not yet been cleared of breakfast, but she couldn't wait. Laying the bag on the table, she unwound the cord from the button closure and reached in. Crumbled lavender blossoms spread on the table, and Iris scooped them away.

Bonnie laid back the folded cloth and there before them, clear as India ink on white linen, lay the black collar. Each thread was a shiny black, and the background was a net for holding the design of two branches from a rose bush. Flower, buds and leaves, clear as a painting.

Packed with the collar were the tiny, leftover scraps of thread caught within the band of paper that came with the thread.

Thread: Cotton and Linen
Launder with care
Color: Ebony Lace

Bonnie stared down at the collar, her breath coming heavily and her throat constricted. Me. That's me. Great, Great Grandmother Cecelia Hadley knew about me years before I breathed my first breath.

Iris looked at the collar and then looked at Bonnie. Dark eyes shiny with moisture. She held out her arms, and Bonnie came into them. Some emotions are just too heavy to be born alone. It takes two.

When sniffles were past, Iris lifted the collar and laid it around Bonnie's neck. With a smile in her blue eyes, and on her lips… "For your wedding dress. Made from white satin."

With the determination of a runner who sees the finish line, Bonnie ate and performed morning duties but the essential part of her was elsewhere.

Sheet of paper. Ruler for exact proportions. Ink. Black, black India ink for the roses. She owed it to the creation in thread that had spent years in hiding to finally see the light of day in a faithful reproduction.

Where had the old lady seen a pattern like that? There was no pattern with the creation. Where had it gone…? Where would it have come from…?

WHERE HAD IT COME FROM? With the softness and absolute certainty of a spring rain, she knew. Grammie Cecelia created the pattern in her own mind. Grammie Cecelia could sketch and draw. COULD DRAW ! That had to be it. It was a pattern that was totally unique to that piece of lace and had not existed until it was created in her head, and shown to the world with her crochet hook and the Ebony Lace thread. Magic.

The little girl, Lacey, had not existed a year ago. Out of nothing was created something. It was just too much to consider. She sighed at the magic of it.

So now, the sheet of paper, the ruler, and the ink.

While in Missouri, Alexander Harper awoke from a drugged sleep and found himself on a pallet in a… hospital…? WHAT was going on? People in white were scurrying around, each one on dedicated mission of… what…?

Then it returned in an explosion. Train. Derailing. Bodies tossed about in the rain. Pa… oh! Too much. Sweet little Rita. Ma… ? He had to find her. There were others asking where to find their… somebody. No one wanted to furnish answers. No one HAD answers.

"Son, do you have a place to go for a day or so until we sort this out? Your mother may not even be here."

No, he couldn't go 'somewhere'. He had to find his mother. He walked the short distance to the small house where he had lived his life. The key was hanging inside the shed door, just where it should be.

The interior of the house was just as it should be. How could that happen when the whole world had been shook, twisted and turned upsidedown? He sliced the loaf of bread and buttered it heavily while he tried to make some sort of sence of it all. Decision. Time to make one.

He'd get clean clothes, and look everywhere. The smaller clinics first. And in hours of walking, he found her. She was with four others in a room presided over by a white coated lady. Your mother? We have no names, come in and see.

He came. He saw. His mother was on a narrow bed under a white blanket. Eyes open. Her face brightened at the sight of him. "Alex! My baby! You're here."

He rushed to her, kissed her cheek and reached for her hand that was placed across her chest, still and pale on the white sheet. She didn't move toward him, so he lifted her arm. Dead weight in his hand. No responsive movement.

"Son, sit down. I damaged something when I was thrown. I don't remember anything, but they say I'm totally paralyzed."

"But Ma! What can they do! Surely there's something… ?" But it seemed there wasn't. What was next was to live with what had happened, and try not to remember what had been.

Ma had a lot to say, like it had been bottled up for the last couple of hours, and must now spill out. "Son, I'm so sorry but there are things to be done. I wanted you to be a boy for a while longer, but now you must suddenly be a man, making a man's decision.

"My condition is permanent. There are things that can be done, they tell me, but every person is different, and there so many injuries, they haven't really gotten to them all. You and I, we must lean together and make plans. Quick plans. When you leave here, you must find help to sell Pa's tack shop. All the saddles and equipment. That should bring some money."

Alex thought… sell Pa's shop? Never! But there, facing him, was reality. No Pa meant no shop. Leather work had not been interesting to Alex, so he was permitted time to decide what he would do. For the last months he had worked for a grocery store, stacking cans.

Food came on trays. Oatmeal. The most nutritious thing that could be furnished in the quantity required, and was least nauseous for the very sick. A tray was brought to Ma. The tray carrier looked at Alex with interest.

"Your… uh, son, maybe?"

"Yes. This is Alex."

The person nodded. "Perhaps he can help you eat. We are so terribly, terribly busy."

"Certainly," Ma said. "Son, take the tray, and she'll show you what to do."

Small bites. Very small bites guided to Ma's mouth, with her struggling to manage the prone position. Ma explained, "They won't let me be propped up. Someone is going to come to see me, and maybe he can help. He told them not to move me in any way."

Tiny, tiny sips of water. Mustn't risk strangling. And Ma talked. She seemed to have it all figured out, and most of it meant that from this moment forward, Alex would live a new life. But then, so would Ma.

When she was tired, he was sent from the room, so she could rest. He could be back in three hours. So he walked away from the clinic and headed toward Harper Tack and Saddle. No key to get in. The key would have been pressed into the soil of the mountain never to be seen again.

Well, the place of business now belonged to him. Walking to the alley he tested the windows. Tightly locked, of course. That was Pa. Still, he had to get in. At this moment, getting into the shop was the most important thing in the world… the ONLY thing. Focus your mind, Alex.

He looked up. A ventilation grid covered a space near the roof. Screws held it in place. A ladder. He'd get a ladder and climb. He'd get into the shop. It was something he COULD do, tucked in amongst the things he couldn't.

He borrowed a ladder and a screw driver from a sympathetic nearby shop owner. A few minutes and he was in the attic, descending the steps that were nailed against the wall. Spare key in the desk. So now he had a way. Back in the ally, he replaced the vent and returned the ladder. By now it was late enough that he could get back to Ma.

He had hardly been there a minute until Dr. Palmer arrived. The expected doctor. Must Alex leave? Oh, no. He must stay because the outcome of this visit would affect him more than any other person. There had apparently been an Xray picture of Ma's spine. The doctor handed the picture to Alex, he felt along Ma's arms and lifted her shoulder, running his hand under to reach her spine.

He pursed his lips, thoughtfully, and nodded his head. Alex watched, hopefully. Carefully the doctor tucked a pillow under her shoulder and hip, carefully adjusting her head so she was facing Alex. He felt along the ridges of her vertebra. Slim woman… no extra flesh. Good. Perfect, at least as perfect as total paralization can be.

With one hand on her shoulder and one on her spine, he gave a quick jerk, causing Ma to flinch and catch her breath. Removing the padding, he eased her down to the flat-on-the-back position. Firm chin, tight lips, serious, piercing eyes behind spectacles. A satisfied nod.

"Mrs. Harper, I'm going to take your hand as if I intended to shake hands, and I want you to see if you can squeeze my hand at all. First, you must think it in your head, and then send your energy to your hand."

Ma, nodded, concentrating. Nothing.

The doctor passed his hand gently from her shoulder up her neck to her ear, pressing here and there. Then he stroked her arm in long, smooth movements. Straightened her arm and tapped sharply on her elbow, causing a sudden intake of Ma's breath.

"Now try it again." The doctor's intense eyes were fascinated on Ma's hand. He saw the faint movement of her thumb from the knuckle to the thumbnail. A satisfied nod, and he told her to do it again.

Nothing.

No matter. He had seen what he has seen. "Mrs. Harper, you have now become my patient. Medicine is continually discovering new things about the wonderful human body. Some things seem to be magic, but does it matter what we call them, if they work?

"Now there is a strong chance of my being totally wrong, but I believe there is a possibility that your grip may return. It will be a long and sometimes painful road for you to travel, but the ability to grip will be extremely important for you, as you will learn. Also, if you can grip, then you may be able to use your arms. That, in your case, will be a magician's best trick. Can you imagine the difference in being able to feed yourself? To scratch your nose if it itches? Also, you might be able to comb your own hair.

He continued, possibly more to Alex than to his Ma. "Imagine the tent pole in a teepee, or maybe a circus tent. It stands straight so the weight is distributed evenly, and all the guy-wires have the same tension. Do you follow me?"

Alex's head nodded rapidly and deeply. He fastened his blue eyes onto Dr. Palmer's faded gray eyes… almost silver, behind the spectacles. "So when a storm comes, the ridge pole can be knocked aside and left leaning. The teepee or the circus tent would have extra strain on some parts and too much laxity on others.

"It would seem to be a small thing to just straighten the pole, but it is often not so easy. The human spine is like a stack of interlocking blocks, and an attempt to straighten them, like the ridge pole, is very different and presents a lesser likelihood for success.

"Your mother's 'ridgepole' has experienced a storm and has been knocked aside. Discovering where the problem lies will be a long journey for the three of us, but if your mother has any improvement at all, it will be worth it. She is young and can live many years, so it is worth what we have to do right now."

He paused, looking from mother to son. "With your permission, I'm having you moved to my clinic, along with three others with similar difficulties. And here is this. I can tell from the look of you, son that you would benefit from helping me. Anything you learn will benefit your mother, and ultimately, you. Is there a way you can be available?"

Alex opened his mouth, but Ma filled it. "Yes, he is available. We have a business to sell, but he can get someone to do that. He will be here when you let him."

The doctor turned to Alex, and was pleased with the vigor of his nod.

And as the weeks passed, it became evident that doc did not hand over a favor. The work was hard. There was help needed for transporting, lifting, feeding, and tending the others. Two of the patients were men who needed help with baths and other personal necessities.

The tack shop passed into other hands at a surprising profit, but Doctor Palmer would accept none of it. "I'd just have to return it to you for your help. I'd have to hire some help eventually, and that person wouldn't be any better than you. What we're doing is very, very, very new, and no one is for certain of the rules.

"Doctors of medicine and surgeons have been working for a long time and have a better idea of what they're doing, but working with bones, the body's framework, is new. It has been called a lot of names, and a lot of them are demeaning. However, the word Chiropractor seems to be the most used.

And Ma not only regained the use of her hands and arms, she actually sat up in the bed. When they talked, she shared the plans for Alex.

"As you know about the train trip, your pa was planning to resettle in Arkansas. Better climate, he thought. Less snow. Let's think about what you really, really want to do, and we can use the money from the shop to let you train for it. Think about the little town of Eureka Springs. Interesting place. Maybe you can remember some kind of business you saw there, that you'd like.

"Stuck here like you are, you have time to think. Don't make a quick decision. Think about everything."

And he did. And he lifted heavy, inert bodies as Dr. Palmer tried this and that and was sometimes successful. He had a notebook where he wrote down his successes. Also, his failures. Each tiny success seemed like a mountaintop to the patient. Mr. Ellis shouted so loudly for joy that he was heard out on the street, and it was only that he was now able to use his ankle to lift his foot and wriggle his toes. Mr. Sheldon actually stood without screaming from pain or falling on his face..

After five months of labor, Ma could lower her legs to the floor and draw them into the bed again. Reason for rejoicing… she could now put on a pair of stockings.

Alex became seventeen with more muscles that he would ever have developed stacking cans of beans.

And another four months of slow, trial and error, Ma touched her feet to the rug beside and lifted her body from the bed. Dr. Palmer stood and watched, and sighed, deeply.

"Alexander, look at that. If we had just known what to do, she could have been doing that eight or nine months ago."

"But, Doctor, we know it now." And that was when Alexander Harper knew he would become that strange person called a Chiropractor. He would become one before it was known that such a thing existed. Before anyone was sure what to call it. He would copy every word of Dr. Palmer's journal and grab every morsel of success from the four cases in his care.

Ma still had a way to go. It took the wrap-around walker to allow her to tend to her bathroom necessities, but she smiled and hummed in the pleasure of her own success. And her Alex would be a… what was it? Bone Doctor? Chiropractor? That sounded better. Bone Doctor sounded like a soup was being prepared, and she grinned at the idea. Her Alex… a doctor.

The thing was, though, there was no school for him to attend to learn more because 'more' had not yet been discovered. He had just spent over a year with the brightest bulb in the business. And he had a copy of the journal.

Alex had turned eighteen the month before Mrs. Estella Harper left the clinic with only a 'walking cane' for balance, if needed. Couldn't afford a fall, especially until the bones and muscles strengthened and sinews attached more securely.

So… they would sell the house and move south. There was still the question of the newness of being a chiropractor. For certain there would not be enough trade to support a doctor with such an unknown skill, or so young, so something else had to be added. Something that was known to be of value, and it would require the spending of money.

Ma was at home, now, and on her own… with care. Alex would again take the train to the little Arkansas town and look around. The other trip had been Pa's trip, but this one would be his. Seen with newer, wiser eyes. And he looked around in Eureka Springs.

Back to the grocery store… no, because it took too much time. Being a barber might have been it, but the town already had three. It was discouraging.

He betook himself down the street to a hotel that had a diner. He'd rest his feet and enjoy a cup of coffee. He'd passed there a time or two, and the aroma was bewitching. So today, in his depression, he'd yield to the 'witch' and humor himself with expensive coffee. Maybe even one of those huge, sticky cinnamon rolls he saw others enjoying.

He seated himself in one of the chairs with wire legs, that seemed fragile but obviously weren't. He turned to face the window, hoping an answer would pass by the glass facing the sidewalk.

It did.

The coffee had just lowered its temperature to sipping position, and he had attacked the outer ring of the roll, when three young ladies passed by. Dressed in white, they were, with saucy little hats on their heads. One of them wore a cape of blue, and the other two carried their capes.

Nurses.

Nurses were valuable and earned money. Now if he could just figure a way to be a nurse and still be a doctor of chiropractor, maybe… Well, it was the best thought yet. It took two more coffees and another roll, but they seemed worth the cost.

He'd pull himself together and go to that 'teaching hospital' he had passed several times. At least, he could look into it. Wouldn't cost anything but a bit of time if he found someone to talk with. There were a lot of holes in the basket of his future, but at least he would have the basket. Caring for sick people could be done by either gender… for hadn't he proved it in the last, almost, year and a half?

He could bring Ma here, and maybe there'd be enough money to leave her at the hotel where he could make sure she was doing all right. It was a really big hotel, eight stories it appeared to have, and a permanent guest for a while might negotiate an affordable price.

Stuffed with rolls and practically sloshing with coffee, he walked out onto the sidewalk, head up, shoulders back and a chin lifted. What a difference an idea makes!

Why, yes! The person to talk with was a Mrs. Cameron, and she was seated in her office. The busy manager left what she was doing to see what he wanted. Likely a salesman.

At the door she took one look. Mighty young to be a salesman, and she was intrigued. It'd only take a minute.

It actually took almost ten minutes of fast, excited words to explain that he did, actually and truly, know where he was, and that he was talking about being a nurse.

"Have you never had a fellow in training?" He finally wondered.

Mrs. Cameron nodded. Yes, they did. But he didn't last long. For some reason, he had seemed to think it was an easy way to get money, but emptying the night soil vessels had done him in. And he had wasted a whole semester slot being a failure.

Alex nodded. Emptying the vessels was something he knew well, and in the 'stonewall' of his duties, that one duty had been just a tiny 'pebble.' Just about everything that could be done with a human body, he had been doing for the last long time. Absolutely, he wanted a space in the next semester.

Mrs. Cameron was interested, but not totally sold on him. "It'll take a deposit to hold the slot, but we'd need the whole amount at least a month before the semester starts."

Alex performed some mental gymnastics. "Ma'am, when I settle my bill at the hotel and buy my train ticket, I'll have $10.00 and some change. I'll need the change for a sandwich to take with me, but I can give you the $10.00 right now."

Mrs. Cameron liked a person who could make a fast decision. A necessary skill for the job. She liked enthusiasm, and he acted as though he'd found a diamond in his own back yard. She took money and gave him a receipt. While she was writing it out, she heard the short version of his next few weeks.

"I gotta sell a house and find a place for my Ma to be here, too. I'm all she's got, and I took care'a her through a long… well, illness." (It would be too lengthy to explain the wreck.) "But I can do that. I WILL be here, and I WILL last the whole year, baring a disaster." He took the receipt and was gone.

To say that Estella Harper was agog and amazed at the story she heard, was understated but she tingled with pride. Just like his Pa. Sees what needs to be done, and does it. So what if she had to spend a year in a hotel room. Just lucky they would have the money for her to do it.

And back in the training hospital in the Arkansas town, Mrs. Cameron turned to her "wardrobe" attendant. "Anna, do we still have that cap we designed for that fellow we had last year."

"Sure do. No way I'd let that be lost!"

"Well, better have a few more made. I'm pretty sure we're going to have a fellow in the fall semester, and I'd bet the farm he sticks it out to the end. Wouldn't that be something?"

Anna grinned, twirling on her finger the white, four-gored cap made of linen. This could be interesting. Better make a couple more of the smocks, and she can fit the trousers when he actually checks in. If he checks in!

## MY NAME IS EBONY LACE

When not occupied with her many duties, Iris leaned over the table and watched Bonnie, wonderingly, as her sturdy hand with prominent knuckles and square pointed fingers darkened the roses over the supporting net of the collar.

Absolutely true in every detail, the image of the lace collar was being reincarnated onto the sheet of paper. Individual threads were truly portrayed with every twist and whorl. Weeks ago, it had seemed to be complete in every detail, but apparently it wasn't.

Such a good thing, Iris thought. It was something that absorbed her restless mind in every facet of absorption. So good, now that she had reached the dangerous age of restlessness.

Doc glanced as she worked at the kitchen table. Better light for working, she'd said, but he was sure it was Iris, the anchor of her attention. So good, he told himself, because so few things totally interested her of late. So good, but when it was gone what could be next? The Ridge just didn't produce enough babies to keep her busy.

"Bonnie, I need to ask. It's about your name. I am the one who wrote Ebony Lace in the book at the insistence of Olivia." (No one ever referred to Olivia as her mother.) "And it was my idea to call you Bonnie. I thought it would be a good name for a tiny girl, but now you're no longer a tiny girl.If you would like to move to your actual name, we can do that."

Bonnie turned to Doc in surprise. "Of course not! Everyone I care about knows me as Bonnie. It fits me. It's just that I thought… well, it seemed like a good thing to do to honor Great, Great Grammie Cecelia. Look at this, Doc. Every group of stitches as even as if they were made by a machine."

Doc leaned forward, studying the collar. "Exactly. Bonnie, my dear, I watched her gnarled, boney old fingers as they made this, the lamplight glistening off her steel needle. At the last, she had to hold it close to her eyes to make sure she saw what she wanted to see.

"But, Bonnie, I might say this. When I look at your drawing, I think it might have been made by a machine, if I hadn't watched it bein' drawn."

"Yes!" interjected Iris. "I wanted to say that, but I thought she might think it was a put down. I been wishin' she'd have other things to put to paper like that. Watchin' her is better'n a sunset… or a weddin' cake."

It was an idea, and Bonnie mulled it over in her mind. Interesting thoughts, but none of them seemed to stick, just floated out on thin air, like the smoke from the kitchen stove on a windless day.

For a while, the sewing of the new white dresses and the aprons occupied her, but not for long. On her seventeenth birthday, she managed to bring down four of the eight squirrels Iris had ordered. A day of simmering and the tiny bits of meat taken from the delicate bones. Iris' light-as-air dumplings simmered in the rich, flavorful juice.

Bonnie was seventeen and ate the left-over dumplings as long as they lasted. She weeded the bushy peppermint plants and harvested them in the early morning, as per Iris' advice. She gathered the stalks, tied them together and hung the fragrant bouquet in the smoke house.

She arose, dressed and pulled herself through another day, while Doc stroked his chin, thoughtfully… now frosted with white. Two years ago he had sailed past age 50, and he had earned every white hair.

On his head the silver had also invaded. He hadn't thought much until he noticed after he had visited the barber in Eureka Springs. Small twists of dark, salted with silver white lay on the floor. He still had a lot of hair, but it was turning fast. No matter.

No one who needed his help had ever complained, or even commented on the silver in his hair. They were more interested in the knowledge under the hair. And he thought about it as he sat in the diner near the hotel. Before him on the tiny round table with the wire legs (that looked so fragile) was the window and he stared out toward the sidewalk.

The diner coffee was extraordinarily tasty. Some said it was because of the mineral spring that furnished the water. It welled up on the side of the mountain and had only to be piped in with gravity. Good coffee.

No one ever complained about the cinnamon rolls, either. Huge and sweet, twisted with butter and spice, they were a meal in themselves. He noted with mild interest that some young people seemed to be bigger on the inside than on the out as they plowed through the second roll.

There was that slender young man who had just devoured two of the delicacies and still had the energy to pull himself from the wire-legged chair and dash out onto the sidewalk as if the idea of the century had just struck him. Maybe it had.

Doc loved the diner. No matter that the chairs were highly uncomfortable. It was a wonderful place to watch people, and there would be no gong to answer. No emergency brought to his doorstep. Stolen moments that were his. Savored and precious.

By the window a pair of nurses passed, giggling and chatting together. Spotlessly white, they walked together. White shoes on the dusty sidewalk… how did they do it? Attractive little hats… how did they stay on? Glue? And he grinned at the suggestion.

The girls walked on past the wide window of the diner, and the next image was one conjured up in his own imagination. Bonnie, with the mop of curls that she constantly gathered in a ribbon, and that just as constantly escaped. Dark, dark, just about one shade short of coal black.

He pictured her in the white dress, so like the one she wore when she rode with him. His mind put a small hat on the curls… there must be a way to hold it there.

That was when a shiver passed from the top of his head to his toes. A nurses' training hospital was right here in town. His beloved 'niece' currently seemed poised on a limb, like a fledgling bird, afraid to fly. She had been that way for at least a year, and he often gave thought but came to no conclusion.

"Would she… Was there a chance that she'd… Hmmm. Well, he'd never know until he plunged in and asked her. Surely that school had an advertising brochure. He'd just step over there and ask. No harm in that.

Mrs. Cameron answered the summons with interest. Two in one day, if this one panned out. The fall semester was filling fast. Yes, they had a brochure. The registration would have to be soon if his niece was to be part of it.

Doc took the folder and picked up the 300 baby chicks Iris had ordered. They were in boxes of 25 each, piled on each other and bound together with cord. A huge pile of boxes almost four feet high and 16 inches square full of peeping, cheeping, scrambling, and trying to peck out each other's eyes. Just like every year.

He slid the brochure into the binding of the chick boxes to make sure it got home. Pokey and Pancake were restless to be going, and took off up the steep hill to Ridge Road with not a hesitation. They turned on Ridge Road, and Doc re-turned his thoughts to the brochure.

He could actually imagine her liking the idea. She was agreeable about most things but enthusiastic about only a few. A bit of enthusiasm would be nice.

A year of study with others her age, those who might be in the same position of flux between child and adult could be a good thing for her. A committed year to give her time to think and plan. Yes, this had been one of his better ideas.

When he had printed up copies of the herb book he had encouraged her to write, he had stirred up no particular interest. Yes, the publisher would distribute them but would not promise success. Still and all, being unusual, it had been a moderate success. As she had not been enthusiastic about it, Doc just managed it with his other duties. When a payment came, he deposited in the bank of Eureka Springs and thought no more about it.

The interesting thing was… and Doc did not particularly believe in coincidences… the current balance on record just covered the cost of a year at the training school. No matter… he would have found a way to pay it if it was what she wanted. This way, however, it might interest her more. It was because of something she did that something else became available.

Well, who knew the mind of a woman, anyway? It was an ancient lament in many languages, but Doc knew only English. And he wasn't certain that he really WANTED to know the mind of a woman. Maybe that was why he had never been seriously attracted to one. Fear… maybe… and he chuckled at what might have been the truth of it.

The mules turned unto the lane and into the yard. Of the farm animals that particularly interested Bonnie, baby chicks came second right after Sparky. Her friendship with the filly had dated back to the days when she could ride a-straddle in the saddle and be safe.

So she met the wagon and helped to lift the boxes of chicks to the ground. There, stuck in the tie cords, was the brochure. "This for me?"

Doc answered with great nonchalance. "If you want. It was free and somethin' to read." He watched as he set the little cheepers loose in the baby pen. He noted that she was spending more time reading the brochure than he had expected.

All right, Lord. It's up to you now… and thanks. For everything.

Together at the table sat Bonnie and Iris, who was taking a chance to get off her feet. Baby number three was making itself known.

"But look, it costs fifty whole dollars just to stay there."

"Right, but that covers uniforms and food. See there, and the use'a the books."

"Hmmm, yeah, and it's a sleep-over. Dormatory. Doesn't that mean a lot of beds in the room?"

"Wonder how many?"

"Here it is. Fifty students in two classes. Twenty five to the class."

"Starts late August… or leastways you gotta check in that you're really gonna be there."

"Down by the diner. Hey, I've seen that place."

Iris sighed, "I haven't. Maybe I can see it when you go down there to stay."

"Who said I was gonna to go?"

Iris just smiled, her dimples a deep dot in her smooth cheeks.

Bonnie grinned and shrugged, grabbed up the brochure, and climbed the stairs to her domain. Sometimes folks knew too much about her life, even before she knew it.

It was a week later that Bonnie was riding along on a call. "Is $50.00 a lot of money to buy information on how to do somethin'?"

"Not if it was somethin' you wanted to know. You got a fair amount more'n that already. You can spend it on anything you like."

"I… got… what…?"

"Money. Folks been buyin' your herb books, now and again. The publisher sends along a money order ever so often. Your money. Buy what you want."

"But if I went to the school for a whole year, I wouldn't be along with you."

"I'll regret that, but it's somethin' that happens. Folks come and go, and things get better and worse, and sometimes a lot better. It's a decision each person has to make. Ridge Road'll miss you, but they'll do the best they can."

Iris was slightly disappointed that Bonnie didn't need a lot of new dresses. Oh, well. She looked really good in white all that dark, curly hair. And she looked forward to the trip. She did get to see the hospital. She even got to look around inside and saw it acceptable. Even exciting.

Bonnie hugged her mother-sister-friend, being careful of the lump in her middle. "I know one thing. Whoever does the cookin', they can't be even half as good as you." She was right.

## THE TEACHING HOSPITAL

The first day of August 1914 was looming just ahead. For Mrs. Cameron, manager of the Nurses' Training Hospital, it came as a dread and an anticipation. Twice a year, August and February the semester divided, and the students studying Medical Text, moved to Practical Experience. The students of Practical Experience were graduated with a quiet ceremony for the parents who so often had footed the bill.

On that day, a new class of 25 students began, and for the next six months would study from the several books that were the currently the most complete and up-to-date in various facets of Nursing, Triage, and Medical Preparation with a short course of Bone Setting. The advanced Bone Setting would be handled in Practical Experience. The course also included Midwifery, a valuable skill hoped for by every student.

So a group of 25 students, mostly excited and somewhat nervous, descended upon the town of Eureka Springs. Their fee of $50.00 had been paid, and it was a bargain of the century. It barely covered expenses and a pittance for the dedicated staff… including Mrs. Cameron.

The same thing would again happen in February. About 50 times during the year that long-suffering lady decided it was not worth it, and she would certainly resign at the next change… and the next semester found her at her place, somewhat excited and nervous, just like many of the students.

At one point, a rule was made that the entire fee must be paid 30 days before enrollment, or the slot would be lost. There were always those in line to take their place. It had also been decided that a class of 25 was the absolute limit for the type of teaching used.

The students were gathered mainly from the county area, and most were excitedly sent and had a position in their home community waiting for them. Occasionally a young lady became unexpectedly pregnant, and her sister (cousin, best friend?) appeared to use the slot, and this swap was generally honored. Babies came when babies came.

The young man with the square shoulders and a decent spread of muscles brought a welcome smile to the manager. His light brown, sun-streaked, stick-straight head of hair, was well remembered, along with the intense and eager hazel eyes. She'd wondered how nursing became a gender requirement? With all the heavy lifting, a young man should do well, and it was 'inside' work, mostly well-paid, and always looked up to.

So when Alexander Harper presented himself for the course, there was something that stuck in her mind, and it was not only that she remembered him so well. Something about his name.

So in the next hour a young lady named Bonnie Harper signed in, she remembered. It was her… uh, uncle? Someone had come in for information the same day as Alex. Hmmm, well, cousins were welcome, though Harper was not one of the most common local names.

Alex had stood with his Ma while she registered herself as permanent hotel guest for the next year. He carried her few belongings up the stairs and thrilled with pride as she walked, though slowly, totally without a cane. He had insisted on bringing the cane, though. Dr. Palmer had thought there was no danger of losing her balance at this point… but better safe than sorry, they said.

The room was small, but neat. Bed, small table, three chairs and a half-sized sofa. Lamp and rug. Nothing else would be expected for a guest spending a night or two. Food could be had at the hotel cafeteria… or the diner next door. This plan would be expensive, but worth it, the pair had decided. It was covered by the sale of the shop and the house in Joplin with not much left over.

It took courage to make this move, but Ma had been insistent. They MUST be together. It had been hard enough to mourn the loss of half their family. Ma had looked around a bit, and the small Arkansas town looked good. And Alex would make himself and her very proud, of that she had no doubt.

Bonnie Harper was directed to the wardrobe room for her uniform, but Mrs. Cameron couldn't resist saying, "Your cousin just checked in."

Bonnie turned, full- faced and wide eyed. Cousin? "Ma'am, I got no cousin."

Set back somewhat, Mrs. Cameron added, "Alexander? He's not… ?"

"You mean a fellow is in the class? Same name as me?"

"Sure as I'm standing here. If he isn't your cousin, he may be as surprised as you to meet you. I had a small thought that maybe the two of you were going to be working together. Well, just imagine that?"

"A fellow, huh…! Well, a body never knows!" But Bonnie knew. Being an only child and being 'adopted' would make her a bit short of cousins. So she made her way in the direction Mrs. Cameron pointed.

They met in the wardrobe room. He was fairly easy to spot, being head and shoulders taller than the others in the room, and being definitely male.

A mischievous idea flitted through her head. Raising her voice a bit she said, "ALEXANDER HARPER ?"

The face belonging to the sun-streaked hair quickly turned her way and answered, "Here…?"

Bonnie made her way through the group toward him. "Pleased to meet you, sir. My name's Bonnie Harper."

"Harper? Bonnie Harper? Well blow me down!" He wasn't exactly sure what was polite at this point. If she was a fellow, he'd offer his hand. Instead, he just stared, his arms full of white trousers and a smock on a hanger. A button down the side of the front, smock. For fellows.

Bonnie saved him. "We'll have time to get acquainted, I'm sure. We're here for a year." With a smile she went on, leaving him watching her departure. Black, black curly hair. Not board-straight like his. Complexion pale while his was tanned. Of course, one couldn't tell from that. She was right, there'd be time…

The first semester of each class was Medical Text, and Bonnie checked into the dorm on the second floor of the four-floored building and found the bed with her name. Hmmm, where would Alex's bed be? Certainly not in here!

And Bonnie, so much of the time alone, stood in the center of the huge room with fifty cots about a foot and a half feet apart. Fifty girls all at one time! How would she ever learn their names!

She turned suddenly and bumped face to face with a name she would never forget. The blond haired girl dropped her belongs and squealed excitedly. "Bonnie! Are you…?"

Bonnie opened her arms for Carolyn and they hugged like sisters who had been separated for years. They had not seen each other since Bonnie's thirteenth birthday, five years ago, but recognized each other like it had been yesterday.

It had been one of the first trips Bonnie had made with Doc when he was called to set a double fracture on her little sister.

A gong called time for lunch, and they went down together. Bonnie confided, "My uncle, Doc Harper, signed me up for this. I think he wanted to get me off his hands."

Carolyn giggled, most refreshingly. "Yeah, and my Pa said he was sending me to learn somethin' and maybe cut down on the doctor bills at our house."

They picked up their tray of vegetable soup, crackers and a desert of bread pudding, with raisins, and found a seat. Bonnie sighed with happiness. "We're going to have the most fun in all the world!"

Carolyn responded, "Yes, unless I don't get a certificate. Pa promised to toss me in the river if that happened."

And they gathered into the room for the first class. A new instructor, a Miss Cartwright, familiarized them with each book they would be studying in this semester, seven in all, and a couple of them were frighteningly thick. She held each book up as she talked about it.

"And we have a new one this year. Not really a textbook, but very interesting and pertains to our section of Northern Arkansas. Much of it is folklore, tested by the users for likely a hundred years. These native remedies were the best they had, and many of them worked quite well. In fact, many of the more modern remedies were made from these plants."

She held up the book and continued, "The school owns these books, as it does all your books, and you are allowed to borrow them for the year. I would advise that you manage to buy certain of them as reference for when you are employed. This little book is one of them, and it is a very handy reference. It would be my suggestion to buy this one, for certain. They will be for sale by the school any time during this year."

Bonnie watched, and rubbed her confused eyes, and looked again. The subject so familiar! She hadn't actually seen what Doc had done with her book, and didn't even remember hearing the title. Doc had assigned it, and she had compiled it, as he had asked. But then he said a lot of folks had bought it and that it paid for her school. Could it be? No, of course not?

But she looked at her copy on her desk. Hmmm, "by Bonnie Harper", it said, right there inside the cover. Scary! Maybe if she was really quiet about it, no one would ever know. Curiosity made her flip quietly through a few of the pages. There they were... her drawings and descriptions. Big as life.

She pushed her hand against her beating chest and quietly returned the little book to the pile. Doc hadn't even told her... but then, she hadn't even asked and had seemed to be interested in other things. Hmmm.

Bonnie's departure from Hadley Lane certainly had not gone unnoticed.

"Looks like Doc's runnin' the show alone."

"How so?"

"He's packed her off to that school over in Eureka. Gonna make her learn more."

"Yeah, you know, I heard somethin' about that. Gonna make her learn to do what she's been doin' without learnin'."

"That's what I thought. Didn't make a lotta sense. The thing is, though, a body needin' 'im, maybe he'll be able to come and maybe he'll get there too late."

Eleanor nodded. "There'll be no waitin' for a baby slow'a comin'. The way Bonnie did. Myrtie's little girl got here just fine."

"Yeah, well, Myrtie didn't have no trouble. What if she was to have trouble, and no Doc there?"

"I don't know. I guess it'd be like it was before we had Doc."

"I wonder how much a school like that costs?"

"Don't know. I'd be afraid if I sent one'a my girls, they'd decide to go to the city and make more money. Maybe marry some big muckity-muck fellow in the city."

"Bonnie won't. She'll be back."

"How do you know?"

"Just wait and see if I'm not right. If she marries somebody, she'll bring 'im here."

"Yeah, well…."

Eleanor again. "Yeah, and I know one thing for sure."

"What's that?"

"Miss Iris gonna miss her like a turtle'd miss his shell. Those took to each other like butter'n honey takes to bread."

A circle of nods agreed with her.

## A WEEK LATER

The training semester started off with a bang and stack of books. It was a whole week before the two Harpers had a chance to bump noses again. The cafeteria, most often referred to as the galley, was the meeting place of everyone… often looking for a leftover to hold them up until the next meal. Young bodies still growing.

Across the table from each other, a saucer of leftover biscuits between them, they began to sort it out. Alex began by saying his own Great Grandads were born in northern England and southern Wales. Being 'adopted' gave Bonnie a slight disadvantage, but from what she did know, they were definitely 'kissing' cousins, if, indeed, they were related at all.

This small conference who was related was usually attended to by the older family members, just to make sure their progeny were not first cousins, or uncle and niece. The way the country was settling, one needed to be sure there was a safe distance between them in the event they became friendly. Very friendly.

No, he didn't have a family here. Ma was over in the hotel, at least for now, and when his year was up, he'd have to decide. Actually, his Pa had just about decided on Eureka Springs, before he… Well, anyway, he was planning on making another trip to be sure.

So Alex had made the trip for him.

"Oh! Your uncle is a real Doctor! Say! That should give you a really good start."

Start to where… ?

A few more words, and they hit the books. And speaking of books, the crate containing Ma's re-read books should be at the station. Days were going to be long for her, locked up in that hotel room. That little book about medicinal plants might interest her until he could get the crate.

He was expected stay at the school, but he could visit his Ma after five for 'a little while'. He'd take the little book on Friday, and get it on Sunday. If she really liked it, he'd get one for her. The school sold them for a dollar. Rather high, actually, but it might be something Ma would like to have for reference.

Ma had spent almost a week in her room, and she had examined every crack in the ceiling and counted the tiles over the tiny sink. She watched as the maid vacuumed her spot of carpet. She offered to do it for herself, but the maid sadly shook her head.

When Alex came with the book, Ma's room was locked. WHAT in the world happened with Ma?

Meanwhile Estella Harper was busily filing papers in the office behind the sign-in desk. She had run out of things to count and had tracked down the manager. A quick explanation of how she was bored out of her skull and would it be permissible to vacuum her own room?

Had the maid not done a thorough job?

Oh, yes! It was just that Estella needed something to do. She had kept house and helped in her late husband's business. She could operate the typing machine and the teletype. She could sweep, vacuum, cook, serve tables, and wash dishes. She could operate the machines in the laundry.

Could something be worked out to permit her to do SOMETHING with her time for the next year while her son was in training? If not, could anyone suggest somewhere close where she could donate a few hours of her day?

She was told to have a seat… please. And in a moment someone else came to her. "Ma'am, are you looking to donate time… because if you are, we can certainly use you. We do not have a budget to pay a salary, but would you consider a swap for the rent of a room, food and the free use of laundry facilities?"

She could… and they did. And she was in position to see her son as he paused in the lobby, casting puzzled eyes around. Who should he ask, and why should anyone know where his ma might be.

"Alex!"

"Ma! What are you… How come…?"

"Son, I was going crazy counting my fingers and toes up there in that room."

"But you…?"

"And just think! They're letting me work out my rent and food! I get to do what needs doing and sometimes I'll get to work in the cafeteria."

"Well, I guess… but…."

"Son, just think! We can save the money for you for your place of business. I just love it here, and the best thing is I don't have as much free time to miss your Pa and little sister. I am so grateful to not be paralyzed, work seems fun."

Well, when Alex put it together, his Ma had always been active, doing everything down to sweeping the tack shop while Pa made saddles and belts. If working in the hotel made her happy… who was he to say anything? Anyway, no one had ever made Ma change her mind, so why should he try?

So he handed Ma the book, which she was pleased to accept and returned to the school, scratching his head in thought. Imagine… Ma earning the money for her hotel room. Clever Ma he had, and that was a fact.

Doc went on his calls, but it was not the same. Rather like operating a buggy with only three wheels. The girl was gone, and there was no reason to think she would ever be back in his house. No blood parent could have missed a daughter more.

He reached birthday number fifty three. He studied the face in the mirror before lathering his beard. White along the edges nearest his ears. Then on each side of his forehead, the curls were a mix of black, gray and silver. Where did his life go, and what had he done with it? A few lives saved and several more lengthened. A little girl who had depended on him for the breath she learned to breath. What else…?

It was on the seventh week after Bonnie had been gone, and he had puzzlingly examined his life in the shaving mirror, that the gong sounded, and hoof beats found their way to the door.

"It's from Miss Ophelia," the runner was breathless. He still had to go to Burnt Tree Junction for the preacher. "Miss Isabel is gone. Doctor, they said tell you it was sudden, like, and she had not complained."

Of course. Isabel did not complain. She plodded on. So what did Miss Ophelia want?

"You, Doctor. She said would you bring the wagon to get her box, and she's be put by her husband. I gotta run. Gotta tell Brother Phil Darkhorse up at the Junction."

Doc nodded and waved him away.

So his duty for today was set. He hoped no babies decided to arrive. It would be the wagon he'd take, and he could get a couple of Clydesdales, but he didn't. It would be Pancake and Puller, with Pokey on a tether. It'd be slow, but by night, he would have old Miss Isabel back where she had spent most of her life. Wishbone Hollow would just have to get along without her.

Dan and Iris would take the buggy to Eureka Springs and collect Bonnie. Iris would be the best comforter he could send her… much better than himself. In the sturdy farm wagon with the trio of mules, Doc Harper set out on a painful journey. The Good Book said to 'give thanks for everything' so he looked up at the blue sky.

Thank You, Lord. For everything. And would You tell Isabel that we'll take good care of her baby, Bonnie. And I thank You for the years You let me have with that little girl.

It seemed that Isabel had said nothing of being sick. She went about her duties at the Kilpatrick's, tidying up the bedroom. She had just smoothed the wrinkles from the beautiful chenille spread and sat down for a breath. She had leaned back into the cushions of the bedroom slipper-chair and closed her eyes. Maybe she dropped off to sleep.

Another dream. Zeke! There he was…big as life and holding out his arms to her… as he often did. She moved toward him, a smile on her face, and before she reached him, the angel came, and they were gone, the three of them.

When Isabel was found, the faint trace of a smile was still among the wrinkles on her face. A great part of the tears shed were from the eyes of Mrs. Kilpatrick who had come to love her like a mother.

Doc's mother and Iris prepared the small body that Isabel no longer needed. A crowd of more than a hundred gathered to honor her departure. Bonnie had cried until she had no tears left, and Iris forced herself to let her cry. Sometimes tears washed away some of the sorrow.

Brother Philemon Darkhorse from Burnt Tree Junction officiated. He had been Ophelia's request.

"Beloved, we are honored to view once again the beloved face of Isabel Hadley. In the perfect marriage, the two persons become one, and that was what happened with Miss Isabel. When Mr. Ezekiel was called on ahead of her, she had no more balance in her life. When half of her true self was gone, she must plod on, and life finally became too wearisome.

"We are glad to say that she is once more with her beloved Zeke, and she takes with her our love. We will remember that as we commit her body to the ground where Zeke was committed. Let us pray."

Bonnie sniffed, dry eyed… finally. She swallowed deeply, and when Doc touched her arm, she walked with him to perform the ritual of acceptance. A bit of the soil beside the grave was sprinkled onto the box. Woodenly, she turned and walked back to the standing group.

Ophelia stood, a lace hanky to her red eyes. Bonnie walked toward her, her hands extended, but Ophelia could not accept her. She reached out a cool hand and touched the fingers of Olivia's daughter, and then jerked back her hand. Her blurred eyes looked up into the face with the dark, dark eyes and dark curls creeping out from the edges of the bonnet.

She could see absolutely nothing of the slim face, pronounced cheekbones, complexion the color of strained honey. Rosy tinted cheeks. Eyes, the blue of the October sky above them. Not one.

This round, healthy face before her had nothing to do with her, and was… had to be… the cause of her loss. Her head knew that was not true, but her heart could not forget. She turned away and leaned against her husband's chest, her shoulders shaking with sobs.

Iris took Bonnie's hands in hers and turned her toward the crowd, holding an arm possessively around the girl's shoulders. The older girl felt her chest constrict leaving her breathless. So little, Bonnie had asked of the person who was her blood grandmother. The only living female relative she had. So little, and she had received nothing.

Bonnie was taken to the buggy, and she sat shriveled inside. Hollow. Grammie Isabel whom she loved had been shrinking away from her, but Bonnie understood that she could not help it. Now she was totally gone. Disappeared. Ophelia, whom she never had, was also gone.

Bonnie was put to bed, and Doc spent the day wandering around the farm. He walked through the pasture to the small cabin where he had lived before Bonnie had needed him. Now he could move back if he wanted to. Bonnie would not need him.

Weariness overtook him, and he opened the door and went in. Familiarity enclosed him like a favorite blanket. He stretched out on the bed and slept.

Two days later, he returned Bonnie to school… at her request. She longed for the books, the other students, the assignments… the structure that her life had begun need.

Estella Harper was happy… or at least as much as she could be with her loss of almost two years ago. She noticed the herb book was written by a lady named Harper. A relative… ? Interesting, anyway.

"Look, Son, we may have a famous relative. This little book is by a lady named Bonnie Harper."

"WHAT, MA ! It can't be! I have Bonnie Harper in my class. I was going to mention it to you. What's the likelihood of two with that name?"

"Hmmmm. Well, maybe her Ma or her aunt. You could ask."

"Not her Ma. She's adopted by an uncle who's a doctor. She's got no Ma."

"But you must ask her. I'd like to know. I know there'd be no one from my name, but this is your name. It never hurts…"

"No, Ma. Forget it. She and I, we've talked. Her folks have been here since the mountains were created." But at Ma's insistence, Bonnie was brought to meet Estella. Circled around the tiny diner table, the three consumed tea and the huge sugar cookie, over a foot in diameter. It was locally popular, and meant to be broken on the plate and the shards shared.

"You… my dear…? This is a very good book, and you wrote it when you were fourteen? My, my, how clever. And it's something useful to every new bride and handy for most ladies who may have forgotten about some of these remedies. I loved reading it. I didn't know half of them."

"Uh, thank you. My uncle sort'a made me do it for something to do. That was before I started goin' with him on calls. He liked me along when he had a layin'in."

"Laying in…?"

"Birth. Havin' a baby. That's what I want to learn in school. I want to learn what I've been doin' wrong, and do better. 'Course, I want to know the other things, too."

"How lovely. Such good plans. Will you work with your uncle again?"

"Maybe. Until I get a place of my own with beds and a place where the girls can come and wait, and be sure to have someone there to help when her time comes. With us, sometimes Doc is ten miles away when he needed to be there. He did an awful lot of bein' on the road."

Alex had looked from one to the other, amazed at all he'd learned just in the few minutes. "Your own place? You mean a buildin' where you wait for the ladies to come to you? Would there be enough business where you live? It isn't a town, is it?"

"No, it isn't a town, but we have a lot of babies, just the same. It's gettin' to where it don't matter to the girls if their Ma is there, they want Doc in case somethin' goes wrong. I'm here to learn what to do if somethin' goes wrong."

It was Estella's time to watch back and forth. "Alex had a certificate of performance from a bone doctor, named Dr. Palmer. He's quite famous. He cured me just by moving bones."

"Movin' bones...? No medicine...?" Bonnie's dark eyes sparkled with excitement. "Oh, my uncle'd like to hear about that. He hates to give medicine if he don't have to. Especially in birthin'."

"Maybe we can meet your uncle sometime. It looks like we'll be here for at least a year."

Bonnie again. "Miz Harper, what was it wrong with you, if you don't mind my askin'?"

"Not at all. I was in a trainwreck. Alex's Pa and sister were killed, and I was paralyzed from the neck down. I was going to spend my life that way, but there was Dr. Palmer. It took over a year, but I can do anything, now."

"Oh, Miz Harper, my uncle sure enough is gonna want to see you."

The two students went back to the school, their heads whirling with possibilities.

## THANKSGIVING

It was in mid-November that Doc received a letter from Bonnie. It had been more than four weeks since he had been to see her, and he was not particularly surprised to get the letter.... Until he read it.

> ... and something else, Doc. There is another student here, a fellow, who is from Missouri and cannot get home for

*Thanksgiving. I really like him, and I'd like to bring him home with me for a visit and to spend the holiday. I was sure it would be all right with you, but there is something more.*

*"He is here with his Ma, and she's staying in the hotel. If he comes with me, that would leave her alone on the holiday. I really like her and would like for her to come, too. Do you think there would be a place for them to stay overnight, maybe two nights? I know it would really crowd us up, but I didn't know for sure until I asked.*

*So if you can let me know. That way his Ma who works for the hotel can tell them she'll be gone.....*

Hmmm. Well, she's gettin' to the age, Doc told himself. And of course she would want to bring him to meet me. She says it's because they're alone, but it sounds like more than that. And if it's a fellow… and he's in the nursing school… it'd be interesting for Doc to meet him.

So a letter was delivered to the school.

*… my dear, don't worry about where they could stay. Remember my little cabin over on Harper Lane? Two bedrooms, perfect for the young man and his ma. We'll count on getting them when we come for you….*

Estella was overjoyed and excited. New people. A Doctor. Not a bone doctor, but a doctor, and it would be good for her son to meet anyone he could in the medical field.

"Son, we'll be sure to take your certificate to show to Bonnie's uncle. I'll get one of those tubes to keep it from bein' wrinkled…"

And the mid-November storm hit the hills of Carroll County, Arkansas. Eureka Springs, Wishbone Hollow, and all of Ridge Road was covered with frozen fog. Every tree, shrub, and grass clump was encased in tubes of clear ice that sparkled in the weak winter sun like diamonds.

The ground was so slippery that basic chore tending was tortuous. The teaching hospital acquired a broken arm caused from a slip, caught by an elbow. There were four broken legs and a dozen sprains.

There were two new babies. The mother of one of them came on a sled pulled by Papa and the baby's twelve-year-old brother, both in the guiding ropes. Four feet were safer than two. Baby made it fine.

On the mountainside, one elderly woman attempted to take out the night soil chamber and slipped. The flat stones of the walkway were as though coated with glass. By the time she was found, it was too late.

The streets were spread with sand when possible. Mostly, stores were responsible for their own sidewalks… especially the grocery stores. The household cooks wanted special things for the holiday meal.

The school was busy with only minutes for food, grabbed on the run. Times like this were dreaded, but they were the best the school provide. First Aid training was stressed, and a lot of it came in.

The storm was also good for another reason. Being so close to Thanksgiving almost promised good weather for the holiday. Two days after the ice-up the sun came out. The school released those who could go to their families, as there were so many who were too far to go home for three days and they could carry on.

Doc came with the two-seated buggy. Estella had packed a suitcase with necessities, and Doc tossed it into the boot. Lovely lady, she was, he couldn't help noticing. Strapping son, as well.

Bonnie undertook the introductions. "Mrs. Estella Harper, meet Doctor David Harper. Doc, meet Alexander's mother. Alex, this is Doc who raised me."

Estella offered her hand to Doc, and it would have been impossible for her not to note the lively dark, dark eyes and hair. And the frosty silver trimming of the curls above his ears. All this… and including the right number of smile wrinkles among the sun-squinches at his eyes.

Iris was at her most excited element. Bonnie's boyfriend! And she brought him home, along with his Ma! And she, Iris, was permitted to make the Thanksgiving Dinner. It didn't matter that she had baby number four under her apron pockets.

She served squirrel dumplings and vegetables for supper. Cornbread and blackberry cobbler. Just a light meal she tossed together before the big day.

The company was properly and enthusiastically complimentary. The school galley never had food like this… neither did the hotel. Bonnie grinned, thinking this was nothing against what would be prepared for tomorrow.

Alex and his Ma were taken to the cabin, and Doc built a good fire to warm things up and last until morning, and then he and Bonnie went home. They rode along in the starlight, silent, just content to be riding along together. Such excitement the day had held. She was sure she'd never get to sleep. Not to be!

She had hardly hit the pillow before she began to dream. Myrtie and her little Lacey. She was almost breathless waiting for the magic moment when the little girl would no longer be with her mother.

Bonnie felt her hands being empty… then suddenly filled with the warm, precious weight of the damp, warm baby. Where there was nothing… magic happened… and there was the baby! How… how… could something so wonderful be allowed to happen this earth of so many disappoints and cruelties?

Suddenly she startled awake. Feeling in the dim light from the window she felt the lamp and the matches.

Snugging into her fleecy robe she moved to where the stovepipe from the parlor came through the floor of her room and on out the roof. It made a toasty corner where a little girl could play. Crouching against the warm wall, she turned to a clean sheet of her journal and picked up her pencil.

Line after line flowed from lead point, and the title was the last thing she wrote, centering it above the 'cotton plants'.

MAGIC FROM ABOVE

Cotton plants and thread of silk
A hook of shining metal…
A picture in an ancient mind,
With skill, are brought together
Gnarled fingers…eyesight dim,

Mind sharp as hardened steel,
Floss threaded through her fingers,
Teamed with remembered skill.
Worked inch by inch and stitch by stitch
With weary gnarled fingers…
Now Miss Cecelia finally rests
But her creation lingers.
A collar Miss Cecelia made
That only once was worn.
But Grammie made the roses bloom
For someone not yet born.
The collar made of black, black thread
Was called Ebony Lace.
Years later, was still shiny black,
When taken from its place.
Thread of cotton, strand of silk,
Black color does not fade.
And for a girl called Ebony Lace
A magic path was laid.
There's magic in the honey bee
And in the evening sky.
There's magic when a child is born
And music in its cry.
There's magic in a rainbow's arch
When showers move on by.
There's magic in a thread of silk
And how a bird can fly.
The Great Magician made it all
Just for the human's eye.
By Bonnie Harper

She put the journal on the desk and blew out the lamp. The bed was still warm, and she was instantly asleep.

Estella was first to read the verse. "Oh, Bonnie! Did you make all this up during the night?"

Bonnie shook her head. "No, I didn't make it up. It was in my head and I just wrote it down. It's about a lace collar my Great, Great

Grandmother made for me before I was born." There'd be time later so show it to her.

It was easy to get Estella to talk, and Bonnie was learning a lot. So fascinating to hear words from someone who was not from the Ridge. It seemed that Doc felt the same way.

Doc listened and sized up the visitor. Age somewhere in the early forties, possibly late thirties considering the age of her son. Clever, too. Knew a lot about the tack and saddle business. Quite attractive. It was a rare pleasure to converse with someone who was not from the ridge.

And Iris. Thanksgiving Day was created just for her, or so she seemed to think. The house was filled with the aroma of roasting ham, and the counter was decorated with deviled eggs. A holiday mixture of corn, beans and field peas simmered on the back burners, sending forth seasoned steam. Pumpkin and apple pies rested on top of the warming oven to stay fresh, and a jar of thick cream was currently lowered in the well to stay as cool as possible.

And, no, she needed no help. Go have fun and be ready to eat at one o'clock. Alex and Bonnie, on horseback, rode into the pasture and woodland. Alex, the city-born, hardly knew how to ride, and Bonnie, the recent lady, rode uncomfortably unbalanced, but Sparky and Midnight dealt with it. There were certain problems connected with humans, and for them it was just a part of life.

Estella wished desperately to show Doc her son's Certificate of Performance, but felt he should be present when it happened. She asked about Doc's business and was amazed when he told her of the growing population all along the ridge. Nothing much was in sight, but she had seen the centipede-leg roads and trails leading to the left and right.

Seemed Doc could really use some help, and though he didn't say it outright, he seemed to be hoping the help would come from Bonnie. Who knew, however, how the year at school would end.

Doc listened as Estella told of humorous incidents at the hotel. Apparently she could do just about anything from operating the typewriting machine to the laundry equipment. Seemed to like it. But she would see changes when Alex completed his year, and how could she know how it would end?

The choices would belong to the students, while the dreams of their elders were held hostage until the end of the year. Estella watched Doc's expressions, and his somewhat guarded statements. He was hiding a lot that he could not say. Why? Sadness... horror... indecision... thwarted plans... what? And why was not this handsome doctor attached to some local woman?

A sound from the kitchen as Iris whipped butter, cream and fluffiness into the potatoes, shuffled pans on the warming oven, and beat smoothness into the cornbread.

Also, the sounds of conversation from the returning riders. Iris had seated her three youngsters at a separate table and fed them. They could then go play while the adults ate. Iris loved being in control of this wonderful kitchen, and knew it could be taken from her at any moment... perhaps by the lovely lady who was visiting. That... however... was tomorrow's problem. Iris was a master of living for the day.

The discussion of food took up the entire meal, all the way to the freshly whipped cream on the warm, flakey crust of the pies. The young pair of student chuckling at the difference between this and what they had at school. No matter... they were not at school to eat.

Iris shooed them to the parlor with coffee, and Dan excused himself for his own duties.

Estella decided it was time. "Doctor Harper, I have..." and Doc stopped her.

"Please just call me Doc or Dave. Saves time."

"Certainly. Doc, I have a question. Have you ever heard of a Bone Doctor?"

A bit surprised, Doc nodded. "I believe I have. My mailbox keeps me fairly well informed. It seems the Bone Doctors are hoping to be called by another name. Chiropractors, maybe?"

Now Doc had Alexander's attention as well as his mother's. Blue eyes twinkling with interest, Estella continued, "Then perhaps you have heard of a Doctor Palmer?"

"I have, most certainly. He seems to be hoping to create an interest in young men to give his teachings a chance. Other than that..."

"Alex, show Doc your Certificate."

Obediently, Alex took the document from the protective tube. Doc reviewed every word (there weren't many) and looked at Alex. "I think you've had a busy year. Does the school know about this?"

"No, Sir, and I'd rather they didn't. I just want to fit in and learn what they teach."

Doc handed the document back to its owner. "I'd like to talk with you more about this, when we have time."

Estella smiled and sighed with satisfaction. One question down and one to go. Not that she didn't know the answer… it just seemed right to let Doc tell the story. "Also, Doc, Alex showed me a book on herbs which had a lot of information. Seems to be written by a Bonnie Harper. Do you have a sister… mother, or maybe an aunt who would have compiled it?"

Doc managed an amused smile. "No, I'm sorry that I don't. All I have is a niece who put it together, along with her own hand drawings, at age fourteen."

All eyes turned to Bonnie, who shrugged down inside herself with shyness also with a wry smile at Estella's cunning question. Alex also was ready to play along.

"You did it?" Alex's eyes widened with excitement. "And here it is… one of our textbooks!"

Bonnie nodded, "But we won't tell anyone. I just want to fit in, and learn all they know about birthing and care of expectant mothers. This ridge has more'n Doc can take care of, and him traveling the whole twenty miles from one end to the other."

Doc turned to Bonnie with a surge of pleasure and amazement. It was truly extraordinarily interesting when folks actually spoke what was in their minds. He had faced years of not knowing what she was about even though they lived under the same roof. How can you help folks along the way, if they won't let you know which way they're going?

But he said nothing. There was one thing he had learned in his years of living. If things were going right, he mustn't break the spell. Another gem or two might escape from that lovely mouth. Had she had so many losses that she, also, was afraid to speak?

Seemed so. Until now. Bonnie picked up on her own dream.

"I've been thinkin', that if there was a place where ladies could come when the pains start... like there is in town... this ridge could use it. Some'a the places Doc has to go to there just about ain't no way to get there, less'n you were born there."

Estelle grinned in appreciation of the description. "Could be Alex is going to be facing the same thing. But when the time comes, he can pick which ever town he likes, and we'll make it work. The Chiropr... Bone Doctors don't seem to be accepted very much. Doc, I haven't told you that I was Alex's first patient, his and Dr. Palmer."

"You? But how...?"

And the next hour was taken up by the story. The scouting expedition, the visit to Eureka Springs, the storm, the train derailment, and best of all, the co-incidence of Dr. Palmer being available.

And Doc Harper had always had a problem believing in co-incidents.

But that would be for later.

## CHRISTMAS, 1915

The students returned to school in a new frame of mind, excited that one more month and they would be in Actual Practice. They would assist and observe, and make millions of notes.

Young women of the town quickly learned the value of the hospital. Sure, their mamas said that babies should begin their lives at home, but the hospital was so bright and clean, and girls in white so eager to take care of them. Food came on trays, and someone took care of the midnight feeding.

The biggest thing, though, was when something went wrong. Mostly it didn't, but even one of the new mothers could tell of a time when it didn't, and the baby failed to breathe. And there were the times the doctor didn't make it in time. It could still happen at the hospital, and it did, but not very often.

And then there were the babies that did not stay alive until birthing time. So often it was those times that the mother just 'didn't never get to feelin' herself agin'. Here, they had a way of 'erasing' something that didn't go right, and letting the woman start over again. Who would have thought that could even be done? Seemed like that'd be up to God, but it looks like He meant for humans to do it. Sometimes.

Among the observers, there were a few students who flaked out on the floor from the horror of the operation… but eventually they came to, and stuck it out the next time. It was something they had paid good money to learn. And, 'by crackie, they were gonna get their money's worth'.

Bonnie, with her pencil and drawing paper, erected a clinic with six cubbys, partially-private rooms, each with a bed. She added an office, and a room for supplies and preparations. And what else would be needed? It would take thought.

If the ladies were there for several hours, they'd need… maybe, tea? And of course, the chocolate 'comfort' drink right at the end. Maybe store-bought crackers in the tin box. Nothing more. One didn't need any up-chucking when the pains hit, for real.

A body needin' more'n tea and crackers was likely havin' that that thing called 'false labor', whatever that was. Happened a lot with first babies, and was partly why Doc really didn't like birthin'. Took up time he didn't have.

Chin in hand, elbow on table, Bonnie let her mind roam. That 'false labor' likely came about 'cause that girl, never havin' gone through it before, didn't actually know what was 'real' labor. Best their Ma or their man, whichever came with 'er, takes 'er home for a day or two. When real labor gets there, she'll know it, and remember for the next time.

There'd need to be a crib room so babies wouldn't be in bed with their mothers. That would be hard to convince to some patients, but the school was firm. Too many deaths occurred when mothers, weary from the birth, overlaid the newborns.

And what else would the building need? Of course, this building was not something that she could actually have, but it was an interesting pastime, and maybe later… Putting it on paper helped to relieve the tedium of having the plans whirl around and around in her head.

Some of her drawing was done on the table in the galley, munching on whatever was found in the school's warming oven.

Often Carolyn brought her books and studied with her, also liking to be near the food.

And Alex came. He complained that he had no dorm, only a broom closet, and the lighting was so dim he was about to go blind. It seemed that caring for fellows, at this school, was definitely an afterthought.

Along with his books, he studied the drawings and dreams of Bonnie. Having no specific dreams of his own at this time, he borrowed hers. Leaning over her shoulder he studied the sketch. "Where's the waitin' room, for the Pa to be?"

Ah! That was something else that needed to be added. Adjusting the angle, she added a whole new wall, and that left an additional small room for something else. Dreaming was fun if you remembered that was all it was.

Dreams were also cheap. For most of the students, money was the blockade that stopped many dreams from coming true.

Bonnie had received a note from Doc, saying that if Alex had a gun, and if he'd bring it, Dan could spend some time with him over Christmas. If not, there'd be one here he could use.

Wherever his feet took him, a young man needed to know how to use a gun.

## CHRISTMAS

Thanksgiving had gone so pleasantly, the 'city' Harpers were invited for Christmas. Iris, still on a rosy cloud from Thanksgiving, insisted that Christmas Dinner would extend over to an After Christmas Dinner as well.

She told Dan she'd need at least three turkeys, and she'd rather have cocks. If he'd get them to her early in the month, she'd have time to have them smoked for the After Christmas affair. Ham, of course, would be for the first dinner, as was tradition.

Bonnie had redrawn the plans for a dream clinic that was far above her ability to acquire or operate. No matter. It was a thing to think on. Also, it was interesting to her best friends.

Carolyn had insisted that when Bonnie finished her latest sketch, she was to give Carolyn the one she would throw away. She might be able to use it as a bargaining position with her Pa.

With a nod and a sigh to herself, she accepted how much fun it would be to work with Bonnie, but Pa didn't send her to school for nothing. There was always that promise to 'feed her to the fishes' if she entertained the thought of settling elsewhere.

Alex leaned over her shoulder, sizing up the drawing. Window position as well as a wide door could be figured in. And the floor… what would be the covering that would be easy to clean? A lot was said about sanitation here in class.

Everyone who could be excused was released for five days. Some must wait for their vacation during New Year's holiday. But Bonnie and Alex both were given Christmas.

Doc came in the two seated buggy with a variety of quilts for wrapping knees and feet. Bonnie insisted Estella take the front seat. The view was better enjoyed from there, and Bonnie had seen the view at least a hundred times.

As they turned into Hadley Lane, they passed by the grove of pines, their shades of green standing out against bare limbs and the brown of the oak leaves. Alex remembered his Ma's love of pines.

"Look, Ma, over there. Those pines grow in a crescent like they were circling a place for a house, don't you think? Almost like they were planted that way."

Estella nodded. "A perfect crescent with a few extra shrubs tossed in for good measure. I noticed that the other time we were here."

Alex turned to Bonnie beside him. "You know… I just thought. That waiting room might should be at the far end away from the screams. It could be scary to first time dad's."

Bonnie squinched her eyes, mentally eying her drawing. "We could do that. What about making the side view the front view, and making two front doors."

"Mmmmm, Yeah. And make two porches."

Doc rode with head turned slightly toward Estalla… as politeness would dictate. That put an ear turned toward the back seat. He glanced from the corner of his eye at the two young people, each leaning into a corner of the buggy.

Bonnie chuckled softly… almost a giggle. "Hey! How about puttin' the pine grove in the back?"

Response. "Yeah. That one over there," indicating the crescent grove with a snuggly-coated elbow. "Sideway on the sheet'a paper."

Doc struggled to keep a light conversation going, rather than to seem to be listening to the conversation behind him.

Estelle, with a grin and a tiny wink, tried to help. It wasn't easy.

"I know what! I'll get a new sheet and make a view of the front with the two doors, and the pines up overhead."

"Sure, and that'd go with the one with the floor plan."

That seemed to conclude the conversation. Alex leaned forward and said, "Doc, where'll it be that I can shoot the gun? I've never shot before. Pa never had the time, and we lived in the city."

"Lots of places, Alex. Look in any direction, and the woods belong to either me or my parents. Dan'll pick a place. He's a better teacher than I am."

Iris didn't need any help, thank you so much. She'd have the meal on at one o'clock. Just as she'd promised.

Bonnie shrugged knowingly at Estelle. "She thinks we'd mess it up if we helped."

Estelle nodded, with a sad smile. "She'd probably be right."

And the whole baked, smoked ham graced the center of the table by the rich-flavored gravy… with satellite creations circling around. Sweet potatoes with marshmallows, green beans with baby onions. Spiced apples studded with plums from along the back fence. Beets, boiled, then skillet-browned with butter, salt and pepper.

Small drop biscuits browned with buttered tops. And that was not to skip over the apple-raisin spice cake, custard pies and a heap of the children's favorite cookies.

Her crowning creation was the triple layer vanilla crème cake with the candle in the center. Birthday candle. It was Jesus' birthday, after all. And it was a shame He did not get a piece. He'd have enjoyed it immensely.

Dan took the young people to the woods with the guns. Bonnie took a few shots, but rather watched Alex's progress, which far surpassed hers. A difference, surely, was that Alex actually wanted to learn.

Doc and Estella examined the drawing Bonnie left in the parlor. Definitely a place of business, there it was… but why?

"Doc, do you have any idea what's going on?"

"Yes, but the question is, how do you feel about it? I've not spoken to Bonnie and she's said nothing. The fact is, I hoped the dear Lord would influence her to practice here. The Ridge is settling fast, and obviously this is a 'lying in' clinic for birthing. One my worst complaints is goin' from one end of Ridge Road the other, and maybe waiting a half a day or more for real labor to start. This is the new thing, and it might just work… in time."

Estella elbow on the arm of the chair, and chin resting on knuckles, eyed the drawing. "But do you know what's going on?"

"No, but if it's what it looks like, your son will have to start from zero somewhere, and that's tough to do alone. Maybe he's just dreaming, as she seems to be."

A series of gunshots sounded in the distance. Doc continued, "Country folks may be more open to chiropractic treatments than city folks. Especially if Alex had some successes right at the start. Folks out here hate pain. Backs, shoulders, arms, legs and even spines. And he has to start somewhere. I understand that the young ladies from nursing school often team up. It lets each of them have a breather, occasionally. I really have no idea what a vacation is."

Estella listened thoughtfully. "Alex will have to decide in a few months what we do next. I have cast it from my mind, and my life has mostly been wrapped around him."

Doc nodded. "I know. Same here. I continually remind myself not to make the wrappings too tight. Decisions must be hers, however I'm encouraged by the drawings. Especially the addition of the pine trees."

Short silence, then, "How expensive would a building like this be?"

"Depends." After a moment of thought, Doc continued, "If it was made of logs, not very much, but a lot longer to construct. We have talented builders right here on the ridge, and dimension lumber builds up fast."

"I just wondered… also the price of land here. I gather that you advise starting in the country for a new sort of practice."

"Well, I really don't know. As far as the nursing is concerned, the rural areas are good… but a male nurse, no matter how practical, would have the natives scratching their heads. For fellows, there needs to be a 'doctor' in front of his name."

"And what would that take? Dr. Palmer became a doctor before he went into skeletal manipulation."

A shake of the head. "Well, you have me there. I haven't a clue. Why not check with him?"

And the door admitted Bonnie with the announcement, "Doc, Alex and I are taking the buggy up to the junction for a sight-seeing trip. We're taking Wildfire. Dan says he will enjoy the exercise." And she was gone.

"Wildfire?" Estella frowned with concern.

"The young son of Sparky. Nothing like his mother, though."

At that moment, Wildfire was tossing his head... his red-brown mane flying in the breeze. He was chewing at the bit and 'dancing' with restless legs. Nothing like his mother were true words. Where Sparky went with the flow, agreeably and leisurely, her son was a restless firebrand.

Tearing around the pasture just for the pleasure of it, muscular legs pumping and hooves thudding on the grass. On the flint graveled surface of Ridge Road, the beat of his hooves could be set to music. Sharp and even, the sounds making a pattern he could repeat for a mile and more.

Today he was overjoyed to be between the shafts of the small buggy with the white flint trail before him. Uphill or down... no matter.

Bonnie held the reins, but she could have hung them on their bracket. Wildfire knew he would be going to the top of the second hill. Alex was looking to the right and left. "I think Ma would like this trip. Maybe we can..."

"Doc'll bring her if you think she'd like it. You know, I've been thinking about the lighting. Lamps won't do. Sure would like the gas sconces like the school has."

"Maybe they're not hard to get. We haven't checked, remember?"

"By turning the plans sideways, it makes that other little room. Was it 12 feet by ...14 feet...?"

"Yeah, I think. How about a portable partition just in case a couple more cubbies were needed."

"There'd be a need for more than six?"

"Doc thinks there'll be a lot of business for you. I heard him say it."

"A lot of business for you, too."

"But it'll take a while. Don't know if Ma and I can afford it."

A quarter of a mile of hoof beats sounded. The scream of an eagle burst forth overhead, indicating he was hunting. The scream might startle a rabbit hiding in a bush, and making it show itself. A clever eagle trick undoubtedly used successfully since God created the mountains.

"It'll be a hard job. Doctors and nurses don't get to shut down, just because it's Christmas. You know what they told us, holidays and storms make accidents."

Another eighth of a mile. "I know. Its bit scary, isn't it?"

"A whole bunch scary!"

While back on Hadley Lane, a trip back to the table meant another piece of Jesus' birthday cake, and a cup of peppermint tea. Settled again in the parlor, Doc thought and chewed, and then bravely mentioned his thoughts.

"Estella, my dear, I know exactly what you're thinking. But we both know that they must make up their own minds."

"I know that, yes, maybe more than you. I worked with Alex's Pa to get a business started. Being business partners will present difficulties, and that very thing has been known to break up a marriage or two."

Wildfire slowed his rhythmic hoof-beats and turned, without direction into an open area. One building sported a sign, CATLOG STORE, and nearer the road was a roadside stand, empty now. It had an attractive shingled roof, a generous counter, and shelves that completely lined the inside rear. One could imagine products for sale, mostly for immediate consumption.

A short walk around, and they returned to Hadley Lane.

"Ma, you gotta have Doc take you up to the junction. There's a view of the lake and the pine trees that you'll love."

"Alex, let's position the lights. How many, do you think?"

"Enough to see by. Maybe even in the broom closet!"

Doc and Estella did, actually make a trip to the scenic bluff which contained Burnt Tree Junction. The city girl stood for long minutes gazing out over Blue Lake and its surrounding border of pines.

Doc stood just as motionless for the same minutes staring at the lady, trying to judge her actions and read her thoughts. It was early in his life that the doctor realized the thoughts and minds of girls and women were uncharted territory, but with this one, he was determined to try. Was she just trying to make the most of this 'vacation', or trying to humor him... or store up something to say to her son..." Or was she maybe sizing up the ridge as an eventual home? It would really help to know.

But then it came time the students were required back at school, so the trip to Eureka was made. Heads together in the rear seat of the buggy, the famous drawing was studied, re-studied and discussed. Enough space here... and where would be the stove... stoves? Considering its length, it would require at least two stoves.

Doc delivered the students and took the lady to the diner, but the conversation remained the same. "Such beautiful country!" and "What do you think of the conversation in the back seat?"

The doctor shared that Bonnie had requested he get an estimate for half of the clinic (with the other half add-on able, later) as something to share in class to others in her position.

The lady listened with great interest. She'd wondered the same thing.

But when Doc found an hour to drop in on Turners Sawmill for an estimate, Simon, the family's estimator, looked it over, stroked his chin and took in a long breath.

"A bit of money in this here picture, Doc. A little trimmin' here'n there'd bring it down a lot."

Doc shook his head. "Actually, I'd like you to add about 10% size to the whole thing to start with. My Bonnie is dreamin' about th' future. Can't really swing it all at once, but we need to know."

"Not good, Doc, goin' half way. Folks puttin' up half of what they want, find it costs a passel more before its through. There'd have to be an outside wall that'd be torn down for the add on. More work, more material. Also, it'd look so bad to see only half what she wanted, she'd never like it. I can price the whole thing, and you could see if she could swing it."

"Do that, please. Shall I leave it with you?"

Simon shook his head. "Cool your heels, Doc. Have a cup of what we laughingly refer to as coffee."

Some seven minutes later, Simon was ready. "Now, if you'd go for a crew (my nephew and little brother) it'd go up faster and wouldn't really cost much more. I was figgerin' in my help, like I usually do."

Doc nodded, so Simon proceeded. "I have walls, halls and a stretched out building, but we can do anything you want. You better stay sittin' while I tell you the price. What I'm lookin' at is about $180.00, unless she adds on somethin' else, like women do. Can you set your teeth in that?"

Doc nodded. "It'll just take me a little time, but I expect to be back with you before summer. Gonna take a little figgerin'." He pitched out the last of the 'coffee' and extended a hand. "I'm thinkin' this here's gotta happen, so there's gotta be a way. This ridge is getting' so many people, I just can't keep up with it. Gotta have a breather somehow."

"Wait, Doc! This here's not a house?"

"It's supposed to be a clinic. Bonnie's gonna graduate with a Nursing Certificate and supposed to be experienced as a midwife."

"You don't tell me! Doc, that's wonderful! 'Course, I see now why it's been drawed so queer. Now, 'course that don't make it any cheaper, but it does bring joy to my ears. There's been talk, of late… Well, you know women! So little Bonnie's a big girl now! Best news I've heard all week!"

Doc, the bearer of the wonderful news, took his copy of the floorplan (the one discarded for the new one showing the lamp sconces.) and drove off. He sighed deeply. He knew Bonnie had not asked for help, and he was determined not to offer it. She also did not inquire how much money was in her book account.

A smile crossed his face at the thought of her book being a text in her class. The school buying a hundred books had spurred the publisher to advertise the fact of its existence. Three public schools and a college had placed orders, and there was still about five months before she would be certified.

Two weeks later he hung his sign on the note box and took off early, heading to Eureka. He visited with Bonnie for the hour she was permitted and returned her at six o'clock. Going back to the hotel, he met Estella, and they went back to the diner.

"Looks like the cost of the building will be $180.00 if they don't add somethin' else. I could help 'er, but I prefer her independence. It'll mean more if she pays for it, since she actually has some of the money."

Estella watched Doc, elbow on the table, and her dimpled chin resting on the knuckles of her right hand. Should she...? She had forcibly restrained herself from mentioning anything to Alex, though he was well aware of her thoughts.

Doc continued, "Bonnie says Alex is waiting for you to say where you'd like to live, thinkin' you was likin' the town here."

"I can like what I need to like until somethin' comes along that's better. I don't gain money by stayin' here. Just workin' out my expenses. Alex will be twenty by the time he's certified, and I know it's young, but he's had to grow up faster than I would have liked." Had she said enough...?

Maybe not, so she'd add a little. "Just 'cause I like the city, don't mean I might like something better. If I'd said I didn't like it here, Alex might not have done so well for thinkin' a me."

Doc nodded, knowledgeably. This was a touchy subject they were discussing. Words were chosen carefully. It was like walking on egg shells, or maybe thin ice. He had never ever... ever... ever... spoken to a woman the way he talked with Estella, not even his mother. Even more so, with so much at stake being Bonnie's future... and maybe his own.

He was not frightened of this woman who spoke so well, knew so much, appreciated so much, and seemed to understand his half-statements. He was concerned at what her decision would be... and would he want to hear it. What could he say, now, and nothing came to mind. It must be time for a bite of the huge cinnamon roll... his second of the evening.

Estelle continued, "Alex will make the decision. I will insist on that… with no deviation. I will go where he goes. He'd all I have. Knowing him the way I do, I think he's testing the water with his own self. He could possibly find someone with a going practice but he doesn't seem to be looking in that direction. He knows he has more to spend than we had thought, due to my deal with the hotel. He also knows he will have to either buy or build, and he is not the artist Bonnie is."

Doc nodded encouragement, and sipped the coffee. (Much better coffee than that at Turner's Sawmill.)

It was a good move, because Estella continued. "I'm not sure the two have even thought of joining forces, but Alex also knows he cannot startup a business alone, especially because he wants to add what is called, 'Skeletal Manipulation' maybe because the other word sounds like another language. Also, there will be special equipment to buy."

Doc again nodded encouragement. He was good at nodding.

"My recovery was a gift from Above. Otherwise, he would have no education, and must spend his life working to have me taken care of… and I might live to be seventy-five-years-old. So you see…?"

Doc saw. He had also noticed that the two students seemed like a pair of friends intent on their education, hardly aware of anything further. Best that way, likely. They both have too much to think on. Well, he'd caught Estella up on everything he knew, so he'd better let her rest.

He checked into the hotel for the night and left before first light in the morning. Puller and Pokey pulled the buggy up the street to Ridge Road with a sifting of snow in the air, their backs and rumps turning white over the gray.

He hardly noticed the cold, so fast was his mind whirling and getting nowhere. He'd spent 'thought' time on each of his concerns and found them returning again to be rethought. What seemed totally clear was that Bonnie and Alex belonged together, in a business sense and that Estella belonged with her son, in a very personal sense. But what would a lovely lady of maybe forty or forty one do with an old gray haired man going on fifty five? Best he get it out of his mind.

It was four days later that he found, in the mailbox, an updated floorplan with the 10% addition he had suggested. So… now would he take it back to Turner's and see how much it was and when could it be started. She and Alex had figured out that maybe they could swing it, if he, Doc, let them put it in the pine grove, and if she, Bonnie, could scrape up half from the books, or maybe manage some other way.

The snow had melted, leaving the ridge moist and fragrant, crisp and invigorating. He slipped her note in his pocket, and saw Dan waiting at the house.

"Doc, you got a spare hour? I've been doin' some thinkin'. It's been a while since we talked business, but here's where we are. I got more'n enough money to buy a farm, but I like this one. I like the way you do business. Iris really likes the house, and the youngens are used to it. Close enough to walk to school. I'd like to think on a long-term plan.

"I'd like to have you keep the $20.00 a month, and instead, let me have all the baby animals that get born on the farm. I have a likin' of animal breedin', and you got too many babies of everything. Getting' crowded. Need to sell some off, and if you like my plan, I'll take care'a the sellin' of all the babies. Be there bein' somethin' born that you like, you could buy it, and I'd still take care'a it like always."

He stooped for a twig of grass, and chewed on the stem end, his eyes fixed on Doc.

"Well, Dan, you gave me somethin' to think on. First I'd say, I want Sparky and her foals. She's for Bonnie. After that… well, give me a day or two."

And that'd make very little difference to Doc's own long-term plan. He could put away the $20.00, but Bonnie was determined to pay her way, and he was button-bursting proud of her for that. The truth was, she had almost enough. He'd check the bank where the royalties were sent, next time in town. But today, he had to go to Turners Sawmill, over on the shores of Blue Lake.

"Friend, I'm afraid you're lookin' at a trifle more'n $180.00. That's with the new addition and my crew. It can be door-key-ready in three weeks, maybe sooner if the weather holds. How does "185.00 sound to ya?"

Doc nodded, his chin squared and lips firm with decision. "Simon, get the boards and nails together and head over to Hadley Lane. We got a little pine grove that needs a clinic."

To himself he said, Somehow, Lord, I know You're putting the right amount of money there. Thanks for everything.

And Simon said, "Good thinkin', Doc. I'll put you in line."

## HARPER AND HARPER CLINIC

(Birthing and Skeletal Manipulation)

On the last day of April, Simon and his crew appeared on Hadley Lane, stopping at the pine grove. The weather had held, thank You, Lord.

As Doc passed it every day, he saw the footing being dug, the floor plan marked out with stakes and cord. He watched the floor joist being laid and the studs raised. Just the sight of it gave him goose bumps.

Estrelle had handed him a check for $95.00, per the instruction from her son. Doc had taken $90.00 from Bonnie's account leaving $5.00 the required minimum balance and added $5.00 from his pocket. He'd take it back next month. He paid half to Simon, and the other half he slipped between the pages of his Bible. Right between the old and new Testaments.

Up at the junction, Doc was accosted by a puzzled neighbor. "That there buildin' goin' up at your place… what's that word Skeleton Man, or somethin'?"

Before Doc could think up an appropriate response, the man added, "Is that somethin' like a Bone Doctor? My cousin over to Siloam Springs, he hurt his hip and a fellow called a 'bone doctor' bumped it with a wad of something, like maybe rubber, and the pain left. Right then. What say, Doc?"

Doc sucked in a deep breath. It wasn't that he hadn't expected this sort of question, it was just that he hadn't yet thought of a suitable answer. "Uh, yes. Sometimes they're called Bone Doctors, and sometimes Chiropractors."

"Chiro… what?"

Doc decided he just as well get ready. He had voted for Skeletal Manipulator against Bone Doctor and Chiropractor, thinking it would be plainer for folks who had never heard of it… which was most of the residents of the ridge. At least, the first question had a positive conclusion… from the cousin's experience. That's what Alex needed most.

Dear Lord, if You got some success You want'a toss toward that hard-workin' youngen, feel free. I'm thankin' You in advance.

During the three weeks Simon worked (one day it had rained) most of the ridge had either stopped by, or knew someone who had. The pine grove was about an eighth of a mile from the ridge road and in plain sight.

These sightings fueled the gossip grapevine.

"You see that monster buildin' on Hadley Lane? I'm bettin' that cost Doc a bundle!"

"Yeah, and it's a clinic. Reckon he'll work outta it?"

"The word is it belongs to Bonnie and a young fella from Missouri."

"What is a Skeletal Manipulator?"

"Beats me. Reckon we'll see as time goes on."

Myrtie Mason, Bonnie's first delivery, heard the news. "You knowin' when Bonnie'll get outta school?"

No one seemed to. Some thought it was first of September. Myrtie groaned. May, June, July and August seemed a long time with already five month gone on her third.

It was mid-June before the owners saw their place of business. With wide eyed amazement they stared at the completion that looked exactly like Bonnie's drawing.

Inside were the six cubbies with the build-in bed in the center of each, and three deep drawers under each. Also, the two cubbies in the room off the waiting room. Three small stoves joined their pipes in a central chimney. Another small stove was in the supply room. Two front doors and two back doors, high windows in the cubby rooms.

Floor covered with black and white checked linoleum tiles. Curtains white except in the waiting room. There, they were red checked, and a few small pillows tossed around. Curtains and pillows… thanks to Iris.

During the last month of school, lists were made of the gadgets and preparations needed to begin business. More money needed. Doc cringed as he overheard the amount of the necessities to be required.

*Dear Lord, we'd appreciate it if You'd see Your way clear to help advertise Bonnie's books.*

The almost-audible echo's erupted from one end of the ridge to the other.

"Did ya see the sight'a that buildin' Doc put up for Bonnie?" and many other versions of the same question.

"I gotta get over there'n look it over. Is Simon puttin' it up?"

"Yeah, him and the crew. That'll take money."

'Course, them Turners… they're fast workers. That'll help some."

"Still and all…"

"Yeah, money is money. A body rides on dollars or he don't get no where."

## THE FIRST SIGHTING

The clinic had been erected and the door locked for almost a month before the persons who actually paid for it got a chance to see it.

It was mid-June before Bonnie and Alex got an excuse for the same weekend. Doc and Estella were waiting on the curb… Pancake and Pokey switching their tails at the new crop of June insects… when the pair stepped out the door. They were quickly on the way before an emergency of some sort called them back.

It was a quiet trip. There was no drawing on their knees for the students to study, and it had been a long day full of accidents as well as two ladies in labor. Knowing it would be a trip of hours, the pair were content to lean into the corners and doze. Doc sympathized. He'd been there many times. Good experience for them both… take rest while you can.

The change of sound of the mules' hoof-beats aroused the sleepers, and they pulled off Ridge Road onto Hadley Lane. Softer… quieter.

Yawning, stretching, and rubbing sleep from their eyes, they began to search for the first sight. Doc whoa-ed the mules directly in front, and the first glimpse was Bonnie's drawing painted in color and shown in three dimension. Unbelieveable. Certain to be. It wasn't there, and then it was.

They jumped down from their places and walked side by side toward the long building with two front doors and two porches with pillars. Silently they gazed, training their eyes from one end of the building, over to the other.

Alex stood with wide eyes, open mouth and breathness. A dizziness stirred in his head, and he turned toward Bonnie with open arms. The arms automatically closed around the girl's waist, and her size felt so good to his arms, that he lifted her and whirled her around… three times!

To keep from falling from dizziness, he set her down, and leaned forward, kissing her soundly on the cheek. Instantly, the enormity of his mistake entered the clearing head, but the shock of it all left him tongue-tied.

Bonnie, also a bit dizzy, leaned forward and returned the kiss. Her aim being considerably better, she managed to reach his lips with hers. Then, with a separation like that of oil and water, they stepped apart and stared at each other. Alex managed to utter a few words.

"I'm sorry, Bonnie. I didn't mean to do that. At least, right here."

"Yes, you did. You quit bein' scared for a minute, and that's what happened. Are you sorry?"

"…uh, no…"

"Then let's do it again." And they did.

The two others, still in the buggy, stared at where the two had been standing. Did they miss something? Sure to have! So they climbed down and followed them.

From room to room they wandered, exclaiming over this and that. Then returning to the waiting room, and they began another circuit. They caught their breath over something they had missed before.

There in the waiting room was the latest sketch that Simon Turner had worked from. Behind glass, framed and hung on the wall. Beside it were several of the more attractive herb plants from the book, also framed.

The small room just off the waiting room was hung with (believe it or not!) some framed x-ray pictures. Estella had written to the Doctor, who had sincerely wanted to hear from her after a year, and he had returned several of the pictures made from the machine invented by Wilhelm Roentgen and perfected by technetium over in Netherlands. The film sheets were to be a gift to Alex… and maybe it would bring him good luck.

The Doctor had explained that several of the positions of the bone might be helpful to Alex in explaining the terrifyingly-new procedure. Especially when explaining to children what he was doing, punching and twisting their bodies.

Moving on to the six cubby rooms, part-partitioned, with built in a bed centered. Lovely wide drawers for storage. A ladder stairway led to the attic, and they both climbed. "Look at the space! We can stand up without bumping our heads."

"Yeah, and there's room for a bed in the middle, and I can stand up on both sides. And over there, a chest."

They stared at each other in the dim light. "Alex, you said you was sorry. Is that true?"

"Uh, well…"

"I mean are you sorry that you wanted to do it, or sorry that you did it."

"Maybe both."

"Why…?"

"I was scared. I still am."

"Scared why?"

"Because you are so smart and so beautiful, and you have so much I knew you were just bein' nice to me because I was sorta alone, bein' a guy."

"What was wrong with that?"

"You wanted Carolyn to be with you. She couldn't, but there were at least a dozen that might have been interested. I expected you to want a girl."

"But…?"

"Then Ma said you needed the money to finish, and you'd need someone to get started with. So did I. She said it wouldn't be a loss, 'cause we could sell my part when you found someone you wanted, and I'd get practice in the deal."

"Uh, well…"

"And I mostly listen to a. She's smart on a lotta things. Pa always listened, and she helped him. Did I do the wrong thing?"

"Maybe. I think you should have been brave enough to say you liked me because I was me, and not that we could lean on each other to get started."

"Are you awfully mad?"

"Not now. But what you did changes things. Doc and your Ma are bound to be puzzled. Almost as much as I am. Let's go down."

Alex started down the ladder. "But, Bonnie, you didn't say nothin' neither. If you liked me because of me, you could'a said somethin'."

"Alex, remember I've never had an actual boyfriend. Or even a pretend one, for a fact. I thought the fellow always said what he felt, not the girl."

Alex was standing on the ground floor watching Bonnie descend. "Bonnie, remember who you're talkin' to. I just got my first job at sixteen, bein' afraid of every girl but my little sister. Then there was the wreck, and I spent over a year with Dr. Palmer tryin' to help ma, and learnin'. Doctor Palmer wasn't too sure about a lot of things, and had no one to teach him. Only what he read and figured out on his own. And he was tryin' to teach me, too. We made mistakes, and Ma and I were scared till she stood up and walked without a cane.

"Then we came here, and I was in a class with twenty-four girls. One girl scares me, so you can believe what twenty four of 'em did. The special thing with you was your name bein' the same as mine that made you different from the others at the start. Later I saw a lot more things about you, and they made me even more scared."

"What things?"

"Uh, well… you knew exactly what you wanted, and you drew a picture of it. I didn't see how I could fit in with your plans. And you are so beautiful and your uncle already a doctor…and more."

"Oh." Bonnie turned her gaze out the window.

In what would be the storage room, they looked at each other thoughtfully. Then Bonnie, "You was scared'a me, and I was scared'a you. We spent a year eyein' each other like a pair'a bull calves, circlin' each other wonderin' if the other calf's horns were bigger. And neither of 'em havin' a mirror to see their own."

"See what I mean? You have a way'a explainin' that's so clear, it scares me. And when I think'a having a patient come in, it scares me again. Not the birthin', I sorta got that down, and you're here. But you can't help with the bones. I'm still scare about how it's gonna go. There's not even books on it. But Doc, well, see what he did with Ma? "

A nod of understanding from Bonnie. "How was I gonna know that, with us bein' afraid of each other, treatin' each other like brother and sister? Even afraid to talk? You sayin' you feel alone… let me tell you about bein' alone. I got no Ma… never even saw her. Had a Gram but she hates me. Too much went on 'afore I got on the earth. I never had a thought to wonder about you."

Then Alex,"But now you know. I'm mostly scared spitless to put one foot in front'a the other. Do you still want to go through with this?"

"Absolutely. You owe me about five years'a stayin' here for scarin' me half to death!" Bonnie found the strength for a grin and squinched eyes. The sunset sent rosy rays through the west window, lighting her face like a lamp.

The sight of it all made Alex so brave, he courageously asked, "If I promise to tell you I'm sorry, can I kiss you again? On the mouth, this time…? I need the practice."

And he did. They stepped out the front door, and the lane was empty. Doc had gone off without them. The remaining eighth of a mile they held hands and swung along, feeling so light… sorta like they had shed winter skin and stepped out in the sunshine.

Nothing was said during supper, or before Doc took Estella and Alex to the cabin where he used to live. It was all too new and strange to be put in words. It would take some time, like breaking in a new pair of shoes. No matter how well you liked the shoes, they needed some softening to feel real comfort. And there was three months more of school to do it in.

Back in school it was different. They had no need to tell anyone. When they were assigned together, it was different. No words for it… just different.

There was no more of thinking one day at a time. Everything seemed out in the future. The clinic was finished, and they would be a pair. No actual words were said. None were needed.

## GRADUATION DAY

Someone, and Doc insisted it was not him, had put a sign on the message tree up at Burnt Tree Junction saying, "WEDDING. Doc's girl Bonnie to marry. Watch for date." That was enough to attract attention all up and down the ridge. Who'd post a thing like that?

The school graduation was set for the last Friday in August, to clear the dorms for the students checking in for the next semester.It was to be a simple ceremony, just for the families of the graduates.

Estelle and Doc found seats beside each other in the galley, the only room large enough. The girls were dressed in street clothes, but wearing the identification hats, and Alex in his white skull cap. He had already been given all the extra caps, but one would be kept for a pattern, just in case another fellow showed up.

Certificates were slipped into a protective envelope, and handed out as a name was called. The Ceremony took only an hour and fifteen minutes, all told, and that included a talk by Mrs. Cameron on how important these students would be to the city and state, and even the world.

Alex was first, and handed over the cap from his head and took the envelope from Mrs. Cameron's hand. A spontaneous applause broke out, obviously in praise of his courage. Bonnie was the next, and she handed over the little top hat, meant only for street wear and for ceremonies, and received her certificate.

It seemed the reaching of the top of the hill for most students, but for Alex and Bonnie, it was just a semi-final step. Their wedding would be the following Saturday in the Church on the Rock, near the junction.

Brother Darkhorse had been notified and the church prepared. Coffee and cookies would be served to the guests. Iris had made about 50 dozen, assorted.

Iris had also created the wedding dress, in total un-be-knowance of the bride. Satin, stylish sleeves, flared skirt (I ain't wantin' 'er to trip). No mother could have been more proud than Iris.

Bonnie's upstairs furniture had been moved to the attic of the clinic. The extra room would come in handy for Iris' expanding family.

The Bride scanned the crowded church for those she knew, and spotted several. Myrtie, however, seemed not to have made it. Bit of a disappointment.

Brother Darkhorse stood the couple facing each other, and told Alex to hold Bonnie's right-hand in his, and cross his left hand to hold her left hand.

"Now look at your arms. You are tied to each other by two triangles, and the triangle is considered to be the world's only totally rigid geometric figure. This is what will hold your marriage together as long as your hands are clasped.

"And now, in the presence of God and your friends and family, I pronounce you, Alex and Bonnie, a married couple, for as long as you both shall live. You may now seal this union with a kiss."

Alex did a better job this time, having had time to put in a little actual practice. Just about everyone would have liked to ask a question, and the few who dared to were told by Alex he would see them at the clinic next week.

On Ridge Road, anywhere there was a crowd and a pile of cookies, there was a party. The widely spaced farmsteads made visiting difficult so the residents made the most of every occasion. So at one point, the newlyweds slipped out and boarded the buggy, already hitched to Wildfire.

Alex pulled her close. "I love you, Mrs. Harper. Are you still scared?"

"All the way down to my toes."

"Me, too."

Wildfire turned in at Hadley Lane because no one told him not to. He trotted along, and Bonnie stopped him at the clinic… totally unprepared for the sight.

Myrtie was there with her husband and sister, labor down to five minutes, and the three of them were becoming very nervous. Door quickly unlocked, she was rushed to number one Cubby, and prepared by Bonnie.

Little Charlie Haskell, just over three, stood whimpering and holding his arm carefully away from his father, who approached Alex. "My Charlie has a sore arm. We couldn't see nothin' wrong, but he keeps whinin'. We went to Doc, and he said he thought he knew the trouble, and likely you would be the best to take care'a him."

Charlie's Pa eyed Alex with a bit of apprehension. He stood before him, eyebrows raised in question as he looked Alex in the eye. He wasn't sure of this stranger dressed in a fancy suit, and no older than his own little brother. What could he do that Doc didn't want to do?

Alex's heart beat a tom-tom, seeming to try to strangle him. He forced himself to breath. The little fellow was certainly as scared as he was, and there was that kid's Pa, hovering over… looking like a storm cloud. Apprehensive. Bound to be.

Alex took the little fellow into the tiny room with the two cubbies, and let him climb up the two steps to the table. He removed the small shirt, and holding the chubby elbow, he felt the shoulder blade.

Yes! Oh, thank you, Yes! He gave a fast glance upward, as he had seen Dr. Palmer do.

Just exactly as his Ma's had been, at Dr. Palmer's first visit. He stretched the little fellow on his tummy, and doing just as Dr. Palmer had shown him… over and over during that important year. A quick twist and a small tap. A quiet little click.

Small Charlie turned his head to look with surprise at Alex. Alex turned him gently and drew him to a sitting position. The little fellow wriggled his arm back and forth and announced matter-of-factly, "Pa. Hurt gone."

Alex felt relief settle all the way from his head into his highly shined shoes.

Mr. Haskell looked from his child to Alex and back again. Alex swallowed soundly and drew in a breath. "Mr. Haskell, if you would like to step over and look at this picture, I can show you what happened. See this bone. Well… " and he explained in his best layman's terms, mimicking the manner of his mentor.

He concluded with, "It would appear that he had a fall and caught himself on his elbow. If he had been older and heavier, he might have fractured his upper arm. As it is, the bone just slipped out of place a little. He should be fine, now."

Doc Harper had taken advantage of fortunate timing that allowed him to give his new adopted son-in-law some wonderful advertisement. Mr. Haskell was a talker and would spread the word.

Doc Harper could have corrected this tiny problem in a moment from what he had taught himself as had most every country doctor.

The father paid the fee, and left. As he closed the door, Myrtie's son announced his presence with loud indignation. Barely an hour after Bonnie had arrived, the strapping youngster faced he world. But Myrtie told her husband and sister that she got to spend the night in the clinic, anyway. None of that bumpy old road back up the hill. They could come for her tomorrow afternoon.

Bonnie moved the tiny rocker into Myrtie's cubby and spent the night tending to the baby and chatting with her friend when she drowsed awake.

Alex stretched out on the bed where he had laid small Charlie Haskell and stared at the X-rays that lined the wall. His Ma's X-rays. Thank you, Dr Palmer.

It was not how he had planned his wedding night, but it was likely a composite picture of what the future would be.

Doc dropped Estelle off at the cabin and drove to the clinic. He tied Sparky to the post and headed for the door of the clinic… then stopped. Whatever was he thinking of? Bonnie did not need him.

So he went back to the buggy and his room, reminding himself of the conversation on the trip home from the wedding. The lovely lady beside him had asked him to answer two questions.

1. "Doc, do you ever plan to marry?"

2. "Do you object to marrying me?"

Put like that, what could Doc Harper say? (nothing… except maybe, "Thank you, Lord! Thank You! Thank You! THANK YOU!")

He spent the night with thoughts whirling and eyes trained on the squares of moonlight that crept across the wall of what what been Ophelia's bedroom.

A room soon to be vacated soon.

Sure to be.

PART II

# CHESTNUT COTTAGE

## THE BOX

An electrical storm had hit the mountains of Northern Arkansas with the ferocity of a herd of wild horses, creating jagged streaks of flame from the blackness of the sky down to the earth. A fire ball gathered from the lightening fire and seemed to roll right up Ridge Road toward the heavily packed buggy.

The young horse attached to the buggy shied away from the bright flash of fire that lit up the sky in the darkness of pre-sunrise, and his left hooves stepped off the rock ledge, slippery from nighttime dew, that bordered Ridge Road. The wheel of the light buggy caught the outer edge of the rock and slipped sideways, pulling the over-balanced horse with it… tumbling them both down a twelve foot drop.

Animal, wreckage, and humans were piled together.

The fall blew out the flame in the buggy lanterns, else there might have been a forest fire in the dry leaves. The scramble of the horse on top of the buggy was a death knell for the two adults in the buggy, and the trappings of the horse wrapped around the neck of the animal and choked him, efficiently breaking his neck before he could scream his rage.

No matter. With the sparseness of the population and the rumblings in the sky, no one could have heard a sound anyway. Angels, forever in attendance over earthly beings, made a quick and quiet transfer of the young couple, and they were whisked safely to where they were always intended to be.

Not all the angels were engaged in the transfer from earth to paradise. Two very important angels remained with the wreckage.

As the buggy fell, its contents were tossed about and several boxes slid down the mountain, scooting on a slippery bed of dry leaves.

It was sunrise before the tragedy was discovered. The weekly mail delivery man was the first morning traveler on Ridge Road, and over the sound of his horses' hooves, he heard the indignant cry of what seemed to be a baby...

Baby? Couldn't be. Bird? No.... It had to be baby.!

That's when the driver halted his team and slid down the steep bank toward the wreckage, now plainly visible. He readily saw the baby but it took precious minutes to retrieve the screaming bundle from the wreckage... soaked to the skin in her night diaper and screaming with understandable rage.

Retrieving a small quilt that had been tossed overboard in the fall, he wrapped her as best he could and took the screaming package to his wagon. He could do nothing for the persons who were obviously her parents, but from the strength of her screams, it seemed likely the baby should survive.

Where to take her? If all other avenues were blocked, there was always the baby box and that was her eventual stop. This child, however, was taken to a house where she would be comfortable and she would never be placed in the drawer.

However...

There was a whispering sound as the metal runners of the drawer passed smoothly over the glides, and, without ceremony, a bundle was placed inside. The wrapping of the bundle was a torn corner of a faded quilt. Inside the bundle was a tiny example of humanity, the Boss' signature creation. A perfect specimen of the creation that He had shaped from dust, for the purpose of his glory.

That baby was not the one retrieved from the buggy wreck.

Also present, though unseen, was Angel 523. The Boss, of course, did not need numbers to keep tract of the heavenly servants he created and assigned to care for the humans, but the finite mind of humans found it quite too much to comprehend the talents and numbers of the heavenly beings. (Psalms 91.11)

When the box and drawer were pushed back to their alternate position, a bell issued a faint tinkle. Chestnut Cottage had received a new charge. The tinkling bell had not been necessary this time, as Betsy Mitchell was seated in the room in the 'nursing rocker' holding a bottle of goat's milk before a greedily sucking mouth.

Everyone up and down Ridge Road knew about the Cottage, of course, and of its necessity to the community. The residents avoided thinking about it, though, because there were always too many untold stories of 'extra' babies and all of them too sad to think on.

All agreed, however, that the box was a necessary thing. A wonderfully necessary thing.

The focus was not the box, actually. It was more on the drawer that gave movement to the box, but the two worked together on an important mission that affected the lives of many.

Located just south of Wishbone Hollow Arkansas, up the hill on Ridge Road and located, discretely hidden, in a grove of pines, was the cottage, shielded from view from the road by a luxuriant growth of crepe myrtle shrubs.

The building which housed the box and drawer was a native stone cottage tucked within a grove of wild chestnut trees, and draped over by wild grape vines… muscadines, they were called.

The massive oaks, spotted here and there, assured a supply of native mushrooms scattered among the dry leaves, each time the weather was right for the spores to produce. It seemed as though nature, itself, was trying to provide assistance to the important work of the cottage.

Today, however, was a happy day… not for the bringer of the bundle, but truly for the recipient, though he didn't yet know it. Betsy Mitchell gave the babe in her arms a couple of minutes more on the bottle, and then tucked her into one of the several tiny cribs in the room.

She drew in a breath of pleasure and smiled as she lifted the quilt-wrapped bundle from the box. This was the favorite chore of her life, and she carried the precious bundle to the nursing chair.

Wet. They were always wet when they arrived. That's what babies did best, right after crying from hunger.

Betsy was the live-in care at the Cottage. An unfortunate circumstance of her birth created an arrest in her development. Though of perfect size and beautiful countenance, when she reached her fifteenth birthday, the Mitchell family was forced to face the fact that Betsy's mental development had stopped at about age ten.

That little circumstance did not seem to bother grownup Betsy, and every ten-year-old girl in the mountains knew how to diaper a baby. Also how to rinse the important cloth paddings, hang them on the line, and bring them in to be folded. And now, at age 31, Betsy did what she did best, care for the little creatures that appeared in the baby box on the average of about 2 a month.

With the anticipation of unwrapping a Christmas gift, Betsy laid back the scrap of quilt to reveal the scrap of humanity inside. Perfect little boy! Absolutely perfect, likely only hours old and already trying to locate his mouth with a waving left hand. Betsy grinned, eyes crinkling with pleasure at the sight.

A lefty, he was, and he did not break the rule. Every left handed baby that had arrived at the Cottage had been male.

No note was tucked in beside him. Often there was a paper with a name, or just 'thanks' written on it. Most times it was soaked and yellow, but it was always saved.

As she cleaned and dried the small bottom, she hummed the rock-a-bye song, and wondered what name Miss Cottrell would give the little fellow. The last little boy had been named Odell Hill (Hill was the temporary last name of every newcomer). Betsy knew her ABC's so this little fellow's name would start with 'P'. She also knew she would not have him very long. Little boys seemed to go fast, and this little fellow was already spoken for.

Adam Percell, from over toward Berryville, had come by with sad news. Coralee had just produced her third girl, and would be unable to conceive again. His chances of having a son were cut off, and every farm needs a son. So he did what any clever man would do. He told Miss Cottrell that when next a healthy little boy appeared, he wished to be first in line.

If it had been voiced up and down Ridge Road that an angel had whispered into the ear of Adam that he must put in his bid for the next little boy, every resident would have chuckled at the idea. How could a little mountain baby be worth the attention of one of God's holy angels?

And certainly there would be no angelic advice before the baby was even born, would there? A smile and a chuckle, but it was something to think on… anyway. Interesting… the way some things turned out.

So Miss Emma Cottrell looked the little fellow over from stem to stern. Healthy. No problems obvious. For certain, Adam Prescott would be a happy man in a day or two when he received the note in his mailbox.

Sometimes things worked out. Tapping the pencil to her wrinkled chins, Miss Emma squenched her eyes in thought. Paul. Yes, that would be a good name for the eventual heir to the Percell farm.

She opened the ledger and printed in plain letters.

July 11, boy, Paul Hill.

She left blank the disposition that would be Paul's fate. Adam Persell was certain to come for him, but one didn't 'count their chickens before they hatched' it was said.

She closed the book and lifted it to the shelf over her desk. How would she know she would be making another entry in less than a week?

## AFTER THE STORM

As so many summer storms do, the heavenly fireworks with its booming thunder rolled over Northern Arkansas, eventually empting its water in Missouri. This did not, however, affect the pile of broken buggy parts, the unfortunate couple and the horse. Their struggles now ceased forever.

Early that day, the couple had camped for a snack and a rest for the horse, then, in their eagerness, decided to travel at night on an unfamiliar road. Their journey had begun at the big river, where the young man had gone with hopes of amassing funds and returning to his home town in Missouri.

While at the river, he had become acquainted with the family of a pioneer riverside preacher and found reason to make a change in his life. The fact of the preacher's beautiful daughter might have been a factor in the beginning, but his conversion to his Maker was real.

He stayed for a couple of years, having convinced the daughter to take a chance on him, and now he was taking her, his earnings, and all his valuable possessions back home. He could just see in his mind the excitement of his mother over his bride, and even more so because the tiny additions to his family. Ma loved babies with a passion. Two of them... little girls... would be such a gift to her.

They would travel to Eureka Springs, Arkansas and catch the train north. They'd sell the horse and buggy for extra funds. Good plans. Made carefully. The plans were even sanctioned by her parents. One could reasonably well expect to lose a daughter when she married. Painful, but expected. Girls must go where the fellow could do best.

So they were traveling in the dark when the fireball shot across the mountaintop seeming to be blown forward by the thunder boom. Of course it would spook the young horse to shy away. The force of the twelve foot fall from the edge of the road, and the crumbling buggy sent the young man and his bride to their reward.

The little one had been cradled in her mother's arm with her face against warm flesh and her mouth sucking in warm fluid. Then suddenly a noise that startled her with a jerk, then the noise was all around her and the protecting arms fell away. The stream of food was halted, and she slid from the warm lap into the cold, hard floorboard of the buggy.

The frightening thrash of the animal alarmed her and she began to cry. Her cries always meant someone would come and remove her from her discomfort. But this time, an hour of cries did not bring help, so she napped exhaustedly for a while on the lap-robe that slid with her to the floorboard.

When her tummy reminded her that she had not gotten her fill, she began again to express herself. Perfect timing. Light was breaking over the hill, and the weekly postal service was on its way.

The postal delivery man could not really abandon his run to take care of the carnage, but he could rescue the living baby. There was a place nearby where a law official could take over. Less than a mile away, Burnt Tree Junction sported a sparsely spaced group of cabins and farms, and a small cottage business or two. He'd drop the little thing off there with the sheriff's deputy and go on his way.

That's how the problem of the wreckage became the duty of deputy sheriff, Burley Collins and his wife, Annie Jo, and she took in the child and she shared the warm goat's milk along with her own little one.

Deputy Collins examined the wreckage for identification and found none. It must have scattered on the wind. The only clue was a necklace with 'Susannah' engraved on the pendent around the woman's neck. He took the necklace and any clothing and small blankets he could see and left the rest of removal up to the Berryville authorities.

Having no other suggestion of the baby girl's name, Annie Jo put the necklace on the baby and called her 'Susannah' until she could be taken to the Cottage.

There would be no drawer with a box for this little one. She was carried safely in the deputy's arms and deposited into the willing hands of Miss Betsy Mitchell. The Cottage would gladly take the extra clothing, diapers, and small blankets that came with her.

Old Miss Emma Cottrell looked at the necklace and thought she saw an omen as to the child's name. The last little girl had been named Rhoda, like a little girl in the Bible story of Peter in prison. Miss Emma loved to use Bible names when possible and here was the perfect one.

The 'S' was the next letter to use, and it matched the necklace. So 'Susanna Hill' was inscribed on the girls' page of the journal, and the tiny girl was added to the eleven others at the cottage. There were bed babies, crawlers and a pair of toddlers among the group. The outside age for residence at the cottage was 2 years, or thereabouts… unless the Cottage became extra crowded. That seldom happened.

Funny thing… mostly the incoming rescues seemed to keep pace with the adoptees , maintaining the number from eight to twelve to be cared for by Miss Emma and Betsy and any neighbor who wanted to share a time with a child or maybe help fold the mountain of diapers that always existed.

The authorities of Carroll County, Arkansas, paid the sum of fifty dollars a month to Miss Emma as resident manager and fifteen dollars to the 'washerwoman', Miss Betsy. Truth was, Betsy did just about everything that needed to be done, and having no other home, thought she was lucky to get to live there.

And Susanna took her place in the line of small cribs and did not remember the wreckage or the fall, nor did she feel the loss of the warm food provider. Angel 310 could possibly have been a help in this, along with the other angelic protection that hovered over the little Cottage.

Back at the wreckage, a clean-up of sorts happened, leaving the buggy to be stripped by locals of anything usable.

At a farm house less than a quarter of a mile away, Carl Prentiss wandered restlessly among the many duties of a farmer's life, settling down to accomplish none of them. They truly needed to be done. Certain to, but maybe not just now. It was just one of those days.

He just couldn't seem to settle down to anything. He really wanted to go hunting, maybe flush a covey of quail… or at least two or three rabbits. So, shouldering his rifle, he headed out into his upper pasture.

About that time a curious young deer carefully approached a small wicker chest, about 2 ft X 1 ft X 1 ft. It was a sturdy, cleverly put together container, made of willow switches and leaving a multiple of breathing openings between the lathes. Clever and attractive. Almost like it was made of wooden lace.

The young deer was about two feet from the tiny chest when the chest made a noise. Leaping straight into the air, the fawn landed on two feet running. Like a wisp of smoke he was out of sight.

Next came the young wolf, recently on his own, and quite hungry. The strange thing looked like it was made by humans, and he knew never to investigate, but he was hungry. He approached and sniffed, touching it gingerly with his tongue. The human smell of the contents made him snort and leap away.

One glance back, and he'd had enough. His strong, young legs carried him leaping through the underbrush.

The man with the rifle trudged on, weapon over his shoulder and his mind whirling. Why did he want to come out here, anyway?

Oh, well, the fence needed to be checked out for holes. It must always be horse and cow tight. Didn't need his livestock wandering up and down the road, now did he?

Nora Prentiss, the man's wife, sighed and wrung out the bath towels from the soapy water and tossed them into the rinse tub. Another day of discouragement. The small ache in her lower abdomen went to reinforce what she knew already. Another month had passed… another month of failure.

There'd been too many months of failure. She wrung the towels from the rinse, tossed them in the basket and, hoisting it to her hip, she headed for the clothes line.

The summer heat bore down. The towels would be dry in no time. Of course, diapers would take even less time, but who cared about that? She had never washed a diaper in her whole married life and hung it on this line. She'd finally insisted that Carl take the tiny empty crib to the barn loft… it surely wasn't to be needed in the house, and the sight of its emptiness brought such an aching, continuing pain.

Carl followed the fence for a way and circled a thicket, and then he almost stepped on a small, wicker box. Hmmm… attractively made, it was. He stopped to examine it. Then he heard the soft moan and coo. Almost like a baby wolf cub.

The hair on his neck raised in alarm. Wolves that close to the house? But the sound was actually not quite right, and why would it come from the little chest? He touched the box with the toe of his boot. Another coo, and it was definitely coming from inside.

Laying his rifle aside, he squatted beside the box, withdrawing the pin that held the clasp together. Lifting the lid carefully, he looked in, and almost keeled over from the shock. He was… without doubt… seeing things.

He'd heard that when someone wanted something bad enough, maybe they could see it where it did not exist. Could that be? Nora's dejection earlier in the day now flitted across his mind for no reason. He had not asked her what was the matter… he knew. Like he had known each and every month of their married life.

But here in the wicker box before him lay a tiny, pink cheeked baby girl. Seeing Carl above her, she puckered and began to whimper.

She'd been patient long enough, and now it was time to get some attention. She'd tried crying, earlier, but even at her age she knew she did not always get immediate attention. However, now was later, and it must be her turn, though she did not recognize the face.

No matter… she was getting chilly and quite hungry. Also very wet.

Late in the night she had fed well and been tucked into the box-bassinette. She had been jostled so little when the buggy capsized it had not fully awaken her, but, of course, now was later. She was fully awake and soaked up to her armpits. Clearly time something happened.

Carl, his heart pounding, knew this could not be a real, human baby, but it certainly looked like one. His hunter's eye followed the trail of scuffed, dry leaves and bent grass stretching up the hill a hundred feet or so. Could this little box have slid all this way without turning over and injuring the baby? If it was a baby?

Carefully, he picked up the box. It was heavy enough, and it still looked like a baby. He followed the trail around the thicket, and there, in a broken heap, was the crumbled bits of the buggy, a few scraps of scattered debris and a dead horse in the middle of the heap. Plain enough to see what happened.

He approached the heap and saw the blood and the evidence that bodies had been removed. His heart leaped again! Could it be that no one knew about this baby?

By now, the little thing was becoming impatient and the whimper was certainly argumentative. Think, Carl… he demanded of himself. But why think? They had wanted a baby for five years, and he now had one in his arms.

He had one that, by some strange quirk of fate, seemingly no one seemed to know about. There were signs of human activity around the wreck, but the box had slid a very long way, remaining intact even disregarding the steepness of the ground. No adult could have been alive in that mess. The buggy must have contained strangers to the Ridge, so possibly no one knew there should be a child.

With pounding heart, he began to convince himself that the beautiful little thing might actually become theirs. His beloved Nora would likely faint from the pleasant surprise.

With the box under his arm, braced over a hip and the rifle over his shoulder he stepped along in rapid strides. When had this little thing eaten last? At least they could feed her, and hold her, and then try to see who she belonged to. Maybe?

With every step, Carl found himself easier to convince. The heart wants to believe what the heart wants to believe, and his heart, for so long, had an empty spot.

## THE NOBLE QUEST

With each step of his lengthened stride, the dry leaves and gravel whispered, '…Baby …girl… baby… girl'. He replied within his mind, *No, Carl. Don't get your hopes up. She's got to belong to someone.*

*But Lord, we been askin' and askin' and…*

*But, Carl, you know how babies come… they do not appear in the upper pasture where you seldom go unless you've got a cow a'hidin' out with the calf.*

*But, Lord, please… please… please. Ain't my Nora suffered enough? Remember, she's Yours, too.*

*Faith, Carl. Remember the faith, and it will be counted to you as a service to me.*

A final word of passion. *Uh… Lord, if we can't keep 'er for always, could we keep 'er a few days, just to look at?*

So he stepped from the last thicket and had a full view of the farmstead. The house, the barn, and the length of clothesline, towels moving slightly in the summer breeze. Also there was his beautiful Nora, the empty clothes basket on the ground beside her. Her upraised arm leaned against the thick pole that held the clothes line taut, and she leaned forward, her head against her raised arm. It was a position he had seen too many times before.

Swallowing the lump in his throat, he approached her. "Nora, baby, I want you to come in the kitchen with me. Something has happened, and I need you to help me make sense of it all.'

Nora sighed, tried to smile, picked up the empty basket and followed Carl into the kitchen where he set the woven willow box on the table. He moved a chair behind Nora and said, softly, "My darling, you must sit down."

Eyebrows raised questioningly, she sat... her eyes trained on Carl. This was definitely something he did not usually do, so something horrible must have happened.

Pulling the pin from the clasp, with one hand he lifted the lid, and with the other he held firmly to Nora's shoulders. She leaned forward and peered at the pink creature who had obviously given up crying when weariness overtook her hunger.

Eyes closed against pink cheeks, both arms raised above her head, she dozed. Nora, in one instance, saw a beautiful doll that could have been ordered from the catalog and the next instance saw the shiny trail of a dried tear on its cheek, and smelled the aroma of a diaper having been too long in service.

Trembling, she looked up at Carl. "She's real, isn't she? Where did you get her?" She asked, helplessly. Unbelievingly.

Face serious and puzzled, Carl answered, "For truth, Nora, I found her in this basket in the upper pasture. Been a buggy that fell over the bluff, dead horse and evidence of grownups taken out of the wreckage. They'd'a had to'a been dead for this little thing to not be missed."

For a solid minute, sixty silent seconds, Nora stared at the tiny person. Then, "Carl, go to the barn loft and bring the big box of diapers. I still got that bottle we thought'd be good for takin' to church and things."

At that moment, a tiny arm flopped down, and eyes popped open. The miniature face screwed up into a full-blown cry. "Go, Carl! Hurry. I'll get the bottle from the pantry."

Carl moved out quickly. Good old Nora... always wonderful at dealing with sudden changes. His heart ached with his pride and love. She was right, of course, deal with the immediate problems and figure out the reason afterward.

Carl returned with the box, mostly filled with hand-me-down diapers and baby gowns given by family members who no longer needed them. Of course Nora would eventually… but, well, it didn't happen, and no one had the bad manners to mention it.

He entered the kitchen to the aroma of heavily soiled diaper reposing in a bucket, and Nora holding the precious bundle, a bath towel wrapped around for a blanket. Miniature arm, fingers spread in eagerness, the tiny girl pulled at the hard rubber nipple. It took only a moment for her to push the strange mouthpiece away, then to taste the flavor of the warm goat milk.

Reconsidering the strange thing in her mouth, she tried again. In her eagerness, she created a solid stream of milky saliva that flowed over her chin and onto her neck.

Carl stood and gazed. He could remember no sight so beautiful, and if this vision before him was to become temporary, he must force the picture into his memory. The look on Nora's face was one of sheer bliss.

She looked up at her husband. "She's perfect."

And followed with a dismal resignation, "We ain't goin' to get to keep her, are we?"

Carl scraped his mind for an answer. "Maybe not, but let's not think on that right now." While climbing the ladder into the loft for the box, he had made a decision. He would sacrifice the time with Nora and the baby to make a trip up Ridge Road for information. He would be unable to relax until he learned more. One couldn't get one's hopes up… then dashed… again. He had to find out where they stood.

From the pot on the stove, he poured a cup of thick coffee. Breakfast leftover. Settling into a chair, he watched. The eager pulling at the nipple had slowed, and a pink tongue pushed it away once more. Alert eyes searched the scenery for something she remembered, found nothing, but settled back in the comfort of a full tummy.

Nora looked at Carl. "Could God've sent… her… to us..?"

"We can hope. I'm going to go back up to the Junction and see what I can find out. You was wantin' more honey from the Bistro, anyway." He nodded assurance that his mind was made up. "You'll be all right?"

"Truly will, Carl. Guess you gotta find out what you can. Baby alone in the pasture ain't a usual thing."

While Carl watched, Nora lifted the tiny body, naked as a baby bird, to her shoulder and patted gently. Obediently, the little body burped, quite nosily, bringing a smile to the faces of the two adults.

Carl stood to go, and his last view was Nora, standing, then walking to and fro in the kitchen, one arm clasping the baby and the other hand rhythmically patting the bare, pink bottom.

He walked away, opting to go through the pasture rather than the road. There might be something else to find, though likely it would be something he didn't want to find.

At the sight of the wreck, he saw evidence of animal attack on the body of the dead horse, but the wreckage seemed not to have been tampered with. Lifting this and that and peering under the destroyed bedding, he saw something that opened his eyes widely.

The tiny, skillfully woven box had a mate. Reaching under a panel, he pulled the bent and broken willow withes toward him. Lining the broken box had been several of the tiny soft blankets favored for newborns. Nodding, he decided the purpose of the second woven box. So attractive the boxes were, the couple doubtless had one for the baby and the other for the blankets and clothes… only there were no clothes. He did, however, find a sack of used diapers. Though not very many.

He put aside the blankets and diapers to pick up on the way home. Reaching the Junction, he saw the Bistro (actually a roadside stand) to be unoccupied. There were jars of honey as usual, and a money jar for the coins. Honor system. Miss Annie Jo would have chores to do, of course, and the honor system seemed to work.

He sat at the provided table for a few minutes and managed to speak with two passersby. Yes, seemed the horse was likely spooked in the summer electrical storm. Deputy Collins had done notified the proper people, and things were taken care of. No, folks didn't seem to be concerned with the wreckage. Occupants clearly not locals.

One old gentleman stroked his chin, "Carl, man, that there wreck happened on your land, didn't it? Me, being you, I'd get that harness leather off that carcass 'afore the rats and squirrels get at it." Nodding agreement with his words, he clicked to the mule, and clomped away.

Carl sighed. What to do now…? He was not assured, and if they were to give up the baby, it should be in a few days rather than a few years with them looking like they were kidnappers.

Starting toward home, he met a pair of neighbors in their buggy headed toward Eureka Springs. Neighbors… he knew them well, so it was natural they'd stop to talk.

With a hesitation in his voice, he asked, "You folks hear anything about a young baby bein' in the wreck. The woman frowned as she tried to think, and the fellow reasoned, "Friend, we wouldn't know, for positive, but if there was it'd'a been took off by that wolf pack. Them beasts can smell blood a mile away, and a young baby'd be no trick for them to… well, to… you know."

With a pleased smile, the woman said, "I think that'd happen. Baby wouldn't be left to suffer. We gotta be gettin' on… you folks come over when you can."

Carl watched the buggy pull away, thoughts racing around in his mind. It had been months… yea, years… since he and Nora visited, entertained or attended gatherings. Just too painful to watch the little ones being born to everyone but them.

Baby being taken by wolves was plausible… made perfect sense… but Carl knew exactly where that baby was. He clicked the horse to faster steps, the sooner to get back to Nora and make plans. Who could understand the ways of God, and who were they… he and Nora… to question God's gifts?

Both of their families lived at least six miles away, over toward Eureka Springs. They'd be notified, of course, and sworn to secrecy. As for the locals, they hadn't seen hide nor hair of Nora for a year and counting. Plenty of time for her to have been pregnant and given birth. If he had not rescued the baby when he did, the wolves would certainly have taken care of her. Ideas and plans pushed their way into his mind, like a mama pig pushing her snout through the ground for roots.

By the time he reached the wreck, he was delightfully pleased at the plans that laid themselves out in his mind. If angels can feel pleasure when a human yields to their guidance, Angel 311 might have smiled. That heavenly being was the last to leave the wreck, remaining to provide a presence at the site of the baby, and following Carl as he had strode down the hill to Nora.

The Boss had ways of testing the faith of those strong humans who continue to trust Him when everything seems to go wrong. The angel had known, before the time the young parents had left the big river, that the little one was destined for Carl and Nora Prentice, sure as apples grow on apple trees. The angel knew that… as well as the eventual path the little girl would take.

That is, if she chose to obey the Boss' instructions. Angel 311 and others would be present all her life, as angels were with all humans. It was a promise, wasn't it?

Taking advice of the old neighbor, Carl unfastened the clips on the leather harness and tossed it over the saddle. One never had too many leather riggings on a farm. He gathered the blankets and diapers and tied them in a bundle. Two buggy lanterns had left their hooks and sailed out in the direction of where the baby was found. He could repair the bent metal.

Nodding reassurance, he promised himself he'd return for a better look later, but now he was eager to get back to Nora. He entered the kitchen… empty except for the new and unusual aroma from the diaper bucket. He smiled, tolerantly, and made his way to the parlor.

There sat Nora in the parlor rocker with the baby stretched out on her lap. She rocked slowly to and fro, humming softly. The tiny girl was now clothed in a snow-white diaper and a soft pink dress that had once clothed his brother's little girl… more than a decade ago. For a long moment, he just stood and watched.

Nora must have sensed his presence and turned around. "Carl! I just remembered way back after we got the big Bible. We read about the lives of the apostles and Jesus, and there was that verse that told about two woman who were helpers. Remember? Joanna and Suzanna! And I said right off to you that when we had a little girl, she would be named Joanna. I said that name felt good on my tongue… and you laughed at me. It still feels good, so let's call her Joanna."

Carl nodded at her enthusiasm, and settled into the other rocker.

Nora had more to say. "You find out anything out there?"

Carl nodded. "Maybe. You rememberin' that name, maybe you remember somethin' else. Those times we went all the way over to Eureka Springs and we looked at the sights and had store-bought ice cream… and how well you liked it? We sorta figgered one thing that was true. Ice cream was really good, but it didn't keep. After it was over, we remembered how good it was, but it wasn't where we could get it all the time. If we'd'a tried to save it, all we'd'a had would have been a sticky mess. Remember?"

Nora watched and listened. What was he trying to say?

"Well, I thought about it on the way home. Didn't find out nothin' about a baby. Someone thought maybe a wolf had got it if there was one. I didn't say nothin'. Fact is, now we got this little girl right here in our house, and she's better'n ice cream. If we was to look at it that she was like ice cream, to be enjoyed as much as we can while we have her… well…?" He looked at Nora's puzzled expression, then continued.

"Could be she's ours. Maybe not. The whole thing ain't figgered out yet, the way I see it… and if we told the Deputy, he'd'a had to look for her folks. I didn't say nothin' 'cause maybe you're right, and she is really ours. So we gotta enjoy her all we can while we have her, just in case somethin' happens later on that we don't like. We'll take a trip over to see our folks and make 'em promise to keep the secret.

"Then after a month or two, we can be seen with her. What folks think happened is none'a our business, less'n they have facts. We'll not be in position to lie about nothin'. One fact is clear in my mind… if I hadn't had the yearnin' to go out with my gun barely after sun-up, she'd'a been dead and that would be that. Where do yearnins' like that come from? How does that all sound to you?"

Nora had listened in silence, face expressionless. "Carl, we gotta call her Joanna. If we'd'a picked up a baby from the Cottage, everybody'd know and it'd still be all right with our folks and friends. 'Member we thought of it a time or two. So the difference is, this little girl knew where she wanted to go, and she came as far as she could. You said she was in our pasture… that should'a counted for somethin'. Shouldn't it?"

Carl thought a minute. Reasoning was well put. "So, Joanna she is."

Nora's smile was a little bit of heaven. "You wanta hold her? You ain't got to yet."

Carl stepped over to the rocker and picked up the tiny mite of humanity. Returning to the chair, he held her out in front of him. His large hands cradled her back and neck as she sat on his knees.

Nora commented, "See how she just fits in our hands?"

If angels can have periods of satisfaction angel 311 would have had a good reason to nod and smile. Who knows for sure about angels, but might not they not enjoy it when the Boss gives gifts to his followers as a reward for their love?

Chestnut Cottage still had 11 young residents. After Adam Percell picked up the little boy who had arrived through the drawer, they had the little girl who came in the arms of the Deputy lawman.

There were many angels present at the Cottage. Angel 310 was to be there for as long as the Boss directed. The Boss must have had reasons for separating the twins, likely the same as when he directed Baby Moses to be put in the river and guarded only by his sister. And when he arranged for young David to refuse the king's armor and depend on his sling and a small stone.

If the total circumstances had been known, the 'grapevine telephone' would have been overloaded all the way from Berryville in the east and to Eureka Springs in the west. Certainly all of Ridge Road would have been able to talk of nothing else for a week or more, and details (right and wrong) would have been aired and re-aired.

The fact was, Carl Prentiss had no way of knowing that the postal routeman had rescued one baby from the wreck and Deputy Collins had deposited Suzanna at the cottage before half the farms had finished the chores and taken care of the milk. The mail was delivered out of Berryville, and the routeman was not a local. Deputy Collins had no reason to discuss and re-discuss what had been taken care of… forthwith. The matter seemed somewhat settled.

For who would have thought to search the woods a hundred yards from the wreck for yet another baby when one had been rescued, and the identity of the couple had been totally unknown on Ridge Road?

Life at the Cottage went on, and everyone had hard work to do. Even old Miz Hattie Singleton had her own work, though it be self-assigned. Every time she could, she volunteered at Chestnut Cottage, and her appearance was heralded with joy. No one could best Hattie when she decided to clean the floor… steps… attic… or even the goat shed. Armed with her own disinfectant (a wicked germ killer called Lysol) she set to work where she determined she was most needed.

The small playroom for the toddlers was a special focus of hers. Being about 12 feet square, it was floored with a shaggy rug, partly for warmth and partly to soften the many tumbles. Every ten days or two weeks, Miz Hattie rolled up the rug and sudsed it out, and then struggled it onto the clothes line. It would be all day drying, during which time the oak planks of the floor would be disinfected.

For at least 2 hours, the room would be uninhabitable. The disinfectant had its own distinctive smell, which the toddlers ignored and which made Betsy sneeze… but there was no way anyone would criticize its effectiveness. Babies can be germy little creatures.

Miz indomitable Hattie happened to be present when Deputy Collins delivered Susanna, and bells went off in her head. Her daughter in law from down past Garland had an attack of 'empty nest-itis' and seemed to develop every physical ailment known to humans. When the last son packed up and left for Fayetteville to a job in a fancy carriage firm, she had nothing to do.

Now, Miz Hattie was good with suggestions and really didn't force them on the general public, but her family often got the total brunt. She took one look at tiny Susanna, and she knew that pink scrap of humanity was the answer to the daughter in law's physical ills.

She rushed a note to her son to get over here quickly and bring Abigail before anyone took this charming little girl. It would give her something to do, and who would be better to raise the founding child than his wife, the 'eternal mother?"

It would have been impossible to determine whether Angel 310 had anything to do with Miz Hattie selecting that day to volunteer, nor did it matter. It was only four days later, that Susanna had delivered her share of diapers to the 'dirty' bucket, she was whisked away to her new home. On a trial basis at first, it was, but no one expected it to be reversed.

During a bout of bravery, the 'birth' of Joanna Prentiss was registered in Eureka Springs. About the original registration of the pair of births, back at the big river, they had been neglected... hence no paperwork would ever be found. Likely wouldn't have, anyway, as Angel 311 had been on the job long before the baby's appearance.

At three months old during a beautiful Ozark summer, Joanna was brought forth for community view. A lot of talk followed, most of it being how wonderful it was that 'finally' Carl and Nora had a baby. And such a beauty she was!

Some speculated on how bravely (and almost impossibly) the pregnancy had been hidden, but then, the couple lived some distance from the church. Nora might have been having difficulties, and maybe wanted to make sure, still it was an interesting trick to play on the community.

Looking the baby over to see who she favored, the majority community vote went to Nora. Same wide-set, chocolate-ice-cream eyes, and dark lashes. However, the chin might have been passed down by Carl. And she appeared to have Carl's wavy hair, though that could change. But the tiny hands... there was no doubt that they were Nora's.

And Nora, herself, was finally resigned to allow herself to actually go to sleep at night, being assured that Joanna would not disappear if she was not kept in constant sight.

Carl had climbed again into the barn loft and lowered the crib he had so lovingly put together almost five years ago. He scrubbed it down and applied a coat of rosebud pink paint. At present time, it was stationed in her parents' bedroom, but soon would be installed in her own room. As soon as the smell of the fresh paint died away, that is.

A breakfast table conversation might be how they would arrange to get her to school. Miss Tillie Temple's private school was the best, so there had to be a way to get her there, and arrangements must be made to have a space for her in a mere five years.

Miz Abigail Singleton, the empty nest mother, suddenly became as healthy as a horse on clover. Her birth children, now grown and with some already married, had hilarious conversations over Ma's new baby… so much cleverer and more delightful than any of them had ever been, if Ma was to be believed.

## HILDA GUNISTON

Greta Guniston was seriously ill, but now there was no more pain. All she had to do now was wait and everything would be good again. She was right… and she never knew when she was being borne away.

Olleander Guniston knew it would be soon. The loss of blood brought about by her eight child delivery (much too soon for the baby) would be too much for her, and he had begun to make plans. The family of nine… now eight… was down to the last step on the stair of survival, and his concern was settled seriously on the living.

For certain the baby would not live. He'd leave the pitiful thing in the shack with its Ma, and the authorities would dispose of the two. Certainly he had no funds for a burial.

So that made a family of eight with one adult. He'd load them onto the ancient wagon (if he went slow, it'd likely make it) and go all the way to the big river. Across over into southern Mississippi, the cotton harvest would be in full swing. There was no cold winter to speak of in Mississippi, and they'd survive together.

When Greta had released her last breath and the unfortunate infant had issued her first tentative cry, he called the children together. So sure he had been that this night would be the last, he had sent Max, age 12, to the police station with instructions to poke the letter through the mail slot and run back as fast as he could.

Max had just returned, breathless, and stood before his Pa. What next in their pitiful life? Hilda, age 14, stood holding the small bit of humanity in her arms. Wrapped in a thin and ragged towel, the baby sniffled and whimpered… too weak to make a louder demand on life.

There beside Hilda, was Lena, age 7 and Essie, age 6, and they leaned against their sister from either side. Lucy, age 2, stood in front of Lena, whose hands protectively held to her shoulders.

Max stood apart with Hans, age 3, nearby. Pa cleared his throat and pronounced. "We're leaving here tonight."

Hilda gasped, "Tonight? But Pa…"

"Yes, tonight," Olleander pronounced firmly. "Max will help me bring the horse and wagon to the door. Hilda will put down that bundle and pack everything we have into boxes. Lena will begin loading the wagon. Now move, everyone. We will be out of town before daylight."

Hilda objected once more, "But Pa, there…?"

"Hilda, obey me. Staying here will help no one, and we need every minute on the road."

Within the hour the shack had been picked clean of every usable item. Hilda lifted up the youngest and prepared to board the wagon.

Pa's firm voice issued forth, an echo in the empty room. "Leave it here with its Ma. It's the best thing we can do."

"She's a girl, Pa, not an 'it'! If she don't go, I don't go."

Pa signed a breath of exasperation. His firstborn had always been bullheaded… too much so for a girl. He'd thought this might happen, and he had a Plan B ready. "Oh, all right. Bring 'er on and get in the wagon."

It was a moonlight night, with the full moon spreading its golden light on Ridge Road's flint gravel covering. It shown down onto a loaded wagon and several heads of sunshine yellow hair. Only young Lucy was asleep, draped across a quilt-covered box. The others blinked tense and watchful eyes. What was next?

Hilda held the baby snugged to her chest. Though the night was warm, the bony little creature could surely not produce any heat. She would soon be crying of hunger if she wasn't too weak, or she just might pass on quietly. Hilda firmed her lips and thrust out her chin. The little girl would likely die of starvation, but she was NOT going to be left to die alone. It would be indecent.

An hour passed in silence, the horse plodding steadily forward. The wagon crunched the gravel while the silent riders stared into the dim future. Climbing a small rise in the road, he pulled the wagon to the right bar-ditch and handed the reins to Max. Leaping from the wagon bed, he walked around to where Hilda sat holding the towel wrapped bundle.

"Give it here," Pa demanded.

"No, Pa! No!"

"Hand her to me, or I will take her by force. I have a plan for her, and you're not going to stop me."

Biting her lip to keep from screaming, Hilda reached the bundle toward her father, who tucked it under his arm and strode into the woodland on an overgrown footpath, treating the infant with no more care than he would treat a stick of fire wood.

Hilda's mind was a whirlwind of thought, and she scooted to the edge of the bench causing her sisters to sit up, tense and watchful.

The vines had barely closed behind the man when Hilda scrambled into the bag she carried for a piece of paper. She scribbled hastily, thrust the note at Max and demanded, "Promise me you won't say where I'm going."

"But, Sis…?"

"Do what I say. He won't hurt you. When you reach the big river, tell him whatever you want to. But now, promise me…"

In the moonlight, she thrust her pinky finger toward her brother's face. "Hook with me on this, quickly."

Max shook his head of golden hair and scringed backward. Then hesitantly extended his own pudgy pinky. Brother and sister vowed a silent vow in the way they had done so many times. Hilda drew their hooked fingers to her lips and sealed the vow with the necessary kiss.

Then, as the group of heads, all covered with shiny blond hair, turned toward her in confused silence. In a stage whisper, she told them, "Goodbye, I love you. Remember me sometimes."

Then, before their wide-eyed stares, she disappeared into the path her father had taken, and the vines closed behind her. In the filtered moonlight she ran as fast as she could make her feet move. Surely there was a river close by where her Pa was going to drown the baby. Certain to be.

What she would do if she was able to fish the bundle from the water, she had not determined. What she would do if the little girl lived, she had not had time to plan. Only one thing she was sure of, her little sister would not die alone if her own arms could only reach her before she drowned. Her heart pounded with the importance of this brave venture.

Within minutes, she saw the path open out into a clearing of sorts, and a lighted window shone through the tree. Strange... most windows were darkened at night to save on fuel. Hiding in a crepe myrtle bush, she watched. Pa walked up to the building, and instead of knocking, he seemed to pull something toward him, only it was too dark to determine what.

In mere seconds, Pa turned and retraced his steps...totally empty handed. Hilda drew in a sharp breath of horror. He'd just left the baby there on a doorstep...? Why, the little thing wouldn't last until morning, and that was sure to be what he wanted. He even had the towel in his hand, so the baby must be naked on the doorstep, or maybe on the ground. Her cries would wake no one and a wild animal passing through the yard... well, it was unthinkable...

At best, the baby would not be seen until morning, and she would be dead. Thoughts and quickly-formed plans raced around in Hilda's head. Moving softly to keep the shrubs between herself and her father, she forced herself to wait until he was again on the path. He mustn't see her, or he might even kill her as well.

Then she slipped on quiet feet between the shrubs and trees to the building. She could at least pick her little sister up and hold her until she breathed her last. It was the least she could do, then she'd make a decision for herself. Hilda, however, had no idea that her future had already been planned, actually years ago, but angels do not divulge such secrets as that until the ordained moment.

Reaching the building, she searched the ground for the baby. No baby. What could Pa have done with her...? There wasn't even a place to hide her. In her weariness, the exhausted girl leaned against the coolness of the stone and felt a nudged against her lower spine.

Turning, she saw what looked like the front of a dresser drawer. It had a solid handle as though it invited itself to be pulled. Hilda pulled, and the drawer opened out before her. It had a box setting there with a soft cloth spread inside.

Hilda's heart pounded. Somehow... someway... this drawer was connected to the disappearance of the baby. She stared at the light that shone in the box. People inside. Help, maybe. Leaning her face into the box she begged with the only words that came to her.

"Somebody help me! Please help me! I'm right outside!"

Betsy Mitchell, the self-appointed night watch of the baby drawer, jerked to attention. Voices…? She'd just rescued a totally naked and very bony little girl child… still breathing, but barely. A challenge! Betsy loved a challenge. Every baby that came from the drawer must have a chance to live. The ten-year-old mind within her thirty-one-year-old head knew this, and she accepted it as her job to make it happen.

But now the voice. She couldn't just open the door. That was a hard-fast rule. It was Miss Emma's job. Clutching the baby, now wrapped in a soft blanket, she dashed down the hall. "Miss Emma! Miss Emma! Someone out there tryin' to get in!"

Miss Emma was on her feet instantly, toes cramming into her shoes and scuttling down the hall. Leaning down to the box, she demanded in her gruffest voice, "Who's out there?"

Hilda, startled by the voice, managed to say, "It's me! Is my little sister in there?"

A young girl's voice. Safe enough. "Wait, there, dear. I'll get the door."

Hilda burst through the open door. "Please, Ma'am. Did you get a baby from outside? She's my little sister! Can I have her… 'cause she can't be let to die without me a'holdin' 'er."

The two adult ladies stared at the distraught girl as though she might have come from outer space. In that moment, the newborn chose to whimper, weakly. Betsy turned quickly to attended to her duty and challenge. Hilda was quicker.

Grabbing the baby, blanket and all, she pulled the little thing to her chest. "I thank you ladies. I'll go now and not bother you."

Miss Emma moved quickly toward the door. The girl mustn't be let to get away with the dying infant, yet what could she say to calm her? She must stall her somehow.

"Miss, could you tell me your name?"

"It's Hilda. I… well, I…" And additional words failed her.

Miss Emma again. "My dear, I think you might be hungry. Could you maybe step into the kitchen for a cup of tea, and maybe bread and jelly? If you take your sister away, you'll both be hungry before you find food."

The girl looked interested, so Miss Emma continued. "We were thinkin' maybe the baby could take a little milk and rest in a crib until daylight. What do you think, my dear?" Miss Emma had a lot of experiences with a lot of people, but this one was different. How should she go about this?

The girl was interested. One could almost see the ideas circling behind her frightened face. Stay calm, and let here think.

Betsy was a statue, darting her eyes from one to the other, hoping for a signal as to what she should do next. Maybe she should try to retrieve the baby.

Hilda tried to think. Tea? Food? Something for the baby? Her eyes darted from one to the other and settled on Miss Emma. So intent she was that she was unaware that Miss Betsy had edged up toward her and eased the baby from her arms.

As though she had not expected an answer, Miss Emma smiled her most friendly smile, wrinkles arranging themselves into a pleasing design. "I'm thinkin' we got cookies, don't we, Miss Betsy? Or maybe Miss Hilda would prefer a bowl of warm oatmeal with brown sugar... and maybe an egg before she goes. That moon is about to set, and it'll be darker'n a hunk of coal out there. Wouldn't want her to be out there in it, would we?"

Hilda had seemingly come to a decision. "If I stay, can I have my sister back?"

Another smile, and Miss Emma tossed away the suggestion. "Of course, darlin' girl. After you've ate and rested, we'll see if we can help you go where you want to go."

Relief, exhaustion and confusion melded into one huge sigh. "You ladies got food for my baby? You got other babies here?"

"Why, yes, my dear. We have several babies that had no other place to go. We take good care of them. If you'll eat a bite and wait until morning light, we'll tell you all about them. Can you do that?"

A quick nod. "I think so, and I'll thank you." It was such a comfort not to have to be brave and defiant any longer. She followed the short, round lady to a kitchen that had the strong aroma of food.

With a cup of tea before her and a cookie in her hand, she watched the lady pour steaming water into a kettle, and toss in a half a cup of oatmeal. Her eyes were trained on the kettle for the five minutes it took. She watched the oatmeal being dipped into a large bowl and be topped with 5 teaspoons of sugar and covered with milk that was yellow with cream.

The bowl was set before her with the caution, "Eat slowly, my dear. It's very hot and you mustn't burn your tongue."

By the time the bowl was half empty, Hilda's eyes drooped and her head nodded between bites. Miss Emma tried to notice without seeming to notice. She suggested, softly, "Any time you're tired, my dear, there's a place where you can rest until daylight."

Hilda put the spoon next to her plate and looked up. "Ma'am, if I was to do that, could I have the rest of this when it gets light, and I have to go?"

"Certainly, my dear. We'll put it up here in the warming oven. It'll be right here in the morning."

The weary girl arose and followed Miss Emma to the 'hobo bed' they called it. It seemed necessary to have that extra bed in an emergency or when unexpected help was able to stay overnight.

Without attempting to dress her in a nighty, Miss Emma motioned for her to lie down, and with deft hands, slipped off her worn, somewhat dirt clogged shoes. Pulling up a light sheet to tuck softly around her, she picked up the lantern and eased the door closed. With a sigh of relief, she made her way to the drawer room where she would certainly find Miss Betsy... deftly doing what she did best.

"How's the baby, Betsy?"

"Skinny and hungry and maybe a whole month early. No matter, I'll fix her up good!" A ten-year-old expression of pleasure beamed out of the thirty-one-year-old eyes. This was certainly something she could do.

Miss Emma nodded her approval and excused herself to her own room and bed, but not to sleep. She stared at the pattern of the moonlight as it traveled across her wall. That girl...

Was there some way under God's beautiful sun that she could arrange to keep the girl and the baby? For a while, maybe?

Obviously, there was a story of horror behind them that she would likely never know. Nor did she especially care to know. The angels knew, and they were always present around Chestnut Cottage, so why should she bother with what did not concern her? Details better left to those more skillful. It had always worked for her.

Miss Emma didn't tell anyone about the angels she knew surrounded the Cottage, because she did not want to explain how she knew. Innocent little babies would be protected against the evil spirits. Bad angels. She liked to think each baby had its own good angel watching over it. Certainly this little bit of a girl needed an angel if anyone ever did, and so did her big sister. If she needed one, then of course she had one. Angels know when they are needed and Miss Emma had needed no one to tell her that. And she didn't need to know more.

If angels can receive satisfaction from human recognition, then Angel 385 might have been nodding agreement with Miss Emma. Not only that but also, Angel 324, who had arranged the handy pencil and paper in Hilda's bag, and nudged her to move quickly and not call to her father. The Boss knew how many of his angels to assign to each job.

It could also be believed that the two angels banded together to get the Pa on the road quickly, and to keep him from counting noses as he got back in the wagon. When the right thing happens just by chance, it may not be just by chance. Who can know for sure?

And now the wagon, drawn by the weary horse, pulled up the long hill at 4:00 o'clock and reached the top. There was a patch of fresh grass, a small park with tables on the hill and maybe a place to get some food with Ollenader's meager pennies.

Also, if the horse had exhibited unbelievable strength pulling the load up the hills, who would ever attribute that to angels, and when pa finally noticed his first born was not present, he realized it was too late to even mention it. It just meant that he had one less 'hand' for the cotton picking, as he would now have to assign Lena to ride herd on the two little ones. No farmer ever let a child under six into the patch. Too many snakes. Too many stickery vines.

Early morning light saw Olleander back on the road, his flaxen-haired brood chewing hungrily on pork jerky strips.

Hilda slept the sleep of the exhausted until 10:00 o'clock the next day, and the late September sun was high. She opened her eyes and looked at the ceiling, then wailed a desperate cry of agony. Ma! The baby! Why was it daylight and so quiet? Where was she, anyway?

She jerked upright and poked her feet into her dirty shoes. She appeared in the kitchen just as Miss Emma was making lunch for the adults.

"Why, Hilda, darling! Good morning. I hope you had a very good sleep."

Hilda drew in a frightened breath and demanded, "Where is my sister?"

Miss Emma turned from her kettle and paused the stirring. "Sweetheart. So glad you're awake. Let's go look at the little girl. She's had her breakfast and a dry diaper and she's likely ready to go back to sleep. Miss Betsy stayed up all night rocking and feeding her. She's doin' real good. Such a wonderful thing for us to have her here."

Hilda followed Miss Emma into the drawer room. Miss Betsy was rocking to and fro and humming softly. "Betsy, my dear, I believe our visitor would like to rock her little sister for a while, while you help me in the kitchen."

Betsy seemed startled at the suggestion, but motioned Hilda into the rocker and placed the baby in her lap, and then followed Miss Emma to the kitchen and her apology.

"I needed to do that, Betsy. The girl is scared out of her wits that we'll keep the baby, and maybe throw her out. I wanted her to see she wasn't bein' guarded, and could walk out if she took a notion. She'll be hungry, and I'm bettin' on the smell'a fried potatoes and onion to help her make up her mind to stay. I'm tryin' to figger a way to keep her here, at least for a month or so. She's been in a bad way 'afore she got here. Starved and no tellin' what all."

For a solid hour, Hilda stared into her sister's tiny face while she rocked. Could it be possible that she would actually live? Maybe she, herself, could stay here a few days, so she could take her time deciding on a place to go.

The rocking incident sealed the immediate future of the two vagabonds. Lunch over and back in the 'office' with the big journal, Miss Emma remarked to Miss Betsy, "Well, we need to put a name in the journal for this little girl while she's with us. Let's see, the last name we used was Katie, so if she doesn't have a name already, then perhaps her big sister can think of a name beginning with "L". Could you, dear?"

Hilda had become wrapped tightly into the event, as new things and words seemed to come at her at an alarming rate. Her mind grabbed at feeling of peace, and in the seeming importance these ladies were putting on her sister. This was her chance. "If I was to pick a name, it'd be Laura. I always liked that name…" She looked questioningly from one to the other.

"Then Laura it is. A very pretty name. Now, dear, she must have a last name."

Hilda nodded, "It'd be Guniston, and her birthday would'a been yesterday."

So Hilda and Laura stayed.

After the passing of two weeks, Hilda had learned the art of drawing milk from the low-hanging udder of the goats. Her teacher was Hiram Jones, 17, who took the teaching of Hilda very seriously. It was good timing, too, because he was needing to have to get a 'paying' job, and his folks had been concerned about leaving the two 'older' ladies to do their own milking chores.

After three weeks, Hilda sat alone on the one-legged stool and hummed as the milk splatted musically into the shiny steel pail. Milk for all the babies. Such a terribly important job, and it was entrusted to her! To HER! Imagine that!

A whispered word to the right neighbors by Miss Emma produced a number of gently worn dresses and underthings in just the right size. Imagine that! Just a coincident, of course. Why would a pair of angels have had anything to do with such a mundane thing as girl's size 12 dresses? And maybe a pair or two of under drawers?

## JOANNA AND SUSANNA

As it turned out, Miss Hilda created her own space at the Chestnut Cottage, and was allowed to stay for 3 years, enabling little Laura to have an extra year of expert care.

When she and Horace, the handiman, legally joined forces, a tiny two-roomed cabin was erected for the onsite 'help'. Little Laura moved in with them and soon shared the cabin with a tiny niece. When the second baby appeared, the cabin was understandably too small, and the Jones' moved on. Good timing. Horace had now acquired and sold enough livestock to afford a place of his own.

The Cottage ladies were not left in the lurch, however. As time went on, there was what became a waiting list for the little cabin.

On the long, lonely trip eastward toward the big river, Pa Olleander had a lot of time to think over the events of his life. Yes, he'd made a lot of mistakes, but none of them had been on purpose. He just seemed to be rolled over with problems sometimes, not knowing how to climb out. From here on, he was gonna listen to the youngens and try to think things through. Could be they'd have a good idea or two.

Young Lena did a lot of thinking. She moved to the back of the wagon with Hans and Lucy. Just as well get started on her new duty. Lena always loved her big sister, and had felt that walking in Hilda's shadow was just the way of things. But now...?

Here she was with a duty all her own. She would be very good at it and help train the little ones the way Pa would want. Also, when they reached the cotton fields, there might be other young ones she could care for. Maybe a nickel here and there would be given, and she might even get to care for a tiny baby. She'd make a cradle board to hang from the tree... the way she'd seen some mothers do. Nodding her head in an agreement with herself, she smiled and drew in a long breath.

She would be wonderful at the job, and who knew...? Maybe she could go to a school and earn a certificate to teach? Anyway, that could be her goal.

She'd just have to insist when Pa tried to turn her away. If she had a teaching certificate, she could live in one place and not have to move. She and Hilda had actually talked about that. She lowered Lucy's head easy down into her lap and ran her fingers through her sister's hair, soft as silk threads. Light as thistledown. Yellow as the petals on a dandelion.

If angels can feel satisfaction when their charges pick up on the agenda the Boss has for them, then Angel 801 might have smiled. The angel knew, of course, where the grown-up Lena could be teaching and how successful she could be. The Boss always knew, certainly, which of his humans would be willing to listen and to work hard for the privilege of serving him.

The angel would also have known how proud Pa would be when it all happened. His own little daughter a teacher. Imagine that! And wouldn't Greta have been pleased! If she had just lived...

Lena stroked Lucy's hair and stared at the full moon... excitement stirring deep inside her. She was now the 'big girl', and Pa would be proud. If angels can smile with satisfaction, Lena's angel might be doing just that.

Pa followed the river's edge down toward Louisiana, doing the best he could with what he had left. A new courage stirred within him.

Created heavenly beings called angels do not, of course, require names or numbers except for those humans unable to comprehend such magnificence. That said, Angel 811 was moving into action, as assigned by the Boss. It often took a soft nudge at certain other humans when something must be done to the assigned person.

Things were happening elsewhere on the ridge. Therefore, when Spike and Daisy strapped their unexpected and essentially unwanted little boy into a cradle board, things were about to happen. The vagabond pair of parents had invested in a jug back up the trail, and joyfully took the buggy and child on down to the edge of Kings River. The tall trees on the bank assured a cool, pleasant evening of happiness as soon as the contents of the jug would begin to take effect.

The little fellow would be no problem. The cradle board was made for hanging, and a low limb was perfect. The parents had discovered the wonderful fact that two or three spoonfuls of the potent liquid from the jog would keep him silently asleep for hours.

Parking the buggy close to the river to capture the cool breeze from the water, they settled in for a night of pleasure... numbed from any troubles that might otherwise be a concern. Angel 811 was there as the cradle board was attached to the low limb. The parents were feeling assured that no animal, two legged, four legged or having no legs at all would disturb him. The horse was loosed, hobbled and placed in a spot of grass.

The breeze swung the cradle board back and forth and around and around, and the snappy black eyes of the baby gently closed. The breeze was the last of the storm from a few miles north, and the water in the river arose quickly, more than a foot an hour. By midnight the river lapped at the back wheels of the buggy, clawing at the sod beneath the wheels, and at two o'clock, the heartless river tugged the buggy gently into the current, which tenderly eased the wheeled conveyance onto its side and moved it down stream.

A quarter of a mile downstream, the buggy shafts stuck in the ground mud, and the human contents were decanted on land. There they lay quietly, having breathed their last some hours ago… just as Angel 811 had known would take place.

The next soft, unexplained nudge was against the featherbed of old Quince Darby. He roused and stretched, and took a sudden yen to catch a pair of rabbits unaware and bring them back for breakfast. His cabin was near that of his son, and the son's wife would fry them up. Good girl, was that Violet. Good cook, too.

His son had been choosy, and that girl was the pick of the litter in the community. She faithfully produced three healthy children and tended her home with an iron hand… as was expected of a good woman.

Pulling on his overalls and tying his shoes, Quince lifted his gun from above the door and set out in the dim light of dawn. He smiled at the world for his good fortune of having had sensible children, enough food and a place to live out his last years. What more could an old man of sixty want, now that his Liza had gone on. He'd be following her, of course, and sooner than quick, if the Good Lord saw fit.

He headed down to Kings River, his favorite hunting place, and breathed deeply of the aroma of the trees and listened to the cacophony of bird songs above him. He listened carefully for every sound… as every mountain man would… for the danger that could lurk in the most unexpected places. That was when he heard the strange mewing noise that stood out from the other, expected sounds.

Hmmm. He squinted through the trees and saw a horse. What was going on? Slipping from tree to tree, he proceeded, and heard want he learned was the coo of a young child getting geared up to demand attention. So he had campers on the river… not unusual, actually.

He marched into camp, gun at the ready as one must always be careful, but there was no one. Except the horse, that is, and what was that swinging from a limb? Also not unusual, for a fact, but where were the adults?

An examination of the ground showed where a buggy had been, and how its tracks led right into the water. River was high, but that was no surprise. Happened every time there was a thunder storm up on the Missouri state line.

He sniffed and looked carefully around. Surely not, but it seemed so. There were folks who couldn't remember how fast a mountain river can rise, and have found themselves where they didn't intend to be. Seems it happened here.

The little fellow in the cradle board had finally had enough of waiting, and he bellowed his impatience loudly enough that if his parents were nearby, they'd have heard. No parents around. Old Quince went over to the tree and looked at the child. Quite young… maybe six months, but the little fellow had a powerful voice.

"Hey, there," he spoke to the child who shut his mouth and stared at the human with eyes black as onyx marbles. "What's the matter, little fellow? You got no people…?"

The 'little fellow' answered with an unmistakable yell of hunger. "Hmmm, well… what can we do about you?"

He yelled 'hello' a couple of times with no answer. All right, the next thing to do was find this kid some help, and he knew where it was. The angel, of course, would not have had anything to do about that idea, or…?

Loosing the horse from the hobbles and seeing no saddle, he picked the cradle board from the limb, put it on his own back as he had seen the women do… fastening it at his waist with straps provided. Then, leaping astride his mount, he plunged through the shrubs to a path he knew of.

The path led straight to Ridge Road and across to a place where he knew the baby would be safe. Chestnut Cottage. Baby box. He knew about it. Everyone on the mountain knew about it, but it wasn't spoken of except in whispers.

The jouncing ride on Old Quince's back lulled the child into silence. Surely something was being done, and he would soon be fed. After all, with the parents he had, he had learned more patience than a 8 month old should be expected to have.

At the cottage, the old man didn't bother with the box and the drawer. He pounded loudly and Miss Betsy answered. Old Quince turned his back to the lady, and she loosened the cradle board and removed it from over his head.

Old Miss Emma appeared, and he figured his duty was done. "Have a good day, ladies. Picked him off a tree where his parents got caught in the risin' river. I knew to bring 'im here."

With that, he leaped aboard the horse and galloped off, there still being time to snare breakfast before reaching his home. Which he did.

Tying the horse to the gatepost, temporarily, he washed up and waited around for breakfast, where he relayed his morning's venture with great detail and relish. He didn't often have such an entertaining story as this to tell his family. And what about the horse... there wasn't anyone to give it to? Oh, well, he'd think about it tomorrow.

Back at the cottage Miss Betsy and Miss Emma knew what to do. The cradle board and the child had both been soaked to dripping, and the little boy was screaming 'hungry' at the top of his powerful lungs. Dried, and fed, he dozed off to sleep, thoroughly worn out from his travel.

So, he needed a name, and Old Quince Darby had been no help. In addition to that, the last little boy had been named Pete, and they had arived, once more, at the letter "Q", the unhandy spot. So few names started with a "Q".

Then Miss Betsy brightened, and asked, "Didn't Old Quince bring 'im in? We could name the little fellow after the old man what rescued 'im... couldn't we?"

Miss Emma allowed they could, and entered 'Quincy Hill' in the book, and assigned him a birthday, that being the day he was brought in since no better one presented itself.

Young Quincy was a good natured little fellow. He'd learned to be, and this place was nice. Soft hands cleaned him and soft voices spoke to him. Food appeared in his mouth, and what else did a fellow need?

While Old Quince finished off his breakfast with butter and sorghum molasses spread on a biscuit, he tried to erase the morning from his mind by admiring the food and the preparer. That Violet, wife of his son, could stir up a biscuit even better than his Liza could, and Liza weren't no slouch.

Sighing in his intense satisfaction, he moved to the front porch where the breeze was best, and leaned his chair against the wall. Time for a good snooze after the morning's activities.

No such luck. Mean old thoughts keep whirling around in his head and keeping him awake. Now, what was going on with that? Settling his chair back on its four legs, he arose and walked to the corral to look at the horse. Right decent animal… been took care of quite well. Maybe he'd saddle up and ride out just to pass the time.

Could be he'd learn who it belonged to, and if not, he'd just take it over to the Cottage. Them ladies taking care of the baby should, by rights, have the animal. Might be worth a few dollars and reward the ladies for their trouble.

No one on the Ridge seemed to recognize the horse, so he sauntered back home. Couldn't seem to get settled down, though, and that wasn't like him. Seemed like there was something he was meaning to do, that he just couldn't wrap his memory around. He tried to take an afternoon nap, but no luck there, either.

After three days of restlessness, he decided he'd had enough. There had to be an answer to how he felt. Time to get that horse where it belonged, and as he couldn't seem to get any rest, he might just as well do it today.

He had just headed over to the house to say where he'd be gone when he met the oldest grandson, a sturdy eight year old. Dark, intelligent eyes and a ready smile, he was the pride of the family. "Grandpap, Ma and Pa sent me to get you 'afore you got off somewhere."

Nodding agreement, he followed the lad to the kitchen where his son and Violet sat, waiting. He settled into the vacant chair and waited to hear their words. "Pa, we was thinkin', Vi and me. Seems you was called, special, to go down and find that little boy, and we wondered somethin'. Maybe it was meant that we should have him."

Old Quince looked from one to the other of his two favorite people and considered their words. His son continued, "Bein' that how you found him was when you didn't even know he was there… that seemed to tell us somethin' special, like he was meant to be ours. That is, if there ain't been no one to claim 'im."

Old Quince nodded. The words made sense to him, being that he was just on his way there, anyway. "Likely you're right, son. I'll go get 'im, right now." And he did.

The ladies of the cottage couldn't have picked a better place for the little fellow if they had tried. He was put back in the cradle board (now dried out and cleaned), and young Quincy rode to his new home on the back of his new 'grandpap'.

If angels can feel happiness when the humans listen to the whispers and nudges, then Angel 811 might have been comforted. The angel's work was far from over, though, and there would be a lifetime of being in 'charge' of young Quincy Darby, and events were in store that would make his family proud. It would happen in year 1917.

When the wars started in a place no one had ever heard of, it was Quincy who attracted the attention of those who assign important duties. It was the strapping lad from Kings River, Arkansas, who led his company into battle to help save the new nation, and it was he who brought his men safely home.

Angel 811 wouldn't have had anything to do with it… of course. And it is thought that even angels do not force stubborn humans to listen… but those who do, were rewarded royally.

## THREE YEARS LATER

Joanna Prentiss reached three, and created her own position in the community. At the tiny church where her parents attended, there was a wonderful upright piano, and at every opportunity, Joanna sneaked away from parents and 'plink-plonked' on the piano key, just barely within her reach.

Carl Prentiss smiled as he thought he recognized skill at his daughter's fingertips. He immediately began to price a piano, (terribly expensive) and a teacher (scarce. All the way to Wishbone Hollow, actually). No matter.

Those with only one child could afford the more expensive toys, and as young Joanna seemed so strongly attracted to the church piano and the 'plink-plonking' of her own fingers, Carl set his head to how to get one of those pianos into his own house.

They were frightfully expensive, of course, but it wasn't the outlay of money that gave him concern. It was how to actually transport the massive thing up Ridge Road and more specifically, down the sloping trail to his farm. Seemed like he might have to construct a special-made wagon for the purpose, and he could certainly do it if it would make his little girl happy.

Something else had been on the minds of Carl and Nora, the formerly childless couple. Now that their family had a little one… why not another one? The little boy they had hoped for at least eight years ago had not shown up, but he must be somewhere. Maybe they had not looked in the right place… or had actually decided not to look and just wait for their own birth child. Now, however, it seemed the time to look for that little boy and the place to start was at the Boy's Home in Berryville.

A little fellow of six, seven, or eight would be a good age to be a big brother to Joanna, and his years would make up for the time they should have had him. For some couples, the baby appears as expected (or not) in the mother's tummy… for other couples there had to be another way.

Carl and Nora had made peace with which couple they were, and, with Joanna tucked between them in their new buggy, they planned the trip, determined to make a day of it. There was ice cream in Berryville, and that always made little Joanna dance charmingly on her toes in anticipation.

The boys in Boy's Home were on the baseball diamond when Carl and Nora pulled into the yard. The head master explained the requirements for taking a boy from the home. They must really want a 'son' not a servant of all work, and he must be fed well and given a chance to go to school. To prove that this was happening, the prospective parents must bring him back to the Home for an examination at six months, and also at a year, before he could become legally part of the new family. It all seemed perfectly right for Carl and Nora… they had no need for a servant.

While the adults were talking, Joanna took it upon herself to find entertainment, and she spotted a swing. The seat board was just a trifle too high for her, so a lad who was reading on a nearby bench, hobbled over to her. He leaned heavily on a crutch, but laid the item aside to lift Joanna into the seat. Then he pushed her gently, causing her to squeal and chortle with happiness as she 'sailed through the air'.

The lad seemed to be enjoying it as well, and continued pushing her until she was suddenly missed by her parents. Nora shrieked concern, but the little fellow called back that he was careful with her. He knew about little girls and swings. He stopped the swing, lifted her down, picked up the crutch and went to the adults.

The head master explained, "Barney, here, has been with us for a year, now. He's had the misfortune to step on a nail that went through his shoe and is giving him some pain. He got tired of being in the house, so he has the crutch to help him get around for a while."

Carl looked at the handsome lad…maybe seven years old. Then at the head master. "Sir, uh… is… ?"

The head man was no dummy. "Perhaps we could go inside for a cup of coffee… maybe… ? Your little girl would be quite safe with Barney, if you should like to leave her outside. You'll be able to keep an eye on her through the window, there."

Settled inside, he continued, "Barney is an unusual case. His parents and little sister were murdered and the house ransacked while he was at school. When he found them dead, he began screaming and ran to the neighbors. The authorities brought him here, saying there was not a scrap of information about an extended family where he might go. At first we thought someone would show up, but it didn't happen. He has done well, and he's very bright with his studies, but he is very lonely. He does not seem to attune himself to a group, as some of the boys do."

It all sound good. But should could this have happened with no delays or fanfare! Had he been just waiting for them? So what if their family was to be put together like a puzzle rather than a picture.

Barney looked like he would just fit the current vacancy. And the situation was clearly all right with the boy.

So Barney rode to his new home in the back seat of the buggy playing with his new 'sister'. Angel 441 would hardly have had anything to do with the day's success, of course, but who would have thought Barney would step on the nail, and thereby not be drawn into the ball game on the field? What would be the chances of that happening, just on the day that a longing for a son became more than Carl and Nora could bear?

So Carl and Nora happily took home the bright eyed seven year old. As a farmer, Carl was very successful… seeming to have an instinct as what to plant where, which animal to buy and when to add a neighboring property to his. So he was obviously able to support a son and give him responsibilities and gifts such as his own horse.

When Outlaw became Barney's horse, the responsibility for the animal came along with it as well. Currying the animal when he had to stand on a box to reach the mane, to harnessing him or saddling him, and to watch for snags, insect bites and any sign of dullness of the animal's eyes.

When school started, he was to saddle Outlaw and ride him to the school, about a mile and a half away… on down Ridge Road. He was to be loosed in the corral the school maintained for that purpose.

But all was not as smooth as would be hoped for.

The lad's days were passed with smiles and activity, but the nights were plagued with memories and scenes he could never erase. There were evenings when everything seemed good, but later there would be sobbing behind the closed doors. Carl and Nora stood outside wondering… should they go in? And if they did, would they be able to comfort him, being unable to imagine the horrors he'd gone through?

Those nights were filled with their own tear-filled eyes as they held each other's hand for comfort to be given and received, and to finally look up toward the ceiling and beg for help. "This is one for you, Lord…" Of course, it always was one for the Boss, but it didn't hurt for Carl and Nora to be reminded 'from whence came their help."

But mornings brought a smile, and the boy managed to rebound and attack the next day with the energy of a healthy seven year old.

With careful planning, Carl managed a way to move the huge piano down from Ridge Road to the farm house, and both children enjoyed the 'plink-plonking' while a teacher was sought. Then there was the trip to Wishone Hollow every two weeks for lessons for Joanna who was now four.

Barney, now eight, went along, listening to every word of the teacher, and even asking a question or two. That was when the teacher suggested Carl get the boy interested in the violin teacher next door. Carl was happy to oblige, though he scratched his head at the thought of both of his children actually having a head for music. Stranger, still, was when Joanna, then at age five, actually produced a few recognizable tunes.

Barney attached himself to the violin like a drowning person to a life raft. Of all the frightening things that happened in his short life… all the things over which he had no control… this little wooden box on his shoulder was an answer. It had no opinions of its own, and answered his every command. After he passed the stage that his bow screeched on the strings, he finally managed to hit an 'A' and the box played an 'A'. Every time. So reassuring!

He began to finger out little tunes he'd heard and matched them to the piano keys. It was another way to send his little 'sister' into paroxysms of laughter to the point of tears.

The musical duet about Mary's little lamb was the first, and Silent Night, Holy Night followed right after Jingle Bells. At that point, there was no stopping them. Actually, with the ear for music they both had, the lessons could very well have stopped, and they would have gone merrily on their way, playing 'by ear'. Papa Carl, however, insisted on teachers and continued lessons, not the least of which reasons was that he could afford it, and leaving a project half done did not figure in the mind of Carl Prentiss.

Good thing, actually, as there was so much to learn that would be needed later by the pair. Angels 311 and 811 would need to have known the Boss' agenda and would have been watchful over the time Joanna was lying in her enclosed bassinette… and Barney's tears and night time loneliness. Both were necessary. The Boss makes no mistakes in his agenda and his assigned angels bring them about… tying together the loose ends of fragmented lives. Bringing widely separated lives together with perfect timing. Working with both ends toward the middle of the human fabric to create a tapestry pleasing to Himself. Assuming the humans permit the Boss to have his way.

Abigail Singleton moved to Eureka Springs following a promotion of her husband. No matter, this marvelous little toy that had come her way, the one named Susanna, could learn to stun the world just as well from that town as any other.

Abby scrutinized her 'daughter' from every angle and was forced to admit she was a bit too uncoordinated to learn dance steps to the perfection that Abby would insist upon. Her crayon art was only mediocre, so mom turned to music. Any tune the four year old had heard, she could repeat, tone-perfect.

Mom decided the girl would learn to play an instrument and the most beautiful and expensive instrument was the pianoforte… a huge instrument that the colonies had abbreviated to 'piano'.

For Abby there was no moment of hesitation, and she bullied the town's most expensive teacher, a middle-aged Miss Stockard, to take her on. Four years old was a tiny bit young… but… a music teacher needs money to live, and this one was no exception. Obviously this family had it. Why not try it for a year or so?

Then, when she put the child on the bench and shooed her mother from the room, she was astounded by the eager look in the eyes of the girl, and the obedience of her pudgy fingers. She had already been taught the alphabet, and was excited to find the letters printed right there on those white strips. Such surprise when the alphabet spoke back to her each time she touched a letter.

Wonder of wonders, 'C', 'C'. 'C', 'C', 'G', 'A', 'B', 'C' sounded to Susanna like one of her favorite tunes… the one that brought new toys. Her small fingers sought, trial and error, for the next sounds of Jingle Bells… and found them.

Miss Stockard, after years of attempting to put music into hands that had none, and watching her efforts slip through the fingers into nothingness, and whose heads were full of other things, was stunned. Could it be…? After all these years…? That she should have a prodigy fall right into her lap? Or piano bench, so to speak…?

Trembling with excitement, she opened the beginner's book with pictures of the keyboard, causing Susanna to giggle most pleasingly, and located the picture positions with her left hand. With her right hand, she located the correct position on the row of white strips.

After the initial half hour (usually a beginner took only 10 minutes or less before they became restless) Miss Stockard gave the mom a glowing report, and spent a sleepless night planning the path she would take, bringing the child to such heights of greatness that would reflect a fair amount of greatness back upon herself.

It was almost as though the forty years Miss Stockard had lived were of no consequence, and that it was on this day that her life truly began. Of course, the job transfer of Sussanna's adopted father, and the presence of Miss Stockard who needed another pupil, were not affected by an angel… certainly not Angel 310! Why would an angel be concerned with a four-year-old little foundling girl in the unremarkable state of Arkansas? Or what part could a child's life could play in the Boss' agenda? Nothing, of course! Anyone could make a case for coincidence.

Certainly. Just coincidence, of course.

Mrs. Abigail Singleton, while initially put out and miserable with the move to the relatively small town, found to her surprise that instead of just another person on the fringe of local society, she was now in position to play a major part in the smaller town of Eureka Springs.

While she was still intensely possessive and interested in her adopted daughter, the trips to the piano lessons, as demanded by both teacher and pupil, became a bore.

Part of the problem was the musical 'stone ear' in which Abby could recognize a melody, occasionally, but the extra ear of a musician was lost on her. The words of Miss Stockard were flattering to hear, but also tiring. So what, that her daughter was talented? Someone had to be, of course, so why not Susanna?

As her social life became more crowded for time, the only thing to do was locate and hire a substitute to go to her lessons with her.

While thinking of this, she also decided there were other things the substitute could do that would free her up even more social duties.

A respectable young lady… maybe girl… could be a governess, of sorts, and could read to the child, take her on walks or carriage rides, prepare her evening meal and even put her to bed. Abby could well afford this luxury with the added salary of her husband, and a 'governess' would add to her own social prestige.

Hence, after a few interviews, she settled on Laverne. Sixteen years old and studious, she seemed ideal. She was even willing to spend the night in Susanna's room, if given an evening off every week. Being the oldest of seven siblings, she had proved her responsibility and skill with younger children. Also, the money was great enough to keep her from wandering away to another employment.

It took only one afternoon for Susanna to attach herself to this wonderful person who had eyes only for her, and not like her parents or their friends whose children were grown. The belated chick loved her substitute mother even more after only one music session where Laverne sat beside her during the lesson and hung onto every note… also every word of praise from the teacher.

When Susanna turned five, Laverne was allowed to give her a birthday party with four of the girls from her school class, as well as taking her to her friends' parties. The wonderful girl would even do necessary shopping, taking Susanna along and making an adventure of it. What a wonderful coincidence for the three of them.

Who needed an angel to arrange things…? Mrs. Singleton could do very well by herself… thank you very much!

And the little girl turned seven with such talented fingers that her teacher could hardly sleep for the excitement of her progress. A concert would be in her near future, and that was certain. Laverne even picked up enough from listening, that she could to play simple tunes.

Laverne turned nineteen and married a young brakeman employed by the railway. His job took him away for days at a time, so Laverne was still free to care for Susanna.

## CABIN AT CHESTNUT COTTAGE

Such a wonderful plan… the tiny two roomed cabin in the yard of Chestnut Cottage originally built to care for the unfortunate Hilda.

After the success with Horace and Hilda, there appeared the need for a waiting list for those wanting the cabin. Washing diapers, milking, tending the kitchen garden, and checking the fences seemed such a small price for free living, being one's own boss and having the chance to earn money by the sale of the baby animals the farm produced.

Horace and Hilda, with baby Laura and one of their own, were again pregnant. With the wonderful start-up money, they were able to purchase a small spot of ground across Ridge Road from the cottage and near his family. The close presence of family was important for parents with small children.

Next on the list for the cabin was Everett Miller, who was waiting with a bit of impatience for his turn at the cabin so he could marry Melissa Smith. Everett was a sizeable fellow, somewhat past six foot tall and with thick, strong shoulders. Loved activity.

Melissa was thrilled with the tiny cabin... her very own kingdom, and all she had to do was wash a load of messy diapers every morning, and somehow get them dry. Nothing to it... she'd been doing it at home for the last five years. In addition to the washing, she managed to be pregnant almost immediately... just as the pair had intended.

In her last month, the excitement grew, and Everett was so excited that he scoured around the farm for something to keep himself busy close by so he would be available for the magic day. September rolled around, and he bent his energy to the fall hay gathering for the animals. Several of the animal babies would be his to sell (or keep to take with him when he left).

It was one of those dry Septembers after a dry August. Hay ripened early, and he hauled load after load into the enclosed corral to become even drier before being pitched into the loft. Beauty is said to be found in the 'eye of the beholder' and such was the case for Everett. The abundance of hay was a lovely sight. He might even have difficulty getting it all into the loft... such a delicious dilemma!

One sunny afternoon he paused and leaned his forearms against the gate post and just stared at the magnificent hay piles. He'd go to the house for a drink and maybe Melissa had something baked... like a cookie. It took a lot of food to keep a big fellow going.

He actually heard the whistle of the Mounaineer as it neared a wide curve. The whistle was supposed to clear the animals from the tracks, and it usually worked. Must be about 10:00 o'clock. One could tell time by the sun unless the day was cloudy... but the Mountaineer was a true heralder, rather like the morning crow of a rooster.

He heard the 'rev' of the drivers on the rails as the locomotive sought for momentum for the next hill. From the sound, it must have a load on... maybe coal. From the hay loft window, one could see the white steamy mule tail trailing out if there was no wind.

Today he did not bother to look. He'd go get a drink and look in on Mellissa, growing so pleasingly round. So the sound of the Mountaineer faded in the distance as he settled down to the tiny table to a cup of leftover coffee and a freshly frosted donut. Across from him in silent companionship, sat the love of his young life, also enjoying a donut.

Neither had an inkling of what was waiting for them by the side of the shiny rails that stretched from Eureka Springs on east to Berryville and then to Memphis in Tennessee.

What was there by the rails was the tiniest of sparks from the friction of the speeding wheels and the dryness of the air and would have died a quiet death except for the extreme dryness of the grass. The spark had landed on a sun-parched leaf in the ditch and was growing dimmer by the second when an errant breath of air flowed down from Echo Mountain. Breathing a momentary new life into the spark, the dry leaf tipped over into the dry heart of a clump of bunchgrass that had been nibbled short by a deer.

The spark... now a tiny ember... dropped into the bunchgrass between the dry blades and glowed rosily... fed on the cluster of dry blades. Even then it might have not have lived but for the burnt blades falling directly onto the growing ember.

Everett finished the donut, kissed the rosy cheek in the chair across from him, and headed out the door. Best he check the mare again. He'd already put her in a stall in anticipation of her coming event, but perhaps he'd put her there too early. It was so hard to guess the exact hour, but he certainly didn't want her hiding the new little fellow in the brush, as her ancestors would have done. There were no prowling wolves to bother this little fellow, but for mom, ancestral memory was strong. Hide the precious baby before he became lunch for other creatures.

The mare whickered greeting but was restlessly pacing in the stall. The human nodded with satisfaction… he'd been right. She was near due, maybe before night.

He stepped out of the barn and faced the east. He stopped still and looked around. Something about the well-known scenery was different. What… ? Hmmm, there was the white mule tail hanging above the trees but the train was long gone. What was going on?

He entered the barn and shinnied up the ladder into the empty loft. Peering from the window, he saw the problem and it made his heart pound with fear and his breath stop from the restriction in his chest. Maybe it wouldn't reach Chestnut Cottage, but the risk was too great to count on it. Forest fires in the dry fall grasses were almost impossible to stop.

He ran to the pump of the stock well and yanked the handle up and down, sending a gush of water into the hollow log drinking tank. Snatching up a bucket, he raced up the ladder that was nailed to the gable of the barn room, sending the water flowing down both directions and soaking the shingles.

As dry as the air was, he'd likely need to do it again, but something else was more important right now. The backfire. First line of defense in outlying farms. He poured a circle of water on the grass around the corral next to the barn wall, and lit a fire here and there allowing it to burn outward away from the barn.

He carefully stomped it out at about twenty feet, and lit another patch. Scurrying up the ladder, he looked toward the tracks, and the white mule's tail was joined by a tongue of a rosy flame. The fire had reached a tree, and that was the worst news the human could have received.

Quickly finishing the corral backfire, he started in on Chestnut Cottage. The walls were of stone… wonderful! But the roof was dry shingles. First make a backfire, and think what should be next.

While working at the backfire, Miss Emma stepped out with a worried frown and asked, "Everett… what do you think? Am I just smelling sun-burned grass, or… ?"

Without a pause, Everett replied, ""NO! Miss Emma, there's a blaze over by the tracks. I'm preparin' for it to get here."

"Oh, Dear Lord, what's to be done? Can I help?"

"Not just yet. You might prepare extra bottles for the babies, and I'll bring around the wagon, ready if you need to evacuate. Crossin' the creek'll make you safe, but it's still early. If I see the blaze from the yard, I'll extend the backfire. I've been through these things before."

Silently, Miss Emma retired to the cottage. "Betsy, gather all the diapers and put 'im in sacks. Might not need 'em, but then again…" She didn't have to explain. Miss Betsy was no dummy.

Melissa, with her mind on other things, sat in her tiny kitchen corner and rubbed her ankles. How come a girl's ankles swelled up when the baby was not even close to her feet… but that was what was happening. It was an old complaint. Some girls couldn't even get their shoes laced up right there at the end.

Everett hooked a pair of mules to the largest wagon and brought it near the cottage door. The mules were nervous, sniffing and snorting and tossing their heads. If they had been loose in the pasture, they'd have run to the creek and stayed there. Mules were just about the smartest animals on a farm. But Jude and Jody were fastened in their harnesses so they just snorted and tossed their heads at the ignorance of humans.

Exhausted, Everett returned to the barn, and leaned momentarily against a post. Smoke smell was stronger. He looked at the wonderful piles of nutritious hay and sighed and shook his head. What if it burned? He needed to extend the backfire. If the fire reached the Cottage and barn, he'd be busy killing the flying sparks created by the burning hay.

He ran the burned patches out to about a hundred feet, and was tempted to turn them loose, but there were the neighbors farther south to consider. He set a small fire between the cottage and the advance flame, finally setting it free to meet the oncoming blaze. The next thing to worry about was the 'wrap-around' blaze that would come in from the side.

A glance at the sun told him it was after 2:00 o'clock. Scooping a handful of water from the stock tank and splashing it over his face and hair, he darted into the mare's stall. Still circling and whickering. Couldn't do a thing for her but trust she could handle it. He leaped aboard Nosey, the young filly who would like to get in the barn with her mother, and kicked her into a gallop toward the goat pen.

Goats were smart… like mules… and the lead nanny was already complaining and tossing her head to the smell of the smoke. Seeing Everett, she knew it was time, and her loudest 'Baaaaa' brought the others into a manageable group.

Galloping around the goats, Everett yelled, "Barn! Barn! Barn!' being once more thankful for the training Horace had given them. 'Barn' meant grain or milking, so they jaunted along in a direction they would never have gone had they not been trained.

Safe in the corral, they began to nibble on the stacked hay as Everett secured the gate and sniffed again. He dashed back to the cottage and saw Miss Emma had moved everything possible to the wagon, except the babies, and Betsy was furtively trying to calm the eleven youngsters under two years old.

He allowed himself a deep sigh for what he was going to do. It was the very last thing he wanted to do, but… well, there was no way around it.

He entered the miniature kitchen and explained in a few sentences to the astonished face and the wide open eyes. "You want me to walk on the cottage roof…? Everett, I'm big as a cow! I can't…"

"Not quite as big as a cow. Besides, a cow's hooves would ruin the roof. Your feet won't. I'll help you up the ladder, and you won't fall. I wish there was some other way, but there isn't."

"But my big fat ankles…!" she wailed. "They hurt!"

His sweaty arms surrounded her. "I know, my darling. But you aren't walking on your ankles, and they are hurting now. So they'll keep hurting, and you can save the cottage. Come, now."

"But the baby, Ev…!"

"Honey, I know about that baby. I done talked to God about him, and God told me it was all right, and the little fellow'll just have to help with this problem."

Melissa giggled in spite of herself. "But.. "

"'Nother thing. Soneone's gotta do it. You and him both together weigh less than either of my other choices."

The ladder was already leaning and a rope with a hook was nearby. He followed her… step by shaky step… and they were now near the top. Balancing her, he helped her step to the rather shallow roof and handed her the rope.

"Now, you hold to the end of the ladder when you lift up the water bucket. Then walk very slow to the gable and let the water run down each side to soak the shingles. I'll be back with the next bucket when you get back to the end of the ladder."

Pulling in a deep breath of determination, Melissa (of the fat and painful ankles) pulled up the three gallon bucket of water and headed up the shingles. Everett watched tensely, but Melissa had always had good balance for things like walking on a log across a small creek. She tipped the bucket and watched the water flow down. It was going to take a lot of buckets seeing how fast the dry shingles sucked it up.

Everett leaped to the ground and ran to the well for the next bucket. On the third bucket, Miss Betsy stepped out and accessed the situation. "Say, Everett, I can do that. If you was to draw up the water in the tank, I can carry it over here."

Thank You, Lord! Also, Miss Betsy! He rapidly filled the tank and took his beater in hand. Someone was going to have to catch that wrap-around flame while it was small. If it got to the back of the corral there'd be no stopping it all the way to Blue Lake. And several farms in between.

Melissa was a trouper. She'd be fine. He wasn't just talking when he said he'd already asked God if it was all right to put her on the roof. Sometimes there was only one person for a job, and this time it was her.

Miss Emma projected into the future. The babies were restless, but it was right to release Miss Betsy to free up Everett to do whatever he knew to do. Eventually, the neighbors would be here… forest fires attracted help, but it took time. A fire that got a good start could wipe out a neighborhood.

With a deft hand, she tossed the oatmeal, sugar, and eggs into the kettle, adding the raisins and spices. Without waiting to roll and out and cut the cookies, she spooned the clumps of dough onto her cookie tins and squashed them flat with the bottom of a drinking glass.

Popping them into the oven, she started onto the next pan. One thing she knew, fire fighters were quickly hungry. Coffee and cookies… and she'd be ready. It wouldn't hurt the babies to fuss. From the corner of her eye, she saw a stream of water trail past the window. A fleeting smile of relief crossed her face, and then she thought of Melissa, tummy like a barrel, and ankles red and raw.

"Dear Lord, help us all!" She hoped that covered everything. There were some jobs just too large for her to comprehend, so she reluctantly turned them over to God.

The first of the fire fighters came on horses, an even dozen of them galloping up the driveway, beaters dangling from the saddles. Like warm butter on a hot rock, the men and boys poured over the farm attacking the wide backfires.

Miss Betsy caught the first man. "Draw me up some more water, mister." Who could ignore a demand like that? No one seemed to think, however, to watch where the water was being taken.

Melissa looked down and watched them scatter, her lips firm in a smile of satisfaction. This was her job. She'd removed her now ill-fitting shoes and set them by the ladder. Tinder bare feet on the rough, sun-drenched shingles were turning her feet even redder. No matter. She and Michael could get this job done. She had long been convinced that her huge, ungainly bump of a belly had to be a boy.

The first pain of labor stabbed her just as she had estimated only six more buckets would have water dripping down all the way around the cottage. Amazing! And she had done it!

Being her first pregnancy, and adding the exhaustion and her burning, blistered feet, she did not recognize the first mild stab of contraction. Stopping and flexing her weary shoulders, she looked around. No sign of Everett, but she had no concerns. She did, however, notice about six of the men circling the hay piles, beating out the flying sparks.

FLYING SPARKS! A sharp sting on her arm, and she swatted what might have been a biting fly. NO! It was a spark brought in on the wind. Looking to the east she could see flames between the trees, and another wagon load of help galloping up the driveway.

Lifting the next bucket, she splashed her head and yelled to Miss Betsy to watch out for flying sparks. Sparks landed all around her on the shingles, dark from the soaked up water. They lasted hardly a second and were gone. What if she had refused to climb up here? The worn shingles would surely be blazing by now! And the babies!

Her heart thumped with pride and satisfaction. She and Michael had won! She'd pushed for the name Michael, as that was the name of God's warrior angel, and her little boy would be a fighter. If guarding angels can be amused at the antics of humans, Angel 297 might have smiled smugly. If the mom could only see the future of her little boy! Surprise and gratefulness would have been heaped on him even higher!

## FIREFIGHTERS

The firefighters to the east had won against the flames crawling through the dead leaves and leaping skyward after reaching the oily needles of the cedars. One by one, the exhausted men limped back to the house, faces blackened with smoke and flying cinders. Streaking rivers of sweat cut through the blackness and soaked into their torn and blackened clothing.

Flying sparks had quit falling on the cottage, and the men at the haystacks were filing back toward the house. Far down toward the creek, she saw Everett coming. She'd just sit down here and wait for him to help her down.

Everett climbed through the blackened scrubs and a few fallen limbs just as the next pain struck her like a blazing knife. She screamed, involuntarily, and all eyes turned in surprise to the heavily pregnant lady standing on the roof.

Miss Emma had just delivered a bucket of coffee and all the cups and glasses she had. She had returned for the huge basket of cookies when she heard the scream. Skin prickled on her neck at the sound... knowing what it had to be.

Everett broke into a run and leaped a fence to get to her. She had sat down suddenly, and was startlingly amazed at the spots of blood on the wet shingles. Turning a painful foot sole upward, she saw the broken blisters and seeping blood from toes to heel. Imagine that!

And then the interman pain hit again. She cringed against the pain and looked at the other foot. Also bleeding!

Everett had reached the top of the ladder. "Melissa, I'm here. You must stand and walk to me. You can."

"I'm bleeding," she wailed.

"I know, but I can't come to you. I'm too heavy for the roof. If you can't stand, then scoot down to me. Right now."

She drew in a breath and firmed her lips. Planting her bleeding feet on the shingles, she scooted downward on her backside, finally standing and holding to the end of the ladder.

"Good girl," he complimented. "Now I'm going to turn around and you're going to hold to my back. I'm going to carry you down."

"But the baby…!"

"He'll just have to take care of himself. You're going to hold to my neck no matter how much hurts you or where. We have to get you down… now!"

So, with young Michael squeezed tightly between his mother's spine and his father's blackened overalls, he descended the ladder. Angel 297 was there and was well aware that the tight spot where Michael found himself would not be the last tight spot he would experience in his life. But that was for later.

Miss Emma had hardly been experienced in this activity. All of her other charges had come already born. Miss Betsy was no better, but Papa Everett did what many fathers before him had done. He coped. Later he laughingly suggested the boy should have been named Sparky, or maybe Torch.

The firefighters waited around, consuming cookies, as it seemed further excitement would be soon. In less than an hour they heard the indignant scream of a baby released into a cruel world. Looking at each other, they smiled knowingly and took their leave.

Each one was forming the wonderful story he'd have and get to tell at the supper table, and with a bit of embellishment, it would make a good story for the rest of their lives.

Miss Emma weighed the newcomer on her baby scales. Nine pounds twelve. Papa smiled with pride, but Melissa listened with unbelief.

"Is that all he weighed…?" was her amazed and only comment.

## YEAR 1903

This was the year that young Quincy Darby turned three. He was the fortunate young fellow who was picked off the tree limb after his partying and inebriated parents were swept downstream in the flash flood.

The snappy, black eyes of the 8 month old had immediately trained themselves on those of the old mountain farmer and recognized a kindred soul. The infant imprinted on the voice and the wrinkles, and the wonderful look of welcome into the human world… such has he had never experienced up to now.

He had imprinted on the old man like hatchling ducks imprint on their mama at the moment of release from the shell… and were like her all the way from the waddle to the quack and were endued with a desire to follow her to the ends of the earth.

So was the mind of the tot who followed the old man, attached to him with the tenacity of a wad of bubble gum. When he learned words, they were the words of the old man much above his age, and whatever the old man's hands were engaged in, there were the dimpled hands of the three year old.

And the attachment went both ways. The old farmer who was retired from his work and had sat relaxed, waiting for the call to his eternal home, now had a reason to stick around. The earth would just have to put up with him until the little fellow was on his own.

The mountain schoolhouse was almost two miles away, but the old man was ready for the trip, morning and afternoon. Perched in front of the saddle, the child and the old man chatted about their day and planned their evening. It was not until young Quincy was eight that he was entrusted to make the trip on his own.

The son and daughter in law watched from afar, pleased with the new life in the old man that lasted until the boy was twelve years old. Young Quincy, now referred to as 'Quince' watched the internment of his rescuer to his final resting place with hard and determined eyes, never letting a tear form until he was alone in the old man's cabin. After a night of sodden pillows and agonized weeping for his loss, he dried his eyes and respectfully requested to be permitted to move permanently to the cabin.

He lived there, contentedly, as a part of the family until 1916. The no-nonsense teacher at the mountain schoolhouse had used the weekly newspaper from Eureka Springs as a teaching aid. That was not so much for learning the content, but more the correct use of words from a free source.

Young Quince absorbed the words from the papers as a dry sponge. The words set his mind free to think thoughts past his small town and the small, southern state of his birth. They sent his thoughts soaring to heights far above those on Ridge Road.

When school lessons were a thing of the past, Quince was still enthralled with the weekly, four-paged document filled with printed words. One Christmas, when he was eleven, he had requested and received a Webster's dictionary. Expensive gift it was... and an example of how greatly he was valued by his new family. The dictionary became his new favorite book.

After he completed the six grades, he continued to get a copy of the paper though often a week or so late), and he consumed every word. He found the country of Belgium on the map furnished by the paper. A squabble of nations was happening, and it raised the hairs on the back of his neck. If they didn't stop that there would be a war!

What was going on... anyway? Where were their brains? He never learned the answer.

At fourteen he went to the small town of Wishbone Hollow for a job... anything that would earn a little money. After trying this and that, he struck onto the idea that would carry him through his teens. He would be a junkman. He would not wait for work to come to him, but would hand out his little bits of paper with his name, and where he could be reached. He would pick up and haul anything that would fit in the six foot by six foot cart he had helped old Quince to make and a horse that was extra to the farm.

He arranged to rent a bed in a shed and a stall for the horse for the first summer in return for assistance when needed. What establishment did not need a strong and willing young man now and again? By fall he could afford a bed inside the house of an elder couple who could use the pennies of rent and the young man's muscles, on occasion.

The hauling job netted a side advantage. Often what was trash at one residence could be sold for a small fee at another one. This gave him a reputation of liking to do favors.

The other advantage was the free time spent behind the horse moving slowly up and down the hills of the small town. It was here that his love of words solidified in his mind. He could read as he rode, and the trash yielded surprising treasures.

There was the day that he loaded on a box of assorted books someone didn't want (how could that be?) and among the assortment, he found a copy of the Bible that could be put back together after a fashion. All the pages were there but the spine was in such disarray that he had to put them together in a bunch of small books. Easier to read that way.

He also found a book on puzzles and tricks and stories that could be put together by use of a code. Code! It was a way to say something without saying it. What a concept! He even amused himself by creating codes of his own.

He thought of his school teacher's fascination with words and the English language. There was a rule for everything, except that the rule didn't always work. Figure that out, if you will!

And then he became sixteen and the newspapers were full of the war across the sea, and the distinct and inevitable possibility of it reaching the hills of Arkansas as new recruits began to be accepted to be loaned to the country of England.

Then there was the family of Peter Pucell. Paul Purcell, the tot who followed the three big sisters into the family, would never remember the three nights he spent in Chestnut Cottage before papa came for him. He was a born farmer (the Boss doesn't make mistakes when folks obey and trust him), and he absorbed every shred of education, eager to earn praise from his father.

He would be certain and ready to take over the farm when Papa was too old, and his Papa woke up every morning, being thankful to whoever left the little fellow in the baby box for him. The way things worked out was only a coincidence, of course, leaving no need for action on the part of the angel assigned to Paul before birth. That was just the way things worked out.

Right…?

Then, over at the big river, Miss Lena Guniston, age seven, fell heir to a duty that should have been far beyond her years. With the passing of Mama and the total removal from the family by her big sister, Hilda, Lena was put in charge of the two youngest children while Papa and the rest of the family picked cotton.

Papa put together a shed, of sorts, at the edge of the cotton field as protection against the boiling south Arkansas sun. That was where the little ones were kept… being entertained by Lena. Before two weeks had passed, she had four other children in her care, whose mothers could pay a few pennies for their care… a charge that was more than made up for in their mother's working time.

By the end of summer, Lena earned her first dollar. She whispered to Papa that the money was going to help her go to school, and Papa smiled and let her keep it. He hoped it worked out that way.

At the end of cotton season, Lena convinced Papa to find something locally to do for the winter… anything! It was essential that she get to go to school and manage to bring little sister along with her. The two little girls succeeded in finding things to do that would add to the pennies. Of course there was no reason that their angels had anything to do with it… but somehow the family survived, and Papa had learned that, though he always meant well, his plans often went awry. Perhaps some decisions could be better made by someone else.

Seemed to work.

In year 1913, the two girls finished the required six years of education, and each applied for a teaching certificate. At the ages of 17 and 18, they were accepted in a new school that was being put up on the banks of the big river. The fledgling Board of Education could hardly believe its luck. Two teachers, sisters, and willing to work at the river, where the 'scum' of humanity scrounged an existence! How could they be so fortunate!

In due time, the two room cabin at Chestnut Cottage was again empty. It was after the forest fire that almost enveloped the baby box and everything around it, that the town of Eureka Springs put together their first paid fire department.

It was well known that Everett Miller had almost single-handedly saved the important building, along with his pregnant wife who walked the hot shingles of Chestnut Cottage with her water bucket, drowning the falling embers.

Melissa's labor began on the roof and ended minutes later in the two room cabin. There were those who insisted that the task of getting her off the roof, while in hard labor, would mark the baby. Maybe it did. Only God and the angels could look ahead, and it was certain that Angel 297 had known from the beginning of time that this would happen.

The hefty young fellow was just over two when his Pa received the offer to be Eureka Spring's first paid fire department superintendent. He had one paid helper who was to also help care for the horses and equipment.

By the time Michael was fifteen, Pa's fire department had five paid employees to take care of the growing community. He was eighteen when the United States entered the war in Europe. The Midwestern states were scoured for healthy young men to send into battle, and Michael was one of the first in line to volunteer.

Who would ever have the idea that Angel 297 would also be in line as Michael signed his name… but then who would have thought of an angel being interested, anyway, in a skirmish across an ocean…?

But then, for those who heed the soft nudging into the direction of the Boss' agenda there may be no need for a physical presence of the heavenly being. At least that was a possibility.

On up the river from where the baby in the cradleboard was picked off a tree an old hunter had a shelter at the mouth of a cave. It worked rather well for his line of business, and the machinery of his business worked well as long as he could get the makin's for the product.

Mostly corn, it took, and the water from a mountain spring that flowed handily beside his place of business. Being close to the river was necessary as it kept the customers from creating a tell-take path to his door.

To keep up appearances that it was a legitimate business, and not one that occasionally created a candidate for the cemetery, he kept an accumulation of item such as several handmade canoes, a few baskets, some cans and small kegs. These were for 'sale or trade'. The canoes were actually made by his hands as his business within the cave did not keep him particularly busy. One might say, that mostly the business made itself if given the right start, water and another item or two.

Good canoes, they were, though they took a degree of skill if one wanted to go a certain place on the rushing waters of King's River. But Old Cobb (who knew what his name actually was) cared not whether the purchaser was skilled. He bought, he took away, and was responsible it he didn't know how to operate it.

Old Cobb liked the location for another reason. Any disposable remains of his business could simply be carried over to King's River and dumped. The swift waters took care of the rest.

It was a 'dumb day' he told himself when he accepted the girl as a swap for a half a dozen jars of his product. At first thought he had decided the girl would be handy for lift and carry work, and maybe even to keep the cave cleaned out of the clutter that kept happening. There was also the possibility that she could cook something besides beans.

Anyway, he took her, somewhat sights unseen, as she had a sticky plaster over her face from the nose down.

"Kept 'er from yellin'. I knowd you'd not want that. She ain't never had a thing to say that was worth listenin' to. I'm only askin' for a half dozen jugs for 'er. I'm throwin' the coon hound fer free."

Old Cobb thought he'd give it a try. Never had a female in the cave before, but supposed it wouldn't change the strength of the product.

He'd heard about not buyin' a pig in a poke' without looking in the poke sack to see if there really was a pig, or maybe someone just wanting to get rid of a mess of baby kittens.

He took off the sticky plaster and told her what he wanted her to do, and she set about it silently. Maybe she couldn't talk. The dog followed on her heels at every minute, looking like he might talk if he just could. It was a bit unnerving.

Then a couple of months down the line, he knew why the girl was so cheaply traded. The girl was one thing, but he'd never want a squalling brat at his place of business, so he told her to get rid of it.

He even pointed down through the trees to a place that had a doctor who would help her get rid of it.

Stubborn girl, she was, or was very bad at hearing, because she became rounder and rounder, and he finally sent her away. She wouldn't go. He cut a willow switch from the river's edge and struck her across the back and was bitten by the dog. He aimed his rifle at the dog, and the beast leaped at him, grabbing his arm and biting to the bone.

The girl took the dog by the collar and walked toward the river, and Old Cobb decided, good riddance.

The girl, however, circled around and went through the trees as the man had pointed, and found the 'doctor'. Could he help her, she asked, now having words.

Too late, he told her, but gave her the brew anyway. The result was that what happened later entered the world protesting the indignity. The 'doctor' was not surprised but told her to take the brat and go. He "didn't never do no killin' and that kid wanted to live pretty bad."

The girl helped herself to a scrap of cloth and wrapped the tiny boy as best she could, and left through the trees, the dog leading the way

Back at Old Cobb's cave, she waited until dark when he was asleep and took some clean strainers he had hung out to dry, and one of his canoes. Loss of blood had made her very weak, but she and the dog quietly moved on.

Easing the canoe into the edge of the water, she motioned the dog to get in, which he did. She wrapped the baby tightly and put him in the bottom of the boat and began to work the oars. She knew what to do, but strength had failed, and her arms were too weak to move the canoe as she wanted.

The dog became nervous and watched closely, occasionally sniffing the baby. If she could just get down to the bridge, there would be someone who could help her so she let the oars rest while she bent over in her lap to save strength.

The waters of the river were not the place for the small canoe, but for some reason, it stayed upright. The dog licked her fingers but could not revive her. Near the bridge, the canoe made a turn and wedged its prow into a patch of willow sprouts.

The dog looked at the bank which was clearly close enough for him to swim to, but he did not leave the boat. Instead he lifted his head to the treetops and barked 'treed' which was the signal that he had a varmint up a tree and the human could now shoot it.

Children playing in the edge of the water recognized the call, and found the canoe, the person, the dog and a crying baby. Rushing home, they brought adults to the scene.

The man who waded out called back. "The woman's dead, but there's a live kid in here."

He started to reach for the wrapped and crying bundle, and the dog growled a rumbling warning in his throat. So the man pulled the canoe up to the bank, held his hand out to the dog. The dog sniffed and decided the man meant no harm, and he allowed him to pick up the crying child.

Immediate help was close, but long term help would be found down the road so after a bit of goat milk spooned into the crying mouth, he and the dog made their way to the small house behind the crepe myrtles.

It was dark when Betsy heard the drawer. She waited for it to be fully returned and the person to be gone, and she lifted out the little fellow. She sighed, as she so often did, when she saw a mistreated child, but she knew what to do.

Miss Emma took down the book and S was the next letter. How about Stuart? Sounded good to Betsy, so Stuart Hill joined the other 11 babies and had a good meal. He made it through the night and on for the next 4 months before he was adopted.

The Findley's gave him a good home. He was the third little boy they had rescued, and when America entered the war in 1917, he was in the line of volunteers. The Findley's had trained him well in the use of a rifle, and he was put in charge of a small scouting mission in southern France.

He and his group were hunkered down, not knowing where the enemy was, and having to do something, even if it was wrong. Sergeant Findley sighed, looked about, and knew it was time to circle around.

He explained his tactic and the men understood. He would go left, and attract gunfire, and they must go right and come from behind. He would meet them when he could.

His scouting expedition was successful and a new hill was taken, but the Sergeant didn't meet them. They plunged on with a Corporal in charge and were given ribbons of bravery.

The Findley family received a flag and his dog tags. A cross was erected over his final resting place in the French soil.

The little fellow who had 'wanted to live' had saved a dozen lives. Just like so many others who fought a senseless war on foreign soil in the name of freedom. The Findley's put a gold star in their window, and it stayed there until the house was torn down, 34 years later.

## NEW OCCUPANTS IN THE 'HELP' CABIN

When Melissa packed up to leave the 'help' cabin, there wasn't much labor to the job. Both families had been generous at her wedding, and much of her plunder had not even been unpacked.

Therefore, it was no loss for her to leave her beautiful, sky blue crockery dinner ware. Service for twelve, it was, and the heavy plates (decorated with hand-painted forget-me-nots) along with the dozen saucers was so heavy that the wall cupboard had to be braced strongly to keep it attached the wall, even though the mugs had their own hooks attached to the wall.

And, in addition to that, there was the matching turkey platter and the gravy boat. Melissa had a good use for the platter. It never saw a turkey and likely never would, but it held a lot of cookies. Those individual, tasty bursts of energy were very popular with young fellows who had a lot of work. So easy to pick up a handful as they came to the kitchen for coffee. The gravy boat made a wonderful container for the bee-tree honey.

So, these, along with the feather pillows and a pair of hand-pieced quilts were in place when Matthew and Nancy Camden moved in. Melissa and Nancy knew each other well, and that made the gifts even more impressive. Nancy smoothed her hand over the forget-me-nots on the turkey platter and determined in her mind to think of something just as wonderful to leave when her time was up.

Matthew, on the other hand, was thrilled when Everett got the chance to move on before his years were up. He and Nancy had married earlier in the year, and now Nancy could be settled in before the baby appeared.

There were currently twelve babies in the cottage. Miss Betsy was just about exhausted beyond her limits from battling a round of runny noses and a fair amount of upchucking. Nancy begged to be allowed to take the night shift in the drawer room… she couldn't sleep much, anyway.

Whoever would have thought something so small inside her could do so much kicking? It was almost like the little fellow was trying to get out, and he had a full two months to go. So Nancy was in charge when baby thirteen arrived in the drawer. That made a record. A little girl it was, and she came with papers that told her name.

Mary Annette Jones. Parents unknown. She was left on a doorstep of an elderly couple, and there was absolutely no one could take her, at the moment, so she must be parked at the cottage. Or so was the message they were given.

Nancy wrapped the shivering, whimpering baby in warm blankets and filled a bottle with goat milk. She settled herself in the rocker with a self-satisfied smile. Just imagine! This was just a taste of the pleasure awaiting her… if she just survived another month of the kicking against her ribs and the squirming around that made her upchuck.

Sometimes it didn't seem possible that birth could happen, but just look around at all the other girls who put up with it and survived. If they could do it… so could she!

## ANGEL 237 ON ASSIGNMENT

Louellen Fisher trudged up one hill and down the other… weary, footsore and exhausted. But, in spite of it all, deep down inside of her was the feeling (hope?) that she was at last doing the right thing. When there was only one thing left to do, then it was time to do it.

A few whispers to herself, and then a nudge from somewhere inside that at last she was going in the right direction. A lot of it was due to the nosiness of her younger sister, Hannah, who went to great effort to be invisible when adults were whispering or spelling words they didn't want heard. Hannah was a very good speller.

The most terrible thing happened almost a year ago… or maybe not quite, but it happened in the middle of the night. Louellen had opened her upstairs bedroom window to the summer breeze, and sniffed the fall air. Smelled like fall when the leaves turned to a rainbow of colors. She loved colors.

Her bedroom wasn't really a room, just a little cubby closet at the top of the outside staircase to the second floor. It became her room when a temperature difference arose between herself and Hannah. Louellen was an open window person, and Hannah could be cold in August.

The door to the outside steps was locked, Pa insisted on it, but in a weak moment Louellen left the window open. Just for a few minutes. She blew out the lamp and crawled into her bed. Propped up with pillows she settled back, and it felt so good she must have dozed off or she would have seen the darkening of the window.

The first thing that happened was that something very sticky was slapped over her face, and strong hands flipped her over and tied her wrists together. The sticky thing efficiently kept her from screaming, but she thrashed around and made as much noise as possible. The headboard of her bed was just through the wall from Hannah's room.

She struggled to the limit of her fifteen-year-old body, but the attacker was stronger. She knew who it was from the profile against the dim light from the window. Also, he had very bushy hair. It was an 'almost cousin' that the family had acquired when Pa' cousin, Bertha, had married the widower with a family. He also had a beautiful house that Bertha acquired by the marriage.

The attack on Louellen had been short, and the invader had hardly reached the window to run away, when she had slid from the bed and scrubbed the sticky thing from her face on the edge of the bedstead…and yelled. Her yell met her sister who had just peeked in the door.

Louellen shouted, "Get Pa! It was Dwayne, and he's runnin' away!"

Hannah disappeared like a whiff of smoke, and it seemed just seconds until the door slammed shut, and the crack of Pa's rifle split through the balmy, fall air. Another shot… and another… and Louellen felt her teeth clench with hatred and the hope that Pa's shot reached the bushy hair.

Imagine such liberties! Just because she didn't like his attention and refused to even talk with him. Here he was, almost twenty. He should know better!

And, here she was, five years younger, and she knew what he did and… well, she had no words hateful enough.He HURT her! Was that any way to get acquainted?

Minutes later the whole house was awake and gathered downstairs. Hannah had cut the cord that had tied Louellen's hands, and Ma was dabbing a cloth against the stinging places where the sticky thing on her face wouldn't hardly come loose.

Pa returned, breathing hard with eyebrows drawn completely together. That meant he was REALLY mad… more than just angry.

"I hit 'im. I know I did when he squealed. Would'a kilt 'em if I wasn't so shook up from bein' so mad."

Ma turned and looked at Pa. "Wisht you hadda."

Pa nodded. "Come daylight and I'll get the sheriff."

Louellen looked at her elbows, bruised and scraped. Ma smoothed on salve, her mouth working as though her thoughts were bleeding through. She turned to Pa and whispered, "No, Ab, you can't be tellin' the sheriff. If you did, then everybody'd know what happened to our girl. We can't do her that-away."

All Pa could say was, "But, Emma, we can't just do nothin'."

Out loud, Ma answered, "Yes, we can. Least wise for a month or two. Give it time."

Pa nodded, reluctantly."…maybe for a few weeks. Then I'll do it! I swear I will."

Ma didn't say anything, but Louellen could tell from Ma's face that the matter was not settled, and that she had an idea. If… well, if it was necessary, there were things that could be done. A thing like this just didn't happen in the Fisher family.

The younger children had been shooed back to bed but Hannah remained, as silent and motionless as a flower on the wallpaper. For once, Louellen was proud of her. If it hadn't been for her quick thinking and sneaky ways, Pa'd'a never even got off a shot.

Then it was about three weeks later when Louellen woke up sick at her stomach. Before the month was out, Ma began to sneak around here and there looking for something… or maybe somebody. She'd go out and now and then and not say where she'd been. No one wanted to talk, outright, to Louellen, but she knew enough to realize what had happened, and it was scary. And she couldn't figure out why it had happened.

It was at three months that Ma had her answer. There was a person who could make all the trouble go away. She'd just plan a trip, or something. Let it be known to the neighbors that she was going for a short visit. Someone was sick and needed her. Just her and Louellen, and they would be away for a few days. Not that Louellen was so sick, but she certainly needed her ma, and her ma was going to take care of her.

"But, Ma, what'll happen to me?"

"Don't you worry, none. I'll be right there with you every minute, and afterward you'll be just like it never happened. It has to be done right away. So get your mind set to it happenin'. Won't be no worse than takin' out your bad tonsils."

Taking out? She had been having a sore throat, and now she had no more tonsils, so they had to be talking about cutting her open. Or something.

"When this gonna happen, Ma?"

"Soon. Likely next week. Sooner the better. Won't nothin' be accomplished by waitin'."

So Louellen walked away and shut her bedroom door behind her. There was thinking… and planning… to do. Right now.

Taking the small suitcase from the hall closet, she went back to her room, but did not close the door tightly. Too much on her mind, and the problem being too serious. Taking her underwear from a drawer and a dress and coat from the closet, she folded them and put them in the suitcase. Ooops! Wouldn't shut.

Taking everything out, she pulled on three pairs of under drawers, and slipped into two petti-slips. She spread two of her winter dresses on the bed and tried on the coat. Yes, it was loose enough to maybe cover the dresses and still button.

So her clean nighty, two dresses, six pairs of stockings. All her underwear. Then her comb and brush and all her ribbons. A pair of light house shoes filled the suitcase. Leaving the suitcase on her bed, she slipped to the kitchen and took a dozen cookies from the jar, and a leftover pork chop. These were wrapped in a tea towel and wedged into the edge of the suitcase.

By now, Hannah was back in her room, trying to think of ways to stay awake. It was bound to happen tonight. It was going to. She had to do something, but what?

Louellen made up her bed and pinned a note to the pillow.

"I had to leave. Don't look for me. I don't want to be cut open. I love you all."

Hannah, a healthy thirteen year old, did not hear her sister leave through the window, and quietly close it behind her. In spite of her efforts to stay awake, she had let her sister down.

Louellen had heard it said that her 'almost' Gran lived four miles away, and she could easily walk it. She'd been there, of course, but what youngen notices the way?

The thing was, now it was too dark to go through the trails that would shorten the trip by almost a mile and would make certain she was not seen. If she could just get there, the old family friend would help her.

The small town of Wishbone Hollow was surrounded by hills, and she had only to reach the path to Echo Mountain, and she'd know the way, but she'd have to wait until daylight. She made it to the house of a near neighbor and crawled into their hay barn. A small whicker from the horse was the only sound. She spread a horse blanket on the hay and curled up in it. She dozed and awoke repeatedly, until finally the first rooster announced morning.

Grabbing up the suitcase and sneaking out the back, she barely missed the neighbor with his milk pail. Slipping behind this and that, she reached the outskirts of town and easily was on her way up the mountains. Gran would be surprised to see her, but she'd know what to do. Reason told her that Gran wouldn't want her cut open, either. And what had happened wasn't her fault at all.

And she had been right about Gran. The old woman was surprised for a moment, and then she paid a neighbor boy to take a note to her parents. It was only right to tell them, though she was sure they would suspect where she was.

She made a late lunch for Louellen and put her to bed. Then she sat at her table with her wrinkled face a painting of anger, and her lips clamped shut. The nerve. The absolute nerve of the whole world. The girl would stay with her, and if her parents seemed unwilling, she would go to the law. That alone would make her 'daughter in law' keep quiet. Nothing like the law to spread news like feathers in the wind. The threat alone would stop them. Sure to.

Well, yes, the parents agreed, under the circumstances. It would be easy for them to spread the word that the girl was sent up the mountain to help her Gran for a while. It made a good cover, and then there would be another chance to dispose of the evidence of the terrible night.

It was a lonely winter for a fifteen year old girl away from her family, home and friends. One nice thing, though, she had a chance to sew, a skill Ma had not the time to teach her. She actually learned something besides the darning of socks. That was usually a girl's first lesson, being the practice of creating new fabric on the heels and toes with the use of a needle and thread, and a bit of clever weaving.

As her size began to expand, Louellen found that she fitted into some of Gran's dresses. At first it seemed funny, then embarrassing. But then, Gran didn't have much company, and there was no place to go. Gran did give her a length of flowered print for a dress that looked nice and actually covered her. Gran also said she had a way of placing a couple of seams that would bring the dress down to whatever shape and size she ended up with.

It was now the beginning of December and Gran computed the weeks and decided she would have to make it until late April. Never had April seemed so far away, but Gran found things to do. By the last week of April, Ma got so nervous that she came, bringing her clothes with her determined to stay until....

Good thinking, actually, because it was on Ma's first night on the mountain that the pains started. There were no near neighbors, so it didn't matter how loud Louellen screamed. The spring sun just cleared the edge of Echo Mountain when a red faced, fist-flailing little girl loudly proclaimed her surprised indignation.

Gran looked worried, and Ma looked like it meant no more than the birth of a new calf. Louellen looked at the tiny thing with a bursting heart of love. With breathless anticipation she reached for the baby and Ma finally handed her over. Not happy about it, though.

Then Ma started getting things ready to go back to town. Already! Couldn't they wait a day… maybe two? But, no, they were on the way by mid-afternoon. Louellen was given the back seat of the buggy, and Ma crawled into the front with the baby.

"Ma? Give her to me, will you please? She really is mine, isn't she?"

"Louellen, honey, you just lie down and rest. The road is too bouncy and rough for you to be sittin' up."

What could she say? She obediently moved the pillow to the edge of the bench and curled up on the seat as the buggy rocked and bumped its way down the mountain.

It was dark when they reached home, and Ma put her to bed and offered to stay up with the baby, at least the first night. Exhausted, Louellen complied, though she couldn't quite understand Ma's change of heart. She'd seemed silent and distracted, so why did she offer to take care of the baby?

Ma didn't want to talk about a name or anything. She acted like the darling little thing might be just a doll. Maybe one of those composition dolls, that looked so lifelike. The baby was wearing the little dress Gran helped her make and looked so cute, how could Ma ignore her first grandchild?

Louellen fell into an exhausted sleep and did not arise until almost noon. She woke up with a start. Baby! She had the baby, and it was over. Bounding out of bed she went to Ma's room. No baby.

Ma was in the kitchen stirring the beans. No baby.

"MA! Where is my baby?"

"Shhh! Quietly, darling. Sit down, and I'll make you breakfast."

"No, Ma! Where is my baby?"

Ma turned to her, full faced. "Louellen, honey, it was all for the best. Now you can be a pretty, sixteen year old girl, and have fun in your life. You have nothing to worry about. Your Pa took care of everything."

"Ma! Did Pa kill my baby?"

"Oh, darling, don't think such a thing. Your Pa just took care of your future, and now you have nothing to worry about. It's like nothing ever happened."

"But, Ma, it DID happen. I'm not like a cow that my calf can be taken away from me. I want to know where she is?"

Ma looked at her daughter with the stern, 'this-is-the-last-word' look that Ma was so good with. "Hush, now, and we'll hear no more about it."

Louellen ate, knowing there were things to be done. Plans to make. Decisions that would affect the rest of her life. Actions that would go against her family.

So it was, that when midnight struck, Louellen, now sixteen, had eased out the door and made her way to the convenient barn. Dawn saw her at the edge of Echo Mountain, and by early afternoon she had reached Gran.

The wrinkled old woman met her at the door, and they wept on each other's shoulders. Gran fed her and tucked her into the bed she had left hardly a day before, then she washed out the dress the girl had made and ironed it dry. She was sure to need it, though maybe she could stall her for a day. It wasn't easy.

It was on the second day that they talked. "Gran, do you think Pa killed her?"

Gran hesitated. "No, sweetheart, I don't. At least I don't want to. I knew they might have done something to you before she was born, but now? No, I don't think so."

"Then where could she be?" No neighbors or family would want her, and Ma wouldn't want that either because of the talk. Her being not only three days old means someone would be taking care of her, and Ma and Pa wouldn't be paying someone to do it. So where was she?

Gran looked sad, weary and old. "Wisht I knew, honey. To my way'a thinkin', you earned that baby. Leastwise, you earned the right to a choice. There's folks that'd adopt a little darling like she is, but that'd take your signin' to give 'er away."

Louellen sat, staring at nothing. Drained and disheartened, she turned and watched as Gran stood and walked to the window. She looked out, up down and round, as though the answer was there somewhere. Louellen sincerely hoped it was.

Gran sighed and turned back to the girl. "I got a whisper of a' idea, but it'll take a promise from you to get me to tell you."

"Tell me, Gran. I'd promise anything. What do I promise?"

"You gotta promise me to rest today and tonight. Then tomorrow I'll help you be ready to make a little trip. I'm knowin' you can do it, because you made it all the way up here."

Louellen's eyes flew open. Gran was magic. She'd had good ideas before. "Tell me, Gran!"

The old woman hesitated, swallowed hard, and announced. "No, not until four o'clock in the morning. I'll give you something to make you sleep, and I promise I'll wake you. If you don't do what I say, you might just faint on the way, and I'd not know how to find you."

Louellen nodded and sighed in the face of good sense. She ducked her head and bit her lip in her mental turmoil. "I'll do it, Gran. You never lied to me, so I know you got a plan."

So, at four o'clock, Gran shook her gently. "Rise up, sweetie. You'll need your time. I got a lunch fixed, and your dress is clean and pressed. You'll eat eggs and biscuits, and then I'll tell you."

At ten minutes until five, Louellen kissed Gran's wrinkled face and smiled. "Thank you, Gran. You're an angel."

Gran shook her head. "No, honey, I just did what your angel told me to do."

"My angel…?"

"Sure thing. You got a angel that has got charge'a you, and I'm thinkin' that angel knows right where your baby is. Now, see you keep that note in your pocket. It's got Aunt Bertha's address all writ down. Worse comes to worse, you'll go there. My poor sister always wanted a girl, and was a mite jealous when you were born even that you were not, well… I know she wants a girl. She'd'a took you in a minute, havin' the chance. Now when you find that baby, you get someone to take you to Berryville to her house, and I'll take care'a things here. Now, off with you."

Another kiss on the wrinkled face and Louellen headed out toward the mountain path that climbed over the foothills. Rested a few minutes at a brook and ate lunch, but couldn't wait. Sore insides were ignored in her eagerness to be off.

It was six o'clock when she stepped out of the trail onto the flint gravel of Ridge Road. Without hesitation, she turned left toward the little settlement of Burnt Tree Junction. She wouldn't go all the way, but must start looking for the tiny, almost hidden sign that said Chestnut Cottage.

The angel watched, and knew the girl, inside and out. Angel 237 also knew this, as the created heavenly beings are always in the know.

But there's that other thing. All angels are not heavenly. There were those who were thrown out in the terrible, heavenly mutiny led by Lucifer. There was a fierce struggle but the Boss was stronger, and there are humans ready to listen to the right voices and ignore the others.

One weary foot plodded before the other as Louellen Fisher turned off Ridge Road and made her way down the tree-shaded lane. Small stone cottage ahead. That must be it. She could rest there, and maybe…

Nancy Camden was again in the room with the baby box. With such a crowded nursery, Miss Betsy was 'dead on her feet', and Nancy couldn't sleep anyway. Her sore ribs hurt less when she was sitting in the rocker, than lying in bed, and the new little Mary Annette was fussy.

Restless, that little girl was. Couldn't seem to nod off even with a full tummy. She'd appeared in the night a day a go, with no explanation from the man who brought her.

Nancy lifted the little girl to her shoulder and hummed, patting the padded bottom in time with the rocker's squeak. She alerted at a sound outside the door. Not the baby drawer, it was the cottage door this time. Time to get help.

Heaving her body out of the rocker she made her way down the hall to Miss Cottrell. "Miss Emma? They's someone at the door. Do I open it?"

Miss Emma was napping and awoke fully awake, a habit born of many such occasions. She followed Nancy back to the door. The knocking continued.

Miss Emma peeked through the slit window. Just a girl. She opened the door and Louellen Fisher just about fell inside.

Helped to the rocker, she sat and looked up at the two people and demanded, hopefully, "You know anything about my baby that got stole from me?"

Miss Emma hesitated. Then, "Honey, we don't know you, and we don't know anything about a baby. Do you know who stole your baby?"

The girl nodded. "I'm thinkin' it might be my Pa. He took her two days ago without me knowin'. I come up from Wishbone, hopin' she was here."

"From Wishbone? You walked…?"

"Had no other way to git here. My baby was to be named Rosemary Louellen, but I didn't get to register her. You got a three -day-old baby girl?"

Nancy looked at Miss Emma and Miss Emma looked back, and then at the girl sitting on the edge of the rocker.

"Miss, you got a way'a describin' your baby?"

Louellen brightened. "Yes ma'am. I got to hold her a few minutes right there at first and looked at her fingers and toes. She's got a whirl of a cowlick on the back'a her head like my sister and a mark on her leg way up here," and she pointed to her right hip. "It's pink and shaped sort'a like a rosebud."

The weary girl grinned with pride. "I already had a name picked out and when I saw the mark, I knew it was the right name. Her name is Rosemary."

Miss Emma nodded. "Her name wasn't Mary Annette?"

Weariness gone, the girl jumped up from the rocker. "Then she's here! That's the name my Pa would'a said. He had a sister that died named Mary Annette. Can I see her… please…?"

Nancy looked at Miss Emma who nodded. Looking back at the girl, she extended the blanketed baby into her mother's arm. Louellen's heart beat so rapidly she thought she might just faint and drop the baby. She sunk back into the rocker, tears streaming down her face.

Peeling back the blankets, she looked into the face of the little girl as though she could never stop. Carefully lifting the gown… not the dress she had made… she looked at the pink rosebud shape just under the edge of the slightly damp diaper.

Miss Emma took down the name book and turned the pages. The last little girl had been named Quanna. The letter "Q" was always a puzzle for finding a name. The next letter would be "R". with a satisfied smile and a poised pencil, she turned to the girl and baby.

"Rosemary, did you say?"

"Rosemary Louellen Fisher. Louellen is my name."

A cup of hot tea and the visitor was bedded down on the hobo bed with firm assurance her baby would still be there, come morning.

Nancy Camden returned to her rocker and sipped tea, her abdomen feeling as if a circus was happening inside. Stomping elephants and swinging monkeys. Tall giraffes waving their heads while herds of wildebeest migrated en masse from her left side to her right… then back again. All inside her protruded belly.

Nancy Camden held the bottle and watched the adorable little face of the new little girl and told herself. "Less than a month, young lady, and I'm gonna to have someone just like you."

If angels can be amused at the words of humans, Angel 237 might have smiled. Little did this human know of what would actually happen.

## ELEPHPANTS, ZEBRAS AND GIRAFFES

Nancy was concerned to the point of desperation.

The circus in her belly now had a 'big top', and the animals were marching around in the parade. Elephants, hippos, and giraffes. There must be a sprinkling of wildebeests, now, and certainly every kind of monkey.

And she was going to have a hungry man appear in a matter of hours. What was the easiest? Beans were his favorite. Could eat them every day, so maybe fried potatoes as well. She dipped the beans into the kettle and added water. While they were soaking, she rendered the fat from a ham and thickened it just a little. Into the kettle it went.

Ouch! A kick from the hippo doubled her over, leaning her head and forearms on her table. Pheeew, today was going to be a bad one…

Potatoes. She flicked off the sprouts where they had started to grow and tossed them in the pan of water. Easier to clean that way. Onions… yes, two large ones. There! If he never got another thing, Matthew would be happy with that. And maybe canned peaches.

She was so, so, so very tired. How could anyone manage to stuff that much tired into one body? Somehow she seemed to have done it. She was just going to have to lie down a while.

The bed wasn't that much better. Easier than on her feet, but the circus tried to move up to her lungs and make it hard to breathe. She struggled her body onto its right side, and that created more room, maybe. The circus was quick to take advantage of it, and she actually saw movement in her left rib cage. Whoever was in there really wanted out. On that one thing, she and the 'whoever' were in total agreement.

In the kitchen, seeming to be the best and most un-scary place for the conversation, Miss Emma and Louellen sat with tea.

"Now sweetie, I'm gladder than you know that you come to us. Tiny babies are our business, and we've had a lot of them. Now yours is here, and we'd like to keep her for a little while, but only if you can stay. I know you have a place to go, but, honey, Berryville is a long ways away.

"Why, a grown man couldn't make it a day less'n he rode into the night. I know you can't walk it, and the little one would be dead before you got there." (If that didn't scare her, Emma'd think of something worse).

Louellen hunched her shoulders together and sipped her tea.

Miss Emma plunged on. "So if you'd just write to your auntie and tell her that you were in a good place where you would be safe, and they were insisting you wait until you and the baby were stronger…?"

Louellen set her coffee mug on the table and nodded. "I would do that if I could. I been hurtin' since yesterday, 'specially after I reached Ridge Road. I wanted to sit and rest, but I was in a hurry. The pains ain't gettin' no better, so maybe I should stay... a day or two, maybe."

Now she had Miss Emma's attention. Pains. Never having experienced childbirth, the after-pains were a mystery to her. "Where at are you painin', honey?"

"...Uh, it's right about... sort'a up here." Instead of indicating a spot on her abdomen, she had crossed her arms across her chest. Miss Emma took in a sharp breath of realization.

"What sort'a pains are they...?"

Louellen frowned in concentration. "Strange pains like they's pins inside'a me tryin' to punch through the skin. And there is achin' over under my arms."

Miss Emma's concern changed. She now knew what to do. "Betsy, dear, would you run over across Ridge Road and get Granny Wise? Tell 'er we need a little advice."

When the ten year old inside Betsy was told to run, she ran, and came back assisting the bent old woman who wore spectacles down on her generously-proportioned nose. Granny Wise was not a trained midwife, but she acted as one, and her patients were glad to have her.

Granny Wise knew about those pains. "How old is the baby?" she demanded. Then exclaimed in horror! "Two days...? Honey, them pains must be givin' you fits?"

Louellen nodded rapidly. Best description she could have thought of.

The old woman turned to Betsy. "Here, you take this girl to your nursin' chair and someone bring me the baby."

Louellen was wide eyed. "You can't take away my baby! They promised me I could keep her here a few days and..."

"I ain't doin' nothin' with your baby. I'm gonna show you how to feed her. You bein' sixteen, your ma or someone should'a told you what would happen. Your pain is just your body tellin' you to feed your baby."

"But..."

"No matter. We'll get this done. Let's fix your dress over here like this, and hold your baby with her head inside your elbow. That'd be the right height. Now, snug her up close against her cheek."

Suddenly the amazing thing happened! Louellen knew, of course, that mothers nursed their babies, but it had somehow escaped her mind that it would happen to her. Rosemary, however, knew exactly what to do.

The first strong tug produced screams of pain from her mother. She straightened up and pushed the blanket wrapped bundle toward the old woman. Granny Wise was not surprised, and gently replaced the bundle. "The first time is the worst, honey. Someone should'a told you this, and let you work up to it. It's somethin' you'll have to do, but it gets better real fast."

Louellen gritted her teeth and settled Rosemary back into position. Shuddering and tensing her muscles, she held steady, and it did, indeed, get better. Maybe a little bit.

Hmmm, well… if it eased the pain, she'd just… Well, of course. She was really a mother, in spite of the awful thing that had happened. And there had been everyone trying to tell her she wasn't.

She snugged the blanketed bundle closer, and Rosemary opened her beautiful blue-black eyes and looked up at her mother. Much as to say, where has this been all this time?

Nancy, who contained the circus animals in her abdomen, managed to put dishes on the table, and to transfer the large, steaming bowl of beans to the table. She looked at the potatoes, sending up their enticing aroma. Bypassing a serving bowl, she moved the skillet to the table and placed it on a thick pot holder.

The 'enticing aroma' did not tempt Nancy. Just as well, because there was no room for food down there with all those animals. Maybe just a little tea.

Matthew loaded his plate with one half potatoes, and the other of beans, thick with ham bits and gravy. He sliced off a chunk of the raw onion and buttered a piece of cornbread.

Then seeing Nancy's empty plate, demanded, "You ain't eatin'?"

Tense and tight lipped, she shook her head and contemplated the tea. Would there even be room down there for that…?

"But, if you don't eat, you'll starve the baby, and he can't even complain about it. Can't you eat somethin'? Maybe a bite'a beans?"

Whereupon, Nancy shuddered violently and excused herself to go to the bed.

At great sacrifice to his appetite, Matthew lay down his fork and his bread and knocked on the cottage door.

"Miss, Emma, I think Nancy'a ailin'. Wouldn't eat a bite'a supper."

"Hmmm, well, I don't… Wait, Granny Wise is here. Let's have her take a look at Nancy. She wasn't due for pretty nigh a month, so maybe she's just tired. She's been sittin' up in the drawer room. Anyway, Granny Wise'll know."

Thus, having done his duty and turned this mysterious subject over to its proper hands, he returned to the food. But it didn't taste quite the same. Could Nancy be…? Was it possible to die from being pregnant? He'd never heard of it, but she… well, she didn't even taste the delicious beans. Fact was, he wasn't very hungry any more.

Old Granny Wise clomped past Matthew, tapping her cane (just for balance) and setting her sensible shoes down with a determined attitude, she headed for the bedroom, the theater of her greatest skill, and tossed back the covers. Miss Emma trailed behind.

She ignored the frightened eyes trained on the face and felt around the bulging belly. She pressed lightly on the dark place on Nancy's lower rib cage.

"Ouch! I really got pains there. Feels like there's a circus'a wild animals tryin' to bust through the bars, inside there."

"There is," Granny informed those in the room. "Them beasts in there… they're wantin' to get out, and they're gonna do it. Before mornin' this young lady is gonna be a mama."

Miss Emma pulled in a sharp breath. "But she's nigh onto a month to go!"

"Nope! It's right now. Tell Betsy to go get my bag, a'hangin' right by the door. She'll see it. Now, young lady, you got things ready like I told you?"

Nancy nodded briskly. "Bottom drawer."

"Miss Emma, look in the bottom drawer and bring the pad. Get the scissors and thread, and heat up the stove."

"Hot water… ?"

"Yeah, for tea. I could use a cup, and there's somethin' for the mama in my bag."

Mama! Sounded strange! "But I can't drink anything. There ain't room down there for nothin'."

Granny snorted, agreeably. "I can believe that. The truth is, we're gonna make room. You're gonna stand on the floor till I fix this bed. Miss Emma, see she don't tip over. We'd have a tough time pickin' 'er up."

Nancy's teeth were clenched so tightly her jaws ached, but when she loosened them, her chin trembled. What in the world was going on with her? Granny Wise turned really bossy, but that was a good thing, wasn't it?

Settled once more in bed, head propped back against three pillows, Granny began once more to poke and tap on the circus tent, causing the animals to stampede. When the firm hand pressed just above her hip bone, she distinctly felt the hippo move over a bit. That made the giraffe slip around, and the top of its head racked against her sore spot.

"Ouch! Somethin' sharp in there!"

Granny nodded. "You bet there is. Knees and elbows feel like hatchets and knives. But don't you worry. When Betsy gets here I have somethin' that'll tame those animals. Right now I want you to start countin' to five. Take two breaths and count to five again."

Nancy nodded, "One, Two, Three……."

A teacup appeared with green liquid. "Now, honey, I know there don't seem to be no room, but this here tea'll just have to find a place to go. Drink it slowly, but drink it all." Nancy did. Afraid not to. Grannie Wise had a very sharp voice.

Granny gently messaged the heaping bulge, and the giraffe moved its head. Nancy finally found that she could unclamp her jaws without her chin trembling. She was tired. Oh, so, so tired. Maybe…

But just then came the knife! A stiletto blade stabbed a sliced path all the way up to her belly button! Maybe farther! Had to be the rhino's horn, but it felt like her Pa's corn knife that he used to cut down the dead stalks. She wanted to scream, but just couldn't get her mouth worked around so she could make a sound.

Granny and Miss Emma were busy with this and that, and when she tried to see where they were, she felt her eyes cross. So she blinked and then closed them. Even if she knew where they were, she couldn't call them. Who'd hear when she couldn't make a sound? Voice gone.

It was then that Sharon opened her tiny mouth and uttered a cry of welcome. More like a mama cat calling to her kits. Nancy wondered, did they really have baby kittens? She couldn't quite remember.

Then she heard Granny tell Miss Emma. "See you mark that one in such a way we'll know it was first."

Hmmm, the kittens were still being born. Quick as she got through with this hurtin', she'd go find them. About then Lydia whimpered her way into the conversation.

The corn knife was gone, now, but there seemed to be something… maybe it was the mama cat crawling on her, but why would it do that?

The reason was that Dorcas had stubbornly let herself turn, end for end, and present a tiny pink foot instead of the top of a head. Granny was having none of that. Miss Emma was holding Lydia, looking for a place to put her, when Granny said, "Come help me here."

Miss Emma tossed a freshly made flannel blanket onto the floor and put Lydia down on it. No other choice. Together she and Granny pushed and pulled where Nancy's muscles had given out, and Dorcas finally obeyed and followed her sisters. Properly head first.

Granny turned to Miss Emma with demanding eyes. "Where at is that first'n? Did you mark it?"

"Sure did. She's wearin' one bootee."

Granny nodded. "Then put two on this'n when you get 'er cleaned up. I'm gonna let this girl rest a half hour or so. She's been through a bundle. So we'll get these three cleaned up and go find their Pa. 'Speck he's in the barn, hidin'."

Her grin exposed a two-tooth gap. "That's where they usually go. Good thing to do. Gets 'em outta the way, and them painin' at the sound that don't help them babies a'tall."

The two women worked busily for a few minutes. "Sure ain't makin' the racket you'd expect with three," Miss Emma observed.

Granny nodded. "Could be they're so glad to be out that they hush up, so they won't be put back. That girl had a right to complain. These here little girls ain't really early. Leastways not a month like she said. Maybe two weeks at the most. They'd done got about as big as they could in the space they had."

"Yeah, she was talkin' a lot about the circus in her belly. I didn't pay any mind, thinkin' they all felt thataway. Seems she really was about to bust."

Then Granny, "Hope this here girl has a sister or someone to help out for a couple'a weeks or three. She's gonna be a few days gettin' over this. Her ribs is spread so they'll never tighten up 'thout help. I got a band over to the house that'll help, but she'll need someone to get her fastened up in it."

"She'll have help." As the words had come out of Granny's mouth, Miss Emma's mind pulled up a picture of Louellen, needin' a reason to not get in a hurry to leave.

Nodding, Miss Emma re-assured, "She'll have help." She swabbed behind a tiny ear, and then continued.

"Louellen, in there, knowin' Nancy needs help... she'll be beggin' to stay. That girl... she sure seems to be made outta extra strong stuff... what she's been through from her parents, and bein' strong enough to walk all the way here. Must'a been six miles if it was an inch. Not only that, she got those nice round breasts. Could be she could help in another way. Maybe for a week or two."

Granny nodded, knowingly. It had been done before. "That'd be help if you can make it happen. Otherwise them little girls gonna be mostly on goat's milk from the start. I'm thinkin' you could take these girls on to the baby room, and I'll work with the girl. We need to finish up, and then she needs more tea to let 'er rest."

Some minutes later Granny wiped her hands and nodded satisfaction for a job well done. "For a fact, that girl must'a got her numbers mixed up. Every one of these three weighin' in at over 5 pounds, and her the size she is. It's a wonder they're all alive.

Yes, it was a wonder. Life is full of wonders. It was surely planned that way.

Nancy was asleep, getting much needed rest, when Matthew was brought into the baby room, eyes grainy and red. Hair a pile of straw from being roughed up, and mouth grim as though he was attending a funeral.

He looked from one to the other of the three little bassinettes. "You say all of them… all three are mine? You're positively sure? And they're all girls?" Smiling, he reached in and touched the pink fingers of Dorcas, and smoothed Sharon's fuzzy head.

Louellen watched with longing eyes. It'd be just about the best feeling in the world to see a baby bringing pleasure to its papa's eyes. A baby deserved that. She hugged Rosemary just a little tighter.

Angel 239 was there. Had been on duty for some months, and the little one had never been in danger.Angels 849, 850 and 851 were there as well. The timing had been perfect. It was necessary for the circus to remain under Nancy's 'tent' until Louellen had united with Rosemary and appeared at the Cottage.

Nancy was going to need a special kind of help, and Louellen was going to need a friend, a friend of a special kind, and the babies would bind the two teenage mothers together.

It was a week later that Matthew and Nancy sat at their table, the first time Nancy was permitted to be up. The meal of meatloaf and vegetable casserole had been created by Louellen who positively refused to join them. The couple had each other, and being there with them would not have helped her loneliness. The fried lamb chops with Miss Emma and Betsy suited her better.

There was a definite pleasure to be sitting at the table with two people who loved her, and encouraged her to eat as much as she could, so she would be able to help with feeding the triplets. They complimented her for being so strong and determined, and being able to travel so far that second and third day.

She'd written to Auntie Bertha who would be expecting her, and explained that she was fine, but would be delayed maybe a month because she had a way to help the people who had helped her.

Auntie Bertha said that would be fine. A bed for her and a bassinette for little Rosemary would be ready when she was.

Imagine! And Auntie Bertha had only seen her once, as a tiny baby, herself. And she was already calling Rosemary by name!

While at the kitchen table, the new parents chattered happily. Nancy teased, "Now aren't you a little bit disappointed we didn't get a little boy?"

Matthew threw back his head in jolly laughter. "Now why would I be wantin' a little ole boy, when I can have three girls! I got braggin' rights like you wouldn't believe. Why, no one in my family has ever done anything like this! Why, they ain't even never seen anything like this."

"Do you like the names all right?"

"Love 'em. They was right there in the Bible, waitin'. Just like they was meant to be."

Nancy sighed with satisfaction and helped herself to the meatloaf. Louellen was a mighty good cook, and she had been making the meals for days, now.

Matthew's thoughts were still on his wealth of little girls. He added, "Besides, we can have a little ole boy anytime."

Nancy swallowed, ducked her head, and muttered, "Yeah… well… Maybe, but not right away."

## ARTHUR STANFIELD

Back down in Wishbone, things progressed.

Seventeen-year-old Arthur was hiding in the shrubbery and highly embarrassed to be doing so. There seemed no other way, as he couldn't just stand around outside the door waiting for Hannah to take her usual trip to the store.

He had spent a horrid and lonely 6 months, and he had finally decided to 'take the bull by the horns' as the saying goes and if he got hurt… well, then he'd just be hurt. He had finally decided being hurt would be better than what he had gone through.

It was dusky dark when Hannah finally made her trip. Seemed the family needed something for the evening meal… just about every evening. No matter. That was no concern of his, but he had to speak to Hannah and his job took care of his days.

Eventually his patience paid off, and the side door by the kitchen opened, and out stepped Hannah. Following along inside the shrubbery, he waited until she was almost out of sight of her house, and whispered. He certainly didn't want to frighten her into screaming.

"Psssst, Hannah!"

The girl startled and looked around. "Arthur, what you mean hiding in the shrubs that'away?"

"I had to talk to you without your family seein' me. I figgered they'd get the law on me if they saw me… quiet as they been about Louellen."

Hannah fully understood. "Then walk with me and walk fast. I gotta get back with the cream."

The boy bravely began, "I gotta find out where Louellen is, and I gotta ask somethin'."

"What…?"

"I want to know why all of a sudden I ain't let to see her when we've been friends ever since I pulled her from the mud puddle when she was five, and I was seven. I've been her friend, and even yours, for nigh onto ten years, so why has that stopped now?" Arthur's eyes were glistening and stern, and his chin firmly set.

"But Arthur, I ain't supposed to talk."

"I know that, but everyone else on this side'a town is talkin' but no one says where she is."

"Lean over and I'll whisper. Somethin' happened that she got sent away, and she don't want'a come home. That's what Ma says to tell."

"I know exactly what happened, but I don't know how things are for her and she in my friend. You have to tell me!"

"Really, Arthur, I would if I could. The thing is, I don't know where she is and I don't even get to talk with her, and she's my sister. We were always best friends."

"But I know you like to listen in. That'd come in handy right now if you was to hear any little thing that would help me find her. I want to hear it from her mouth that she doesn't want to see me no more. I ain't done nothin' to hurt her."

Hannah nodded. "We all know that. We know who done it and I wisht Pa would'a hit him. I wisht he'd'a got his head blown off." She shrugged, and added, "'Course that'd'a put Pa in the jail and then everybody'd know."

"Hannah, I tell you… everyone knows already. I want to know if she's still alive, and if she is, where is she. I want to know if her baby is alive. I think ten years of bein' a friend to 'er owes me that much. I keep thinkin' you can tell me somethin'. I remember you even listenin' in on me and Louellen. Didn't matter. We didn't say nothin' you wasn't supposed to hear. Now tell me…"

A long sigh, and she opened the door of the little corner store. "Come with me, and stand behind the shelves. All I heard, and it wasn't my fault 'cause I want the same thing you want. I heard that she might be at Gran's house up on Echo Mountain."

"Your Grandmother? Where does… how can I get there?"

"Well, she ain't really my Gran, but she's a friend and she likes Louellen. That's where she'd go. She snuck out in the night and didn't let me know, but I think she went there. If she did, then Gran would know where she went from them and would help her. I don't know about the baby."

"You saw the baby…?"

Hannah nodded. "A little girl, but I didn't get to touch her or hold her, and by morning she was gone. I don't know anything about that. Honest to goodness, and I really want to. The baby was my real, true niece. Do you believe me?"

Sadly he did. "But you can tell me how to get to Gran's house."

"I can, but it's hard. She ain't got no address, but I been there several times. Find me a scrap'a paper, and I'll do my best to remember."

Within minutes, Hannah left with the cream and Arthur left with the scrap of paper tightly clasp in his hand, and the hand thrust deep in his pocket. One very tiny clue to her where-abouts, and he'd make it enough. Now, how could he leave his good job for the maybe four or five days this would take? It wasn't IF he would go, but when. He would go. He had been treated unfairly by the town, and he was going to put an end to this, one way or the other.

He'd worked at the livery stable for three years, and he knew the boss liked the way he curried the horses and cleaned the stalls. Someday he hoped to be the driver of one of the carriages. Really good job, that was. Consequently, he had a little money, and he never asked for time off.

Angels 239 and 781 may have been together, because, wonder of wonders, he was given the time off as well as the loan of a horse. Not a carriage horse, but one that pulled the cleaning equipment. Perfect! Wonderful!

Now to get away from home. The last thing his parents would want for him was to locate that girl who disgraced her family, and then certainly the disgrace would rub off on them if he found her.

He could lie, but that had never worked for him. So, just tell the truth. The note said:

Ma and Pa, I've gone to do something I have to do. I'm seventeen now, and I know you know that, but sometimes I'm treated like I was ten. This is something I need to do, and I'll be coming back home in less than a week, if you'll let me Arthur.

And that was the truth. That sentence about them letting him come home was a key to his confidence. When you had only one child, you wouldn't throw him out for one little offense… except for one thing. They would know exactly why he was going but not where. Even he did not know where.

So when he turned up, finally, at the house Hannah described, he knocked on the door, dead tired and hungry, but encouraged. It took a while to convince Gran, but she finally relented. He'd need to go on a certain path… due south… and he'd reach Ridge Road without going back to Wishbone.

He was given a sack lunch, fed well, and sent on his way. Gran watched as he disappeared into the trees, and then shook her head. May the saints and angels help that girl. Her folks certainly ain't doin' it.

Gran had actually wasted her breath, because angels seemed to be already on the job.

Late in the day he rested by a stream of water for a while and he ate from the lunch packed by Gran. He took the other tiny package from his coat pocket. It had been a purchase bravely made, and if not accepted, would be tossed into a ditch by him.

On the bed of moss by the stream, he spread the tiny pink dress, and it it looked just as pretty as it had in the store. Beside the dress he lay the tiny doll, its cloth body a soft pink, except for the head that had brown yarn hair and embroidered face. He studied the two items while he ate. Maybe they would say to Louellen what he couldn't.

He reached Ridge Road late in the evening. It would be another night in someone's barn, but no matter. He was close. When the roosterswoke him, he eased down from the barn loft and slipped through the fence, brushing bits of hay from his clothes.

He took a left turn, as instructed, and began to watch for the lane that Gran thought might be somewhat hidden. And then he saw the tiny sign. Chestnut Cottage. The lane wound through the trees.

The sun was high when he knocked on the door and tried to tell the woman he was a friend of Louellen's and had they seen her?

Betsy knew right off this person would never get to see that girl. Obviously, the poor girl had enough of him, so Betsy slammed the door in his face. Not to be deterred, Arthur rounded the house to the kitchen door. A soft knock produced a grandmother-looking person. He spoke fast.

"Please, I need to say something to Louellen. Just let me see her and I'll leave if she wants me to." The woman hesitated, so Arthur reached in his pocket and brought out the dress, holding it up. "Her Gran thought she might have been here, and I brought a present. Please tell me where she is?"

Miss Emma put two and two together and decided whoever violated her would not bring a gift, and likely wouldn't be wanting to speak to her. Decision made. "Young man, just stand right there and I'll see what I can do."

After the initial shock of a fellow asking for her, she couldn't imagine it to be Arthur, she peeked through the window. There he stood with a pink baby dress in his hand. Her heart melted, but her stubborn head remembered the terrible months she had experienced.

At Miss Emma's urging, she stepped through the door. No one would see the old woman's crossed fingers behind her back. The young man needed all the luck she could wish him, but she would already know that he had the best. She knew about angels... nor than she would ever let be known.

"Wait, Louellen, before you make up your mind. I come all this ways, and you're rememberin' how far it is, gettin' my mind clear in what I wanted to say. First off, I ain't to blame for nothin' except wantin' to see you and hear from you that you were alright. Here it is that I seemed to lose a friend, and I don't know why. I wasn't let to know where you were, and even Hannah couldn't talk with me. I figgered she knew somthin'... nosey as she is. I was right.

"I've seen you with mud caked on your bloomers and cryin' with a splinter in your finger. I think you were five and six then. You saw me dirty from workin' in the yard, and my skin peelin' off from sunburn. I think I was maybe seven or eight.

"You saw me all upset over a test I thought would be too hard, and you wanted to help. I loved you for offering, and it helped. You saw me with a ripped shirt from fallin' out of a tree and didn't laugh even if it was funny. I helped you get your swing rope untangled and you hugged me. Now, I could go on and on, but I don't want you to get tired. You remember all them things as well as I do. It was my thinkin' that they all put together added up to a friendship, and in my mind there ain't nothin' been changed. If that friendship ain't no more, it must be 'cause of how you feel about me.

"I know everything that happened to you, and I know it wasn't your fault and you weren't likin' it a bit, and Hannah was hurtin' the same as me. The thing was, I couldn't get to you to tell you, and that wasn't fair.

"So there's nothing' I can do to change anything, but I gotta know how you feel, so I won't bother you no more. I know you gotta go to Berryville, and it's likely a good thing. It ain't the end'a the world. I know I gotta stay in Wishbone leastwise till I get older and learn to do what I want. Someday I'm gonna have a beautiful carriage, and a pair of horses, and charge money to take rich folks to fancy places. I don't know if it'll be in Wishbone, but some of that may depend on you.

"There ain't no difference in my feelin' toward you, and I can't see how some little bity girl could change that. I was hopin' I could bring her the first present she got so you'd believe me that there ain't been no changes.

"The way I see it, there's mail delivery to Berryville, and we can both write. I'm thinkin' it'd be better'n nothin'. Maybe I could take the train over there a time or two, but we both got a couple years till we can be face to face. I always figgered it'd be you and me sometime, and it still could be.

"If the folks here'd let me camp out in the barn, and maybe feed my horse, we'd have time to talk tomorrow before I need to get the borrowed horse back. That'away I'd be sure you knew I was still the person who pulled you outta the mud puddle. Maybe I'd get to hold Rosemary a minute or two. I've never got to hold a baby that new to the world, and I'd really like to if you would let me."

Arthur held out the tiny stuffed doll. Louellen took it, fingering its miniature legs and arms while she looked at Arthur's feet. "It's just that my folks told me things that wasn't true, and I believed 'em. I wasn't seein' how you could feel the same about me, when everyone else didn't. I didn't even know about Hannah bein' hurt, and I figgered nothin' wasn't never gonna change."

She lifted her eyes to his very sober face. "You gotta be hungry, and I ain't got no manners. Come in, and I'll get something for you, and ask about you stayin' over."

Arthur stayed two nights, and at daylight on the third day he was in the saddle and headed down Ridge Road. It'd be no trick at all to be in Wishbone by late evening, and on the job the next morning. Ma and Pa deserved an explanation, and he had the next six hours or so to plan it.

It would take that long, for a fact, because the words had to be carefully thought out.

## MISS EMMA THE PLANNER

Some folks plan better than others, and Miss Emma was up there with the best. At Chestnut Cottage, nothing was ever the same, one day to the next, except for the fact tht babies that got hungry and got wet. Everything else and everybody were woven around those two occurrences. That was the whole reason for there being a Chestnut Cottage in the first place.

Consequently, Louellen would occupy the hobo bed for at least a month, sharing a room with four little girls needing to be kept fed. Along with Rosemary, there would be one other little girl, and the three would be rotated every three days. Nancy had to have a bottle available to top off the tummies in her bedroom, but Louellen managed the other two quite efficiently, in addition to short times throughout the day.

Granny Wise had convinced Miss Emma that it was NECESSARY, and the girl must be made to remain for at least a month before going to Berryville.

Granny's word was law.

When the time came, Matthew hitched up the mares with the gentlest gait to the most comfortable buggy he could borrow. With an early start, he was able to deliver Louellen to her Auntie Bertha before nightfall and head back in the morning. That way he would know where Louellen would be, and that was very important to Nancy who ached to be taken along, but it just wasn't feasible.

Letters zipped back and forth from Berryville to Wishbone, and Arthur worked every paid hour he could get and saved every penny. His parents had decided that, when he actually left, they would help out. Maybe even buy him the horse he wanted. It was painful, but they finally realized that children were not bought and owned, but just rented for a while. To keep in touch with their Arthur, whom they so carefully reared, they would have to compromise.

At age twenty one, he was living in Berryville with a good job, and was paying out the cost of the carriage he drove. He also had moved his 'ladies' in the house with him. Aunt Bertha witnessed the legal union, smiling as though she had been responsible for it all, and maybe she had been. She had certainly been compliant with the nudges of the angels.

When Nancy remembered the rule at the cottage, 'Three years or three babies' she was pale with fright. Here they had three already and no place to go.

Miss Emma, the arranger, shrugged her well-padded shoulders and showed the girl the new rule. "Three years or three babies, unless the babies were triplets'. There were answers to every question if one just thought about it.

Matthew, always good with his hands, hired himself out to a builder in Berryville. The sale of the animals he had acquired while in the cottage had set him up well when he moved Nancy, Sharon, Lydia and Dorcas to Berryville.

The four little girls grew up together, just as they were meant to do. The angels knew how the book would eventually end.

It was some years later that Matthew would build his own house and had ordered a load of a special wood from the saw mill in Burnt Tree Junction. The one down on the banks of Blue Lake.

Jonathan Turner delivered it and got a glimpse of the three lovely young ladies who were within a gunshot range from the mill, and he had one of them in his sights. Didn't matter which, because they all looked pretty much alike.

A lot happened quickly between the Turner young men and the 'quad' of young ladies, but something else came first.

David and Dottie McAlester were next to occupy the cabin at Chestnut Cottage. That agreeable couple, through no fault of their own, failed to produce the child they desired. They left the cottage at the end of their three years quite well set up for their own business. With them, they took one fortunate little boy, and a pair of lucky little girls… all three of whom had arrived into their lives through the drawer.

Sometimes things worked out.

## SUSANNA AND JOANNA

Why the loving and excited parents of the twin girls were not permitted to stay on earth and rear their daughters can never be known, but so are the many ways of the Boss. The path to His eventual purpose for them seemed to lay in the spooked horse and an overturned buggy in the electrical storm, followed by the sudden taking of the parents to their reward.

Still and all, the upset occurred just at the time of the weekly run of the mail delivery. The mail carrier knew what to do, and he did it. The parents were beyond any need for emergency assistance, but one baby was calling out with a good set of lungs while the other baby slid down the mountainside into the place where she was obviously meant to be. Just goes to show, the Boss knows what he's doing.

Susanna was taken to Eureka Springs at the age of eight, and her governess was moved with the family. The most expensive and well known music teacher was employed, leaving her former teacher in deep despair.

Miss Yulalee did not take just anyone. She was considered a 'finisher' accepting only those students who knew the rudiment and showed extraordinary ability. That, of course, would take in Susanna.

Joanna stayed with Miss Stockard who thought she could 'finish out' Joanna quite well all by herself. At her age 13, the teacher began to get her ready for her first concert/recital which could take place at age 14. It was going to be a wonderful year for the old teacher.

Barney Prentiss, the seven year old rescued from the Boy's Home, had been instructed by Mister Bryan, who also instructed another boy named Christopher. These boys would be seventeen at the time of the recital, and Mister Bryan considered them prime age and skill and paired them as an instrumental duet.

Violin duets were popular, and the instructor put them on a very difficult classical piece called 'Indian Love Call'. It was sure to bring him much acclaim that would result in additional new students.

Truthfully, he would have taught these boys for nothing, if he had had to, but he didn't. They both had parents eager to pay.

The boys would perform in suits with a black tie... bow tie because of their young ages. The girls were instructed to acquire a 'formal' dress which means something that they would never wear again and that cost enough to be appreciated by wealthy concert goers.

Joanna was taken to the bigger city of Eureka Springs to locate just the right dress. Nora would have chosen white for her, but the girl insisted on the glistening gold of a summer sunshine.

Her mom was soon to admit it was an excellent choice... both color and style... along with her taller-than-average height and her black, black hair. Stylish black patent leather pumps and pale golden stockings completed the outfit, and her hair was lifted into the popular sausage curls held in place with combs.

Simple, actually, but oh, so attractive for a young girl. The same was said by the sales person to another little girl of about the same age.

Miss Yulalee, herself, orchestrated the selection of Susanna's dress, and the governess, barely twenty, was in no position to argue, even if she'd wanted to. Also, the classical selection contained a lot of notes and not a great lot of melody. Quite difficult to accomplish, as any concert goer should recognize.

The concert was to be held in Bentonville, and Joanna's parents considered her brother, Barney, to be capable of providing for her safety, especially when Mister Bryan and Miss Stockard were also going, along with several students. Parents would come later.

There were those who went earlier, and that included Susanna and Laverne, with instructions to do a little shopping for items not available in Eureka Springs.

When it was time for Susanna to take the stage, Joanna looked on and knew she was getting' sick from nerves and her eyes were playing tricks. For there she saw her yellow dress on another girl with black, black hair just like hers. And, horror of horrors, the girl was playing her selection! What was going on? Was there a magic mirror… maybe? Was she Alice in Wonderland, from her childhood story books?

Barney tried to calm her, but he was also astonished, and was concerned that Joanna might not be given the stage, as it appeared that she had already been there.

More horrified than those two, was Miss Stockard who saw her wonderful acclaim being yanked from her before it was given. How could there be another girl like Joanna, and she was excellently executing the same musical selection. The castles she had built in her mind were crumbling into dust before her very eyes and she was being buried in the chaotic stone-pile.

The Master of Ceremonies was in no way nonplused. Two entries later he brought on Joanna, just in the position she had been placed on the schedule. Heart beating a tom-tom, she curtsied to the audience and seated herself. Then, as usually happened, her fingers took over, having been thoroughly practiced on what to do.

The MC, noting the puzzled looks among the audience, located the first girl and held her in the wings. At the end of her piece, Joanna was given the applause she was due, but there were still frowns and glances at each other in the audience, hoping to see some sense of it all. As beautifully done as the piece was, it was not usual to be treated to it twice in the same program... with the same performer.

As she left the stage, the MC stopped her and left the two girls staring at each other in the wings. "Friends, I ask for your attention for a few remarks before the next number, which is a deviation from the schedule. We have just witnessed the coincidence of the century. I am now going to treat you to the un-rehearsed piano duet by two 14 year old girls who, I am of the opinion, have never met. We are fortunate to have two pianos on stage for another rendition, and we will now take advantage of that fact.

"Girls, step forward and seat yourselves at one of the pianos, and on my direction, you will begin your pieces together."

The Master's heart was beating even harder than that of the girls, as this could be either a high point of his life, or collapse in a dismal failure. His whole future now rested, so to speak, on the shoulders of two children.

The girls, however, were troopers. Licking their lips and squaring their shoulders, they settled their dresses on the benches and turned their eyes onto the man with the baton. Just as they had been trained to do.

Twenty fingers took over and performed... just as they had been trained to do.

At the close of the rendition, as the last sounds died away, the applause became a roar, with everyone standing. Three solid minutes of clapping and a few appreciative whistles. The acclaim seemed to go on forever. And forever.

That three minute space of time essentially laid the pattern of the lives of four young people. Possibly five, including Laverne. There were still lessons to learn, and some years of age to live through, but when Sussana's 14-year-old eyes settled on the handsome face of Barney, she sighed in appreciation of one of God's better creations.

It seemed obvious to the world, and to both sets of parents, that these two girls were twins, or at least very close relatives, though the Prentiss' were painfully concerned. After a lot of meditation on the subject, Carl explained the result of his reasoning.

"Look at it this way, Nora, my love. If she had been placed in a basket and set on our doorsteps, we would'a naturally had first claim on 'er. It just happened that her bassinette didn't slide far enough."

Nora nodded. Sounded good to her.

It was when the fellows were past 21 that the four were reunited permanently as a musical quartette that would be available to churches and other assemblies for both voice and musical renditions. There was even a place for Laverne and her new husband in the matters of booking, transportation and care of costumes.

Requests came from as far as Fayetteville and Bentonville, and even Fort Smith and Little Rock. Christopher, the violinist, was also a composer, and new songs appeared with regularity. Money appeared as well.

The double wedding was held in the country church where the Prentiss' attended, a stone building called Church on the Rock. An event of the year… maybe longer.

The Prentiss parents were no dummies. Carl had an enormous house set upon his ample lands, knowing that between engagements, the four would need a place to stay… and also there would eventually be children.

There were.

## YEAR 1917: WAR IN EUROPE

Anyone who read the papers would have been a total fool if they had been surprised when war broke out in Europe. When rich folks with nothing to do, started meddling in matters that didn't pertain to them, something was going to happen, and it would affect a lot of other people.

A very 'important' young fellow was killed way over in one of the European countries, and someone else used it as an excuse to be angry, and maybe use the crises to acquire more land for their own country. Unbelievable, actually, how it happened, but it did happen just that way.

Also, anyone who read the papers, knew that eventually America was going to be pulled into it like dishwater being sucked down the drain, carrying everything along with it. And Quince Darby, barely past eighteen, read the papers. Always had, ever since being introduced to them by the mountain schoolmaster.

The young man knew he would do his part, just as he had in his adopted family and in his city of Wishbone Hollow. He wasn't exactly sure what he could do, but he was young, strong and intelligent, and could 'shoot the eyelashes off a frog at thirty paces' so to speak. Not that he had ever been called on to prove it.

Sure enough, along with the preparations and the anticipation of America to enter the war, he read that England was already in the war, whether they wanted it or not. They had seemingly held back on preparations, hoping it wouldn't happen, but what happened was that they were forced into the war without enough preparation to adequately defend themselves, both in weapons and in humans.

His brain told him he could sit back and wait, and it would take a while for the world to find him on the backside of a mountain in the middle of a small state in the south. They'd get to him eventually, and then he'd go anyway.

So, he stepped forward to offer his services for whatever that meant. Men were needed. If not him... then who...?"

He made the trip to Eureka Springs and was bundled onto the Firefly locomotive and sent on to Bentonville. The locomotive had already taken several more and had picked up a contract to furnish wool blankets to the Red Cross... blankets that would eventual warm the young men who were lined up in the recruiting office. Crates would be packed aboard in southern Arkansas and sent up to Little Rock, later to be picked up by the Firefly, transferred to the Screaming Eagle and on to St Louis.

At Bentonville, Quince was prodded and poked, tested and questioned, and consequently determined to be A1. Of course. He'd have had it no other way. He was then put in the package of those accepted, sent home and told to 'be ready'. He felt he was already

'ready', but he did as instructed. Two and a half months later, he was called up.

He would be sent to England on a supply ship along with the wool blankets and a lot of cans of food. There was even milk put in a tiny can so it wouldn't spoil. What would they think of next? Quince was not afraid… though later he thought maybe he should have been.

England was a buzz of excitement and a fair amount of fear. They were in a fever to get done some things that they should have already gotten done, knowing what was looming just across the channel, a scarce 20 miles away. There were already a few potholes in the brick streets of England made from explosives dropped from the dirigibles that floated overhead like so many mammoth balloons.

Quince Darby was poked and prodded again, not to determine if he was acceptable, but to determine the best use of his talents. This person had answered his test questions in such a way that was obvious in an important area. His tests were flagged for further review. He had great ability with the language… surprisingly great… and that was sure to be of value.

He had written his answers concisely and plainly. Wouldn't he be a marvel with messages to be sent to the battle lines… or maybe translating and condensing incoming messages to be forwarded to those making decisions? Sure to be!

Then, of course, there was the fledgling code room where messages and scraps of messages were studied to determine whether they might be false… meant to throw the English off track… or could they be pieced together with information from here, there and yonder so that together they made sense? Which? Much like a jigsaw puzzle with several pieces gone, and the picture must be completed without them.

The enemy Nazi were obviously using one word to mean another, and it must be determined when this was done, and how. This took a mind with the ability to look at words from the inside out, and from backward to frontward. Not only that, the enemy was becoming more and more sophisticated, and the puzzles were becoming more difficult to solve. Tests indicated this young man would be one of the best.

But then, this young man could shoot the weapons with the best, and he was badly needed on the line, certainly as an officer. True, success in the field would be a small triumph, needed as it was. But should he be put there with all its risks, when success in the code room could save many more lives?

Which?

When passed through the first station, his records were annotated, "keep this one in England. He's like gold." So, where would their gold coin be best spent? After much thought, he was put in the code room.

The code room contained such a valuable amount of hand-picked intelligence and protected so many minds so badly needed, that it had been dug underground and covered over with impenetrable layers of protection.

The decision makers thought they had made this decision, but had they…? This young man had been picked off a tree by a special person with a dedication and guided with care by a Power much greater than the English Officials.

It was finally with nods of satisfaction that the decision makers sealed his fate.

This young man, in perfect health, was accustomed to the wooded mountains, the rushing streams, the sunrise and sunset and the view of mountains on top of mountains on top of mountains. He was used to living outside in the elements and breathing the freshness of air off Blue Lake and the waters of Kings River. He had grown up with space.

Disregarding all this, he was consigned to the underground, even deeper than a mole would ever go in his search for tree roots. He was enclosed with thick masonry on four sides, and the very air he breathed would be forced down from the land above that was under attack.

He came face to face with the enemy, of course, but the enemy was piles and heaps of papers… not men with guns. The enemy was millions and millions of words, and many of them were in an unfamiliar language. New words to learn. A whole new language to memorize.

Among the coded messages, there were the supplies to be divided and somehow shipped to where they were the most needed, regardless of the difficulty of getting them there. Someone had to make these decisions. Someone had to see that they were carried out. The persons with th guns need to be cared for.

Food, ammo and fresh troops. It all started here. Lt. Quince Darby squared his shoulders and breathed deeply. This was his job and he would do it.

He was assigned a desk that faced a blank wall of dull and chipped masonry and was given a booklet of the known codes and told that it was already obsolete, but it was what they had until they got something better.

He was told that there were those who were working on mechanical devices that would make the job quicker and easier. Supposedly. Hopefully.

He nodded silently and looked at the solid gray walls and at the narrow bed. Totally adequate. No more… no less. Small chest and a chair and a clothes rack extending from the wall. On the bedside chest was a clock with very loud ticks.He could manage.

He was taken back to the desk and the messages, papers and scraps of notes. His guide looked at him with sympathy. "Sir, I was told to say you could just go through papers today… maybe get acquainted with them…?"

Quince nodded and said, "Thank you."Just as he had been trained to do by the old man.

## LANORE GILSTRAP, BENTONVILLE

Lanore had boarded the Firefly headed south from Eureka Springs and looked around. Disappointment clouded her face, though she was just a tadd embarrassed about it. Why should she expect a roomy car just for her? It was full cars that kept the locomotive running.

She scanned the car for a seat, and it seemed totally full. But no, there was a hand waving in her direction. She made her way toward it, holding to the grips along the aisle.

A young man stood and motioned her toward the cushioned seat by the window. Settling in place, she smiled her thanks, taking in the sight of him in a glance. Almost twenty, and she had seen a lot of young men but, well… one would have thought she would be married by now, as she was considered such a good 'catch', whatever that was.

Her first thought was that any young man was out for what a friendship with her would bring him, rather than how much he loved her. Grandmother had warned her of the problem… as had her parents and others.

This young man slid in beside her, folding his long legs in a manner intending them to be out of the way. It wasn't easy.

She glanced from the corner of her eye. Worn pants, clean. Work boots, somewhat worn. Hands rather rugged, knuckle skinned but healing. Nails clean. At that point she turned her attention to the view outside the window.

She rather liked to ride the train, and for the last half a dozen years had rode alone to visit Grandmother in Eureka Springs. So, this time she'd visited for a week and was now headed home.

She rather liked the power in the wheels rather than the clip-clop of the carriage horses. She liked the well-shaped seats, and she liked noticing the fellow passengers, but that was not likely if this young man was going all the way to Bentonville. Most likely he was. There were no scheduled stops on the way.

He spoke. "Ma'am… I mean Miss? Sorry to be crowdin' against you. There just ain't much room in these seats."

"Oh, you aren't crowdin' me. I have plenty'a room."

A few houses and businesses passed the window, and the Firefly steamed its way out into the plowed fields and tree-covered hills.

"I don't get to ride very much," he confided. "Takes away time I need to keep busy. This trip is necessary, though, and it'll maybe give me more time. Either that, or maybe it'll let me get more done."

Her curiosity was instant. "What do you do when you work?"

"I cut down trees. I have a chunk of land out by a lake, and it grows huge trees, good for sawin' into boards. Only I got no saw to do it with."

"What are you usin' now?"

"Mainly a choppin' ax and it brings the tree down, and it'd make a log cabin, but not lumber boards. It's just me out there workin' and I don't get enough done. I think I'm fixin' to change that."

Lanore smiled inwardly. Fellows didn't usually talk with her this way. *He actually seems to think I know what he's talking about. And he hasn't once commented on how 'beautiful' I am.* Intrigued, she responded.

"How'll you do that?" she asked.

He smiled her way, and his face crinkled in a friendly way. "Saw an advertisement sometime back. Company over in Bentonville that carries all kinds'a workin' machines. I was told that if they didn't have it they could get it."

"What is it, another kind of saw?"

"Sorta of. It's more of a machine that can be put together that can saw all the way through to the end of the tree trunk in just a few minutes. Has a motor that runs on Kerosene. Gonna be hard to get it down to my place, but maybe it'll come in pieces."

"Where is your place?"

"Ever heard'a Blue Lake? No, well it's up off Ridge Road outta Eureka. From up top of a hill the road goes down, pretty much straight down, till it gets to the lake. My land borders up against the lake. Lotta good fish in there, right handy to catch a body's lunch."

"Hmm, well, that sounds interesting. Does your family live with you?"

"Naw. just me. 'Course there's the muleskinner."

"Skinner?"

"Uh, well, some folks call 'em a muleteer. So far I've just sold logs for log houses, but that's slow and heavy. I think that new saw is the answer to bein' faster. Still need the muleskinner, though, 'cause everything has to be hauled up the hill, no matter what it is."

"Big hill?"

"Really big hill. About the size of that one out there," and he jerked an elbow toward the window.

Lanore looked. It really was a big hill. She contemplated life beside a lake at the foot of a hill like that. Sure to have a bit of charm, once one got used to it.

"Say, my name's Woodrow Turner. They call me Woody, less'n they're mad at me."

"Pleased to meet you, Woody. I'm Lanore." She made a habit of never mentioning her last name. It always seemed to change the situation, and she was enjoying this conversation.

A few hills, mountains and rivers later, Woody confided. "Sure hope I can find that place. Don't get around in Bentonville too much. Kills two whole days that I could'a been workin'. I usually have good luck with folks tellin' me where to go."

Lanore, with a streak of bravery, responded, "I live there so I know it rather well. What's the place you're lookin' for?"

"It's a place called Gilstrap Equipment and Tool Company."

Lanore startled at the sound of her family name, but settled quickly, admitting, "I know where it is. It's actually on the way to my house. I can show you."

"I'd be much obliged, Miss Lanore, if it wouldn't be too much trouble. That'd save me some time, and likely I could get the night train back."

The Firefly chuffed into the depot, hissing steam. One thing about that lumberjack, she'd noticed, he had manners, and assisted her though she didn't really need it. She had a carriage waiting and insisted he ride with her.

His first thought was how much did this saw rig cost, and then he divided it by the sale price of the logs minus the salary of Shorty, the stocky, bearded driver who ruled over the mules.

His second thought was how much fun it was riding beside this beautiful lady who had actually seemed interested in his conversation. Being a lumber jack really thinned out the girls who asked questions like they actually wanted answers.

When they reached Gilstrap Equipment and Tools, she allowed him to help her down and led him into the large showroom and then continued back to the office. The man behind the desk looked up and smiled.

Woody began to wonder what was going on. Some kind of a trap? Then she said, "Pa, I met this here fellow on the train, and he happened to be interested in some kind of a saw for cuttin' up trees. His name is Woodrow Turner, and I brought 'im on in. Niles is waitin' outside, so I'll leave him to you. Bye, Woody. It was a fun trip." And she was gone.

Poor Woody was totally wordless, but 'Pa' took over. "Woodrow, is it? Let's look at some pictures and get this thing narrowed down."

Yes, they could order it in parts and have it shipped to him. It came with directions… easy to put together, they promised.

The prices were a bit staggering, but he saw exactly what he intended to have in a year or so. Right now he'd have to get along with a much lighter version that did the same thing, only it would not last as long. But it was one he could afford… almost. Buying the adjoining 60 acres had set him back a trifle, but the fish in the lake were a big help.Couldn't go hungry with them flopping around and jumping outta the water. Also a turtle or two and a few rabbits. Free food all around him.

His twelve by twelve log cabin didn't hold much but the stove, bed and a bench.Pa lived up top of the hill, and Woody's better clothes were still there, along with a place to stay to get his breath when things became too much. It was going to take the better part of a year to actually be able to look over the heap of duties.

Yes, they could order it in parts, and they did. It came with directions… easy to put together… and it was. Pa'd helped.Folks along the ridge were beginning to want dimension lumber rather than logs. Made the buildings they built go up a lot faster, and it made straight walls some ladies preferred. Who cared if it wasn't as warm in the winter and didn't last for a hundred years like the logs?

When a body was in business, they had to have what folks wanted to buy and he had to manage a little more time to make it available. For one thing, he needed to work out another trip to Bentonville. That young lady was really messing up his dreams, and thoughts of her were arguing with his goal of having money for that piece of land that bumped up against his land on the west.

Good trees over there, and it'd pay for itself in a couple of years, if he stayed on the job and worked hard. The thing was, where would Miss Lanore be in two years, and right now he had no idea if he even had a chance… her Pa and his money and all. Reason told him that would be a major obstacle.

Probably an obstacle higher than he could manage.

## NEW NAME AND ADDRESS

While in Bentonville, Bertrand Gilstrap kept saying, "But you only saw him on a five hour train ride. Lumberjack living in a cabin on his lake? What are you think of, anyway?"

Didn't matter. Lanore was smitten, and what would she do if Woody did not follow up on the introduction? The way he talked to her... just like she was anybody else. Quite disarming.

Waiting for his move wasn't easy. The decorum of society, however, demanded it. There were certain things that well-bred ladies did not do.

Woody managed a trip back practically within hours, and gave her an address. She could send her mail to his Pa's house, Joe Turner, Burnt Tree Junction. Pa lived just up on the ridge and he'd check in regularly for her letters.

It had not been an easy courtship, but it proceeded. In the matter of a year and a half, Lanore was Ms. Turner and living in a log cabin not quite as large as her parents' parlor.

To say she was amazed at the work it took just to exist would have been to put it mildly, but there was never a minute that she thought she should have done differently.

It the last weeks of her first pregnancy, father-in-law Joe appeared with an armful of gray/bown fur... having eyes, nose and a pink tongue. It also had long, leathery ears made of velvet. The blackish-brown skin stood in rolls on her back and in furrows over her eyes.

Perfect gift for the little boy she would have, but from the first moment, the little creature knew he belonged to Lanore, and she knew it. The lonely bride giggled with pleasure and lifted the ears, one in each hand. "I know your name, little girl. You will be called Butterfly." And she was.

Dogs would come and go, but Butterfly was the constant companion and guard for her new mistress. Once acquainted with dogs, some folks would spot right off that its Ma would be a thoroughbred Blood Hound, but the bone structure and overall shape had been tempered by a visiting salesman, most likely being the alpha male of a local wolf pack.

As an anniversary present for her first year of marriage, little Clive was born, bringing with him the tall and stocky build of his Gilstrap grandfather. Other sons would appear with amazing regularity.

## MICHAEL ALLEN MILLER, SARGAENT US ARMY

Michael, the little fellow who began his life after being squashed between his parents during a wild fire battle thrived as he had been meant to do. His Ma had been stationed on the roof of Chestnut Cottage to kill sparks with a splash of water, and it was while there, labor had started. Michael's Pa assisted his Ma and himself down the ladder.

That had been his first tight squeeze, squashed between the bodies of his parents while they tended to an emergency, but there had been many more. Husky, broad shouldered and muscular, he had more than his share of boyhood scrapes, but his wit had brought him through them, mostly unscathed.

Then the war started.

And now he had turned eighteen and stood proudly in line to offer his services to his government. Pa, who operated the fledgling fire department in Eureka Springs would just have to get along without his able assistance. Tucked within his resume were two lives rescued from third floors, and many hours manning the pumps that sprayed water on the flames, and countless, exhausting nights that had been spent beating out forest fires.

All of this had built layers of muscles onto his strong frame. This fact was duly noted in his first examination and so remarked on his records. Those in charge of making these decisions were on the lookout for young men like Michael, as there was a lot of Europe to be covered by young men, themselves weighed down heavily with weapons and ammo.

Being almost a half a head taller than average, was also noted. They'd found that taller leaders were more readily looked up to, especially in the heat of danger. So Pfc Miller was promoted to acting Corporal before he left the shores of America as he also had an education and could write and converse in good sentences. Not every strong young man from middle America had been so favored.

So, when Young Michael crossed the international date line on the American ship, Revenge, he turned 19 years of age. Also, this month, the Royal Flying Corp of England was assigned to the bombardment of northern France, in the region of Rouen, on the Seine, and Toulouse.

Scarce manpower able to manage the hastily-built, light aircraft and the absolute necessity of strategic bombing, meant nothing was to be wasted. Especially manpower. And most specifically, American manpower. For that reason, targets must be accurately marked to be seen from the skies.

Additionally, the most favorable time for the attacks was dusk, when vision from the ground up was impaired, and when there was still time for the fragile aircraft to return to England as soon as possible. If, indeed, the aircraft was still successfully unharmed and moving through the air.

One very dangerous way for this to happen was for the ground support to somehow get themselves to the target with flares, get them lit and placed, and still get themselves to safety out of reach of the bombs. Physical strength, intelligence, and the ability to act under pressure were the goal when selection these important 'point' persons. Also, important was the demand for leadership of the special small, active squads.

Somehow, Sgt. Miller found himself in charge of a crew of five before he was 21, and his four crew members were even younger than he. Instead of anno, they were loaded with flares that were light weight, but took dry matches to ignite. That made the new unstable, strike-anywhere match the important trigger of the operation.

The 41th Royal Flying Corps was assigned to target an ammunition factory that had been taken over by the Nazi forces and must be destroyed before they came into full operation of ammo. The factory was served by a railway of double lines of rails and locomotive transports. These targets must be highlighted with pinpoint precision, so the flares would be visible when the bombers flew over, and the lighting must be timed to allow the men reach safety.

In this particular instance, the safety for the men was to be the waters of the Seine River. With Sgt. Miller were Pvts. Carmichael, Hammond and Sanders, who were Americans, and Bowman and Simmons from England.

They infiltrated carefully and individually. A group of five together would attract too much attention. Roughly drawn maps were of little use but were all they had. It was decided that, on signal, three would meet at the factory and two the railways.

Michael was assigned the railways with orders to plant the flares about 100 yards apart and wait until the signal, which was to be 6 of the light weight SA5 aircraft high overhead. Two bombs would be dropped from such a height that they would burst in the air. That was meant to signal the ground crew to be ready as the squadron of 300 planes was in route.

It was hoped that the sound of the aircraft motors would cause the German guards to look up and aim their weapons to the sky, giving the ground crew time to light the flares.

Hearts pounded, and blood ran cold as the young Americans at the factory tried to swallow their fears. They were furthest from the safety of the river but must somehow reach it before the blast from above.

Crouched in hiding, they waited, finally hearing the 'bumble bee' buzz of the advance aircraft, and they crawled forward, knees and elbows raw against the sharp gravel. A pattern of four flares was set on one side, and Carmichael and Sanders were left with matches. The sergeant and Hammonds crawled forward in the gathering darkness.

A shrill whistle from Sgt Miller would be the signal to light the flares and flee. Michael Miller, the master of tight spots, how squatted on his haunches, matches in hand. Their meager shelter was an oil tank, and the ground was covered with spillage. Would the match flame ignite the fumes from the ground before the wicks were lighted…? Maybe, but somehow it had to be done.

And now there came the six forward aircraft. Breathlessly the ground crew waited for the bombs bursting in the air, and there they were. The factory was suddenly a beehive of activity and Michael had a mental flash of a wasp nest being kicked by several 12-year-old boys. The collected count of the stings was well over twenty. What faced him now was worse than wasp stings.

A drone… a flash and a volley of shots from the ground, then the burst of bombs in the air. Michael struck the match to light the six flares. On the fifth flare a burst of flame from the fumes of the spillage surrounded them like the burning houses he knew so well. Falling to the ground and rolling, he caught the sleeve of Pvt. Hammond and felt the flame. The 'flash over' was quickly gone and the oil-soaked ground caught fire. The flames crawled outward.

The force of the flash-over had knocked the private backward onto the gravel, and the leg of his uniform caught fire. Michael knew they could not run. With his bare hand he scooped the flame toward Hammond's boot before the fire had a solid hold onto the fabric.

He hoisted the private on his own back and continued crawling over the gravel. By the time they reached the rail tracks, the private had gained his senses and his feet, and the pair, stooping as low as possible and still managing to run, they dashed through the black darkness to the meeting point.

Rocks and shrubs that had been unnoticed, made themselves known in the path. Then the whistle came from the water, and the low call, "Here, Sarge".

The two teenage soldiers plunged into the shallow edge of the water with profound relief. The calf of Pvt. Hammond's leg and both of the Sarge's hands were burned, and the cold water felt good. For an instant.

Then came the 300 aircraft squadron. The flares were lit, but the light planes were so fragile it was hard to pinpoint a target, allow for the wind, and let it go. Misses happened, and out of 300 bombs, there was bound to be one or two mishaps.

Ground fire erupted, and the air was alive with flashes, lighting the water where they stood. The fizz as fire hit water was deafening and terrifying.

They ducked under water as long as they could, but one had to breathe, and that was when a small aircraft above them began to spiral toward the water, one wing in flames. The non-burning wing hit the water first, momentum spinning the flaming wreckage over the water surface.

A pilot had to be in the plane, and only the wing was afire. The Sarge called to the closest person, "Bowman, go for the plane." The private did, with the Sarge close behind. With raw palms he held to the sinking wreckage, as Bowman pushed himself into the cockpit head first.

"Got 'im, Sarge. Pull me back out."

The pilot was freed, and held above water as the last of the plane disappeared. The icy river water swirled and pulled at their soaked uniforms.Pvt. Bowman had grown up on a fishing vessel and knew what to do in water, so between them the pilot was taken to the shallows.

At that moment, the flame on the oil–soaked ground reached the oil tank, and it exploded, sending arrows of burning oil in every direction.

"DUCK UNDER!" sarge commanded, grabbing the pilot's chest with his left arm and holding his nose with the other. Grabbing a breath himself, he went down into the water. It was over in minutes as the burning streams of oil reached the water and were carried away with the current.

Michael felt the struggle of the pilot who was 'coming to'. Such a relief! The two men might have risked their lives rescuing a dead man, but this one was alive!

In relative safety, they pulled themselves to the shore and worked their way north. The pilot managing to stand, and walk between Carmichael and Sanders. "Uh… wh…? Where at am I?"

The four Americans cheered softly. That dialect could only have come from their country. "Where ya from, flyboy?"

"Alabama. You fellows American?"

"Some of us. Sarge is from Arkansas, and three of us from Mississippi. Two are limeys."

It was two weeks before Sgt. Miller was permitted to go on another patrol, and then it was only with padded gloves. Leaders like Sgt. Miller were too valuable to be kept out of action. That mission had been only the first of his close calls and tight escapes.

The angel who had been present at the forest fire at the Chestnut Cottage, on Ridge Road, had known, of course, that Michael, who was named after the warrior angel, would see more and tighter places than the one between his parents on the rescuing ladder.

And over the English Channel the bombproof, underground code room was busy, day and night. The problem solvers became so engaged in their work they had trouble pulling away to get needed sleep.

Lt. Quince Darby was one of those. The hardest part of his job, it seemed, was working underground. One night after he had been there a week, he became semi-awake, and the reflected light from the open door of his room lit up the solid dark walls and the flat, low ceiling.

Not exactly sure where he was, it seemed that the ceiling was becoming lower and lower, and the dull walls closing in. For a mountain man to be squeezed to death by masonry walls, it was horrible enough to drive him insane. He tried to scream at the walls to get back but he could not hear his voice.

Finally, he gave in to the inevitable and shut his eyes waiting for his certain demise. Someone came through the door. He tried to warn the other fellow but still could hear nothing, though he seemed to be screaming at the top of his lungs. The fellow put his hands on Quince's chest and shook him.

"Wake up, man. You're havin' a dream."

When he came to his senses, he tried to apologize. The rescuer would hear none of it.

"Forget it, man. Happens to all of us, and I figured it'd happen to you sooner or later. The thing to do now is go down the hall and get a drink of water, and maybe somethin' to eat."

Lt. Darby tried to thank the co-worker, but was waved off. "Think nothin' of it. This here ain't human, workin' down here like fishworms. But we have to do it. Can't be expected to be in our senses all the time."

That had been the last of the nightmares, but the enclosure was tormenting, nevertheless. The morning after the nightmare, he actually climbed the stairs to daylight and looked around, reassuring himself that the ceiling really couldn't come down in his face, and that there really was a world above him.

Life had begun scary, as it had been told to him that he was picked off a tree limb in a cradle board… and that saved his life. He'd survived. So here was another scary thing. Get used to it, man!

He'd only spent three days in Chestnut Cottage, but what a life he had been given! Someday he would be through with this hell on earth, and he'd be back there hunting the woodland surrounding Burnt Tree Junction, and fishing in Blue Lake.

Sgt. Michael Miller was the first of the pair to come home. Having no other option, he wore his 'dress' uniform with a rainbow of medals across the front. He was advised that he must not remove them, as that would desecrate the missions he had so skillfully completed. So he wore them all the way back to Ridge Road.

When it had been noted that Sgt. Miller had a record of returning from precarious operations all in one piece and also bringing his crew back with him, he went on one mission after another, following the heat of the battle as it proceeded northward.

There were dams to blow up to eliminate a power supply. Railways to blow apart. Surveillance here and there, along with tossing a few of the new little things called grenades into selected buildings. One after the other. Destruction became his goal, and the resulting debris was right there before him. Facing him. People hungry and homeless. Little children torn apart and left behind when parents fled.

Just sigh and move on. Nothing could be done, and the living must be protected.

On his journey homeward, Michael stood on the deck of the ship and gazed at the expanse of water. Turned his mind off. Refused to think. And finally he was in his home town. Wishbone gave him a hero's welcome, and congratulated him while he wished he could hide.

At home, he rolled his uniform into a ball and crammed it into the back of a shelf. His mom, Melissa, of the fat ankles and water buckets, found it and carefully removed it. Taking it outside, she poured on a can of kerosene and with her cleaning brush removed every speck of foreign grime, perspiration and shipboard odor. She cleaned around every medal and tightened two loose buttons.

When the smell of the cleaning fluid had been carried away on the wind, she folded the uniform into a box with the small bags of lavender, rosemary, oregano and sage as protection from insects. She pushed the lid down tightly and sealed it with loop after loop of heavy cord.

With a final sigh, knowing it was protected now from any varmint known to attach wool or cotton, she relegated it to the upper region of the attack. Slipped into a burlap sack, it was suspended from a high rafter. She turned with one last action and pushed her tongue out to its limits and pronounced, "So there!"

Melissa would much rather have set fire to the kerosene soaked garment in a celebratory bonfire, but its destruction was not hers to commit. There would be others... Michael's future son, perhaps... and they must be made aware of the cost of their freedom.

Michael walked the streets of Wishbone looking at every house. No burned out hulls or blown out walls. All was well. Then he went to McCafferty's and sat in an obscure corner and studied the customers.

Unaware, they were, of what had been aborted... disaster being drowned in the blood of the neighbors' sons. Here there were no tiny planes that spiraled out of the sky streaking flames, or children herded into hidden country locations to save their lives.

He rejoiced in the sight of tots in the arms of their moms, chortling with glee at being alive.

The boy with the nickel and his look of total expectation that a nickel thrust at the clerk would produce a pair of sandwiches... certain to. One for himself and the other for his little sister. Confidence, not dulled by destruction.

Michael nodded. It would certainly be that way forever... except there had been no peace treaty after the war he had just left. What in the world was an Armistice, anyway...? Wasn't it just a promise to ceasefire and let the enemy rebuild, so he could attack again?

The aroma wafting from the grill... bacon, sausage... or the bubbling steam from the chile caldron reminded him of the time he and the private with him were so hungry, they chased down a loose chicken, old and tough. No matter.

They'd split it with their knives and divided it, including the fat and the bloody liver. The liver went down first, raw. No fire could be permitted while on surveillance. Soon nothing was left but feathers and gnawed bones, and they were pathetically and thankfully glad to have caught the fowl. It sustained them for the next two day.

And he sat there, alone, the customers sensing somehow that he must be left alone for a while and they averted their glances.

His face was a mask of puzzlement, discouragment and dogged determination.

And eventually Lt Quince Darby was released. It seemed there was a lot of filing of documents be done, and the preservation of methods that had been successful… should they ever be needed. Needed… what for? Had the war not been won? What was that thing called an Armistice? Why was it not a signed Peace Treaty?

He had spent the whole of the voyage home strolling on the deck. In all weather, even reveling in a rainstorm, the wind cracking the canvas overhead like the explosion of bombs he had never heard. He could look up and around, and nothing blocked his view but the raindrops.

For now he was going back to Burnt Tree Junction.

He, being not a resident of Wishbone, came home unheralded except by family… his adopted brothers and sister. He paid his dues as he accepted their congratulations over his many medals, and then scrounged up his old fishing pole. With bed roll and matches, along with his rifle, he headed four Blue Lake.

Turner Sawmill owned about half of the lake shore and actively advertised for visitors… hunters and fishermen. Either side of the lake was good for hunting, and a swinging bridge with cable handholds had been strung across the neck of the hourglass-shaped lake.

The north side was cool until midday, because of the mountain under Ridge Road. The south side had afternoon and evening shade. The southside would be shared by the headstones of the departed, many with no name. No matter. The remains were not the persons. They were not there, anyway, having gone on to their reward. Still, there was a certain comfort in the shallow, weathered mounds and the slanting stones.

Then, behind the cemetery, the mountain arose with alarming suddenness. Shrubs and vines clinging to the stone ledges by their toenails, so to speak. Flat places here and there sporting massive hickory trees, furnishing a favorite nut for making candy.

An eagle family had called it home for as long as Quince could remember. Gone were the four walls closing in on him, and the notes of the competing birdsongs arose to a pleasant roar within his troubled head. An exciting and wonderful roar!

Quince made his camp by an overhanging rock bluff… not really a cave. He was tired of walls. He made a circle of stones for his fire, and lived on fish, rabbits and a raccoon or two. There were hickory nuts, and if it had been spring, there would have been berries. He gathered the drying leaves of the blackberry plant for tea, baited his hook and lay back on the dry grass.

Occasionally he could catch a sound of humans… maybe buzz of the sawmill across the lake as it ripped through an oak tree trunk. Someday, he'd see them about some lumbar for a house, but not any time soon.

He thought and thought of the past year, and then actively proceeded to purge the sights and thoughts forever from his mind. They would be replaced with sun, wind, rain and birdsongs. The processed food from cans and paper wrappers would be only a memory as he feasted on the wildlife… fur-bearing, scale covered or protected by a shell.

A tickle across his arm turned to out to be a woolybear caterpillar… sometimes thought to be able to predict the temperature of the coming winter. Quince had no wish to know the weather, so he flicked the creature into the air with a forefinger against his thumb.

The insect hit the surface of Blue Lake and was instantly snapped up by a channel catfish, measuring at least 15 inches. Immediately, Quince felt the jerk on his line.

The signal. His own lunch would soon be served, and what would it be… ? Maybe a bluegill, or most likely a mud cat, from the weight on the line.

Hung on a green hickory spit over the coals, the channel cat issued an aroma that could almost be tasted. The fish was most likely the one that had snapped up the woolybear, but the man had only sliced a fillet from each side and tossed the rest back in the water. Food for something else.

He knew he would again be human, sometimes, but it would take a while and he was so, so willing to wait until that happened.

## TURNER'S SAWMILL

Lanore Gilstrap Turner spent a lonely year, in spite of the help of the bloodhound pup, Butterfly.

Things changed with the birth of Clive, and everything being so new, she had now time for loneliness. Woody built on a room that would be the temporary nursery, and he hired a pair of woodcutters, as the new saw, however small, speeded the production of dimension lumber, and the demand was almost too great to fill.

Men were coming back from the war and needed homes.

He sorely needed someone who could make estimates for customers, as he, himself, must be in at least four places at once.

Following Clive a year later was Simon. Where Clive was stocky build, Simon was long and drawn out like his father. Next came Jackson, and he was like neither, but truly himself. By now, Lanore had, not a house, but more like a series of connected cabins, each hastily built onto to meet an immediate need. Woody could not afford to let his builders make paying customers wait so it was his wife that 'made do'.

It was rather like the old saying, 'The shoemaker's children go barefoot.'.

As the sons reached school age, they must be hauled up to Ridge Road to the schoolhouse, and at age seven, Clive was on the reins of the cart, and the mule had no doubt as to who was boss.

After Jackson came Mark and Edward. Clive was through his four years, which was as high as the school went at that time. Edward was born, and two years later came Carl.

Woody was burning with ambition to provide not only food and clothing, but a life-long occupation for his sons. That meant he must be prepared to purchase any nearby tract of land that became available before it was sold to another. So profits were horded for this purpose.

His land ownership climbed up the hill and leaped over to the evening shade side of the lake. Not much flat land there, but the trees clinging to the mountainside were very valuable. Not only that, they could be sawed down and allowed to roll to the lake, and then floated across.

Bertrand came along in time to be animal tender, sorely needed by now as the distance of the job sites became more and more lengthy.

Next born was Joseph, and in later years it was speculated on how they would ever have made it without Joseph, son number eight. He seemed born with the mechanical instinct that kept the multiple buzz-saws running.

After nineteen years of marriage, Lanore's house was still the hodge-podge of quickly added-on sheds but she coped. There was no time to do otherwise.

The 'business' came first. The young men had all sorted out a position suited to their abilities and quickly fitted themselves into it.

Clive was the mountain man who spent time among the trees, marking which would be felled next. He maintained the new growth and, armed with a sharp hatchet, he trimmed sprouts that would sap strength from the main trunks of young trees, allowing them to grow tall.

Simon, quick with his figures, could determine almost to the nail what it would take to produce a house from the sketchy drawings he was shown. He could estimate the hours involved if the Turners were to be the builders. He was often gone, for this reason, as he must check the location to accurately determine the cost labor bringing the lumber.

Jackson and Mark were the 'muleskinners'. They were the ones who loaded the flatbed wagons and double-mule-teamed the lumber up to Ridge Road, and on to the building site, if they were to build it.

Edward would come along, and Mark, who would stay with the job, batching on site and sleeping wherever they could while they began the foundation.

Jackson would return for the next load, bringing Bertrand along to help where he could, and Jackson would stay to help with the structure when possible.

The average house could be framed and boarded up in a week, weather permitting, and usually the homeowner did his own shingling.

Joseph, however, stayed with the buzzing mill, directing the log pushers who positioned the logs before the blade. That freed Papa Woody for the million other things demanding attention.

It was Simon who actually looked at the string of cabins where his mother lived and worked, and knew something had to go. On a scrap of paper he designed a new house, six generous rooms down stairs, and five bedrooms up… each having windows and a door onto the balcony that surrounded the upper story.

It would be constructed totally around the existing mess, which would then be demolished and carried out as soon as each room was completed. Lanore put up with a lot of noise, but otherwise the tight family schedule was essentially uninterrupted.

Sawdust in the beans never killed anyone.

It was about this time that Lanore's grandmother from Eureka Springs was no longer able to live alone, and had come to stay. She turned out to be enough help in some areas to offset the extra effort put forth for her, and she was grateful, though lonely. The few friends she had left were still in the city, and not able to see her for a visit, and letters were very unsatisfactory.

Lanore regretted the loneliness of her grandmother, but could do nothing. She was to remember this period vividly about 30 years later, when the memory of these days would take on a life of their own.

## THE MUSICAL GROUP

The twin girls who had been separated and then rejoined, had moved onto the property of Carl and Nora Prentiss.Large house, made for two families. Worked out beautifully.

The popularity of the quartette increased so rapidly that they were away a lot of the time, but as each of the children were born, there were the grandparents ready to take over. Carl and Nora, the sad childless couple, now had tots and school children all over the place.

Total bliss!

The singers specialized in the old favorite hymns, and a number of new ones composed by Christopher. The former governess, Laverne, and her husband found a house in Wishbone and were available for scheduling and transportation, costume creation and whatever was needed. Churches and civic organizations lined up for an evening of entertainment from this group.

There were occasions of outdoor entertainment in brush arbors, but that meant depending on the weather to cooperate.

Hilda, who had rescued her little sister, had married Horace who "could do anything' and lived across Ridge Road from the Cottage. Laura, the rescued baby sister, turned out to be a pleasure to all around her. It was agreed by everyone that Hilda made a wonderful 'mother', and tucked her brood around her sister, and they all thrived. It was no surprise to the angels. Of course.

Laura at age 10 and 11 became a capable helper, and when not needed for seeing her nieces and nephews off to school, she could be 'borrowed' by the Cottage. After all, a lot of years had passed, and Miss Emma and Betsy were getting on, as it was said.

Laura, at that age, knew everything that was done at the cottage, and her touch with the babies was amazing. She knew how to take care of the garden produce for later, and cooking was her exquisite pleasure, as she considered the kitchen her own personal realm of expertise. At her sister's, the kitchen had to be shared, but Miss Emma was glad to turn the cottage kitchen over to her.

Then she began to have paid employment in other kitchens. The Cottage missed her as they would miss the sunshine, but life went on, and Miss Emma would give her last ounce of strength to keep coping.

Nancy Camden, of the circus in her belly, was grateful her two sons came one at a time. She lived in Berryville where Matthew worked as a builder to keep them eating regularly.

Nancy's friend, Louellen, now married to Arthur, her life-long friend who had 'seen her with muddy drawers', had managed to acquire the carriage horses and the beautiful carriage he desired. He was very much in demand by the elite of Berryville.

Rosemary, Louellen's un-planned-for baby, grew up with the triplets almost as though they were quads… born 2 ½ days apart and nursed by whichever 'mother' could provide the sustenance at that hour. They sailed through ages 15 and 16, and by 17 they had become fairly proficient in the skills a girl should know.

They were, however, together so much, that the young men of Berryville, who would have courted any one of them, found 4 girls about 3 girls too many and did not know how to dis-entangle the foursome.

Therefore their romantic life was somewhat slower than would be expected if they had been 'singles'.

Arthur's son, Rosemary's half-brother, was being primed for the carriage trade like his father, and it was his occasional job to see that his sister and the triplets were safely delivered to social events. Gave him good practice in his driving and certain other skills required of young men coming into 'courting' age. Certain to.

So it was when Arthur's business success enabled him to build a new home with a massive carriage house on the site. The job would take a couple of months, at least, and it seemed only natural that he would give the job to the Turners.

Simon Turner, the job estimator, was first on the site and the first of the young Turner men to be seen by the girls. In addition to being talented and a hard worker, he wasn't bad to look at, and Dorcas saw him first.

And Lanore, ever aware of any situation concerning her family, was prepared for the eventual onslot of brides. Miss Dorcas was invited for a visit, and she was welcome to bring a friend. There would be a cottage prepared for them and transportation.

And Dorcas might have declined an invitation if it had been for herself alone. She'd done practically nothing alone all her life. So when the invitation included friend(s) she accepted, and there began a round of parties, sing-alongs, barbeques of a whole pig and any other means of entertainment available.

So that was how the four inseparable girls would meet a choice of young men, brothers, who were totally and inexorably tied to the valley and their work. There were other young workmen living on site, and many had wives with them.

Absolutely made to order, it was.

This, however, could not be permitted to hamper the busy load of lumber making and house building and much of it was some distance away. But the beautiful shores of Blue Lake provided entertainment until the fellows were back.

Dorcas was first to go, and her early spring wedding with Simon provided gossip material for weeks. By fall, the other three had made their choices and were settled in… each in their own private cottage. Meals were still taken in the 'big house'.

With the arrival of children, the family 'big house' concept became unwieldy, and gradually Lanore's nest began to empty. By Christmas, only Simon and Dorcas (pleasantly rounded) remained. Lanore wisely eased away whenever possible, and took many excursions on the far shore of the lake. A much deserved rest.

It seemed that Dorcas and Lanore could actually be friends, and that would be mostly because of Lanore's willingness to step aside.

Then, with the efficient crew that Woody had, he decided he could also 'step aside' somewhat and spend time with his beloved wife. And he did.

For the next year they made trips to town just for the ride, they spent time on the far shore of Blue lake and attempted to renew old friendships…, which worked out not as satisfactorily as they had hoped.

Gradually Woody, who had gone top speed all his adult life, and who had now accomplished what he thought was his life's dream, was not able to adjust to 'taking it easy'. He lay in bed instead of rising early, and on their excursions, he preferred to nap under a tree and let Lanore go on alone.

It was in the summer of the second year of his 'retirement' that she left him sleeping in the morning, as he seemed to want to do, but when she went to wake him, he was gone. Suddenly and quietly, seeming that when he had finished his assigned duty on earth, he left. With nothing to pull him forward and nothing depending on him, he just refused to continue to live.

Ridge Road residents from Eureka Springs to Berryville were shaken from their emotional foundations. If that could happen to Woody, it could happen to anyone. All available residents attended the funeral, and Lanore put steel in her spine and made it through the day, wishing sincerely that this barbaric procedure would end and let her grieve in solitude.

In a week, Ridge Road was back to business as usual. Woody's sons had already been running the business, and they just continued what they were doing. The daily covered wagon hauled the school age children to the ridge returning later to collect them.

The new families were busy with the act of living, and Lanore was nowhere. It was not as though Woody would appear sometime before midnight, sweaty, shivering, laughing or irritated by some small mishap. Woody was not going to appear again in this life.

Like the southern lady that she was, Lanore squared her slender shoulders and looked forward, hoping for a place to be. There were no places left, and no one needed her.

She still spent a lot of time on the lake shore, mostly wandering aimlessly trying to attach her attention to something useful, if not interesting. Not easy. And she spent a lot of time thinking of her Granny who had spent the last months of her life in the valley.

Lonely for her old life. Sighing, and moving forward day by day.

She made trips to the fenced plot with the headstones, Woody's spot now growing over with new grass.

"Grass widow. That's me,", she realized with a start. It was the signal to 'move on' with whatever her life would be.

She stepped into the small boat and picked up the oars. Pointing the prow toward the mill, she stroked, telling herself that SOMETHING must be done, and she would set about figuring what. But help, when it came, was from a totally unexpected source.

Begging for a duty, she was given the pan of peas to shell. She gratefully seated herself on the porch in the breeze, and began. She had hardly shelled a pint of the needed two quarts when Dorcas joined her.

Settling in a nearby chair, she sipped her cool tea and followed her mother-in-law's gaze across the lake. The craggy peaks rose suddenly about a hundred yards from the lake shore, and the late afternoon shade had crept out to the water's edge. The scene appeared cool and restful.

Dorcas set down her tea glass. "Miss Lanore, I would really like to say something, but I'm afraid you will think I'm overstepping my relationship. Please understand that I say this because I love you and I know you are not happy. I can't bring back Mr. Woody, but I did have an idea. I can't afford the time to take you to visit your friends, but what if your friends could come here?"

Lanore paused and eyed her daughter-in-law with interest.

"If the fellows were to build you a roomy house with a lot of guest rooms, we could advertise for other ladies who are alone to come and live in one of the rooms. We could have 'help' come to take care of everything so all of you ladies could just visit or whatever you wanted to do. Think on how much fun you could all have, talking about your youngens, the past, and just anything you wanted to."

Dorcas hesitated. Had she said too much? ... not enough...? She glanced from the corner of her eye to the face that had suddenly acquired a lot of wrinkles. A silver stream of liquid etched down the wrinkled cheek and she visibly swallowed an uninvited lump in her throat.

Lanore set aside the peas and turned to face the younger woman.

"Dear girl, listen. Move your chair over here so you'll see the same scene I do."

The puzzled Dorcas, with concerned eyes, did as instructed. Surely she had committed the worst of indiscretions. How could she make it go away? How does one un-say what was said with the best of intentions?

But Lanore pointed. "See that grove of pines there on that craig? Those trees have roots that entirely wrap around those rocks. Back behind them is a patch of moss surrounded by violets.

"That yellow strip that appears to be vanilla pudding is a bed of Brown-eyed-Susans. The patch gets bigger each year. Deer come down to water just about every day. I've walked around over there and looked at it for hours from this side of the lake. I often thought the mill should have been over there where the morning sun is bright and warm, and the summer shade is cool in the evening.

"We'll do what you said. We will make a home for lonely, old ladies who have begun to feel they are a worry to their children. There are some who just wither and die because there is no one their age and nothing to do. Life is more than eating and sleeping.

"We'll start with the big house, and plan for at least two wings with rooms as needed. Simon can sketch it out in less than an hour.

Everyone can help. I have never asked for anything, and I have worked for 35 years taking care of everyone. We will start it next week and continue until it's done. I will go over there each day and watch, so I'll be ready to help with decisions."

She looked toward the amazed Dorcas. The beautiful young woman was goggle-eyed and open mouthed. Her eyes plainly said, "Who is this person! This lady who is suddenly giving orders and deciding what's to be done without talking with Clive and Simon.

Lanore smiled and continued, "What's more, my dear. The name of the place will be Evening Shade. This was such a kind thought you had, and your words were just what I needed to put me on the right track again. After supper, we'll get the boys together and let them know."

For something to focus her whirling attention, Dorcas reached for the pan of peas, and her capable fingers began to expertly split the pods and release the tasty green globes. And she listened.

Miss Lanore had opened up like a cloudburst on a spring rain, and described room after room, the kitchen that would provide the meals and the indoor privy for those who would be unable to navigate the path. There would be a handrail down each wall so a cane would not be needed for every indoor step.

The rooms would be arranged for either one or two residents, owing as to whether company or solitude was wanted. There would be a cost, of course, to cover the expenses and the wealth of help that would be needed. This home would be welcome to families up and down the ridge… not because they wanted to get rid of their older family member… but because they wanted the best of care for her, and their own busy lives would not allow for that.

Dorcas tried to follow the stream of words, amazed at their coherence. It was no wonder Simon could look at a sketch and know how it would appear. That's where he had to have gotten the ability. Then she smiled slightly at the thought of how the coming evening would go. The fellows would likely be more stunned than she, and would be rendered speechless.

They were. Not only that, the foundation was marked out the very next day, and no new jobs were taken for the next three weeks.

The central building was completed. The wings with their side rooms would quickly follow.

The newly erecting Evening Shade was the gossip of the ridge, and no one could think of enough words to describe their amazement. Eight different families sent a delegate to see when it would be in operation, and could they be in line for a room.

A pontoon bridge, of sorts, was constructed across the waist of the lake. It consisted of floating platforms 10 feet by 12 feet chained together and meant to rise and fall with the current height of the water. It swayed only slightly and was great fun for the children to run across.

There were boats at each end of the bridge for those less steady on their feet, and the furniture began traveling across the lake. First to be furnished was the west wing consisting of a hall and ten guest rooms, five on each side.

Each guest room had a carpeted floor for warmth and safety, and a minimum of furniture. A bed and a bookcase. A comfortable chair and desk. A wardrobe closet and a dressing table with mirror. Anything else the occupant wanted would be furnished by them.

The dining room consisted of tables, four feet square and four chairs each. The huge 'parlor' had stuffed chairs and a number of small, moveable tables. Later there would be a bookcase and open to receiving any gifts of books that happened.

Lanore moved herself into room five, farthest away from the kitchen. She wanted to make it plain that she was only a resident, not the manager. Rosemary and Sharon moved in as temporary housekeepers and cooks until others could be hired.

The first guest to arrive was old Miss Gertie Carmichael. She was assisted into the boat and rowed across by her grandson and Dorcas' fourteen year old. She sat and smiled sweetly as she looked about her, clearly enjoying the ride.

She chose room one nearest the kitchen and the indoor privy, and had only one question. "Be there a reason for me not to change the color'a the curtains?" Assured, she pointed to the bedspread in her boxes and demanded the grandson spread it on the bed. He did.

Next came Bertha Eldridge followed by Carlotta Infield and Loretta Brooks. By the end of the week, the west wing had 9 rooms filled, and the saws and hammers were noisily working on the east room that would furnish ten more room, that being the goal for the moment.

The fee would be $25.00 for each month, and though that seemed a bit high, nothing was said. It did, however, cover everything, all the way to a 'night person' who could be aroused by the bell cord in each room. A roommate was permitted, to split the fee, but would be charged $10.00 for their food and laundry service.

Most of the ladies who moved in knew each others quite well, but Lanore, not being local, or growing up with the ladies, had a lot of new friends to make. A whole new life, in fact.

It was Catherine, Bertha and Gertie, actually, who thought of the musical group, Burnt Tree Junction's own contribution to the current music world.

"Do a good job, I hear tell." Gertie nodded approval of her own words and took a sip of tea from the no-nonsense cup furnished by the kitchen. Good cups… these! Meant to keep the liquid warm to the last drop.

"That's that I hear. My folks went to Eureka once to listen to 'em. Didn't take me. Said the weather was too bad, but it was mostly 'cause I've had too many birthdays." Bertha sighed with the realization that the musical was just one more thing she missed by being old.

Catharine, (Called Rinnie by her friends), nodded knowingly, and stared out the kitchen window past the billowing white curtains. Allowing that subject had been covered, she commented. "Good tea. Wonder if it was from Dorcas' garden?"

"Likely," came the reply. Her eyes had followed Rinnie's gaze out toward the craggy peaks to the south, and the small patches of vegetation clinging to the protruding layers of volcanic material. "It'd be my guess that a body could have a tea garden right there on one'a them ledges and grow about any tea a body'd want to drink."

Gertie set her cup carefully in the saucer decorated with violets. "My folks always set a store by a tea garden. Got all kinds… they have. Been handin' out 'starts' to anybody who wants one."

Then Bertha, "Then when you tell 'em, say to fix up a few starts and we can go put 'em in the ground past the window." Bertha topped off her tea cup from the pot, with an air of the matter being taken care of. Bertha expected no less, and, for a fact, her suggestions were mostly very good ones.

The conversation went on from subject to subject, but the herb garden and the singers stuck in Sharon's mind. Outdoor musical for the residents and as many of their relatives as could make it. Some afternoon would be right and have the festivities start just as the shade of the mountain began to cover the flatness of the lawn.

She'd talk with Lanore and see if it would be suitable. The tea garden she dismissed, seeming that the ladies were going to take care of that themselves.

So the west wing was filled and half the east room spoken for when the musical family arrived and made their way across the floating bridge. Carrying cases contained the trumpets, and the accordions, mostly called 'squeeze boxes'. They were advertises as 'lap organs' and designed for times when space and transportation were a premium.

The piano keyboard was just made for Joanna and Suzanna, and they set their instruments on the platform provided. Audience benches were already being filled as an early October breeze flowed down the mountain.

Lanore sat with her family, her handkerchief at the ready for the tears she knew would come. Better than she had ever dreamed, and here it stood and would be her home for the rest of her life... among friends who remembered the same things she did. And had had the right number of birthdays.

Young folks could never understand the importance of that... and would not until they were old.

Song after song taken from the old hymnals from the old country. Tunes from the masters and words from a loved vocabulary. Then, as darkness settled, they moved to newer tunes, mostly written by Christopher.

The singers were 'put up' in the partially finished east wing, and fed a hardy breakfast. Evening Shade Ladies Home had been official and enthusiastically put of the map of Ridge Road, northern Arkansas.

And a pair of twin girls who were never meant to be a part of the ridge were tied inescapably to its vine festooned trees, its flint gravel road and folks who made it what it would be for decades.

## CHESTNUT COTTAGE AMONG THE CREPE MYRTLES

Years had passed and Miss Emma had slowed down considerably.

Miss Betsy was not far behind, but it would have killed her to think she would ever be moved from the cottage because she was no longer able to do everything as she used to. She still had a lap and could still spend a night of light sleep in the drawer room.

Laura Guniston, young baby sister of Hilda, grew up just across the road from the cottage and seemed to be 'everybody's girl' to any who needed help. That meant she spent a lot of time with the babies.

Harley Infield, great-grandson of Carlotta Enfield a new resident of Evening Shade, re-discovered Laura when he was delivering a load of apples and fresh corn his family had sent to the cottage.

He was loading the sacks into the pantry when he came face to face with Laura heading for the chicken yard with a pan of crumbled cornbread and a lot of crushed egg shells. They stopped dead still and stared into each other's still-familiar face. They'd spend a lot of time conversing across the aisle at school.

"Laura! That's gotta be you!"

With a bright smile she reassured him. "Course, Harley. It always has been me, even when we was whisperin' across the aisle. Looks like they got you a'workin'." And she eyed the apples appreciatively.

"Yeah, and say. What's goin' on with you? This here your job and can you get time off? I'd sure like to take you where we wouldn't have to whisper?"

"Where'd that be?" Laura demanded with an impudent grin.

Harley pushed his hat back from his sweaty forehead and raked his work-calloused fingers through his sun-streaked light brown hair.

He grinned through his last few freckles and winked a wicked-dark brown right eye.

"Well, first off I'd borrow my brother's courtin' buggy and hitch up my chestnut filly. We'd then take us a ride up and down the ridge till we learned whether we could still stand each other! You play your cards right, and I might come early sometime and take you to Wishbone for Ice Cream."

Laura shrugged and walked past him to the chicken yard where she threw the scraps to the flock of half-grown Rhode Island Reds. The little roosters in the flock were destined to be chicken dumplings next winter.

Harley waited in the doorway until she returned. She faced him with piercing eyes and announced, "In your dreams. What you got to offer?"

He grinned and leaned against the door blocking her entrance. "Young lady, I got me the prettiest little filly you ever rode behind. I got a pair'a mules that can pull anything, and my last litter'a Hampshire pigs numbered thirteen. All of 'em already sold when they reach 50 pounds."

Laura faced him soberly. "That all you got?"

"No. I got dreams of havin' a place of my own. Looks like I can buy my old gran's place with her goin' down to Blue Lake with her friends. It's a good place 'cept pretty much growed up right now."

"What'll you do if you get it?"

"Thinkin' I'd rent it out for a year on two till I figger out what I'm gonna do. That could likely mean learnin' what you're gonna do."

They stared at each other like a pair of red-bone hounds deciding whether to be friends or fighters. After a long stare, he replaced his straw hat on his head and turned to go.

Staring at his retreating back, she called, "What's that filly's name?"

Over his shoulder, he called back. "Princess. Why?"

"Wanted to know what to call her when I rode 'hind her watchin' her swing her tail."

He turned and called back. "Laura, where at would I find you again quickly, and not after 10 years, like now?"

She walked to his wagon with him. "Mostly around here. It's my sister's house through the trees. These ladies need me, and I like it here. You know that I was here as a baby."

"Heard about it. What about tomorrow about sundown, where'll you be?"

She smiled. "Either here or acrost the road."

"Be ready!" and he winked wickedly. Once more.

She watched until he disappeared behind the crepe myrtle shrubs. A quick little thought flitted through her agile mind… one that created a small shrug and a crooked smile. Did fellows with beautiful dark eyes and brushy black lashes pass them on to their daughters? Just a thought!

Then she turned and entered the cabin where she took down the book that determined who got the 'help' cabin next. On the next line she wrote Laura and Harley.

She showed the entry to Miss Emma, who ask, "He ask you?"

"Not yet but he will. The Morley's got another year here, and there'll be time. "

Miss Emma nodded, contentedly reassured.

The Morley's stayed as long as they could, and when they packed to leave, Laura Guniston and Harley Enfield stood before Brother Darkhorse and promised to love each other till death did them part.

The Enfield family gave a party that lasted till the wee hours. The moon was high when Princess waved her lovely tail and trotted to the Chestnut Cottage tucked within the tall crepe myrtles.

Harley lifted her down to avoid tangling her skirts in the darkness. He set her on the ground and took Princess to the stable behind the cottage.

The filly whickered conversationally and began to nibble the straw in the manger while Harley walked out into the moonlight toward the lighted windows of the "help" cabin and the open door.

He closed the door softly and stared at the beautiful Laura. Life was perfect. Until there was a soft knock on the door.

In Chestnut Cottage Miss Betsy had sat in her usual place… waiting. Most of the time nothing happened, but not this time.

285

There was the soft sound of the drawer on its oiled rollers. She waited until it was pushed back into its usual place inside the cottage.

She moved over to the drawer and took out the infant, fussing slightly at being disturbed. She opened the blanket, and there he was pink and healthy. And whimpering.

She paused for a moment, and then made an executive decision that was not easy for the ten-year-old girl. Miss Emma had been a bit 'tottery' today and had retired to her room.

With a determined look and firm lips, Betsy stepped through the back door and walked to the cabin. She rapped sharply with her worn and knobby knuckles.

"Miss Laura? Miss Laura?"

Laura opened the door to face a concerned Miss Betsy. "It's the drawer, Miss Laura. Just happened when I heard you drivin' in."

Laura looked at Harley. Meaningfully. Questionally. His shoulders drooped, but he nodded. "Go. I'll be here when you get back."

Laura went. She lifted the soggy bundle from the box in the drawer and laid him on the diaper table. Pealing back the blanket that had seen better days, she looked in the face of the tiny boy, his whining stopped and his black eyes tried to focus on this new person.

Miss Betsy stood by with the naming book. "Miss Laura, we have "D" next. We could name him Donald?"

Laura nodded agreeably and took the book.

Cleaned and re-diapered, she deposited the little fellow in Miss Betsy's waiting lap and returned the book to the shelf. Little Donald Hill was now properly enrolled in Chestnut Cottage for a few weeks or months. Miss Betsy would hold him all night this first night… as she always did with 'newcomers'.

As she had with Laura, herself… when she had been poked through the opening and into the drawer… naked and wrapped in a ragged scrap of cloth.

Laura tiptoed past Miss Emma's door where soft snoring could be heard. Then she slipped quietly through the kitchen door and crossed the few steps to the 'help' cabin. The lamp had been placed in the window to guide her home, though it wasn't needed in the moon light.

Laura paused at the door and drew in a breath. The words that came to her mind were, "Full circle". She turned the knob, and there he was. Her Harley.

Hers forever.

*'FOR HE SHALL GIVE HIS ANGELS CHARGE OVER THEE, TO KEEP THE IN ALL THY WAYS. THEY SHALL BEAR THEE UP IN THEIR HANDS LEST THOU DASH THY FOOT AGAINST A STONE"*

*(KJV Psalm 91: 11-12 and repeated MATHEW 4:6 & LUKE 4:10)*

# ADDITIONAL BOOK SERIES BY JOANN KLUSMEYER

**The Great I Am Bible Story Series for Kids**
*6 books*

**The Young Pioneers Adventure Series for Kids**
*5 books*

**The Wentworth Triplets Mystery Series for Young Teens**
*3 books*

**The Footsteps in the Canyon Adventure Series for Young Teens**
*4 books*

**The Burnt Tree Junction: Historical Fiction**
*6 books*

**The Ozark Mountains Historical Fiction Series**
*7 books*

**The Taming the Wilderness Historical Fiction Series**
*7 books*

**The Sheltering Stones Historical Fiction Series**
*5 books*

**The Trilogy of Wishbone Hollow Historicial Fiction Series**
*3 books*

www.ingramcontent.com/pod-product-compliance
Lightning Source LLC
Chambersburg PA
CBHW070444030726

47503CB00004B/893